STUMBLING UP

A Loser's Guide to Progression, Book 1

RECK WELL

This is a work of fiction. All of the characters, organizations, and events portrayed in this novel are either products of the author's imagination or used fictitiously. No generative AI was used to write this book.

Published by Dragon Tomes Publishing, LLC
Topeka, KS

Dragon Tomes Publishing
www.dragontomespublishing.com

Name: Reck Well, Author
Title: Stumbling Up: A Loser's Guide to Progression, Book 1
Description: First edition/ Kansas: Dragon Tomes Publishing, 2025
Subject: Fantasy fiction
Cover Design and Chapter Art: Henrique "Morpheuz" Neves
ISBN: 978-1-963198-08-9 (paperback)
ISBN: 978-1-963198-09-6 (ebook)

The ePub version of this title meets WCAG 2.1/2.2 Level AA compliance standards. A free, downloadable braille-ready file (BRF) for this title is also available at https://louis.aph.org.

I dedicate this book to my family.

Jen, Missouri, and Miranda.

May we always find a reason to laugh.

Contents

Part IV

The Hunt

PART I

Trial Dungeon

Chapter 1

QUARTER-LIFE CRISIS

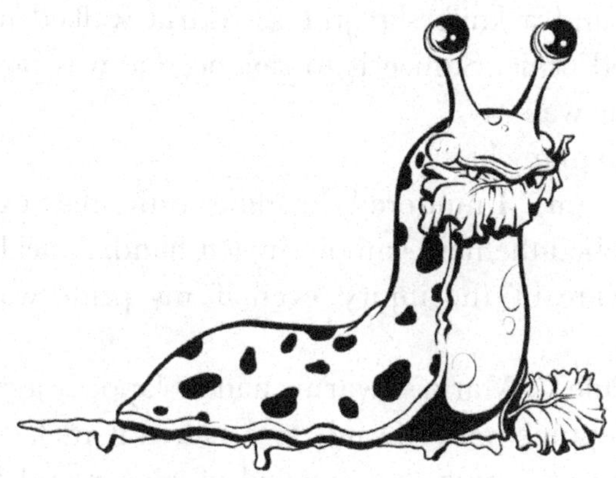

"You're late," Marta's words echoed painfully.

I squinted at her, the head chef of the *Ram's Horn,* trying to formulate a reply. The drums hammering my skull from Leo's drunken birthday bash didn't help.

"At least I showed up?" was all I had.

There was no anger in Marta's stare. It just lingered, heavy and still, letting me know she expected better.

Meanwhile, I was busy trying to limit sensory inputs, focusing on the worn white tiles of the kitchen instead of the smells of dinner. I put my stomach into a mental death grip to prevent a further escalation of how I'd spent the first half of my day.

Marta was a master of her craft. Guilt bubbled as she continued to frown at me. I owed her. She'd been very patient over the last year with my fumbling attempts to become a real chef.

"You're on dishwasher duty today. I can't afford anyone seeing you cooking and looking like this after last week."

Wincing, I bobbed my head in agreement. Dishwasher duty was my least favorite role at the tavern, but the one I received the most.

Last week, I was on onion duty for our signature caramelized onion soup, and I rubbed my eye. Cue bloodshot tears, snot, and a knife slip just as Marta walked in with a regional food critic. Suffice it to say, no one was pinning his review on the wall.

Welcome to my life.

"Yes, ma'am," I muttered, heading to the rear exit of the tavern. I rubbed the new skin on my left hand. A healing salve had taken care of the injury, even if my pride was still in tatters.

"And Cole?" Marta's warm hand slapped against my shoulder, stopping me. "Drink and eat, it'll make you feel better." She put a mug that smelled of ginger and honey in one hand and a small bowl of cinnamon-spiced gruel in the other.

And that's why I loved Marta—she cared. Sure, she could make you feel like an ant when you screwed up, but she was also the first to offer you a hand up.

I took a sip of the warm beverage and almost gagged at the contrast between the sourness in my mouth and the soft bite of ginger.

The dish station sat behind the tavern on a covered porch. It was always too hot or cold, but it was easier to heat the water out here, and the compost didn't stink up the kitchen.

One of the other kitchen assistants had already prepped the station. The sink was full of warm, sudsy water. A fresh dishcloth sat neatly folded, ready for action. Flies buzzed over the compost bin.

Whoever'd gotten the station set up hadn't bothered to

empty the bin. I didn't blame the poor sod who had covered for me. I was also irritated with myself.

Taking a deep breath, I tried activating one of my meditation skills, [Monotonous Calm].

Nothing happened. Damn hangover.

I took another long sip of the ginger tea. At least I didn't accidentally trigger my [Self Critic] skill.

Before diving in, I drained my cup of tea. The ginger had already begun working on my stomach. The gruel still took an iron will to attempt to eat, even though I knew it'd be for the better. When Marta handed you food, it was generally worth eating.

On the fourth spoonful, my headache receded enough to work. I still wasn't feeling great, but I could function.

Mica, one of the waiters, popped out with a stack of dishes. He gave a friendly head bob before ducking back into the tavern. The early dinner crowd was starting to finish their meals. If I didn't start moving, the teetering pile of dishes would reach a catastrophic size.

I threw the dishrag into the water, watching it defy expectation and float for a moment. Then, just like my life, it succumbed and slowly sank to the bottom of the sink.

Leo had been the last of our little trio to get the quartermark of mediocrity. We'd had such dreams as kids. We were going to travel the world and slay monsters.

I reached into the water, grabbing the rag and the first plate.

Growing up, none of us imagined being stuck in Woodsten, relegated to scraping half-eaten congealed food off plates. The naivety of youth didn't include a reality of broken builds, dungeon breaks, and a slowly eroding frontier.

The thought sparked a dim memory, a fleeting glimpse into yesterday's celebratory day drinking.

Leo was grinning like a fool as he swung his axe wildly, taking out imaginary enemies. Tandy's face, flushed with drink, egging him on. Her auburn hair was curly and unbraided, shining in the sunlight. I was elated, happy, floating on a sea of grog.

I gripped the sink's rim, the memory throwing me on the cusp of understanding. What had we done?

My gut quivered. I dropped the plate I'd been scrubbing into the sink. My mind warred with itself, needing to know what we'd done but terrified of the hints my mind provided.

I began walking through the day from the beginning. We started the celebration early, each securing a rare day off from work. Even Tandy had managed to wrangle it, which was no small feat considering her grandmother.

It should have been joyous, but Leo was in a shitty mood. I'd been determined to cheer him up. At twenty-five, he still hadn't gained a class, cementing his status as [Broken], a loser who couldn't interface with the [System].

Even the most optimistic stopped calling it a 'phase' at twenty-five. This wasn't something that he was going to outgrow. We'd known for a while, but there was such finality to this birthday.

This was all our lives now.

I wasn't much better. I'd failed at what? Three professions? Working for Marta wasn't so much a career as a job. I never really picked up any useful skills, no matter what trade I tried.

I was one major bill away from moving back in with my parents. If Tandy hadn't gifted the healing salve to me at the winter solstice, I would have been short on rent when I cut my fingers on the onions.

We'd toasted Tandy, the only theoretical success. Her braided hair had started the day tight and perfect, just like her family's expectations. Tandy was never shy to complain, so when it was her turn to toast, she spoke to our collective misery.

"To seventy-five more years of the lives we've all settled

for." The acidic words burned us all the more in her firm voice. Leo took the first of many long drafts of his grog.

My mind returned to him grinning like an idiot, dancing around our campfire.

What had we done to cause such a reversal in mood?

It hit me. A flash of gray, dreary walls. The pimple-faced bureaucrat from the Guild who updated the Woodsten quest boards.

It was the one building everyone avoided because it was full of vultures. The only reason Woodsten had an Adventurer's Guild presence was its frontier outpost status. Sheep and trees made the town's economy, not [Adventurer] loot. The cities that thrived on the frontier were along the major passes through the mountains, not in our forgotten backwater.

Only one local group had bothered to join the [Adventurer] ranks. They took care of twisted wildlife and the occasional bandit that cropped up. Not much older than us, that group had been bred to be [Adventurers]. They had investment, mentors, and education. They'd learned the fighting arts, magic, and class strategies needed to be successful.

Tandy called them *Team Abs*, and they were as pretentious as they sounded.

The lot of an [Adventurer] might sound romantic, but for anyone untrained, it was a surefire way to die young.

The hangover haze burned away with a single, horrible realization. I remembered the rough texture of the paper under my hand as my pen moved. The recruiter's grin as my signature dried. Understanding sank through my chest like a lead weight, settling deep in my gut.

Generally, I avoided looking at my stat sheet. It held nothing but disappointment for me, so I braced my psyche as I brought it up.

To my horror, all my [Mundane] classes had been grayed out, and [Provisional Adventurer] had been granted. A

[System Notification] alert hung in the corner of my vision, a spot that my insobriety had blurred out this morning.

Mentally expanding the alert, my worst fears were realized.

[Quest Granted: [Trial Dungeon]

Congratulations on taking the first step to fight the Incursion. You have now been given the temporary class of [Provisional Adventurer] with all the inherent growth opportunities. Please note this is an interim designation as your worth is measured.

[Mundane] classes and skills have been temporarily disabled as [Adventurer] baselines are calculating. Please move to the nearest [Trial Dungeon] or face consequences.

You have been granted [3] attempts to pass the [Trial Dungeon], and your life will be forfeited upon failure. More details will be provided upon entering. Beginning levels are calculated based on your base attributes during your twenty-five-year tutorial.

Adventure onward!]

"Upon failure, your life will be forfeited?" I read the sentence out loud, the horror sinking in.

It was widely believed that the [Trial Dungeon] experience was the [System's] way of balancing out the rewards of the [Adventurer] class. For the unprepared, it was a death sentence dressed as a quest.

I was going to die.

I had no skills to survive a dungeon. I was a failed farmer turned failed blacksmith turned mediocre line chef. Had Leo talked me into this? My head throbbed as I tried to remember.

An image floated to the surface: Three pens moving on three separate sets of paperwork. Relief hit first, at least I wasn't alone. Then the guilt landed. We hadn't signed up for a party. We'd signed our death warrants.

All *three* of us were going to die.

I stumbled over to the compost bin, my stomach in revolt.

Looking down into the mess of vegetables, a much larger than average banana slug looked up at me, tentacles waving in welcome. Two tiny fangs clung to a small piece of lettuce.

A [System Notification] alert pinged.

[Congratulations - You have unlocked Richard, the Fanged Banana Slug, a [Rare] [Companion], a level [redacted] entity. His slime is eternal, his fangs decorative. 1/1 [Companion] Slots used. Adventure onward!]

A dry voice sounded in my head.

Good day, ahem, Cole. My name is—

I bent over the bin and introduced myself, letting Richard know in explicit detail just what a hot mess I was.

As first impressions go, I nailed it.

Chapter 2

DRUNKEN CONSEQUENCES

You're lucky we're already bonded.

"I'm sorry," I said, immediately hating how whiny it sounded. I was apologizing to a slug. This was a new low.

A gentleman might have helped Richard out of the compost bin, but my stomach clenched at the thought. I didn't want to add to my disgrace. Instead, I leaned against the sink, trying to face it all.

Two yellow tentacles breached the top of the bin. They waved in the air, almost sniffing before focusing on me. Inching forward, a tiny, fanged mouth appeared.

We had banana slugs in the forests around Woodsten, but I'd never seen one fanged. I'd never heard of an [Adventurer] bonding with something so slimy. At almost a foot long, he was the most enormous banana slug I'd encountered, which wasn't saying a lot.

"I'd help, but I'm not sure I trust my stomach..." My voice

trailed off as I watched Richard shimmer with a soft yellow energy. Bits of compost and unmentionables slid right off him like water off a duck's back. My yellow companion pulled the rest of his larger-than-average body onto the rim of the barrel.

One of the first skills I picked up as an [Adventurer]. No one likes a dirty—never mind. So you're Cole?

By the tone of his mental voice, I could tell that Richard found me as wanting as I saw him. At least we could commiserate in our disappointment.

"I am Cole, newly minted, unprepared [Provisional Adventurer]." I stood, straightening my shoulders, lifting my chin, trying to strike a heroic pose for the foot-long slug.

The stained apron must go, but I can work with this.

Doubling down, I grabbed my plate scraper, thrusting it into the air like some magical heirloom sword. I tilted my head to show off my five o'clock shadow and 'chiseled' jawline.

Even better. At least you have a sense of humor. You're going to need it when the monsters show up.

Richard undulated forward, his long body balancing easily on the barrel's rim. I watched in fascination as he stretched forward, bridging the gap between the barrel ledge and the countertop. I wasn't sure how useful a self-cleaning slug was to an [Adventurer], but he was unique.

As a kid, I dreamed of returning to Woodsten as a hero in shining armor with a dire wolf by my side. The wooden scraper lowered slowly. Richard was a slug, and I wasn't a hero but a [Provisional Adventurer]. The [Trial Dungeon] stood in our way. So few souls who attempted it passed.

"We're going to die," the words slipped out. I had to stop thinking about it. My stomach did a slow flip. Thankfully, there wasn't anything left to lose.

You might, but I'm [Immortal].

"Sure, and I'm the King of [Adventurers]," I laughed.

"My first act is to outlaw [Trial Dungeons]." I got the distinct impression that Richard wasn't impressed by my mockery. "Lo, my famous [Immortal] banana slug, are you ready to tackle the quest before us?"

His ego seemed mollified, but Richard didn't reply. Which got me thinking, did I need to finish the dishes?

I looked at the unappealing leaning stack of plates. Congealed gravy mixed with mashed potatoes and limp pot roast. Do I finish them? Is this even my job anymore? The buzz from the compost pile clogged my thoughts. If I only have a week to live, do I want to spend one more day working next to the trash heap? Do Tandy and Leo realize what we've done?

A cool, slimy touch knocked me out of the mental spiral. Richard stretched across the gap between me and the counter. His eyes looked up at me, concerned.

We'll figure it out together. Without warning, his body glided forward, up my arm.

"What the hell?" I shouted as he wrapped himself around my shoulders like a python looking for a meal. Except he didn't squeeze, he just settled behind my neck like one of Tandy's cats. I absently wiped at my slimy arm, only to find it surprisingly dry.

You're fine. Soon you won't even remember I'm here. Besides, where else am I going to sit? I move too slowly to keep up with a human.

The back door opened, and Marta stuck her head out. "You're falling behind, Cole." She did a double-take, eyes furrowing. "Is that a...? Nope, I don't want to know." The door shut with a muttered, "Kids these days."

I went back to dishwashing. Knowing Leo, he would be out of commission for a while yet. He slept late most days, even without a hangover. And Tandy, even if she were a newly minted [Provisional Adventurer], would take care of her family obligations first. I had time.

I started scrubbing. No part of me wanted to be on Marta's bad side. Quitting this week would be bad enough.

"I'm just going to finish up work, and then we can figure out the [Adventurer] life," I said aloud for Richard, but mostly myself. I needed to calm the incessant churn of anxieties running through my head.

Richard, the Dishwasher Assistant. Not the role I was expecting.

Every seventh dish or so, a yellow glow would extend from my shoulders, causing all the dirt and slop to fall away magically from the plate I was about to dip into the dishwater. It surprised me every time.

Richard had been right. He was easy to forget. If I focused on him, I'd note the oddly cool wet presence wrapped around my shoulders, but otherwise, he just melted into the general sensation of wearing clothes.

I fell into the rhythm of the job: scrape, dip, scrub, rinse, dry. The waitstaff kept the pile of dishes high, and the kitchen emptied my dry rack every hour.

My thoughts drifted to Marta. She had taken me in after I'd quit the forge. Put me to work on the morning shift making breakfast. Instead of harping on my failures, she kept me busy and gave me a paycheck.

I'd been close to heading home, tail between my legs, and she saved me from facing my parents and the unending work of the farm. As much as I wouldn't miss doing dishes, I would miss her.

A dry voice entered my thoughts. *Cole, keep washing dishes, but we've got a problem.*

My back itched as I tried not to turn around.

I thought we'd have more time before the monsters started showing up. I was wrong.

Monsters showing up? What the hell was Richard talking about?

You must neutralize the threat before it initiates its sonic attack.

My heart raced as my eyes scanned the dish pile for a

potential weapon. The only two options among the butter knives, mugs, forks, and plates were a small paring knife and a mid-sized iron pan.

I pretended to dip the three-inch knife into the dishwater, my knuckles white as they clenched the handle. The cast-iron pan had burnt au gratin stuck along the rim. I was going to die smelling of potatoes.

Ready or not, I was about to meet my fate as an [Adventurer]. To face my first monster encounter. Richard coiled tighter on my shoulders. I spun, raising my pan like a shield.

Then I saw it.

A duck.

An oversized, menacing duck with murder in its eyes.

Richard shrieked in my mind.

It's a bogquacker! They eat ***slugs****, Cole! Slugs!*

Chapter 3

DUCKING AND DODGING

The mallard was the size of a goose. Green, shimmering head feathers surrounded two beady, red glowing eyes. Its bright yellow bill opened to reveal a line of serrated teeth.

Richard mentally shrieked and ducked behind my neck. A lot of good he was going to be in a fight.

The bogquacker took a deep inhale. Instinctively, I thrust the pan between us, as the air rippled in front of the duck unleashing a [Quack Attack].

Au gratin went flying as the sonic boom ricocheted off the pan, reflecting most of the attack back at the duck. It took all my strength to keep the pan steady as it shook violently.

The attack stopped suddenly with an abrupt cough. I wasn't sure if the spell rebounding or a stray chunk of potato caused the bogquacker to pause.

Either way, it wasn't going to last long. I had to act.

Lowering my shield, I got a good view of the monster. The

demonic duck elongated its neck, letting loose a distressed honk. Something was violently ejected from its throat and flew through the air. The duck's head shook as its red eyes focused on me.

The bogquacker grinned, showing those gruesome serrated teeth again. It inhaled, preparing to unleash another [Quack Attack]. I knew what to do.

Stepping forward, I locked my leg as I kicked. The laces of my boot hit the feathered menace squarely in the chest. Air whooshed out of its lungs with an oof before my follow-through punted the bogquacker into the night.

A shower of downy fluff filled the air as the surprised bogquacker rocketed into the trees. Glowing red eyes wide, I watched as the duck smacked into a tree trunk. Some birds weren't meant to fly.

[Bogquacker defeated. You have earned experience. Further details and rewards will be aggregated and awarded upon [Trial Dungeon] completion.]

The system was a cheap, reward-hoarding weasel. I needed the loot to *survive* the [Trial Dungeon]. Mother-ducker.

I took a breath, trying to invoke my mundane meditation skills, which I no longer possessed. System be damned.

Richard was shaking, glued to the back of my neck. He'd scrunched up as small as possible. I shivered as an ooze of fear-induced slime dribbled down my back.

"Hey, buddy, it's alright." This was awkward. Bogquackers were no joke, but most in Woodsten had dealt with one of the feathered grumps in their lifetime.

I put down the now perfectly clean pan. Even some of the years-old baked-on crud had been cleaned off.

Mentally, I made a note to think about starting a bogquacker-based cleaning service if adventuring didn't work out.

I'm sure it looked ridiculous when Marta poked her head out the back door. I had one arm over my back and another under, trying to reach Richard, who, beyond logic, was glued to the one part of my back I couldn't quite reach. As I twisted to get a better angle, I saw the door quietly shut.

It was the middle of the dinner rush. I understood the practicality of letting quivering slugs lie.

"Richard! The duck is gone. You're fine." Nothing got through to the creature, and my twisting and turning only made it worse. So I did the only thing left to me: I went back to work.

Scrape, dip, scrub, rinse, dry, and repeat. Over and over, the monotony soothed my frayed nerves in ways only provided by monotonous labor.

Leo had teased me for being jumpy throughout our entire childhood. I had never wanted to follow him into the woods on his many attempts to pick up a [Class]. The wilderness along the frontier was a dangerous place, and bogquackers are the least of the worries. Growing up, my parents had told endless stories of their struggle to secure their farmstead.

Eventually, the warm yellow glow of Richard's cleaning magic reached out and enveloped a particularly gooey plate in my hands.

"Back among the living?" I asked, trying to keep my voice nonchalant. I didn't want to scare him back into hiding. My slug was sensitive.

Richard didn't answer, so I kept going. I could tell he'd started to unwind his body, adopting a more relaxed position. His magic continued to reach out and assist. The station grew darker as time passed, and the ebb and flow of the evening traffic changed from dinner plates to tiny sticky dessert plates. Ale mugs gave way to teacups.

I reached for the next dish, only to find the stack empty.

Marta stood by my station, her stern arms crossed and her eyes narrowed in appraisal.

"Are we really done?" I'd lost track of time. Had it already been eight hours?

"Aye, lad, we're done for the night. I'll take care of the compost. You did well." She hesitated, then her voice softened. "I heard a rumor. I'm thinking this is your last day here?"

My throat closed up as I nodded. Marta ran a strict kitchen, and most thought her a cold Easterner, but she cared about us. She cared about me. I'd belonged here.

"Well, do yourself proud. You're always welcome back," she gave me a sad little smile. We both knew I wasn't coming back. One way or another, this was it. Before either of us broke down, she saved us both. "Only you could get a pan *this* clean."

Marta held up a shiny, new-looking mid-sized cast-iron pan. My bogquacker shield.

We laughed, and she handed me my last week's wages as we shook hands.

With my back to the Ram's Horn, slug on my shoulder, I hesitated before walking away. I waited until Marta swung the back door open one last time. For a moment, I heard the familiar clanks and shouts of the kitchen staff. Marta started calling out the end-of-night orders to the closers. Then the door swung shut, cutting Marta off with a finality I felt in my heart.

Someday, you'll return.

Richard's voice echoed in my head. As unlikely as his words were, I smiled. It was a nice sentiment.

Woodsten was a fairly robust Outpost built on wool, lumber, and trade. It sported a minor trade route that led to one of the larger mountain passes. As such, it had a few taverns and shops. I'd recommend one tavern, The Ram's Horn, over all the others. Its kitchen was well run, and the food was tasty, no matter what the food critics say.

To be classified as an Outpost, Woodsten sported a half-finished palisade and an Adventurer's Guild hall. We also had Team Abs, the local band of [Adventurers], and a well-run militia. The town held almost a thousand souls and thus had a decent residential footprint.

I lived in one of the old boarding houses. The building dated back to the origin of the town and was as drafty as a person might suspect. It was cheap enough that both Leo and I could afford our own rooms. Ours sat across the hall from each other, unlike Tandy, who lived above her family's wool store.

This is why I was so surprised to find Tandy, not Leo, sitting cross-legged, leaning against my door, napping. She rarely visited our humble quarters.

Her well-groomed auburn braids were back, not the chaotic mess she'd had in my last memory. A green wool cloak wrapped protectively around her slouched form.

I reached down to wake her and was stung by a hornet. My yelp of surprise woke her up.

"Took you long enough," she muttered sleepily as I looked for a stinger in my hand. A whole swath of my fingers was reddening with a line of blisters.

"Be careful. Do you see the hornet that got me?"

"Sorry, that was me. I haven't attuned the cloak to recognize you as a friend yet." She punctuated her explanation with a yawn.

I backed away, realizing my mistake. Tandy was far and away the smartest of our trio. She'd been the darling of her family, a [Sage] potential genius who wove with skill and magic. She stretched and stood, reaching down to pull up a heavy backpack.

Tandy ran her fingers down the lining of her cloak to find a stitched-in fabric tab with a sewn-in activation rune. She frowned as she gripped the tab with the tips of her fingers.

"It's not going to work, remember? We're not [Mundane] anymore." The words came out more bitter than I'd intended.

Tandy stepped aside, frowning as I edged towards the door lock, key in hand. Her magical cloaks could be keyed to specific owners who controlled the cloak's magic through an activation rune.

Tandy's skill set allowed her to [Override Ownership], a rare skill in polite company that could reset garment ownership keys even in the absence of the original owner.

While she'd undoubtedly made the magic cloak and was thus immune to its defensive properties, she probably wasn't keyed as an owner. It looked brand new, and Tandy's grandmother wouldn't have willingly let something that expensive out of her shop.

"Well, I dyed this one with nettle and kept the sting, so be careful."

I nodded, carefully keeping distance from her as I unlocked the door with a click. The pain from the sting was already subsiding, but I wasn't going to get near her anytime soon.

Nettle-infused garments were used as chastity belts and low-grade [Adventurer] gear. It wouldn't cause lasting physical damage, but the sharp pain would make anyone hesitate.

I ducked my head into my room. It looked like the same pigsty I'd left this morning. I closed the door, turning to face Tandy.

"Uh, why don't we meet up after I have a moment to change?" I still wore my damp, stained apron from work. I avoided her gaze by plucking an errant bogquacker feather from my sleeve.

"Oh, please. It can't be that bad." She moved forward, causing me to jump back for fear of the nettle.

The door swung wide, revealing all my sins. My bed was covered in dirty laundry, underwear on full display. The room was small, holding two tables covered in crusty dishes and bits of junk I'd pulled out of the trash. A lone, ratty towel with moth holes hung next to a shelf containing my three books.

Everything was lit in soft light from the cheap glow moss I'd carefully kept alive.

Tandy and I had never been in the same socioeconomic class. Leo and I often wondered why she'd chosen us as friends. We both tried hard over the years to keep her in the dark about how different our lives were.

I didn't want my friends to take pity on me. Leo knew, but he was only a hair better off than I. He was only paid more because he was willing to take more dangerous jobs.

Face burning, I slid past her, just barely avoiding a sting. Quickly, I threw a blanket over the laundry and collected the dishes, putting them in a bin under my desk. The treasures I'd pulled out of the trash stayed, most of which I hadn't fixed or figured out exactly how they worked, but I would someday.

My hands slowed. Or maybe I wouldn't.

I turned back to Tandy, embarrassment forgotten. "My memory is fuzzy, but is this your fault or Leo's?"

"Does it matter? Whoever's fault it is, this is our reality." She said it in the matter-of-fact way I'd always appreciated. Unlike the other girls in town, I never had to guess where I stood with Tandy.

"It was Leo, wasn't it?"

"Of course. Who else?" Tandy sounded as tired as I felt. "He's always the one getting us in trouble. Do you even own a backpack?" She looked at my hopeless mess with an air of judgment. "We're going to need to get out of here before monsters attack the town." Ever practical, she was already trying to take the next step.

I like this one.

I mentally waved Richard's comment away.

"I do. It's just under the bed. Richard, can you sit on the table?" I extended my arm, making a ramp for the mollusk. "This is Richard, by the way. He's my newly bonded animal companion."

Richard obliged, gliding slowly to take his place. A tentacle waved at Tandy. She raised her eyebrows in a classic expression that meant, *a slug, really?*

I nodded guiltily, as though Richard had been a choice. As though I'd contemplated a dire wolf and chosen the slug life.

"We've already been attacked." I shoved an arm under the bed and reached for my pack. "A bogquacker came at us while I was working at the dish station. Found it!" I pulled the pack out, holding it up triumphantly.

Tandy leaned against my desk, lightly petting Richard. One look at my pack, and she covered her mouth. I could tell by the creases around her eyes that she was laughing at me.

"What'd I do?"

Richard sent me a mental image of cobwebs in my eyebrows and my old, crusty, stained pack in hand.

Tandy grinned, "I couldn't replicate your style if I tried." Her voice softened. "You know, if we die in the trial, that could be the last backpack you'll ever own."

Before I could think of a reply, the city bells broke our revelry, chiming in a disharmonious alarm.

Woodsten was under attack.

Chapter 4

NEVER A DULL MOMENT

As a [Mundane] person not in the town militia, my role was clear during the infrequent monster attacks. Evacuate to one of the pre-identified fortified buildings scattered throughout the town, then bunker down and wait out the attack.

The fortified buildings also had weapons handy for distribution. We'd never had an attack in my lifetime such that we needed those weapons, but I'd heard stories.

All [Adventurers], local or passing through, were expected to join the town's defense. Between them and the militia, most attacks were handled relatively quickly. The boarding house where I lived was not a fortified building, though. It was so old that a stiff wind could blow it over.

"Do you think the attack is because of us?" Tandy's voice was panicked.

"Doubtful," I said, with more confidence than I felt. I started shoving supplies in my bag. What did an [Adventurer] need? I grabbed a few pairs of clothes from the pile on my bed and raided my meager snack drawer.

I grabbed my blacksmith hammer, belting it into a leather holster. I hadn't worn it since I'd left the forge, but it was the only thing resembling a weapon I owned. The weight of the hammer pulled at my hip like an old friend.

I eyed the rest of my room. The quilt my mother had sewn, the projects I'd started, my books, it was impossible to decide what else to take.

"Cole, we've got to go. You can come back for your stuff later."

As soon as Tandy said it, I knew she was wrong. We weren't coming back. Not to this life.

I grabbed my mom's quilt. It was thin through years of use. Examining my workbench, I plucked the tools I'd built over the years—the tiny screwdrivers, tweezers, the sharp knife, my fine filers, and the most expensive item in my kit, a small magnetic strip. Finally, I grabbed the mechanical drill set and my lucky nails.

Then I reached up, my brain telling me only to grab one book, but my hand snagged two. I shoved them both into the bag.

I left Dad's farmer's almanac. He meant well when he gave it to me, but I'd never felt the calling to the fields.

The city bells hadn't stopped clanging. Tandy had one foot in the hallway, watching for movement.

My building's activity was hit or miss at this time of day. Many residents were having dinner with their families or swapping stories over a mug of ale. They were likely sheltering in place.

I grabbed the cloak Tandy had given me years ago. The dark blue and forest green pattern had twigs and leaf debris stuck in it from our last camping trip with Leo. I put down my pack, whipped my apron over my head, and replaced it with the cloak. I couldn't delay any longer.

"I'm ready," I whispered. The words weren't true but, as Tandy's white face swiveled towards me, I realized we'd run out of time.

"Someone's in the foyer," Tandy whispered. We stood silently, ears straining to hear.

You forgot something.

Richard's silent voice made me jump. Tandy gave me a dark look before trying to peek down the hallway.

I scooped Richard up, placing him on my left shoulder.

Tandy beckoned me to the edge of the door. Peeking around the corner, I saw what had her on edge. Multiple shadows moved in the gathering space of the house. My hand instinctively jerked to my hammer.

I ducked back into the room.

"This can't be because of us. Can it?" I voiced my fear in a low whisper.

Monsters could spawn and were attracted to [Adventurers], but this seemed too coincidental. The city hadn't had an actual monster raid in decades. Our quest warned us of consequences if we avoided the [Trial Dungeon], but it'd only been a day.

"Unlikely." The dry look she gave me brokered no room for doubt. Not only was my anxiety stupid, but we didn't have time for it. "Is there a back exit?"

Pushing me out of the way, careful not to brush her cloak against my skin, Tandy took another peek at our foes.

I like this girl. I may have picked the wrong companion.

I ignored Richard's jabs and answered Tandy's question. "Not exactly."

She glanced back at the unease in my voice. Seconds later, we were coated in a shower of splinters as a throwing axe slammed into the doorframe. The invaders had noticed us.

Tandy only missed getting hit by a hair. Eyes wide in shock, she looked at me as the side of her face began to bleed from embedded splinters of wood. We'd run out of time.

If we stayed in my room, we were dead meat. Our only chance was the ancient escape tunnel in the rear stairwell.

I pushed past Tandy, got stung, and pulled at her to follow. She resisted at first, to grab the axe embedded in the door frame. With a tug, it came loose. I ran, pulling an off-balance Tandy behind.

The founding of Woodsten had been rough, and all the original buildings had escape tunnels dug for emergencies. I just didn't know if this one was intact.

Hurry, they've begun to chase us.

As though I needed more fuel for my sprint. The door to the stairwell swung open easily. I jammed a wooden stay against the base of the door. It wouldn't stop a monster for more than a few seconds, but we needed every moment.

To the right, narrow stairs led up to the second story, but to the left was a wooden hatch with a metal padlock.

I pulled at the lock futilely for a second until I remembered my tools. Dropping my pack, I started rummaging through it.

Tandy took a quicker route to our goal by swinging the throwing axe down hard on the lock. It shattered as the old brittle mechanism gave up before our desperation.

Like a badass, Tandy lifted the hatch with a bloody hand and didn't hesitate as she stepped down the dark stairs of the tunnel. I grabbed a clump of the glowing moss they'd put in the stairwell. We needed some illumination.

The wooden stairs groaned under our weight. The sound didn't help my sudden fear of being buried alive. Little puffs of dust billowed up with each step.

I turned to face the stairwell. Keeping the hatch cracked mere inches, I wanted to get a glimpse of our pursuit. My hands sweated as I held the inner locking mechanism. The stairwell door swung open, and two pairs of black scuffed boots entered.

"Where'd the initiates go?" The man's voice was rough,

and his accent hard to place. Who were these people? They certainly weren't monsters.

I was unsure what Richard could pick up from my mind, but he must have thought it was a question for him.

Not monsters - worse. They're [Raiders], Cole. Hostile flagged.

Of all the tick-infested sheep in the realm.

The [Raiders] would discover the smashed lock in moments, so I quietly lowered the hatch and slid the locking bolts into place. My mind raced at the implication. They weren't simply raiding the village. They were looking for us. Who else would be considered initiates?

My night vision shot, I turned back to Tandy, hardly able to see.

Tandy was at the edge of my light, a specter beckoning me on. I shivered. There were reasons Leo and I had never explored the tunnel. Many of the early settlers had lost their lives, holed up in collapsed tunnels. The stories of kidnappings and worse haunted these tunnels.

It felt like entering a tomb. The temperature started dropping and, the further we went, the darker it seemed. Roots dangled from the ceiling, and brushed our faces like thick cobwebs. I held the clump of moss out like a beacon of hope, trying to banish my fears.

The escape tunnel felt like a sheep that'd gone missing years ago. It was overgrown, forgotten, and felt more than a bit feral.

The air was stale and earthy. Old rough-hewn wooden supports sat like silent sentinels. Our pursuers had begun banging on the hatch, trying to break in.

Tandy was suddenly in my face, the blood stood in stark contrast to her white skin, "Do you know where this tunnel leads? Has the exit collapsed?"

I shook my head. "I have no idea. I..." The tremor in my voice stopped further words. Tight, confined, dark spaces weren't good. I took a deep breath, missing my meditation skill for the second time today. "The monsters had boots."

Richard's voice echoed in my head. *They're [Raiders].* Another thump. They were going to break through.

Tandy pulled the moss close to our faces. "Boots? Are you sure?" It felt like she looked into my soul for a moment.

I nodded. "Richard thinks they're [Raiders], tagged as monsters. And I think they're looking for us." If a group of sentient [Raiders] was after us, it had to be because of our [Provisional Adventurer] status. The best way to keep Woodsten safe was to leave.

"Well, I guess it doesn't matter if there's an exit." She sounded resigned. Tandy had reached the same conclusion—we were screwed.

She walked back to the last set of supports. The light from my glow moss only gave me a dim impression of her actions. Tandy ran her hands along the supports, as though searching for something.

I scrambled back as I realized what she was doing. We'd been taught that the fifth support had wedges with a long rope built into the frame. Pulling these wedges would collapse the tunnel, theoretically sealing those fleeing off from their pursuit.

Of course, the whole mechanism was decades old.

Tandy found the wedges, and her fingers clawed at the safety mechanisms. I heard a ping as the metal safety pins bounced off the rock floor. She backed away, lightly holding two ends of an old rope.

The tunnel was suddenly lit as our foes broke through the hatch. My heel caught on some debris, causing me to stumble to the ground. Undiscernible, very human voices could be heard. We'd run out of time.

I kept my eyes on Tandy while still backing away on all fours. This wasn't going to end well. Collapsing the tunnel was a last-ditch, desperate effort because it could collapse the building above, and maybe even the entire tunnel.

Is she going to collapse the tunnel on us? I take it all back. She's a lunatic! Richard coiled tightly against my neck. *Cole, I'm glad I chose you! You're the reasonable one.*

"Tandy, I don't—"

She looked back at me, teeth white with a maniacal grin, "They're coming, Cole. The [Raiders] are coming for us."

Knuckles white, holding the ropes, Tandy pulled. She yanked hard, and with the safety pins missing, the wedges sprang loose. Time seemed to slow as the two support pillars near us ponderously leaned forward. The left column snapped, and everything sped up as the ceiling came down.

A cascade of rubble crushed our pursuit, just as a gust of dust enveloped us. I lay on the dirt floor, coughing, and wondering if this was it. I prayed to the nameless gods that we would survive as the floor bucked. Eventually, the collapse stopped.

I'd lost the moss. The only sound breaking our tomb's silence was my raspy breath.

A system message flashed in front of my face before I dismissed it.

[Raiding Party defeated. You have earned experience. Further details and rewards will be aggregated and awarded upon [Trial Dungeon] completion.]

"Tandy?" The word came out in a sharp gasp. Every breath took in more grime that cut my lungs like razor blades.

Did I search for my friend, possibly buried under the rubble? Or should I retreat to find breathable air? My mind didn't see a choice.

Coughing, I reached for Tandy. She had to be alive.

[Base Skill Assessment: Complete

Quest Update: [Trial Dungeon]

Notice - You have not prioritized the [Trial Dungeon] in the first 24 hours. By consequence, the time allotted to complete the quest was reduced. Countdown transparency protocol enabled. You have [48] hours to complete this quest.

Congratulations - For better or worse, you've chosen your friends over survival. [Party] capabilities granted for [Trial Dungeon].

Congratulations - You have survived [2] expeditionary forces. [Mundane] Skills are granted for the [Trial Dungeon] attempt.

Adventure Onward.]

I've barely survived escaping the Raiders without skills. Now the oh-so-generous system returned my [Mundane] cooking skills, just in time to die?

Two days isn't a lot of time. We're going to need some luck.

Screw luck, we needed a miracle.

Chapter 5

NOTHING TO SEE HERE

You hard-headed son of a goat. When are you going to wake up?

Consciousness was both a blessing and a curse. Two tiny teeth pricked the side of my neck.

I know you're awake, idiot.

The problem was, I wasn't sure I was. Eyes open or closed, the view was the same. Darkness.

I remembered searching for Tandy and found her aggressive cloak. I flexed my hand, making sure it still worked. The shock had made me jerk, slamming my head into a rock.

A system indicator blinked in the darkness. Expanding the alert, it helpfully informed me of two statuses I intimately felt: [Bruised] and [Concussed].

"Did we make it? Tandy?" The words were thick in my mouth. Everything was dry and caked in dirt. It felt like a magical carriage had run me over at top speed. Nothing seemed broken, but *everything* was going to be bruised.

I raised my hand to see if the roof had collapsed further. I traced the new ceiling gingerly, then sat up carefully to avoid repeating my mistake.

My mind felt like it was trying to run through water. As the memory of Tandy pulling the column supports drifted forward, I grew more frantic.

"Tandy? You here? Richard, can you see? Do you know what happened to Tandy?" Tandy *had* to be alive. There was no other option.

Before my slug could respond, a soft groan came from the darkness. I crawled towards it, hands outstretched, searching.

"Cole, is that you?" Tandy's voice was groggy, but didn't sound pained.

My fingers found the hem of her cloak. I jerked away, belatedly realizing it hadn't stung. Had the enchantment broken? I crawled forward along the fabric, finding her prone form.

I brushed the rubble off her body. She was cold, but seemed whole.

"It's okay, you're okay," I mumbled the words as I moved a couple of stones. My aches and pains melted away through my gratitude for her survival.

Let me help, but one glow-worm joke and it is light's out. Also, the skill has a long cool down, so don't expect this for every hole you fall in.

What was left of the tunnel was bathed in a soft yellow light.

For a moment, Tandy looked dead. Dried blood from her face and several new cuts had stained her clothes. Her skin was covered in dust and dirt. My heart clenched.

Tandy must have sensed it. She grabbed my hand.

"I *am* okay." She held my hand until our eyes met. "I'm here, let me help you."

She sat up, the remaining rocks falling to the floor. We patted the dust off each other slowly, trying not to sully the air too much. It was reassuring just to feel each other.

As the shock of it all receded, I examined the tunnel behind us. It'd collapsed entirely.

Maybe I should have felt something for ending the [Raider's] lives, but I didn't. They chased us here, some sort of test from the [System]. Ideally, we could have spared their lives, but nothing about this moment was ideal.

I'd examine what that said about me *later*.

With Richard's light, we both limped towards the presumed exit. I kept coughing. The quality of air had improved, but the cave-in had kicked up a lot of dust.

As we walked, the tunnel grew larger and deeper, several offshoots joining ours. Arrows had been scratched into the wall, pointing forward. We debated briefly about trying the side tunnels, but ultimately agreed that getting out of town was best. Who knew if there'd been more than one [Raiding Party]?

I found an old torch hanging from one of the nodes in the wall. It lit quickly, allowing Richard to take a break as our sole provider of light.

Footstep after footstep passed. I triggered one of my [Meditation] skills, [Monotonous Calm], and was surprised when it worked. Small mercies.

The skill stopped my mind from spinning out into what-ifs in moments like this. It allowed me to focus on one foot in front of the other. Part of my mind noted how the rough, human-carved tunnel gave way to a more natural cave wall. Dirt and wood support beams became rock and stalagmites.

Markers pointing the way were still present, so I didn't question the change. I was tired, my body ached, and my life narrowed down to taking the next aching step.

"COLE!" Tandy snapped her fingers in front of my nose. I blinked and focused on her face. "Are you with me?"

I nodded, unsure why she'd interrupted our trek.

"We're here, we made it."

I leaned against the cavern wall, exhausted, and looked around for the first time.

When the tunnel had turned into a cave, I'd assumed we'd just walk out into the forest. Everything had melded into the death march to the end of the trail. As I examined our surroundings, there were obvious signs that my foggy brain had missed.

Thankfully, Tandy had been paying attention, as the cavern we were currently in had metal footholds sunk into the wall, leading up to what appeared to be another hatch ten feet off the ground.

I stared at it stupidly for a moment. It felt like we'd been trying to escape for hours.

"Are you alright?" she asked.

"I don't know." The words came out thick. "I used one of my [Meditation] skills, but it normally doesn't affect me like this."

Tandy was suddenly in my face. It was so quick, I almost jumped out of my skin. She looked nothing like her freckle-covered self. She looked like the victim of a kiln explosion, blood, sweat, and dirt mixed in wiped splotches. Her braids were disheveled.

"You look awful." The words came out before I could stop them.

She looked at me square in the eyes, her expression disapproving. I mimicked her, not knowing what else to do, and stared back. She was lucky none of the wood fragments had hit her eyes. She was fortunate the tunnel hadn't collapsed on her head.

"And you have a concussion. You know better than to trigger a mind-based skill when you've hit your head. Turn it off."

Commanding the skill to turn off was like mentally wading through molasses. It was slow, and my mind kept getting distracted. When I finally shut it off, the internal click was painfully sharp. A throbbing headache replaced the out-of-body numbness.

Tandy nodded, watching me wince. Her face changed to her typical "I told you so" expression.

"Let's get out of here," I muttered, setting down the torch and grabbing the ladder's lowest rung. Richard refrained from commenting, thankfully, as what little concentration I had was spent clinging to the side of the wall.

At the top, the hatch was bolted into rock.

Every motion caused muscles to ache painfully, and my head kept threatening to turn the world sideways. I looped my left arm firmly around a rung as I tried to figure out how to open the hatch.

A rusty bolt had locked into place, the tip disappeared into a bored hole in the stone. I grabbed the knob trying to slide it free. Rusty flakes fell off the mechanism, but it didn't budge.

Let me help.

Richard glided forward, rubbing against the hatch. A gooey slime trail followed in his wake, coating the mechanism thoroughly. I watched in amazement as the goo began to bubble.

"Should I be worried if this drips on me?" I watched, my nose only a few inches away.

Not as long as you stay on my good side. Give it a try now.

I grabbed the knob and pushed at the bolt. It was still frozen, but the effort caused it to shift, which was promising. I wiggled it, watching as rust and goo glooped off. Another shove, and the whole bolt shifted. The hatch was unlocked.

Now was the moment of truth. I wasn't sure what would greet us on the other side, but we couldn't stay in the cave. Our torch was already sputtering. I longed for clean air and a dunk in the creek. At this point, I'd settle for death on the tip of a [Raider's] sword if it meant fresh air.

I reached down, finding comfort in the fact that my

hammer was still looped on my belt. If it came to it, I wouldn't go down without a fight.

I grabbed the hatch handle and pushed. Nothing happened. I shifted, angling my shoulder, and shoved. The hatch moved, and a shower of dirt rained down on the two of us.

Spitting grit out of my mouth, I got the first bit of fresh air since we'd entered the tunnel. It smelled of the sweet mossy pine of the Heltenic Forest around Woodsten. As I pushed up a few more inches, the hatch groaned, revealing a moonlit patch of forest that could have been anywhere around the city.

Scanning the ground, I found a pair of boots standing in my limited field of vision.

A deep voice greeted me from the surface. "It's about damn time."

Chapter 6

WHOSE PARTY?

A beefy hand wrapped around the lip of the hatch. Crap. I pulled at the handle, trying to close it, but it didn't budge. We were screwed.

"Leo, is that you?" Tandy's shout echoed in my head. I should have recognized his voice, but it still felt like wool had been shoved between my ears.

Leo removed all doubt, however, when he yanked the hatch up. Thankfully, I still had my left arm firmly looped in a rung, or his enthusiasm would have flung me off the ladder. Above, my six-foot-tall, straw-haired giant of a friend grinned down at us.

"Can you believe I found you guys?" He reached down, gave me a hand, and pulled me up like a toddler. Tandy scrambled up, too dignified for the toddler treatment.

"Honestly, I can't. How *did* you find us?" I asked. I slowly scanned the forest, trying to figure out where we were. The trees blended into anonymity in the evening air, making the spot look like every other part of the Heltenic Forest.

"I'm a [Provisional Adventurer] now, and we're in a party!" Leo stated it as though pointing out the stars in the sky.

I looked at Tandy for an explanation, wondering just how hard I'd hit my head. If we were in a party, why hadn't I gotten a notification? Even drunk me wouldn't have agreed to Leo being the [Party Leader].

I'd follow Tandy into the pits of hell, or in the most recent example, an escape tunnel abyss. But Leo? Never. I loved the guy like a brother, but he was missing a few tools from his mental toolbox.

Tandy, thankfully, had answers. "The party functionality didn't trigger for me until I regained my [Mundane] skills. Do you have a water canteen, Leo?"

My mouth puckered at the word water.

"I got my [Mundane] skills back, and it didn't trigger for me," I blurted. Tandy took a slow drink, swishing the water in her mouth. My words were thick, as the anticipatory saliva mixed with the dust in my mouth. "I don't see how these things are connected."

Tandy handed me the canteen, and I greedily took a long pull.

"I suspect it's the [Concussed] state. It's impacting you more than I think you suspect. Being in a party allows us to track each other on a mental map. I've followed Leo's progress as he's tracked us away from the city. I mentioned it to you at that first fork."

Had she? I couldn't remember Tandy saying anything.

She did, but you were in the middle of your [Monotonous Calm] skill.

I scooped Richard off my shoulders, holding him before me. I stared him right in the tentacle. "Did *you* know?"

Was I the only one worried about where the tunnel let out? About whether Leo survived the raid? Or if another band of [Raiders] were going to be waiting for us at the exit?

Yes, I'm part of your party, too. Richard's tentacles extended with an air of innocence. *You didn't ask.*

"Uh, Tandy? Why is Cole talking to a slug? How hard *did* he hit his head?" Leo broke in, destroying my moment.

"That's Cole's special friend, Richard."

"He's my animal companion." Special friend? Who said that? Richard got a dark look as I returned the mollusk to his usual perch on my shoulders. "He's also a complete dick."

Leo looked at me, wide-eyed. Then looked at Tandy, who covered a grin.

"*Richard's* a *dick?* That tracks," Leo said with a straight face, before bending over in laughter. Tandy started chuckling, not able to hold it in herself.

I tried covering my embarrassment by taking another long drink of water.

I don't get it.

Water shot out of my mouth as I lost it. It was good to laugh. The three of us had pulled each other out of ditches more times than I could count. We'd handled disappointment, change, even first loves together. We stood on the cusp of hell laughing at a dumb joke, and I had no regrets about my company.

Whether it was the laughter or the water, someone thought I'd suffered enough.

[[Concussed] status has ended. All attributed adverse effects have been removed.]

[You have been invited to join [Your Mom's Party]. Do you accept the invitation?]

The fog over my mind slowly lifted. I mentally acquiesced to the [System's] request. Only one idiot in Woodsten would name our party that.

[Congratulations - You have joined [Your Mom's Party].

[Tandy Selvedge] has been designated [Party Leader] with all additional attributes granted.]

My mind expanded as new tabs opened up on my interface. I could sense that Tandy was hurt, but slowly healing. That Leo was strong. I even had a sense of Richard.

Looking inward, I could bring up a map that included a small part of Woodsten and the entirety of the escape tunnel we'd traversed. It showed every place I'd been since becoming a [Provisional Adventurer].

"I still can't believe you didn't tell me about this," I muttered.

Under your [Monotonous Zombie] spell, would you really have listened?

Point made.

My [Mundane] classes and skills were viewable, and I had a vague sense of where my [Adventurer] classes and skills would appear, assuming I passed the [Trial Dungeon]. The sheet gave me a dull impression of having some information filled in.

Yet every time I tried to bring it into focus, a notification indicated I had [1 day, 23 hours] to enter a [Trial Dungeon].

"This map skill *is* incredible. It would have saved us so much trouble when we were kids." So many of our plans and pranks had gone sideways, even with the most detailed planning, due to the unforeseen logistical challenges. "So, Leo, tell me about our [Party] name?"

Leo smiled widely. "Like it? I blame the two of you. The [System] forced me to pick everything since you two were knocked out. I know you're upset about Tandy being our Team Lead, but she's cuter than you." He said the last bit *loud*, earning an eyeroll from Tandy, who had been hip deep in [System Notifications].

She was the right choice for [Party Leader]. Already, I could tell she was stitching together our next steps.

"So, what's the plan, oh fearless leader?" I picked up my pack, trying to find the bag of granola and berries I'd brought for a snack.

"We need rest." She waved off my protest. "It's late, and we need to sleep. The [Trial Dungeon] looks to be up by the foothills of Bear Ridge, so it's only a day's hike away. Leo, is there a good camping spot nearby? Preferably one with a stream?"

I couldn't argue with her logic. Examining my map, I expanded the view. Off to the west, towards the mountains, was a gold star indicating the position of the local [Trial Dungeon].

Leo was much more familiar with the Heltenic Forest than either Tandy or me. Depending on the season and village needs, he'd been working off and on as a hunter, trapper, and lumberjack.

We flipped the tunnel hatch back down and followed him cross-country until he found a deer track that led in the right direction. The conifer forest stretched before us, filled with damp ferns, patches of dogwood, and a rare oak. The moon was full and high in the sky when he pulled us towards a clump of trees I recognized.

It was one of the old forts we camped in as kids. Several trees had woven together to form a barrier of sorts from the rest of the forest. We'd spent hours weaving branches together and placing stones for the fire pit to make it a fort worthy of our childish adventures. A small brook ran nearby, making it the perfect spot.

Immediately, we set about our chores. I borrowed Leo's axe to break down some wood for the fire. Tandy went to clean up and get a pot of water for dinner. Leo cleaned the site, checked the fire ring, and set the dry kindling.

Before I knew it, I sat clean, wrapped in my mom's quilt, watching the fire crackle as dinner cooked.

All was right with the world.

We were close enough to the Ursine Wall to hear the evening bells. The deep, mournful toll of the Everbear's Guardians filled the evening. No one in Woodsten had seen one of the sentinels that guarded the mountains from the wild, [Corrupted] monsters from the east. But on a cold night, we could hear the bells even down in Woodsten.

Some believed the nights the bell tolls signaled the death of one of the guardians.

I gazed into the fire, listening to their tone. I'd always taken comfort in it. Their ancient magic kept the world safe. I stared in the flames and, let my mind drift in the wispy, ethereal lick.

"Are you still meditating? I can't believe you still do that." Leo's voice was a harsh interruption to my semi-trance. Always ready for a good-natured jab, he kept me grounded.

"I'll stop meditating when I stop leveling it." Maybe I had hit my head harder than I thought. That was a low blow to a man who couldn't level. Leo had never earned a [Mundane] class or skill.

"Sure, like [Self Flagellation] is a specialization worth having." He said it with a smile and a raised eyebrow.

I turned beet red at the deserved poke. He might not be able to gain a class, but every time I progressed, I'd end up with the most idiotic specialty.

"It's been a rough enough day, no reason to keep pointing out I'm hanging out with two losers." Tandy was carefully braiding her hair, restoring order and tidiness. We'd pulled the remaining splinters out of her face in the moonlight.

She looked better, but the scratches would take a while to heal.

"Do either of you remember Leo's birthday? Tandy, I can see how Leo and I got here, but you? Why did you sign up to be an [Adventurer]?" I was lying a bit, because I couldn't understand why *any* of us had signed up to be [Adventurers].

Sure, my life wasn't amazing, but had I hated it *that* much?

Leo poked at the fire with a stick, causing a fountain of sparks. Tandy pulled another piece of hair into the weave of her braid. It'd been a while since we sat around a campfire. The kids who hunted imaginary goblins and built forts in the trees were long gone. A memory of Tandy catching a frog and chasing Leo around with it surfaced.

Man, that guy *hated* frogs.

Tandy leaned close. "Your cloak has a hole in it."

Leo and I shared a look. Tandy could be stubborn. But we both knew she'd tell the truth if you waited long enough. I stayed silent, the epitome of patience.

Everything you own has holes in it.

She fingered a gash in the weave I'd gotten last year. She'd given it to me a few years back. "Why didn't you ask me to mend it? It would have been this easy."

She muttered [Seamless Fix], and I watched in awe as the cloak glowed a soft golden light as the holes wove themselves whole.

Tandy had slowly been pulled away from Leo and me to do her family's craft. She had skills and purpose. Leo and I... we were just stumbling through with sweat equity and dumb luck. It's not that we stopped being friends. We just hung out less. Our various jobs and responsibilities didn't allow our off-hours to match.

"I was going to, it's just been a while. And you've got more important things than me." The words were true enough, but they soured in my mouth.

Tandy just nodded and looked at Leo, shivering in his tunic.

"And you, Leo? Where's the cloak I gave you last year?"

I winced. Leo looked at her and shrugged. I knew he had lost it this past winter logging. It'd been ripped to shreds when a tree fell in the wrong direction, catching him in the aftermath.

"Uh-huh." Tandy stood, walking to her pack leaning against a tree. She muttered, rifling through it. "Here it is." She held up a woolly sweater, dyed a girlish pink, obviously sized for her.

Leo opened his mouth, I'm sure to point this out, when she spoke her second skill of the night.

"[Shape the Weave]."

I watched in wonder as the sweater reformed itself to fit our lumberjack friend. He was a head taller than Tandy, with broad shoulders, but it fit perfectly when he pulled it over his head. The sweater was still pink, but the fabric stretched effortlessly over his frame. The color worked with his blond hair.

"I bet neither one of you remembers Leo's birthday clearly." Tandy's eyes were glued to Leo, already knowing my answer.

"Sure don't. You know how I get when I drink that much," Leo said with the dopey grin that made him impossible to hate.

Tandy was unsurprised at his answer. "I wasn't drunk at all. So, Cole, if you want to blame one of us, you should blame me. And if you don't want me to be the [Party Leader], I'll understand why."

Leo and I glanced at each other briefly. It's all it took to know we were of the same mind.

I scooted closer to Tandy, seeing a lone tear trace down her face. I put an arm around her shoulders, ignoring the ache in my back. Leo joined us, leaning into the other side of Tandy.

"You don't think you can get rid of us that easily?" Leo nudged her, getting a small smile.

"Yeah." I squeezed her against me. "Like it or not, you're stuck with these losers. I just want to know why."

Tandy let out the breath she'd been holding, and it was

like an emotional dam broke. Tears ran freely for a moment, as we sandwiched her between us, trying to convey our love. We might be doomed, but we were sticking together.

Eventually, her voice soft, she began telling her story.

"I don't know if you two knew this, but I *hate* sheep."

Chapter 7

ALL FOR ONE?

"I'm not one to hold sheep hatred against a person, but it does seem a rather large leap to [Adventurer]." I knew my words were tinged with bitterness, with poison. But I was having difficulty letting go of the low probability we would survive the [Trial Dungeon].

The fire popped. Silence sat between us as darkness settled on our little camp. We sat beside each other, but not as close, with our backs to the wilderness. The trees loomed ominously in a way they never did when we were kids. Perhaps I was just less fearless.

I couldn't meet Tandy's gaze, so I focused really hard on poking the fire with a stick.

Tandy sighed and pulled out her practice weave. She'd had this square of cloth as long as she'd been a [Weaver]. It glowed a dull orange-yellow between her fingers, the edge unraveling as she used a disassembling skill.

"Cole," her brown eyes raised to meet mine, glowing in the reflected firelight, "I don't want to be a [Weaver]." She said it heavily, like it was a confession. Misery sat in every line of her face. The cloth under her hands glowed again, causing a tear to form.

"Duh," Leo said, breaking the levity of the moment.

I elbowed him. But it *was* an obvious statement. She'd been saying it in different ways for years. We knew the girl who carelessly romped around the countryside with us when we were boys wouldn't be happily tied to a loom.

What wasn't obvious, however, was why that led us all to the Adventurer's Guild. Many options in life don't risk life and death like [Adventurers]. Even this path didn't have to involve us. I gestured for her to continue.

"I hit level forty last week." Now, *this* was a secret. No one revealed their true levels, even to friends. And level forty was unfathomable. At that level, Tandy was a [Master Weaver], a feat people could spend their whole life chasing and never attain. She would have received a personalized mastery title.

Doing this at twenty-five was impossible. If it were true, it meant she had [Sage] potential and was on track to be the greatest [Weaver] of a millennium. Her face showed none of the expected happiness at the achievement. She looked away, slumped on the stump, not a trace of triumph in her body.

Her hands gripped the practice cloth tightly, pulling the weave apart. No skill glowed, as the fabric broke.

"I went to the circle. My mom, my grandma, and the aunties were waiting. It was like they knew. They expected it before I did. My grandmother's eyes shone like I had done something so special." Tandy's voice was harsh, angry at a feat I couldn't imagine—making my parents proud?

She took a breath, almost a sob. It took everything in me not to reach for her. Tandy continued, quieter. "I lost it. I told them the truth. For the first time, I let loose. I *didn't* want this life they'd carefully mapped out."

She picked at the torn fabric, pulling out individual threads. "For the last five years, I have barely breathed without fabric in my hands. The constant practice of following their expensive guide to progression. They never bothered asking what I wanted from life."

Leo and I looked at each other. I'd suspected Tandy's family had a progression guide, but Tandy would never admit it. I wondered how much that guide had cost her family.

It had always surprised me that the girl with the most potential in Woodsten would hang out with the two guys with the least potential. It was starting to make sense.

She'd never helped us, and I was beginning to see why. Making her family proud had cost her nothing less than her own dreams for life.

Tandy's hands glowed again with a skill, and the bundle of threads in her hand changed color to maroon, her favorite color.

"I knew it was a mistake. My mom was angry. My grandmother refused to look at me. It was a mistake, but once I started talking, I couldn't stop. The levee broke, and I couldn't stop myself. I couldn't tell them fast enough; every resentment I'd held for the last decade just bubbled out."

Tandy's shoulders slumped with the admission. "I never wanted the family tradition and the life of the loom. I didn't choose to have [Sage] potential. To be a [Threadmarked Weaver] at twenty-five." She said the last with a mocking singsong. Her hand glowed, and another bundle of threads turned pink, matching Leo's new sweater.

The rejection of her calling sat between us, a hot coal that slowly burned at the bonds of our friendship. While Leo and I had grown up to become outcasts for our [Broken] builds, she'd been the town belle and her family's pride.

I'd tried to keep a tight lid on my jealousy. Leo had been less successful over the years, as his fate as a [Broken] solidified.

[Threadmarked Weaver]. The words hung between us. Only a handful of folks in the region had personalized [Master] classes. All but one were in their eighties.

"At least you have a class," Leo said bluntly, his face downcast.

Tandy winced. She knew she'd broken the unspoken rule: never bring up your system attributes in front of Leo.

She picked out another bundle of threads from her cloth and carefully chose her words. "Sorry, Leo. Honestly, you're the reason I kept at it so long. I felt so guilty for having the one thing you wanted that I just sucked it up. I put what I wanted into a tiny box and buried it deep. I worked on my skills so hard because…" Her voice trailed off.

"Because you had to try to deserve them," I finished her sentence. I'm sure I was part of the reason, too, with my unhappiness over my lack of progression and disappointing specializations.

I put a hand on Leo's shoulder and squeezed. The tension left his body, and as he raised his face, it held the fake grin we were all used to.

"It's alright." We were all way too good at burying our feelings.

The lie sat heavy between us. A small moth fluttered into the campsite, its delicate wings beating gently as it narrowed in on its focus. The fire popped loudly as the moth died in a blaze of glory.

We were all intimately familiar with class-based shame. My father had once lectured me that we all were 'valued' village members. We all produced. Those fancy classes didn't mean much as long as you had a roof over your head and food on the table for you and your family.

At the time, I'd worked as a low-level [Smith]. I'd come home raging. Four years of labor, of working at the forge to slowly gain the skills I needed to make a go at the profession, had resulted in a Class Specialization of [Nails].

I'd quit the next day, eventually finding my place at the Ram's Horn. Years under Marta had resulted in a similar outcome. I'd gotten a [Gruel] Class Specialization, and my fellow [Chefs] dubbed me the 'Master of Mush', making me the laughingstock of the kitchen.

Marta kindly took me off the breakfast shift.

"Later that day, I met with you to celebrate your birthday." She leaned into Leo with the unspoken apology. "I didn't expect it to go the way it did. I just knew I couldn't return to being a [Weaver]. Signing a guild contract was something I knew my family couldn't take from me. Couldn't talk me out of being. I can't escape the hope that there is more to life."

The threads in her hand glowed as she triggered another skill, changing the fabric color to the blue and green of my faded cloak.

That was the crux of it. That irritating quality I [Self Flagellate] myself with, hope. Even after my specialization failures and Leo's inability to attain a class, we both kept trying. Kept hoping that one day, something would change.

Change was here, for better or worse.

"It's going to be okay." The words were meant for Tandy and Leo, but I also believed them. An adventure with the three of us *felt* right. We were returning to our roots, to the times I cherished the most in my life. "Leo, you've already gained your first class. Sure, it's provisional, but we'll make it permanent."

He gave me a nod with a small, genuine smile peeking through.

"And Tandy, a blind donkey could see you weren't suited for the [Weaver] life. You're one of us, and now you're with us."

Tandy's hands glowed a brilliant orange gold. The tattered practice cloth she'd been disassembling wove together before our eyes. The three colored threads were braided in and out of the new design.

Did she trigger multiple skills at once?

I mentally shrugged at Richard's question. I'd long ago accepted that Tandy could do impossible things.

Hot tears sprang from her eyes. "Thank you." She gave me a look that made my throat close up. "I've never wanted my stupid family's legacy. I've hated it and hated that it kept me away from *this*."

"Being in the forest?" I asked with a grin, trying to make a joke.

She glared at me. The joke had fallen flat. "No, not the forest." Her voice softened momentarily. "Here. With you. Out in the world." Her words were so soft as she glanced between us. The fabric in her hand shone perfectly in the firelight.

"I thought I'd have to leave without you two." She mimed throwing the mended cloth into the fire before continuing. "You both surprised me at Leo's party. You demanded to come along when I told you I was going to the recruiter's office." She pulled the fabric back, clutching it close to her chest.

"Of course," I said. The platitude was unsurprising, even expected. I think I even meant it. The poisonous knot in my chest began to dissolve.

Of course, I'd follow Tandy.

"Besides, don't you both hate your jobs? I mean, I *hate* wool. I hate sitting inside carding wool, the shuttle rhythm." She brought up her tear-streaked face, defiance shining in her eyes. "I *hate* sheep!"

Hating sheep was anathema in sheep country. She's said it before, but I never really believed her until now.

Leo and I shared a glance. He knew exactly what to say.

"Fuck sheep!"

I laughed, remembering all the moments I railed against my assigned shepherd's watch on the farm. "Yeah, fuck sheep!"

In the insanity that we were running off to be honest-to-god [Adventurers], sheep could go to hell, too. I'd never have to take a shepherd's watch, make gruel, or hammer a nail again!

Tandy started giggling. We all did. High on the stupidity of what we were about to do. She scrubbed the tears off her face as we laughed. Neither Leo nor I cared if she was the Grand Magus of Weaving. She was our friend.

You hear that?

Richard's mental voice was low and urgent. I strained my ears. We'd been talking, as though we'd sat at Ram's Horn over a pint. The Heltenic Forest was too close to the wilds to be completely safe. It'd been a mistake to let down our guard.

Rustling. I squinted into the darkness, but my eyesight was shot.

I stood up, tense. Tandy and Leo were looking at me, confused.

I can feel passive skills, so it's not a simple forest creature.

I took several steps beyond the campfire, signaling Leo to grab his axe. A branch cracked under the weight of the creature. Whatever it was, it was big.

Had another monster found us?

Chapter 8

SHEEP LOVERS

Another branch cracked. I swung my head to the left, finally making out a human silhouette. Richard was coiled around the collar of my shirt, his head stretched forward as though he could pierce the darkness.

Got it. My [Identify] skill triggered. Do you know a guy named Ched?

I groaned and waved off Tandy and Leo.

"It's just Ched," I told them.

"Hey, sheep fuckers. Sounds like you finally noticed me." Ched walked closer to our ring of trees and stepped into the firelight.

We'd grown up with Ched. He'd been a darling of the town and one of the kids who had successfully trained into an [Adventurer].

He'd never bullied us outright, like some of the other kids.

But he'd always had this arrogance that informed you of your lesser status. Less than Ched.

Becoming an [Adventurer] hadn't improved things. He frequently walked around town shirtless with his double-sided battle axe draped across his shoulders and his abs on display. He was the face of *Team Abs*.

It didn't help that Tandy had dated him for a very short time. I guess abs can bedazzle anyone for a short period of time. Leo glared at Ched with the hatred of a thousand suns. It didn't take a genius to understand why.

"What do you want, Ched?" By Tandy's tone, she was just as over Ched as the rest of us.

The man grinned, his tight cutoff shirt stretching over his biceps as he swung his axe, embedding it in a log. The fool posed, putting a foot on the log as he ran a hand through his dark hair.

"I was ordered to check on you." He didn't say it, but I heard it anyway. *On you* ***losers***. "The city gets attacked. An escape tunnel collapses, bringing down half of Aunt Milli's boarding house. And the only three missing are you all. Plus," he pointed at Tandy, "someone's grandmother is trying to get the militia to dig you out of the rubble."

The three of us exchanged glances. "No one realizes we signed up to be [Adventurers]?" Tandy asked.

Ched grinned. "No one but me. See, I got what's known as an escort mission from the [System]. It seems like it's worried you'll skip out on your duties and fail to show up for the [Trial Dungeon]. So I'm just here to help you find your way." He drew out the line, making helping us 'find our way' sound like a threat.

Before Tandy or Leo lost it, I stepped in. "Well, Ched, hopefully, escort quests give good rewards. We were camping out here tonight and headed to the [Trial Dungeon] in the morning."

Ched's expression soured, confirming what I suspected.

He'd been hoping to force a bunch of runaways into the dungeon.

Sighing, he sat on the log beside his axe, cutting off any chance at further heart-to-hearts. None of us were going to talk in front of this moron. While I rolled out my bedroll, Leo stoked the fire. Tandy was already lying down, the furthest away from Ched as possible.

It took us all a while to fall asleep. I was unsettled. We were on the cusp of the most significant change of our lives.

Despite a hazy memory, I'd realized something after talking to Tandy. This was *my* choice. This wasn't another job to get by, not something I had to do for my dad.

I had decided to join Tandy because I wanted a change. And the nervousness in my stomach wasn't Leo's cooking, but the reality that what I chose mattered in a way it never had in Woodsten.

This wasn't [Farmer] versus [Smith] versus [Chef]. Lives depended on us. Our lives.

Ched's snores broke my thoughts.

This man is the most annoying version of you humans, isn't he?

I grinned at Richard's commentary. The slug was stretched out in front of the fire. He *loved* the heat. It was counterintuitive. I figured he'd dry out or cook that close to the fire. As close as he was, I'd burn immediately.

Tandy was also struggling with everything. She'd put her practice cloth away, but had been muttering skills most of the night.

I turned my head, watching her try to trigger another skill. "[Weave True]!" She'd been pointing at the boughs of trees, but as far as I could tell, nothing happened. Not even a whisper of power, and she'd been at it for almost an hour.

"You okay?" I whispered, realizing Leo had started to doze.

"I *know* I can use my weaving skills to help us. I just haven't figured out *how*." A crease had formed between her eyebrows, a sure sign she was about to melt down in frustration.

Her voice was too loud, causing Leo to mutter sleepily. "Mhmm... like those strangers in the rumors. That group, uh, *Fellowship of the Rim?* They... waltz into dungeons and clear 'em like it's nothing. You'll do that, Tandy. Snap into place. You'll be a killing machine..." His voice trailed off into an oblivious snore.

Tandy's frown deepened at Leo's ramble. Even awake, he was clueless to her moods, a trait I sometimes envied. I tried to return to her original topic before she ended Leo.

"Tandy, the skill will come. In the meantime, I saw in your pack that you have some daggers? They'll do damage. If your [Weaver] skills aren't a good fit for a fight, you can still do damage. Plus, you're the brains of this operation." Which was true. Tandy was the thinker. Leo, our muscle. Which made me... the guy with the sentient slug?

"I want you to be right..." *But I'm afraid you're not.* She didn't say the words, but they were implied.

It didn't help me silence my doubts about my abilities. She wouldn't be convinced until she did it, and I'm not sure that was even enough to convince me.

I turned over, trying to get comfortable. It wasn't worth arguing with her in this mood. I was already struggling myself.

The campsite was rocky, and none of us had brought tents. My body was still bruised, adding to the discomfort. I watched the blinking stars as Richard fell asleep. Snore snot bubbles broke with each breath. The little sluggo was curled up dangerously close to the flames. One wrong twitch and he'd be cooked.

Maybe I'd get a dire wolf after all.

Tandy muttered on, lost in quiet frustration. The Everbear constellation twinkled down on me. He was the protector of [Adventurers]. I'd never given him much significance, but having him in the sky felt good tonight.

Eventually, sleep came to us all.

I woke groggy, unsure why. It was the middle of the night. As I looked for Richard, I slowly realized that two fangs had been firmly embedded in my ear.

I'm glad you finally decided to wake up. I've only been yelling at you for the last ten minutes.

I started to reply, but he cut me off.

Silence! Do not move. Just open your eyes and look up.

He thankfully let go of my ear as I gazed up. At first, I didn't know what I was looking at. It seemed someone had connected the dots of the constellations as I slept. A silvery latticework glistened in the starlight. My eyes widened as I saw a cocooned form slowly ascend a fir tree by a long strand of thread. I followed the glistening line until I saw her.

We'd made one of the most elementary mistakes a prospective [Adventurer] could make. We'd assumed we were safe.

I didn't have to have Richard use his [Identify] skill to know that the dog-sized spider was a widowmaker. The species wasn't common, but it *was* one of the few human predators in the Heltenic forest.

The spider wove traps for sleeping prey that would snap shut if they stirred. It was known for picking off each person individually until someone woke up, causing the rest of its trap to trigger. The species was deaf but quickly caught any sudden movement or vibration through its sticky web.

Scanning the campsite, I realized Ched was in the cocoon.

I tried to brush away the twinge of guilt. If anyone at this camp knew better, it'd be Ched. Poor, stupid idiot. He probably relied on his [Party Leader] Theo for wards at night. Theo could have taken out the widowmaker with a single spell.

Ched's cocoon dragged against the tree bark as he was pulled higher. He was likely alive, just paralyzed by a bite. I looked to my party. If we could, we'd save Ched. And if we couldn't, I'd likely be mourning more than him.

"The spider is deaf, so we can talk," I said, tracking her progress with my eyes. "Are the others awake?"

Leo chose that moment to give a loud snore, answering one question.

"Cole, is that you?" Tandy's urgent whisper was good news. "Do you see it? Whatever you do, don't move."

You're lucky Leo's such a heavy sleeper. If any of you sit up, it's game over.

I ignored Richard as I answered Tandy, "I see it. What are we going to do?" This was the moment I'd been fretting, with life and death balanced on our decisions.

Heart racing, my mind chose this moment to play a memory for me: [Adventurers] talking about finding entire camps covered in webbing, sacs with dry husks pinned against trees.

The spider pulled Ched's cocoon against a tree trunk. I watched it slowly wind threads from its abdomen, anchoring Ched in place. The spider's legs moved with agility as it wove a net around the cocoon.

As if finished, I could see it looking down at us. I froze, watching as it used an existing layer of webbing to pull itself out between the trees. Once solidly perched, the spider began pulling more thread from its abdomen, stretching it across the camp fifteen feet above our heads.

The three red streaks on its belly confirmed it as a widowmaker.

I waited for Tandy to tell me what to do and realized the truth. She didn't have an answer any more than I did.

I can help.

"How? Are you going to cut it with a sarcastic comeback? Bite it with your two mighty fangs?" My comments may have been mean, but I was stressed out.

I am an [Immortal] fanged banana slug!

"You talking to Richard?" Tandy hissed, unimpressed.

I watched the spider stretch two threads together. The widowmaker lowered its mouth and added a thick dollop of glue that glowed with a red, malevolent magic. The threads were magically reinforced to pull tighter if a victim struggled.

"Yes, it's Richard. And I don't care if you're the King of the Forest Slugs. There's nothing a banana slug can do against a monster like this."

There's nothing a human [Chef] can do either. Minimally, I'll give it indigestion.

He was right, but the idea of sacrificing Richard made my stomach roil. Somehow, despite myself, I'd become attached to the little sluggo.

"Are you two done fighting over who's less useful? We need to figure this out, or we'll all die." Tandy was irritated, while Leo was still blissfully unaware of our predicament.

The three of us sat in silence. Richard's tentacles were scrunched close to his body, and I recognized it as a thinking face. The dark spots on his back glistened. Sleeping almost in the campfire hadn't dried him out at all.

Slowly, his tentacles uncurled and swung in my direction as though staring me down. He maintained tentacle-eye contact as his body undulated toward the spruce wrapped in webbing.

"Stop moving, Richard, you're going to bring her down on us." Tandy's voice was tight with anxiety.

I move too slowly for it to notice me.

Eyes focused on the widowmaker, breath held, I waited for him to be wrong. The spider kept gluing its webbing together, oblivious to the foot-long slug with a plan.

"He says he's too small."

*Too **slow**.*

I smiled, ignoring him. "What's your plan, Richard?"

I'll inch towards the anchor point on this spruce tree. Once I'm there, I'll spring her trap. Once she's focused on me, the three of you can escape.

"But springing the trap on you will kill you. That spider will eat you alive." I stopped speaking momentarily as the spider scanned the campsite. My heart thumped in my chest.

The slug kept inching forward towards his target. There had to be an alternative.

As the threads trembled above us, I saw the Everbear twinkle as it watched.

I'll be fine.

"Richard, don't be a dick!"

I sent a silent wish to the heavens, hoping my slug didn't kill us all.

Chapter 9

ON [IMMORTALITY]

I wasn't a genius at reading slug emotions, but the more Richard smiled at me, the less convinced I was that he'd survive his plan. It was a terrible plan.

The slug had slowly slimed towards the spruce. Every couple of inches, he looked back with a one-fanged attempt at a reassuring smile.

This wasn't what I wanted. To start my career as an [Adventurer] by running away. By killing my animal companion. Even if a slug wasn't ideal, he was still *my* slug.

"I think I can help. I have a skill that might make the entire webbing collapse on him," Tandy said thoughtfully.

How was that going to help?

"Thanks, Tandy," I muttered as she unbelievably took Richard's side on executing this 'plan.'

I'm [Immortal]. Besides, you can get a less sarcastic companion if I die.

The spider was sitting at the center of the campsite, spinning out its web, utterly ignorant of the approaching deranged slug.

"You're not [Immortal]." My chest tightened. "I don't want a *different* companion. Just because you're not what I would have chosen doesn't mean you're not welcome."

We both know you'd rather I was something else. This is your chance.

The words stung. I didn't know what to say; the truth hurt. Richard left a long, slimy trail that glowed faintly yellow in the campfire light. A pang of guilt wriggled in my chest. Perhaps I *had* made the dire wolf joke a few too many times in the day we'd known each other.

Last words? I'm going to unhook this widowmaker in a moment.

I didn't know what to say, so I said nothing, like a coward.

Richard had reached an anchor for the spider's trap. A thick glob of her glue sank into the tree trunk. He looked back, giving me a toothy grin before turning and chomping on the glowing anchor.

The widowmaker paused as the thread vibrated. A drip of red ichor dropped from its fangs, falling into the fire. The goo flared with a loud pop—the glue was flammable.

Richard paused in his gnawing, hoping the spider would ignore him. She watched, head tilted in confusion. Probably wondering what a bright yellow banana slug was doing picking a fight with her.

Another glue droplet pooled on her fang before raining down into the fire. A flare brightened the campsite with another loud pop.

Inspiration hit me like a hammer. "Do it! Break the anchor! Tandy, use your skill when it breaks!" I shouted almost instantly regretting my decision as Tandy looked at me, horrified.

I could see it in her eyes. She didn't think her skills would work. I'd just doomed us all.

Richard didn't hesitate. He gnawed with renewed vigor, snapping his teeth down on the bundle of threads. Filaments twanged as they broke, and any question the widowmaker had about Richard's intent evaporated. Her long, spindly legs pulled her abdomen off the web nexus, and she raced towards Richard's position.

As she moved, Richard, the hopefully [Immortal] banana slug, triggered the trapping magic. The web structure launched at him, wrapping him in an immobilizing grip. The widowmaker descended to examine her catch.

Richard struggled as the filaments squeezed him. I'd risked everything on this moment, and I suddenly wasn't sure it'd been the right call.

"Here goes nothing." Tandy's voice was strained as she summoned one of her skills with a shout. "[Tighten the Weave]!"

The air vibrated as though fighting the skill. Tandy's face was taut with strain.

Nothing. Sweat glistened on Tandy's face. My plan was backfiring. I frantically looked around, trying to think of something I could do.

"Work, you useless skill!" She shouted at the system. Every line on Tandy's face was edged with determination. "[TIGHTEN THE WEAVE]!"

The air quivered again. This time, she reached for the webbing above our heads. Her finger glowed molten copper as it made contact with the threads. The world snapped as her magic took hold, streaking across the webbing.

As Richard struggled, the entire web structure snapped shut on him. The webbing collapsed into a tangled ball, which captured the widowmaker as well. Richard and the spider struggled to free themselves.

Ched's cocoon dropped as all the supporting anchors vanished. He hit with a dull, soundless thud.

More bands of filament wrapped over the spider and

Richard's bodies, forming a cocoon of wet, sticky, ever-tightening webbing.

It was my turn to act. I reached for a stick sitting in the fire. The widowmaker, who had some immunity to the sticky properties of her webbing, had started to free herself. Several legs were pushing to give her an avenue of attack. She bared her fangs, ready to plunge them into my helpless yellow slug.

Richard wriggled ineffectually.

I jumped towards the tangled mess and slapped the fiery embers of my stick into the cocoon.

The sac ignited as though doused in oil, and the flames whooshed as they rushed down the filaments. The spider, trapped in its fiery grip, couldn't escape. It writhed and screamed.

Desperately, the widowmaker used a skill and shimmered. It slipped through the fibers, popping out of the cocoon. The spider landed feet first. With teeth bared, she snarled.

Rearing up on her hind legs, burning filaments still clinging to her body, the three stripes on her chest glowed with a menacing power. Her beady eyes locked on me with hatred.

I braced for her attack.

Just as she launched, Leo flew in with Ched's axe. He buried it squarely through the spider's head. The swing broke through her carapace, causing her ichor-producing organs to be exposed to the fire.

If Leo hadn't killed her himself, the explosion of ichor ripping her body apart did the job.

The three of us watched as her bodiless legs twitched. I swatted at a floating ember of her husk as we got credit for the kill.

[Widowmaker defeated. You have earned experience. Further details and rewards will be aggregated and awarded upon [Trial Dungeon] completion.]

"Did we just kill a real monster and live to talk about it?"

Leo asked, grinning as he tried to pull Ched's axe out of the corpse.

"I hope so." I kneeled beside the tangled bundle of webbing. As I examined it, trying to figure out how to get to Richard, the glow from the widowmaker's magic faded. The burnt cocoon began disintegrating.

Frantically, I dug around searching for Richard. Where was he?

Flames still moved through the layers of webbing. Dread ate at my stomach as I had to slow down or get burned. The air reeked of burned hair and smoldering silk.

"Richard, are you in there?" I didn't hide the panic in my voice. Like it or not, I cared about the slug. Finally, I hit something slimy.

I held my breath. Was he dead? Did I kill him by setting everything ablaze?

The edges of the filament glowed red, eating at the last layers. A faint yellow shone through.

The cocoon slowly eased as four smug tentacles poked out. Another pulse, and Richard slithered out from under the last layers. He looked dry and charred, but whole. I couldn't erase the relieved grin on my face.

How'd you know I would not immolate with the spider? Maybe I'm just immune to its venom.

"Calculated risk. Weren't you going to sacrifice yourself anyway?" I wiped sweat from my eyes, waiting as his outrage grew. "Besides, everyone knows banana slugs are resistant to fire. You were practically sleeping in the fire pit."

"Did he make it?" Tandy asked as she and Leo joined me.

They'd prioritized Ched's cocoon. Cutting through it, they'd confirmed he was still alive. He leaned against a tree, trussed up and dazed but in one piece. Richard was everyone's concern now.

"He did," I said as I cradled the singed mollusk.

"Good boy." Leo scratched under Richard's chin.

It'd been *my* plan that saved us. Well, our plan. I crushed my indignation.

Richard basked in the team's affection. They gave him the win. I didn't *really* mind.

You could have killed me, you know. Resistance to fire doesn't mean immunity. You're just lucky I have a ***strong*** *resistance.*

Tandy held him now as he rolled so she could scritch his belly. His mental voice had a fake outrage as he leaned into Tandy's attention.

"A good cook doesn't burn their dinner."

Richard gave a mental sigh. *You're going to be the death of me.*

The acrid smell of burned webbing hung in the air. I'd made the right move for the first time in years.

With a rakish grin, I called his bluff. "I thought you were [Immortal]?"

The slug sat up in Tandy's hands, using a tentacle to flick a glowing ember off his back.

[Immortality] is relative.

Chapter 10

MEREDEATH

"I like the heft of Ched's axe," Leo said as he swung said axe around. It sang in his hands, whistling as it cut the air.

I bet it's got a handling [Enchantment] on it. It's a Rare [Enchanted Axe of Singing].

Richard's [Identify] skill was more useful than I thought. Tandy had been picking up the destroyed campground. It was a clear sign she was stuck in her head.

"Great job with [Tighten the Weave]. I'm glad it worked," I said to test the waters, and I watched her response.

Tandy kept packing as she muttered, "Yeah, we got lucky."

She confirmed my theory, she still didn't believe in herself. In her skill's utility.

I frowned, bending down to help nest the dishes for packing. I reached over and put a hand in front of the towel she'd been trying to fold.

Tandy finally stopped to look at me, so I continued. "You did it. You used one of your skills in a fight. It's exactly what you wanted. Why don't I get the impression you're happy about it?"

Tandy set the towel down and sat back. "I wasn't sure it was going to work. It almost didn't, but a spider *weaves* its web, right? I spent most of the night staring at the canopy, trying to figure out how my skills would be useful in combat. What will I do when the next one fails? When there's no web?"

It was unsettling to see Tandy so unsure, especially about her skills. She had the '[Sage] potential,' that supreme confidence in her skill set. The surest-footed in our group, at least until Leo got liquor in him.

But now, we were all in uncharted waters.

"It didn't fail. It won't." Neither of us believed my words. Tandy returned to folding at the meaningless platitude, so I touched her shoulder. "Hey." I choose my next words carefully. "*If* your skill does fail, *we'll* figure it out together." Now that, I meant.

She gave me her half-smile, which meant I'd gotten her superficial agreement. I decided it was good enough. Fake it until you make it.

The charred husk of the widowmaker was sitting not five feet from us. We had to be doing something right. Tandy moved to collect some of the uncharred loose webbing draped across the trees.

Not wanting to push my luck, I turned to our latest problem. "So Ched, you ready to come out of that cocoon?"

"I've told you six times, I want out!" He struggled against the bonds of the weave. Although it'd lost the tightening powers of the spider, he was still trussed like a festival goose.

"Great, what can you tell us about the [Trial Dungeon] to help us survive?" Leo asked, holding Ched's axe across his shoulders, mimicking the [Axeman].

"I told you, I can't share any information. If I could, I would, but there are rules."

"You need to do something for us. Last night was a complete failure of your escort quest," I chimed in, joining the conversation.

Ched sat quietly until Tandy put it together. "Unless his quest had an 'or' clause. Either he gets us to the [Trial Dungeon] *or* we die as a punishment for not making it."

"Is that true?" Leo was starting to lose his temper and, with the guilty look on Ched's face, I didn't blame him.

Leo lifted the axe and swung it hard. For a brief moment, I thought he was going to hit Ched. Wood chips flew as the axe head sank into the log, not a foot away from our spider-bound captive. He bent down until he was in Ched's face. "*Is it true?*"

Ched's face was white as he gave a slow nod, then looked away.

As much as I hated Ched at that moment, I took one look at Leo and decided I needed to step in. We weren't going to kill Ched or leave him here wrapped up like a present for some other lurking monster. There were limits to what I'd allow our collective anger to do. I pulled out my belt knife and began sawing at the webbing.

"What are you doing?" Leo demanded. I knew he was going to need to be appeased.

"I'm doing what we should have done an hour ago: freeing the idiot."

Ched's body sagged in relief as the fibers loosened. "Thank—"

"Not so fast, you still owe us. We saved you even though you were prepared to let us die. I think," I pretended to look around, "that shiny axe of yours would be a good repayment for our trouble."

Ched looked at his prized axe. I stopped cutting to let him think.

Leo leaned over and pulled the axe head out of the log with a yank. Glancing up, I could see him trying to hide a grin. He hadn't wanted to kill Ched. He just needed justice in the form of a new, very sharp weapon.

"Yes, fine." Ched was smart enough to understand he could buy a new axe. For us, it was a huge win. We just scored a real [Enchanted] weapon. Surviving the [Trial Dungeon] just got a little more possible.

After cutting Ched free, we finished packing up and headed out. Every minute we spent packing felt like an invitation for another monster. We packed fast.

Leo led as he knew the route best. He twirled the new axe in his hand as he walked. Tandy followed, fiddling with the ball of uncharred webbing she'd snagged. Ched was next, unarmed. He kept muttering about his quest.

Richard and I brought up the rear of our group. I monitored Ched while Richard watched for anything sneaking up behind us.

Hours passed, and the mossy forest of giant trees gave way as the land sloped upward. The trees were stunted, and the undergrowth became sparse.

The [Trial Dungeon] portal was in the foothills of the Ursine Wall, the mountains separating civilization from the wilds. It got colder as we trekked, and pockets of snow sat in the shadows.

Leo had linked us up with the main trail up to the ridge. The morning fog had given way, and the view was incredible. Woodsten looked so small nestled in the forests, with the Eastern road snaking in and out of the city.

The narrow trail opened up onto a saddle between two mountains. We'd made it to Bear Ridge. Over the millennia, a pocket formed at high altitude, causing an alpine lake to form. The basin also sheltered the area from the harshest blizzards.

This is where a small [Adventurers] post sat guarding the [Trial Dungeon] portal.

Woodsten sent supplies for the area administrator, Malyc, who stood arms crossed in the middle of the path.

"You're late." Malyc was an odd fellow. He wore the robes of one of the bureaucrats of the Adventurer's Guild. He'd come to Woodsten seeking an isolated post and had begrudgingly become a mountain man to survive. Everyone knew he preferred his books to the challenge of Bear Ridge.

Tandy raised her eyebrow. "According to our quest log, we have twenty-two hours before needing to enter the [Trial Dungeon]."

A woman stepped out from behind Malyc. Her clothing was unlike anything I'd ever seen. Her hair was dark at the roots, fading into an unnatural slate blue that framed dark lines elongating her eyes. She wore all black, contrasting with her pale skin. Her thin pants were dotted with holes, and her white skin peeked through a design I realized was a skull.

"The countdown is to *finish* the dungeon, not enter it," the woman cut in. She raised a clawed finger to rub at her forehead as though we'd already caused a headache.

"Oh shit," Tandy said. Distracted, I hadn't even triggered the quest dialogue for the [Trial Dungeon]. Tandy was on it, though. "She's right. We are so screwed."

"Yep, I hope the dungeon spits out my axe when it's done with you." Ched tossed the insult as he walked over to confer with Malyc.

Leo stepped forward, still in his pink sweater, holding out a calloused hand to the new woman. "My name's Leo."

She looked at his hand as if he were a small child who had brought her an unwanted worm. Reaching out, she daintily touched the ends of his fingers. "Meredeath."

Leo's face blossomed into an interesting shade of red.

Trying to be suave, I stepped in to save my friend. "Hi, I'm Cole, and that's Tandy. What's your role in all of this?"

I didn't extend a hand, but I may have held my breath as her eyes scanned me.

"Is that a slug on your shoulders?" Meredeath stepped forward out of curiosity. She held her finger out towards Richard, and I realized she didn't have claws. They were painted extensions of her nails.

She waited, fingers stretched as though letting a dog get a sniff. I don't know what Richard did, because she smiled and lightly moved to scratch his chin.

Her scent coiled around me. It was a dark, woody musk reminiscent of secrets and dark promises. I hated how much I liked it.

I tried not to stare, but a skull amulet sat right between her breasts, almost pulsing with power.

"Cole, did you hear me?"

I blinked, looking back up into Meredeath's face. I could feel the heat in my cheeks as I stammered, "No, I missed it. What did you ask?"

She smiled self-satisfied. "What's his name?" I stared at her stupidly before she stepped away. "The slug?" she added helpfully.

The spell had broken, and I found my voice. "Richard. His name's Richard."

"If you two are done, we must get into the [Trial Dungeon] *now*. We have less than a day to complete our quest!" Tandy was almost panicked.

I should have been, but this mistake confirmed what I already knew. We would fail the trial.

"Why are you here?" I ignored Tandy, wanting to get one more word. I wanted to prolong this moment to avoid focusing on my imminent death.

"I'm here to join your party," Meredeath said over her shoulder as the silver chains on her boots tinkled as she walked away.

Chapter 11

SWALLOWED BY THE DRAGON

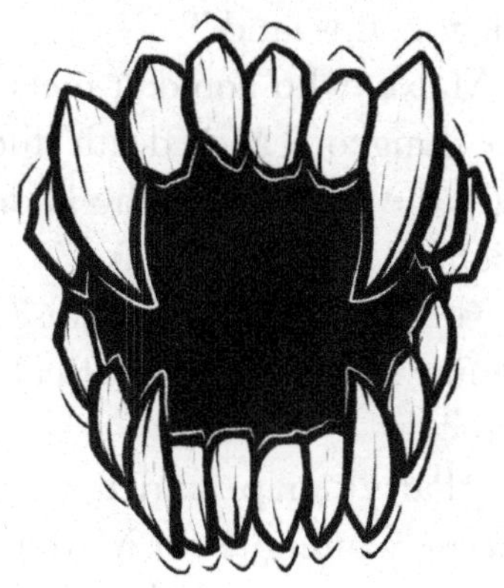

"Tandy, just send her an invite." The more people we had fighting on our side in the dungeon, the better off we'd be.

But Tandy was being stubborn. "Why should we? I haven't seen one shred of evidence that she'd actually help us."

Meredeath's face darkened, something I didn't think possible.

Malyc saved me from making a complete fool of myself. "As the Adventurer's Guild representative, I formally request that you add Meredeath to your party. I can vouch that she is deadly in a fight and has the same motivation you do for surviving the dungeon."

"There is no better motivator than death," I said, chuckling weakly.

Tandy opened her mouth to speak, but Malyc silenced her with a glare. "The young Cole is correct. Additionally, her quest has a rider. Her entire party must survive for her to be successful."

Tandy didn't have a counterargument to that. She frowned at Meredeath, then asked a question none of us expected. "Meredeath, do *you* want to go with us?"

Meredeath's stony expression lightened as she thought through Tandy's words. "It's been rare that I've been given a choice since I came to... this land."

She looked at Malyc, who couldn't meet her eyes. Was he forcing her into the dungeon? Meredeath studied us, searching for something. I got the impression she hadn't found it when she shrugged. "Might as well give it a try."

Tandy must have sent the invite, because Meredeath broke out laughing. "[Your Mom's Party]? Really? I guess some things are universal."

I checked my [Party] map, and it showed a black dot, which was appropriately ominous for Meredeath.

We walked in silence towards the [Trial Dungeon] entrance. It sat on a windswept cliff facing one of the valleys in the Ursine Wall range.

Leo and I had snuck up to the valley when we were kids to catch a glimpse of the portal. We'd imagined a magical, shimmering doorway to a different life. Instead, it'd been a disappointing white arch amid a ruined city. No showy magic. No gateway to adventure.

Wind whipped over the cliff, buffeting us harshly. I put a hand on Richard to pin him in place. It was as though the very mountains were trying to warn us away from the attempt.

The arch sat just as I remembered. A thin structure, sitting ten feet tall, with the arched curve tapering sharply as it reached for the sky. Malyc took out a thin white rod covered in runes. It seemed to be made of bone.

The Guild Representative faced us stiffly. He cradled the activation rod, looking at us with eyes devoid of emotion. "You will have three chances to prove your worth. If you expend those chances, you will forfeit your life. If you finish the [Trial Dungeon], the [System] will make your [Adventurer] class permanent. Your experience and loot will be calculated and paid upon exit. I will warn you, death is not the only way to fail this dungeon."

I shivered. Death wasn't the only way to fail? What the hell did that mean?

"As in the life of a [Mundane], *how* you achieve your goals matters. *Enter and seek glory.*"

His tone was somber, and the message rehearsed. I had questions, but his last statement had a finality that brooked no query. Tandy and Leo were frowning at the multiple ways to fail clause, while Meredeath enigmatically ignored everyone.

As Malyc stepped towards the gate, the rod in his hand shook violently. The wind suddenly abated, and the sound of the cliff left. An envelope of silence fell over all those in the arch's shadow.

I squinted, searching for any hint of a shield. Outside our bubble, the trees swayed, and the lake rippled. We'd just been ripped apart from the rest of the world.

Are you paying attention? The rod and gate are relics from another time. My [Identify] skill doesn't recognize either.

I stopped looking for a shield and refocused on the gate. Malyc slotted the rod into a node like a key. A curtain of liquid silver cascaded to the stone floor. The liquid portal pulsed slowly leaking a magical smoky green fog into the ruins.

This was magic. This was the adventure I'd yearned for as a child.

"Well, losers, I guess it's time to die." Leave it to Ched to spoil the moment. "Leo, you could save me a lot of trouble by handing my axe over now." Arms crossed, he stood several paces away, looking nervously at the gate.

Tandy looked at him. I caught a faint copper glow on her hands. "Any last tips for us, Ched?"

He sneered. "Like I could say anything helpful enough to save you."

Tandy shrugged, winking at me as she walked confidently into the portal. Leo gave me a tight smile as he walked forward. His knuckles were white on the handle of his axe as he stepped into oblivion.

Meredeath took a step towards Ched. I could see the interest in his eyes from here. She gave her message in a low whisper, but it echoed in the portal's silence. "You and I both know that they give escort quests to... winners, right? I'm not sure why Leo has your axe, but I bet it's a fun story."

Angry, he stepped towards her only to trip and fall. Meredeath walked away, stepping through the arch without hesitation.

Ched flopped around. "Who the hell tied my shoelaces together?"

Turning my back on him, hiding my smile at Tandy's joke. Where Leo and Tandy went, I would follow. Gathering what little courage I had, I walked towards the gate. It shimmered back a distorted reflection.

Richard bit sharply into my earlobe, delivering a message: *Hold your breath!*

The portal sucked me in. It pulled at my ears, clothes, and pack. Richard clung to my shirt as it whipped us around. The silver glow of the mirrored entrance gave way to a fleshy, red pulse that squeezed us forward. It felt like we were stuck in a straw, with the mouth of a leviathan sucking us forward.

With a wet, sickly pop, we were free.

The cavern was fleshy and wet. I bounced as I hit the floor with a slimy splotch. The air was tepid, humid, and smelled of decay. This had to be a nightmare.

Tandy and Leo were sprawled on the ground, while Meredeath balanced on the squishy floor with ease.

"What the hell is this place?" Tandy asked as the floor rippled under us.

"We're not in Kansas anymore." Meredeath mumbled under her breath before speaking louder, "Isn't this the dungeon you imagined?"

A glob of goo hung from the ceiling above my head. It bobbed up and down, hanging by a long, cloudy thread like an elongated raindrop. I rolled out from under it, sitting up and examining the rest of the room. Large white boulders sat in a horseshoe ring around us, with grotesque twins hanging from above.

"This is so gross." A goo drop had fallen on Tandy's head, and it stuck to her fingers as she tried to wipe it out of her hair. "Why does it smell so bad? It smells like Leo's morning breath and Cole's ambiance after drinking a pint of milk."

Meredeath's knees bent easily to accommodate another ripple across the floor. She looked at me with a raised eyebrow. "Lactose intolerant?"

I did not know what she was talking about, so I shrugged.

Richard clung to my shoulders, his usually inquisitive tentacles curled inward.

It hit me. The image my mind had conjured as I'd fallen through the portal. The boulders sat in a familiar pattern. I looked at the cavern's rear for confirmation.

An uvula dangled between two giant tonsils. We were in the mouth of a leviathan, about to get the tongue-lashing of our lives.

Slugs cause indigestion.

"Do they?" I whispered.

Chapter 12

HEART

Tandy finally managed to get to her feet, but she was covered in slime. Her hair rose on the right as if a giant dog had licked her. "I hope all dungeons aren't this gross, or I will cut my adventuring career short. One of you needs to become a [Water Mage]. Either that, or we'll need to invest in cleansing potions."

"We need some crystal wash," Meredeath said, her elongated black fingernails poking at one of the molars.

"Whatever the hell that is." Tandy was irritated. "Are we going to start this dungeon or brush its teeth?"

The [System] must have taken this as a clue that we were ready to begin the crawl, as it triggered a message:

[Quest Update: Welcome to the [Trial Dungeon]. This is the final test to receive your [Adventurer] status. You have three attempts in the [21 hours] remaining on your clock. Health, Mana, and Stamina stats have now been unlocked.

Beginning levels for these are calculated based on attributes during your tutorial period. Your continued choices will influence final classes and skills achieved, assuming you survive. Adventure Onward!]

As the [System] notification faded, three bars appeared in the corner of my vision. Focusing on them, I realized they were meant to represent my health, stamina, and magic, all of which sat at 25/25 points.

Great, now I knew precisely how unequipped I was to be an [Adventurer]. It was incredibly unfair. The [System] and the guild expected us to tackle a dungeon without a single combat ability? They might as well line us up outside a slaughterhouse.

"No skills?" Leo was focused on his stats. "How are we supposed to survive the dungeon?"

Meredeath gave him a deadpan stare. "With your brain? Although I can see where that'd be a disadvantage for you."

"At least you have your axe, and Cole's got Richard, for whatever he's worth. No offense, Richard," Tandy said distracted, her face plastered in a frown of concentration. "Some new [Party] features have opened up. I'm just going to activate them."

Whatever she did, it felt like she'd taken the air out of the room. My ears popped, and my head felt like it'd been put inside a drum. My mind unrhythmically pounded, pulled to the left and right.

Leo groaned as he doubled over. "What did you do? I feel like I just got food poisoning." His words echoed painfully in my head.

It was like a discordant band was tuning its instruments in my head. I'd focus on one, and as soon as the sound started to isolate, it'd sharply hit off-tune, losing me.

Isolate each one. Richard's words floated across my consciousness.

I focused on a deep, resonant drum. The strike of the

mallet was inconsistent. It hit square, sending a powerful thrum through my body, but then would strike the drum hoop painfully, canceling the expected resonance. Part of me recognized it was Leo—his strength, his commitment. When it hit, the sound shook my soul.

As I accepted the dissonance as something I recognized in my friend, it faded into the background.

Richard's words came back to me: *Isolate each one.*

The next instrument was a fiddle. It danced along a hundred notes, reeling freestyle. The notes taunted themselves, with an off-key hint at a sabotage attempt on the melody. Something deeper clawed to be free as the bow frayed under the fiddler's hand. In my mind's eye, I could see Tandy reweaving the bow and strings as she snapped them with her pressure.

The painfulness of the tune faded.

I'd only heard a cello once, when a troop of performers had been making a tour of the frontier. They'd traveled with several wagons, affording the storage of such an instrument. The sound I heard now was reminiscent. I could tell what the instrument desired: a lingering, haunting melody. However, each stroke of the bow produced a muffled, muted sound. The strings would squeak.

I couldn't grasp why until I imagined the player: Meredeath. She played, but the strings bit into her fingers. A mixture of blood and tears dampened each stroke of the bow.

As my understanding grew, my mind allowed the sound to fade.

The last two instruments played in my mind. I listened to a music box from another era, off-key. Slowing with each rotation, it kept plunking out one more note. Each time I drew closer with my mind, the box would reinvigorate, the music louder, the tune more off-color, less understandable. It was all other, alien, and immortal. The song of a mysterious slug.

The tune faded.

Finally, there was one last beat left. Although I knew it was mine, it was confounding. The method eluded me. A drum? My head winced, bringing a bright drum hit to mind. Sharp, clear, and direct, none of this mimicked my inner melody.

It sounded too hollow, too weak for a drum. Each hit caused a stringed resonance. Was I beating a stringed instrument? The idea caught, and I couldn't let it go. I imagined myself holding an old, frayed guitar, hitting it with the palm of my hand.

I snapped back into my body, head clear. I felt rather than saw threads of connection running between myself and the team. Each thread held information. I could pick one up and understand whether they were healthy or sick. The magic danced along their nature like Tandy, power like Meredeath, or the strength of Leo.

I looked at Richard, who had two tentacles giving me side-eye. For a fleeting moment, I understood why we were bonded. I glimpsed his feigned [Immortality]. As the minutes passed, the insights I'd gleaned faded.

A [System] notification blinked in the corner of my vision.

[Skill Acquired: You have gained a new [Meditation] skill, [Stillpoint]. When mental overload strikes, you reach inside for the stillness to recognize each beat. Centered, you can organize incoming chaos into sensory bundles and categories to be revisited or ignored. This skill is passive.]

[Skill Acquired: You have gained a new [Party] skill, [Heartbeat]. While not your team's strongest or most intelligent, you have heart. This platitude rarely comes with perks. However, with this skill, you can feel the connection between yourself and integrated team members. Status, knowledge, and insight will flow through these connections if you pay attention. Warning, as the heart of the team, you are more susceptible than your teammates to see what you want to see. This skill is passive.]

[Skill Acquired: You have gained a new [Party] skill, [Partial Rapport]. This allows for sharing basic data between party members, including enemy identification, and alerts for low health, stamina, and mana. This skill can be upgraded if team cohesion statistics warrant such an upgrade. This skill is passive.]

Well, look at that. It'd been a while since I'd gotten a new skill in [Meditation], and I'd never earned two skills at once, much less three. I was not sure what any of them would do for me in a fight, but it was a nice boost of confidence.

I could *feel* that Tandy had resolved her internal turmoil at the threads of information, so I repeated Leo's initial question. "Tandy, what did you do? This is incredible."

She also turned your brains into spaghetti. You need to read the warning labels before you do these things.

Leo was leaning heavily on Tandy. Tandy looked exhausted, and Leo was actively sweating. He looked to be in pain.

"I turned on [Team Synergy], [Overlap], and [Rapport]. Which may have been a mistake." I could feel the guilt in Tandy's expression, so I didn't press.

Didn't stop Meredeath. "Are you insane? No, not insane. You saw the incentive script. You chose this on purpose." Meredeath's voice dropped to an accusatory hiss.

[Heartbeat] skill or not, I hadn't read the truth of Tandy's decision. It looked like there was some hidden potential bonus we could get if Tandy turned on enough [Party] skills.

"We need every advantage we can get. None of us was prepared for this." She waved at the teeth and the beckoning throat. "If we're going to survive, we must take risks."

Meredeath, green eyes flashing, stepped forward, her heeled boots sinking into the flesh of the dungeon. "If you kill us before we get started," she pointed at Leo, "it won't matter."

Tandy and Meredeath matched energies. I could feel them

pulsing through our bond. My dad always claimed that guilt couldn't stand in a staring match. Tandy looked away first.

"I'm sorry," she whispered. "I had no idea it'd be that bad."

"You might be the designated [Party Leader], but you can't make decisions like that for all of us." Meredeath's words sat heavy, and Tandy gave a slight nod of acquiescence. Meredeath's green eyes bored into Tandy for a moment before continuing.

"Did it work? We only got [Partial Rapport]. Leo might have a headache for the rest of his life if we can't get his mana higher. Did it work?" The words came out through gritted teeth. I realized Meredeath was angry, but also reacting to the attempted skill acquisition.

"The [System] did grant a bonus upon completion of the [Trial Dungeon], but nothing that helps us right now."

I kept my mouth shut. I didn't want to give anyone hope that the new skills I got would be helpful in any way. None of them were combat-ready.

Meredeath sighed. Her anger receded, but the tension across her forehead stayed. "Let's share our base health, mana, and stamina. I want to see what we're working with."

Tandy, Leo, and I shared glances. We all noticed she didn't share *her* stats. It was a standoff. I looked at Meredeath. She wore her clothes like armor, closing herself off from the rest of us. Wherever she was from, it shouted she wasn't from *here*. She didn't *belong*.

I could understand that, so I stepped forward. "I'm at 25/25/25 across the board."

Tandy frowned, thinking I was taking Meredeath's side. I responded to her silent accusation. "Look, my gut says if we're going to survive this, we're going to have to trust each other."

You sure you're thinking with your gut?

I ignored Richard.

"Leo, man, what's your stats?" I spoke more gently, trying to coax it out of the guy.

"I'm at 50 health, 90 stamina, 10 magic. When we'd earned the [Partial Rapport] skill, it warned me that I didn't have the minimum mana to earn it. Then it granted it anyway." His voice was taut. He was paying the deficit in other ways.

Mana illness, he's taking a debuff to his health.

Tandy and Meredeath were still standing off.

"Guys, we need to work *together*."

Meredeath sighed, pulling off a ring with a blue inset emerald. "Put this on. It'll boost your mana by 10 and should get you out of the deficit."

Leo took the ring, ready to protest that it wouldn't fit. Magically, as it changed hands, it grew to accommodate his size. He slipped it on an index finger, and the relief was immediate.

Where'd she get a [Minor Ring of Mana]?

Good question, but I wasn't about to interrupt Tandy. "I'm worse than Cole on health and stamina. I've only got 10 of each."

"Good thing you have mana, or you'd be dead." Meredeath's eyes narrowed. "How much mana *do* you have?"

"Two hundred and fifty," Tandy finished quietly, as though her having more mana than Leo and my total stats combined was something to hide.

I started to protest the unfairness, but I stopped myself. *This* was Tandy.

She rushed to make herself smaller. "I don't have any magic, though. No spells, nothing I can use it on."

"What about you, Meredeath?" I put all my spine behind the question. Green eyes flashed at me unhappily.

"Believe it or not, I'm the one in the group who can take a hit. I'm at 100 health, 50 stamina, and now 30 magic. I've got several magic items on me and, before you ask, no, I didn't steal them. They were gifts, mostly from my mother." She unconsciously touched her necklace. "She must've thought I needed talismans to protect me."

"Alright, are we done with math? I'm ready to hit something!" Leo emphasized his point by smacking a tooth with the flat of his blade. The hit resonated, sending vibrations through the air, causing me to wince.

A deeply unsettling sucking sound followed. Leo backed away, wide-eyed, as two teeth pushed themselves out of the dungeon's gumline.

These teeth weren't molars. I stepped back in horror as several more dropped from the ceiling. The teeth's roots transformed into armored legs that looked like stout, angry crabs.

Richard's [System] identification message was shared across the team thanks to [Partial Rapport].

[Root Canal - Level ?? - These sentient teeth are a real toothache. Immune to most damage types, they are susceptible to crushing and drilling damage. Slow to attack, they are difficult to survive.]

I looked at Meredeath, waiting for her to jump in front of us. Take the heat while we figure out what to do.

She caught my panicked look and grinned, waving as she jumped down the beast's throat.

Chapter 13

CHEW TOY

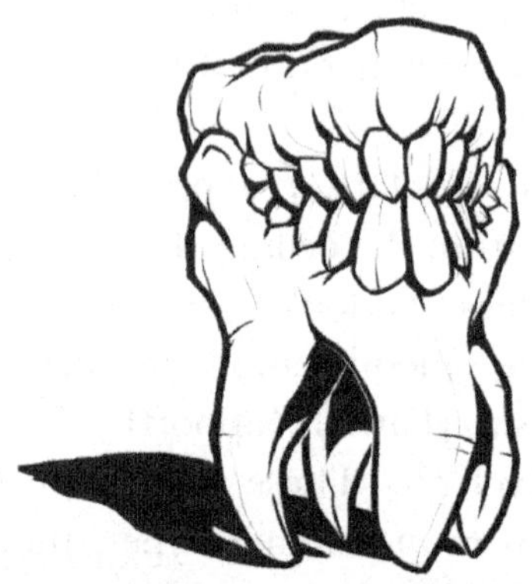

A discolored cuspid hit the ground with a splat, turning our attention away from Meredeath's disappearing form. It sank tooth first into the spongy floor of the dungeon.

The cuspid's roots morphed into legs only to wave frantically in the air. It looked like an overturned beetle unable to flip itself right side up.

I watched with odd fascination as I unclipped my hammer. The familiar charred ash handle was reassuring.

I had [Smith] skills. Maybe, like Tandy, I could adjust them for the [Adventurer] life?

I ran forward. Bringing my hammer up. I was going to target the weakest part of any object—the joint. The four root leg segments came together in a divot in the tooth's center.

The best skill to use would be [Nailed It] as aim and velocity of my blow would double.

"[Nailed It]!"

[Skill Failure: [Smith] skill [Nailed it] requires a metal medium, or minimally a nail. Target does not meet the criteria. Cooldown is doubled for skill failure.]

The head of my hammer still smacked the joint exactly. Even without the skill, it was a heavy blow.

The monster sank with the hit, some of the impact absorbed by the squishy floor before the whole thing shattered. Fragments of tooth and chitin flew, coating my hammer and arm with monster guts.

"I found their weakness!" I shouted triumphantly as I watched two additional teeth push themselves out of the gumline behind Leo.

Richard shifted. I felt the light tapping of a tentacle.

I'm just patting you on the back. Now, all you have to do is flip each of these and hit them perfectly with [Nailed It] on cooldown for the next fifteen minutes.

"Do we stay or follow Meredeath?" Tandy asked, and I could tell she hoped to follow Meredeath despite my success. She didn't have enough health points to make any battle trivial.

Leo held his double-bladed axe, eyeing the mobile tooth crustations. We exchanged a look that mirrored my thoughts. Even just hitting them straight on, *how hard could this be?*

I'd stepped back towards my friends as two teeth ran up to their fallen comrade.

"Ready?" Leo asked, with a feral grin. He didn't wait for me to nod, running towards the root canal. "It's time to pull a tooth!"

Still covered in the viscera of my last victim, I followed Leo with a little less enthusiasm.

Leo had gone for the tooth on the left, which left the canine on the right for me. The tooth braced as I raised my hammer.

There were no obvious weak joints, so just tried to hit.

The hammer came down with the might of a former [Smith] apprentice.

It smacked hard. Vibration burned through my arms painfully as the hammer rebounded explosively off the tooth's crown.

It was all I could do to hold on as the hammer swung backward over my head, almost braining Richard.

Watch where you swing that thing!

I fell backwards, off balance by the unexpected result. As I sank into the slimy floor, I couldn't take my eyes off the nightmare fuel in front of me.

Cracks raced along the face of the cuspid. Two dark cavities opened, revealing inset red eyes.

My blood froze, my self-preservation instincts blared in alarm to run.

A third crack split horizontally, revealing the serrated maw of a predator. It grinned.

"The teeth have teeth!" I yelled like an idiot.

Chomp. The tooth bit deep into the leather of my boot, grazing my foot.

I swung my hammer with one hand across my prone body. The edge of the hammer skittered off the tooth ineffectually.

It bit deeper this time, breaking through the boot into the top of my foot.

The searing pain made me gasp.

Instinctively, I yanked my leg. If I lost the boot, so be it.

The root canal held on, legs trundling forward like a dog with a chew toy. Teeth biting even harder to keep its prize.

My health bar dipped as my flesh gave, and I thrashed in its jaws as we played tug of war over my foot.

Richard clung to my shoulder, riding me like I was a wild bull. The useless slug.

Leo fended off his attack, swinging the flat of his axe in a pattern that kept the teeth away. Tandy stood at the esophagus of the dungeon, fiddling with the draw of her bag.

No help was coming, so I decided to save myself.

I kicked out with my right foot. Not in the tough enamel but right in the teeth.

As I made contact, the teeth shifted, loosening like baby teeth, and the creature's eyes widened in pain.

I bent my right leg and put all my strength into another firm stomp aimed at the front row of teeth that disappeared into my boot.

This time, the teeth went flying. It was the root canal's turn to stagger backwards. Its mouth was agape, as the whole row of top teeth was missing.

With a whimper, the monster retreated to the gathering horde. It kept eye contact with me, hatred boiling as it disappeared into the dozen root canals.

My foot ached. Blood and saliva mixed as it oozed out of the holes in my boot.

I pulled myself up slowly, watching Leo. If another root canal attacked, I wanted to be on my feet.

Leo swung his axe sideways, smacking the carnivorous tooth with the flat of the head. It flew through the air, bouncing into a row of dormant teeth.

"Any luck?" I asked, shifting weight off my injured foot.

"I think I can kill them if I hit it right through the middle," Leo said, determination written on every line of his face.

More teeth dropped from the ceiling, and the roots transformed into legs as soon as they hit the floor.

These weren't molars.

The teeth were coming for us, and I wanted to opt out of this dental emergency.

"Go for it, man." My foot throbbed as the fetid smell of rot grew. Leo could be the hero. Although I doubted we were going to survive this fight. Maybe Meredeath had been right after all.

Leo spun his axe before him, looking like an entire wrecking crew. He stepped forward as though he were our elected champion.

I limped towards Tandy, clipping my hammer onto my belt. Every step made me wince.

Her auburn braids glistened in slime as she fought with her pack, trying to pull a length of coiled rope from the bottom. With one eye on Leo, I kneeled to assist her.

The unnatural light of the cavern shone off Leo's axe, the edge glowing in a deadly promise as it whirled through the air. He looked like the heroic champion, muscles flexing under Tandy's pink sweater.

"I've got this," I whispered to Tandy, taking over the tangled mess. Without asking questions, she left me with the bag as her focus turned to the other end of the rope.

Tandy tied the end into a loop, then tried to wrap it around one of the molars.

Leo stood between Tandy and the attacking teeth while she worked.

My hands shuffled through Tandy's pack, moving the rest of her possessions out of the tangle. With effort, I found the other end of the rope and pried the whole wad out. With the end in one hand, I worked on untangling the mess.

I couldn't believe how much rope she'd fit in her pack as loop after loop untangled. I'm sure it was caused by some overpowered [Weaver] skill, like [Infinite Tangle].

Saliva dripped from hidden glands as the dungeon's tongue twitched uncomfortably. The gaping holes left by the root canals oozed blood and mucus. Everything felt hotter, like an infection had taken hold in the mouth.

The sentient teeth seemed unbothered. They bumped into each other, all eyes on Leo, as they gathered courage to attack.

Finally, I'd reached the end of the knots and threw the

complete coil to Tandy. She gave me a small smile as she sawed a length of the lasso between the molars, like a reluctant bit of floss.

My attention returned to Leo as he rode a ripple in the floor forward. His calf muscles danced, balancing perfectly.

One well-worn tooth stepped forward on nimble claws. It sat, an unlikely champion, with rounded enamel and a stout frame.

Leo, muscles bulging like a bronzed god, whirled his axe above his head. The weaving axe pattern elongated, building higher to give more heft to an attack.

The [Enchanted Axe of Singing] whistled as it came down, blade hungry.

The sharpened edge of the axe hit the little monster square. The creature sank into the ground and, to my horror, shifted. Leo's axe was turning to slide off the top of the monster.

With most of Leo's momentum, the axe plunged into the dungeon's fleshy tongue in a spray of blood.

Tandy and I didn't have a chance to react as the dungeon howled. A gust of wind blew, moist and angry, from the dungeon's throat.

Leo tugged valiantly at his axe, trying to free it from the floor.

His foe, barely over knee-height, ran straight at him. With a malicious grin, it aimed for maximum damage. In the last second, the creature lowered its head and triggered a skill.

The asshole accelerated forward, hitting Leo right in the family jewels.

Ouch, that had to hurt.

Leo doubled over, clutching himself. The root canal backed away, bumping into the axe still embedded in the floor. The dungeon howled in pain again.

This time, the floor under my feet gave.

With Tandy's pack clutched in one hand, I watched helplessly as the tongue of the dungeon flexed. Root canals flew in all directions as a roll of the tongue pinned me to the roof of the mouth. Smothered, I suffocated.

My lungs didn't have to wait long as I was rolled along the ridges of the mouth, then casually tossed back. Swallowed without consent.

My fall was messy. As a kid, my favorite pastime had been swinging off a rope into the local swimming hole. My mom made sure we knew how to swim as soon as we mastered walking. In the summers, we'd sneak off with her unofficial blessing to amuse ourselves endlessly in the creek.

I fell in love with the swing of that rope. Hanging on to the knot until I hit the maximum arc of the swing. Letting go, and for a few seconds, I flew.

This was nothing like that. It was a slimy cartwheel, as the tunnel forced me down through gravity and muscle. I spread my arms, trying to catch tension on *something* to slow my descent.

The tunnel walls glowed, as though only a bit of flesh separated me from the creature's soul.

If I closed my eyes, I could feel the pulse of the dungeon. Richard clinging to me. Tandy's panic.

My fingers flexed, searching for purchase in the sinew, but it was useless. Everything was slick.

My hand caught on a bone pressing against the tunnel. Scrambling for a grip, the esophagus undulated.

My fingers clawed.

I dug into a bit of sinew. I twisted my hand to hold on, but my weight pulled me down.

My grip broke with a pop.

I fell head over heels over slug tentacles catching glimpses of Tandy above.

Finally, the tunnel began to narrow, and my descent slowed. The flesh sagged, slowing me further as I approached a hole only a couple of feet wide. I spread my feet, my injured foot throbbing, and came to a halt.

I stood, feet on both sides of a bottomless chasm.

"Well, I'm not dead ye—"

My words cut off as Tandy slammed into me.

What precarious hold I had on the ledge evaporated.

Tandy screamed as I tumbled into the abyss.

Chapter 14

[REASSEMBLE], BREAK DOWN

Gravity pulled Richard and me through the terminal hole, dumping us into free fall.

[Root canal defeated. You have earned experience. Further details and rewards will be aggregated and awarded upon [Trial Dungeon] completion.]

My "Fuck you!!!" scream echoed in the dark cavern. A light source flared below as I watched a foamy, acrid lake rapidly approach.

The smell of bile confirmed it. I was about to bathe in a lake of stomach acid.

Richard clung to me as I held my breath, waiting for impact.

I belly-flopped right into the lake, knocking all horded air out of my lungs. The liquid ate at my eyes, so I squeezed them shut. Awkwardly kicking, I tried to get my head above water. Inhaled acid burned my lungs, daring me to cough.

Between my hammer, Tandy's bag, and my boots, I just sank.

When my feet touched the bottom, I kicked off awkwardly, hoping it'd give me enough momentum to break through to the surface. A small part of my brain told me to let go of the bag, unhook my hammer, detach Richard, and slip away.

My lungs burned as I hit the apex of my jump. Instead of panicking, all I felt was the heavy weight of regret.

Then something grabbed my shoulders. Breaking the surface suddenly, I didn't care if it were a monster, I just sucked in giant gulps of air.

Lungs satisfied, I began fighting for my life as I was hauled across the water like a hooked fish. Kicking and thrashing, my eyes were blurry.

One of my feet brushed the bottom of the lake again. The water was shallower here. If I could get enough leverage, I could toss my attacker.

It's Meredeath, you idiot.

I stopped fighting, and the helping hands relaxed their grip. Wiping the frothy lake water off my face, I tentatively opened my eyes. Everything burned slightly, like I'd received the season's first sunburn. As my vision cleared, the dark-clad Meredeath stood in front of me.

Her clothes and hair were damp, probably my fault, but otherwise she looked in perfect health. A glowing orb bobbed above her head, and the ring on her right hand glowed quietly.

Sheepishly, I gave a head bob of thanks.

"What took you guys so long?" she asked as we watched Tandy fall from the ceiling. She screamed too, but had enough presence of mind to ball up before hitting the lake.

All my anger at Meredeath deserting us drained out of me. Seemingly, she really had expected us to follow her.

"We tried to fight the root canals."

"Huh." Meredeath began wading out to retrieve Tandy. "I can't tell if you guys are brave or stupid."

Stupid.

"Probably both," I called, ignoring Richard as I shivered by the cavern wall.

The place smelled atrocious, like a compost bin in the kitchen when it hadn't been turned frequently enough. Chunks of half-digested food floated in the liquid.

The walls rumbled, sloshing the lake. Ripples formed, affecting each other and generating a foamy aftereffect. I decided it was time to stop ignoring my notifications and immediately regretted the choice:

[Indigestion Event - This terrain is undergoing acidification because of an indigestive event. Acid levels will increase until the irritant is removed.]

[You are [Acidified]. Lose one health point every thirty seconds until this environmental condition is removed.]

I looked down, realizing the waves were licking at my boots. I took a step back, wondering how I hadn't noticed the burning in my feet. With every step, my feet sank into the spongy floor, creating a puddle of acid.

Focusing on my stats, I discovered that my health had already dipped to 20/25 health points. It wouldn't take long for the lake to kill me, and even less time for it to kill Tandy.

[You are [Diseased]. Bites are one of the worst sources of infection. Bites in an acidic lake of biological pathogens are even worse. The numb feeling in your foot is not a good sign. You will lose one stamina point every ten minutes until you cleanse yourself.]

Tandy had bobbed up with Meredeath a few feet away. She looked a lot more put together than I felt.

"We're in trouble. There's an [Indigestion Event] that has given me an [Acidified] debuff, and I'm losing two health points a minute. I've got less than ten minutes, and Tandy has even less."

A giant blob of something green floated by, caught in an invisible current. I tried hopping on it to escape the goop, but it sank under my weight.

The walls of the cavern, the stomach, stretched and gave as I tried to climb, but no matter how much I struggled, I couldn't get my body wholly out of the soup.

Meredeath watched quietly as I wore myself out.

Soaked, my skin itched everywhere. The muted throbbing in my foot worried me more. My eyes burned, and everything had a hazy halo effect.

Meredeath looked perfect. She was damp, but for all her journey to rescue the two of us, she looked like she'd just taken a dip in an alpine lake. It had to be magic.

Uncharitably, I was grateful that Tandy looked as bedraggled as I felt. Out of frantic energy, I stared off into space numbly.

"Any ideas?" Tandy was exhausted. She leaned against the wall, her hand sinking in to mid-forearm.

"I can't believe how this stuff affects you. I must be immune." Meredeath looked at us, almost bored, unimpressed with our lack of self-preservation. She looked at us like we were complete buffoons for not preparing acid resistance upon entering a dungeon. My eyes narrowed. How could *she* possibly be immune?

Anger flaring, I replied, "Yes, it's affecting us. You need to help us *losers*, or you'll be without a team and, according to Malyc, that means you'll fail the dungeon too."

She abandoned us to the hangry teeth above, then acted superior? I was done.

That her gear and skills backed up her attitude just pissed me off even more.

"Hey, guys! Anything I can do to help?" Leo's voice called cheerily off-key from my outburst.

The cavern vibrated, sloshing foamy acidic liquid everywhere. Richard whined as a wave broke over my shoulders. My health points kept dropping.

"Good to know you have a backbone after all," Meredeath murmured, giving me a wink. What the hell was wrong with this woman? She tapped her ring and threw another light ball out of it, towards Leo.

"My vision's still hazy, can either of you see him?" I squinted, trying to make out Leo, but everything was still foggy.

The idiot has embedded his axe across the hole and is standing on it.

"Do you have any rope? Can we climb up to you?" I called. It was the obvious solution, although I wasn't sure how much weight the shaft of Leo's axe could take.

"I didn't pack a rope." Well crap.

Tandy broke in. "If we could find *my* pack, we'd be fine."

I frowned. "What's in your pack?" I held up the bedraggled bag that'd almost drowned me twice.

Tandy looked at it stupidly before her face split with a huge grin. She sloshed over to me, hand outstretched like I held something precious. I happily let her take it.

Tandy plopped her bag onto a green floating chunk as she rifled through, pulling out a small slice of the same type of rope I'd untangled an esophagus ago.

She held it up like a long-forgotten messiah. "[Reassemble]!"

The skill pulled her up off her feet. Meredeath grabbed her other hand, helping support Tandy as the magic took effect. The rope's end glowed with Tandy's warm golden magic as it tried to restore itself.

"Ouch, what the hell?" Leo's curse rang out, a good sign.

Tandy started sliding again towards the middle of the lake. I helped Meredeath as I wrapped my arms around Tandy's waist.

The rope snapped together. One end held tightly in

Tandy's hands, and the other tied to the distant molar in the dungeon's mouth.

As though the [Trial Dungeon] knew we'd outsmarted its trap, the water level dropped dramatically. I ignored my internal warning bells, grateful the water level was only hip deep. My eyes finally cleared, and I could see Leo waving with a stupid grin.

"I have little health left. Do you mind if I go first?" Tandy's voice had an edge to it, and for the first time, it hit me how fragile her base stats must be.

Meredeath looked unconcerned, so I spoke up. "Of course, I've got a few more minutes. Let me give you a leg up." I bent down, cupping my hands so she could get some lift. The faster we got her out of the water, the better.

"Climb on up!" Leo yelled as she stepped onto my hand.

Tandy climbed up onto the rope, grabbing as though her very life depended on it.

The cavern rumbled, the water dropped even more, and something long and sinuous flashed below. Was it a fish? A snake?

"Did you see that?" The question was out of my mouth as Tandy climbed higher.

"I sure did." Meredeath eyed the water suspiciously. It was frothy greenish-yellow on top, but the liquid underneath was a dark brown. It wasn't hard to understand that this was an oversized stomach. A giant seed pod floated by, half-digested and covered in slime. "Is it me, or do the walls seem... closer to us?"

I squinted at the walls, but it was hard to tell. The light from Meredeath's orb ring wasn't too powerful, but it looked ominously close.

"Maybe closer. More worried about what's in the water with us. Tandy, how are you doing?"

"Better now that I'm out of the cesspool. My health is climbing, but now my stamina is draining."

She had little of either. We'd just traded sure death for a slow death.

"Do you have a skill that will knot the rope? If you had a perch, it wouldn't be as much of a strain." I threw my idea out, nervously hoping as something rubbed against my calf.

"I can pull you up!" Leo shouted down as Tandy's body surged upward. The rope slid through my unprepared hand, biting into my palm.

The cavern rumbled, sloshing Richard and me.

Pulling her up wasn't a terrible idea, but I noted my health was down to 11. Did we have enough time to pull us both out?

Leo needs to shut the hell up before he kills us.

"This isn't straining my stamina at all!" Leo boasted.

Realization dawned too late; Leo's yells triggered the stomach-quakes.

The cavern shook violently, geysers of acidic juice spouting into the air, showering us with filth.

"Leo, shut up!" My words came out jangled as I was tossed left and right.

The acid reflux didn't stop this time, each choppy wave splashing up as they collided. Tandy was above the splash zone, but Richard and I were getting scrubbed on the washboard.

Worse yet, the rope sizzled under a gelatinous splash.

My situation grew more dire as something long brushed against my leg. I unclipped my hammer and watched the water.

"There's something in here with us," I called to the team, eyes glued to the froth.

Meredeath was on guard, calling on a skill. "[Claws of Death]." Her face twisted in pain as her fingernails slowly elongated.

A dark aura shrouded her body. It was hard to get a good look at her now, and she *felt* dangerous.

"Cole, look!" Meredeath's call hissed across the lake as she pointed to a roiling spot of water. A mass of thin white ribbons covered in tentacles thrashed.

Suddenly, something wrapped around my ankle with a bone-crushing grip, and pulled me under.

My scream was cut short as my vision and mouth filled with the miasmic soup.

Chapter 15

THE TIES THAT BURN

To my horror, I swallowed the frothy sludge. The acid burned all the way down. With lungs on fire, I fought aspiration as my stomach roiled.

[You have been [Poisoned]. All health regeneration has stopped. If you already suffer a health debuff, you will lose an additional health point per thirty seconds.

Currently [Poisoned] stacks with [Acidified]. You lose two health points every thirty seconds.]

My health bar had already turned a brownish-red color due to my [Diseased] state and was now shot through with a sickly green. The bar pulsed with anger, as though judging me for my poor decisions. My eight health points would vanish in a flash at the rate of the double debuff.

I had to do something fast.

It dragged me through the lake, as if my foot had become

caught in the stirrup of a runaway horse. The joints in my leg ached with pressure.

Desperately, I called on [Heartbeat], tugging on the string connecting me to Meredeath, begging for help. Water and debris overwhelmed all my senses, so I used [Stillpoint] and slowed everything down, ignoring all but Meredeath's thread. I needed *help*.

Suddenly, Meredeath was there. We collided as I raced by, except suddenly my ankle was free. Bobbing up, I gasped for breath.

Meredeath reeled from our collision. The lake was in absolute chaos.

The water frothed with movement. Splashing as ripples and waves smacked into each other, throwing droplets of acid into the air. Mixed in the surf were tentacled threads rolling and churning through the water as they rubbed against friend and foe in a frenzy of excitement.

A tendril snaked up the rope towards Tandy. Leo looked ready to jump in to save her. Precariously balanced, he wobbled indecisively on his axe.

Meredeath, who I thought had been reeling from our collision, instead had used the momentum to spin faster. She dipped her claws in and out of the water, a maelstrom of death. Red foam and dead bodies of the creature bobbed in the surf.

To free me, Meredeath had left the base of the rope dipping into the water. Even with Leo pulling Tandy up, enough was coiled in the lake that I could see white wormlike threads coiling up after Tandy.

I'd admire their ability to climb a vertical surface if they weren't monsters.

"Meredeath, Tandy's in trouble." Our worm death dealer stood, checking her surroundings. Her claws showed a dark ebony, tips dripping blood. She looked feral as her eyes scanned the lake, searching for her next victim.

I got an [Identify] on them. Richard shared his notifications.

[Ribbons of Hunger - Level ?? - These tentacled strips of unending hunger will voraciously assault anyone in their territory. Immune to acid and poison, they are intestinal parasites. Fast to attack, they have little resistance to physical damage, relying on overwhelming odds.]

She started moving towards Tandy and the rope, but her progress was slow as the ribbons of hunger targeted her. The white ribbons rippled under the surface, tentacled skin flashing in the magical light of Meredeath's glow orbs.

I felt helpless as a ribbon coiled around Tandy's foot. Within seconds, the monster tossed her into the lake like unwanted garbage. Two more worms wriggled towards Leo, pushed by their need to feed.

I'd made it to the lake's edge and found a dry patch of stomach lining. Richard clung to my shoulders. With my feet out of the lake, my health stabilized. Regeneration was cut off, but I wasn't losing ground either.

One worm pushed onto the shore next to me.

I brought my hammer down on the creature, pinning it for a closer look. It writhed, trapped under the head of my hammer. The monster was only a couple of inches thick. Instead of fish scales or a slippery eel skin, the suction cups of an octopus lined the beast. The monster slowed as life drained out of it.

Do something! You will all die if they reach Leo.

Dead seriousness replaced Richard's usually jovial voice. He slithered down my arm, looking up at me. Acid and poison pocked his discolored skin, turning it green.

I holstered my hammer, the crushed ribbon of hunger no longer moving.

You need to throw me at the rope. His little eyes looked serious.

"If we miss, you're dead. You won't be able to get out of the lake in time." I said my fear out loud. He may have been right, but no part of me wanted his life riding on my throwing arm.

Then don't miss. Besides... I'm [Immortal]. He arched his back with a brash grin, all bravado. I didn't dare question his [Immortality] right now. Instead, I grabbed him by the tail, prayed to the god of slugs, and threw.

If he was indignant about being thrown by his tail, it was lost as the foot-long banana slug cartwheeled end over end through the air.

I held my breath and maybe closed my eyes.

He hit the rope with a loud squeak.

That throw had a lot of... enthusiasm.

His voice had returned to the dry sarcasm I'd learned to expect. Smiling, I saw his bare fangs descend on the incoming worms.

That's my slug. I sent him a silent wish of luck and waded in to help Tandy.

My health had dropped to a mere five points.

Tandy had worms dragging her under. I grabbed a hand with one arm and pulled her towards Meredeath. Her head popped out of the froth, eyes wild as she gripped my arm.

Her fingers slipped.

Using both hands and all of my leg muscles, I hauled her towards Meredeath.

"Hold her still, I'll take care of them," Meredeath called, diving for Tandy like a predator on the hunt. She whirled in the water like a tornado of claws, using some unknown skill.

Meredeath struck with surgical accuracy. The parasites evaporated in a spray.

I carried Tandy's limp form slowly towards the wall where she could sit out of the lake. Meredeath joined me, taking the majority of Tandy's weight.

Not six feet from the rope, my body spasmed as my health dropped to a mere three points. Flashing warnings alerted me to the helpful fact that death was imminent.

I hesitated, torn between helping Tandy and getting to safety quickest.

"*Go,* I've got her," Meredeath's harsh voice broke the tie.

Richard clung to the rope, midline. Slug slime trailed behind him like a triumphant banner. His fangs gleamed as he dispatched his second writhing target.

I ran for the rope as though my life depended on it.

My health was down to two. Skin was such an insufficient barrier to stomach acid.

With a leap, I grabbed salvation with both hands, pulling my body out of the gastric stew.

I hung, feet tucked under me, out of the lake, and watched [Acidified] blink out. My health didn't improve because I was still [Poisoned], but it wasn't decreasing anymore.

I arduously pulled my body up. Looking inward, I realized that hanging onto the rope drained my stamina every half minute. This meant that, at tops, I could cling for another nine minutes, and that didn't count my [Diseased] debuff or any feats of strength I'd need to go up the rope.

I struggled, manually pulling myself higher. Unlike Tandy, Leo wasn't pulling me up.

My stamina drained faster. I had to get higher so Tandy could join me. She was going to need to get out of the stew, too.

Suddenly worried, I looked down, checking on her.

Meredeath had propped Tandy on the shore, the only relatively safe spot other than the rope. Meredeath fought like a cornered rat as dozens of ribbons of hunger followed her ashore. Tandy was slumped unconscious behind Meredeath, her body splayed out like a marionette without strings.

Dread crept up my throat as I examined her too-limp form. I followed the outline of her foot. It dipped low, back into the miasmic surf, surely stealing the last of her life.

My sheep-hating weaver friend, who just wanted to escape Woodsten, was gone.

I hadn't gotten the notification yet, but I knew.

Her body lay on the shore like an abandoned shell. Empty. Lifeless. The tension in her brow, the strain in her jaw, gone. Her face held an odd, serene expression of relief.

Reaching out with [Partial Rapport], I felt a void where Tandy's warmth had been. The [System] confirmed what I already knew with a message.

[Your [Party Leader] Tandy Selvedge is [Dead].]

My hand slipped as the death notice blinked in my head. One of the strings holding me up had snapped. My heart ached unbearably for an unwavering moment before a dull numbness washed all feeling out.

"Tandy!" Leo shouted a heartbroken wail. The rope shook as he reached futilely for his abandoned friend, hands pawing at the emptiness between them.

The walls convulsed, reacting to Leo's shout. A wall of rotten digestive juice coated me from head to toe. My vision flickered red as my health ticked down.

One health point. My fingers burned as my arms shook. The rope was slipping. I was slipping.

In all the days I'd dreamed of being an [Adventurer], in the stories we told of our [Trial Dungeon] success and failure, I hadn't imagined the taste of bile. The slosh and sizzle of burning acid as it marked my skin. Or the desperate fear in a slug's face as the cool brackish water closed over my body.

[You, Cole Thornfield, are [Dead].]

Chapter 16

SKILL CHECK: TRUST

Tandy paced, even in death.

Her footsteps sloshed on the dungeon's tongue as we waited for the rest of our party to die.

The [System] reset the dungeon mouth, and each root canal returned to its original place.

Tandy muttered to herself, trying to determine what we'd done wrong. What could we do differently? Why wasn't the rest of the party dead yet?

I had the same thoughts, but had dipped into using my [Meditative State] skill. The questions bubbled up in my mind, and I acknowledged my frustration as I let them go.

Besides, what was the point? We couldn't have survived that deathtrap even with the perfect plan.

My thoughts turned darker. What bothered Tandy the most wasn't that we failed, but that she'd been the first to fail. Catastrophic failure wasn't something Tandy Selvedge did.

I stared at the portal rune on the fourth incisor. Cole Thornfield, however, was used to this sort of thing. I closed my eyes, feeling for the team. Leo was close to joining us. Meredeath and Richard seemed fine.

Saliva slowly oozed through my pants as I sat cross-legged on the floor. I had full health and stamina when we were portaled back into existence, and all my state conditions had vanished. It was as though perfect health erased our failure.

"I still don't understand why I have so little health and an untouchable pool of magic." Tandy finally plunked herself next to me, gray shawl across her shoulders. She picked at her cuticles, a long-suffered habit I thought she'd outgrown. "I have the most advanced [Mundane] class of our trio, but it's useless."

Leo and I had always wondered why the [System] hated us. Not so much why it favored Tandy, but why it favored *everyone* else?

It never made sense why Leo couldn't gain a class. The man *worked* for a living. He hopped from job to job, always giving 100%. For years, he treated every job as an opportunity to earn himself a class.

I couldn't claim the same work ethic, but I'd earned classes. I always studied and practiced the basics studiously, focusing on my progression. Then, out of the blue, the [System] would grant me the most inane specializations.

Theoretically, people should celebrate specializations, because they rarely earned them. Some folks didn't get one until they were deep into their professions.

Not me. I'd get a colossally disappointing message as soon as I hit level 10 that I'd specialized in the most mundane, idiotic thing. It would focus on an attribute I had worked on, but not something significant, prestigious, or practical.

At least Tandy had magic. It didn't do her much good yet, but if we figured out how to survive, it should. Admittedly, she was going to have a hard time surviving. But so was I.

I was an anchor that was going to hold us back short and long term.

"Cole, snap out of it." I raised my head. Without realizing it, I'd slouched over, holding my head in my hands. Tandy snapped her fingers before my eyes. "Your [Self Critic] skill is at it again. This has nothing to do with you."

Bringing up my active skill display, I found Tandy was right. [Self Critic] had quietly triggered. It'd slipped into active like a sly parasite on my psyche.

Turning it off manually, I immediately felt better as the spiral let go.

I triggered my daily [Meditation] based skill, [Analyze]. I wasn't sure how it worked, except that it boosted my thoughts. Problems were easier to solve. The skill lasted half an hour, as evidenced by the clock counting down in the corner of my vision.

There had to be a logic behind it all.

"Okay, Tandy, let's think this through. I've got three active classes: [Smith], [Chef], and [Meditation]. All with specializations. I guess four if you count [Provisional Adventurer]." I wasn't telling her anything she didn't already know, but saying it out loud felt wrong. People didn't talk about their classes and skills.

I knew, however, that if we were to solve the puzzle, we'd need to share. I was also hoping that Tandy would, for once, open up about her build. She'd already walked away from her family legacy. What did she have to lose at this point?

Her brown eyes searched mine. This was the moment. We'd been best friends most of our lives, but had never bridged the gap about our classes. We'd avoided the topic when Leo was around, trying to spare him the pain.

Her reluctance had always gone beyond Leo's feelings and the general taboo, though. Tandy's family had always been obsessively secretive about her progression.

"What classes do you have?" I realized I'd never flat-out asked her until now, as the question hung between us.

If we were going to be a successful adventuring party, we had to trust each other. She was still hesitating.

Was she going to open up or keep her family secrets? I watched as she stared blankly off into space, locked in an internal battle. Her jaw clenched.

I pushed. "Look, we've got to figure this out. It's time to go all in, Tandy. Trust me. Trust in us." We'd been friends for a long time, but we hadn't made that last leap of faith to family. I'd measure the words and say them kindly, but firmly.

I saw when she picked her chosen family over her blood. Eyes rose to meet mine, full of determination. My entire world pivoted as she spoke. "I have one class. You already know the level."

Just one? Impossible. Everyone had at least one side class. My mind raced, and I concluded she must have abandoned all her side classes in her narrow-minded pursuit of [Weaver].

So I asked the next logical question, "How many abandoned classes do you have? I've got five: [Farmer], [Shepherd], [Weaver], [Janitor], and [Builder]. I still can't believe I got [Builder] from our little forts we built as kids, and you were always more involved than I was. You've got to have [Builder]?"

I suspected most of our village had a similar array of abandoned classes to mine. They weren't challenging to pick up in childhood pursuits unless you were Leo. Three was the sweet spot for active classes. Tandy was hyper-focused on one. It was unusual, but possible.

Maybe that's what it took to be a [Sage] potential.

Anything over five was nearly impossible. The grind to demonstrate proficiency, much less progress, was insurmountable. The [System] inactivated classes that weren't used, causing you to abandon your associated skills.

I'd held onto [Smith] because I used [Basic Heat Tolerance] and [Steady Temperature] all the time as [Chef]. I'd pick up a shift at the forge once a month for a little extra cash, allowing me to keep my other [Smith] skills active enough, like [Pound], [Nailed It], and [Hammer Time].

"... and that's why I have [Builder]." Crap, I missed a whole segment of what she said. Concentrating, I followed her discussion thread, trying to figure out what I had missed. "I earned it by accident. I hid it from Grandma for years because I loved making those net forts of ours. Even though it was against the *plan*..."

She trailed off sadly while lost in the memory. I remembered the day her mom stomped into our tree hideout. Furious, she'd [Unbound] the fort with a wave of her hand.

Tandy had fallen hard, bruising her shoulder. Leo and I were lucky to escape with our lives.

Tandy's mom had been pitiless, hauling her off crying without a backward glance. Our childhood ended that day.

Everything changed. They forbade Tandy from hanging out with us. Leo and I couldn't come close to her towering webs of thread, so we gave up. A curtain had been drawn, keeping everyone at a distance.

Until Leo's twenty-fifth. Until now.

Tangent aside, my [Analyze] skill clamored for the segment of conversation before she talked about her [Builder] class.

Awkwardly, I interjected. "I missed it. Did you say you had other abandoned classes?"

Tandy looked away. "[Herbalist]. I used to help my dad pick flowers to use in dyes before they discovered my ability to [Weave]." She never talked about her absent dad. Although my mind itched to have her elaborate and dig in on *that* mystery, I refused to lose focus.

So far, in our comparison, we were different, but not by too much. She had two abandoned classes to my five. I moved to the next logical question. "How many skills do you have active?"

She frowned, and I knew I was pushing my luck to get her to share this data. I offered my skills, hoping it'd tip her over into sharing.

"I've got…" I brought up my internal stat sheet. "Oh wow, I've got thirty now."

I hadn't noticed a skill related to Richard until now. Frowning, I read the most peculiar description of a skill I'd ever seen:

[Companion] (from [Error - Class Not Located]): Allowed user to bond with [Richard, the Fanged Banana Slug].

It was yet another mystery about Richard that needed to be solved, if we ever got time and he was in the mood to talk. I'd never seen the [System] admit an error.

"Are you sure you want to know?"

I mentally shelved my thoughts about Richard. Tandy was still hesitating. She looked away as though ashamed, and a faint blush of embarrassment colored her cheeks.

"Out with it. It can't be that bad." She was a level 40 [Threadmarked Weaver]. She had to have at least double or even triple the skills I had.

Confident, self-assured Tandy wouldn't meet my eyes. "I have a little over two hundred skills," she meekly squeaked.

Holy shit. *Hundreds of skills.* That wasn't just an advantage; she played a completely different game. No wonder her family guarded their secrets.

Her hesitation was due to her having been afraid to embarrass *me.* I felt like an amateur in life. This must have been what Leo felt as we tiptoed around him.

I took a breath, grounding myself. Tandy was a generational talent. The whole of Woodsten knew it. Being jealous of her was like envying a hawk for its wings.

"Okay." I forced a smile. "Well, *that's* a difference between our builds. Damn Tandy, good job!" It stung, but I was proud of her. "I can't imagine Leo has skills, considering he could never earn a class. I have to think those skills influenced your magic points. Is weaving classified as magic? Has your grandma talked about anything like that?"

She tightened her shawl around her shoulders like armor against the fetid air between us. She was comically out of place. Tandy'd spent most of her life in a [Weaver]'s studio with her family or working at the town's shearing barn. Well-manicured, she'd always had perfectly woven braids and carefully controlled emotions.

Now we sat in the literal mouth of a dungeon, warily eyeing the dormant teeth. Saliva soaking into every bit of cloth, her hair escaping every attempt to tame. I was equally ridiculous, the third cook at a second-rate tavern, mostly relegated to dishes and gruel. I sat playing [Adventurer], covered in bile with my old hammer attached at the hip like a real weapon.

We were out of our respective comfort zones. But we were trying. I was proud of us, of her.

Tandy started to answer my question. "Mom and Grandma, they—"

The dungeon inhaled sharply. Tandy's shawl slipped from her shoulders.

[Your [Party Member] Leo Patch is [Dead].]

Chapter 17

FIVE POINTS PER [FLORIST]

Runes glowed on the top jaw of the dungeon. Energy gathered above our heads, whirling into a portal. I could see Leo, or rather, his body in the void, falling towards us. A gruesome injury cut across his face and torso, splitting him almost in two.

His flesh and sinew knit together as he got closer to us, until he fell through the portal, smacking into the floor with a wet plop.

Leo bounced up to his full six-foot, bearded lumberjack self. Eyes wild, he crouched as though expecting an attack.

"Cole, wait," Tandy said in a quiet warning, pulling me up short as I stepped towards Leo.

Examining him, I understood, seeing his white knuckles glued to the shaft of his [Enchanted] axe. He was still living the nightmare of his death.

I put my hands out wide, looking non-threatening as possible.

"Leo, it's us. You're safe. You died, but we get three chances, remember?" I kept my voice calm and level, as I felt his panic through our [Partial Rapport].

Tandy stood nervously. "It's us, Leo. Cole and Tandy, you're okay."

His red-rimmed eyes locked on mine, and I shivered. I'd never seen my friend so freaked out. The [Enchanted Axe of Singing] slowly lowered to the ground and slipped from his fingers as humanity returned to his eyes.

He brought his hands to his face, probing the unbroken skin, searching for the ghost of the life-ending tear across his body.

I looked back at Tandy for reassurance, but she looked as out of depth as I felt.

"I'm whole?" Leo's words were tiny, broken. They were harsh, not in the normal jovial tone of my friend.

"Yes, you're fine. We're here. Three chances, remember? Tandy, want to get some water?"

Leo let out an ugly sob of relief. Dreams of adventure never included the nasty feeling of choking on monster bile as it ate your skin or being ripped in half by the gods know what.

I stepped forward and wrapped him in a hug. "We've got you."

Tandy joined in, adding her warmth.

Three-fifths of [Your Mom's Party] hugged it out. I'm sure we were an odd sight, a huddle in the mouth of a leviathan. Clinging to sanity through the comfort of a familiar bond.

Eventually, we grew self-conscious. We were [Adventurers] now, and group hugs weren't sexy. Imagine if Richard had caught us?

Tandy held out a canteen for Leo, asking the question we'd been avoiding. "You want to tell us what happened?"

"Are we safe here?" Leo eyed the neat rows of teeth.

"As long as you don't try to perform dental surgery." He gave me a hard stare. I rushed to reassure him. "We're as safe as we can be in a dungeon. No sign of any root canals."

He took a long sip from the canteen, as though stalling his words. "I jumped into the soup, but I was too late." His voice caught. I sympathized. When I saw Tandy's prone body, I thought my heart had been ripped out. "I lost it. All I could see was red. It didn't take long for Meredeath and me to finish the ribbons of hunger."

It sounded like a [Berserker] skill.

"The room slowly drained, revealing another chute, except it was clenched shut. I wanted to come back here and find the two of you, but Meredeath convinced me that pushing on was better. Any knowledge of the next zone would benefit our next attempt."

I couldn't argue with the logic, but I wasn't sure I would have reached the same conclusion. Meredeath was oddly experienced for a [Provisional Adventurer].

Leo's voice shook as he continued. "Richard tickled the chute open, don't ask. He sat on Meredeath's shoulders as we traveled through a never-ending intestine filled with parasitic traps. Long tendrils waved from the walls, attracted to sound. If they found you, tentacles popped out of the walls and shredded your skin. We moved slowly, step by step, squeezing by tendrils, pustules, and tentacles."

I could feel the tension in his voice.

"I fucked up." His eyes sought mine, as though he needed my forgiveness. "I brushed a pustule, and it blew up, filling the air with spores. I immediately started coughing. The tendrils wrapped around me as a wall opened with a giant tentacle. I didn't even have time to defend myself before I got ripped…"

In two. My mind finished what he couldn't.

"Hey, it's okay," I said mechanically. But was it? The image of Leo's body falling, skull bare, scalp pulled back, his torso shredded, stuck in my heart right next to Tandy's limp body, blistered and inert.

I found better words. "Next time, we'll do better. Not die."

Leo looked up for the first time in his story, a small smile cracking his face.

"Not die, right? Why didn't I think of that?" His smile had turned into a chuckle.

Tandy looked at us as if we were crazy. She handed us both a wrapped sandwich from her pack. She'd thought of everything. It was a peanut spread with crushed berries. The sweet and tart were a welcome distraction from the grossness of the dungeon.

Leo's disposition improved with food. Time helped too. I suspected something about our [Adventurer] class helped blunt the most traumatic events.

I broke the silence of our chewing. "Leo, have you ever wanted a pet? Something like Richard?"

Tandy laughed. "As though there's anything like Richard."

Leo shrugged. "Not really. I never wanted a pet. I always thought they were too much work. Plus, they're always at a lower level than you, so how much help could they be?"

"Richard's been pretty useful." He'd saved my life a couple of times now.

"For a [Fanged Banana Slug], he's incredible." Tandy's words dripped with sarcasm.

"You forgot he's [Immortal]." I grinned.

"Allegedly," Tandy bantered back.

"But what level is he?" Leo asked nonchalantly. Tandy elbowed him, and they shared a look. Whatever that was about.

"It's blocked out. I figured I'll find out once we lose the provisional part of [Adventurer]."

I sent a mental poke towards Richard. He was either out of range, or something prevented longer-distance telepathic communication in the dungeon.

"Yeah, probably," Tandy said. "If we live long enough, considering I have the threat profile of a wet kitten."

Finished with lunch, I unhooked my hammer and checked for rust. My fingers traced each indentation as if it were an old friend.

My [Analyze] skill had been working in the background. It didn't speak in words, but the logic kept threading together. If my hunch about Leo was correct, I'd cracked the puzzle.

"Leo, can you bring up your class interface?"

A shadow passed over his face. "Class interface? I haven't. Never had a class to look at. Let me try it." He blinked at the interface, awe temporarily clearing the strain from his face. "Oh wow, there it is! I've got the [Provisional Adventurer] class," his voice slowed, "and a bunch of… abandoned classes?"

The first part of my theory proved true. Abandoned classes signified a considerable waste of time. Most folks had a couple, but who spent significant time across a wide range of skills?

Leo. Leo had toiled across dozens of professions. I suspected the [System] could not grant him an actual class, so it simply shunted them into the abandoned category.

"How many abandoned classes?" I asked, trying not to sound excited. This bit of information would prove my theory. I suspected we got credit for classes, whether active or abandoned, and our skills.

The calculation for Leo should be straightforward. He had no skills to confuse the numbers. With 50 health, 90 stamina, and 10 magic, he had 150 points across the categories. If I were right, it meant he had 30 abandoned classes—an inconceivable number.

"Let's see, I've got [Forester], [Chef], [Shepherd], [Florist], [Fixer]..."

"You were a [Florist]?" I asked, curiosity overwhelming the need to solve the mystery.

Leo turned pink. "I-I don't know why it thinks that!" There was obviously a story, but I decided not to press. "I haven't been *anything*, remember? I'm the no-class guy. It's claiming I've had thirty abandoned classes."

Of course, Leo had thirty abandoned classes. He didn't know how to stop trying.

I plugged the number into my calculations, and to my utter amazement, they worked.

By the Everbear, I'd solved the puzzle!

"Five points per class." The secret bubbled out of me as I looked at Tandy. Her fingers jumped as she did the mental math, comparing her numbers.

Her eyes sought mine. "And a point per skill."

I nodded in affirmation. The leap in logic took us to the next logical conclusion. I spoke the last rule out loud. "Each class and skill stacks towards either health, stamina, or magic."

She frowned at my statement. "That'd mean most of my [Weaver] skills go against magic? I can't dispute the evidence, but it makes little sense."

"Can you tell me what's going on?" Leo had lost his patience with us.

Tandy, thankfully, stepped in to explain. This was reason number 231 why I didn't want to be the [Party Leader].

Had we stumbled upon a mathematical secret of the [System]? It *was* unusual to have so many abandoned classes. Coupling that with the low percentage of the population that became [Adventurers]... it was possible.

What made Leo's life miserable as a [Mundane] made him epic as an [Adventurer]. This was a secret worth more than any dungeon treasure.

As though frustrated with our breakthrough, the dungeon convulsed. Thick gobs of saliva hung on the walls. The jaw of the beast slowly closed.

Leo had to crouch significantly to avoid the moist, spit-soaked ceiling of the cavern.

The dungeon's teeth clenched, then ground together. The floor rippled in distaste.

"What the hell is going on?" Tandy shouted, eyes jumping around looking for the first root canal to break free.

What's up, loser? Richard's mental greeting rang in my head.

"It's Richard!" I pointed to the sudden slack in the anchored rope. Within minutes, an oversized Richard slowly came into view.

He was wrapped in a makeshift harness, dragging something up the beast's throat.

The dungeon burped, giving us all a stench worthy of its irritation.

A little help, please? Meredith is heavier than she looks.

Chapter 18

AERIAL ACROBATICS: DUNGEON EDITION

Okay, it's not that Meredeath's heavy, [Enlarge] is wearing off! Hurry!

The dungeon groaned as Richard dragged Meredeath up its esophagus. It took everything in me to run towards the wet burps gurgling up.

Richard was just over the lip, the dungeon's uvula bobbing and tonsils twitching around him. An oversized harness wrapped around the struggling slug, as the strain muted his usually vibrant yellow skin.

The harness was an intricate masterwork that carefully distributed weight across Richard's chest. The slug was shrinking slowly as his skill wore off. He'd given up on moving forward and heavily excreted a blue, gluey slime to cement him in place.

The rope dug deeply into the flesh of the dungeon, and I struggled to get enough traction to pull any meaningful weight off Richard's form.

The floor vibrated in a gastric warning of a suppressed barf. I *did not* want to be swimming again. I dug mercilessly, finally getting my fingers around the trailing line. Pushing my heels into the floor, I tried anchoring us all.

Richard sighed as some pressure released from his body, but my hands burned. How had my little Fanged Banana Slug pulled Meredeath this far? My forearms burned, and, sure enough, my stamina bar plummeted. Richard quivered beside me, his [Enlarge] skill wearing completely off, and I took Meredeath's full weight.

"Leo, a little help!" I hissed. I needed his muscle. Adjusting my feet, I stood in a low squat using my legs as leverage.

Slowly, the rope inched up. I couldn't believe Richard had made it this far. He must have burned an epic skill or two. I needed access to *his* class details.

Okay, I can trigger [Enlarge] again, but this is my last refresh for the month.

"Do it!"

I glanced back, realizing that Leo was almost to us. The man was hyper-focused on the rope in my hands and wasn't paying attention to his feet.

What is the fool doing? Oh shit, [Peel]!

Leo's giant foot came down squarely on Richard. Immediately, the full weight of Meredeath hit me, and I staggered forward off balance. I saw Leo comically flailing as it looked like he'd just slipped on ice. Ass over teakettle, he landed and bounced, smacking into me.

I went headfirst into the abyss. My grip on the rope broke entirely.

[Enlarge]! [Heroic Moment]!

The rope under me snapped taut at Richard's skills, but it was too slick to grab.

My descent started to pick up speed when I saw Meredeath. Wide-eyed, she braced for impact.

I twisted my body to the side, narrowly avoiding a head-on collision.

We were both coated in slime. I began sliding past, scrabbling for any hold, modesty be damned.

My fingers finally caught on the belt of her harness. The rest of my body swung past us. I held on tight, causing the line to jerk.

Eyes closed, I didn't know if Richard could sustain us both. When he didn't move, I slowly opened an eye, only to close it again.

My face was pressed against Meredeth's inner thigh.

My arms ached as my stamina plummeted. But it was the burn in my ears that was unbearable.

I took a deep breath, no time for dignity.

At least it was a good sign we weren't moving. Even if Richard wasn't pulling us up, we weren't free-falling either.

Dangling from her harness, my face awkwardly plastered to Meredeath, I wouldn't last long. My stamina bar was down to twenty percent as it started draining again.

"Well, hello there," Meredeath said. "You know we've just met, right? Normally, you buy a girl dinner first."

Was that a joke? She was a lot calmer than I was.

My feet dangled uselessly. My fingers dug into the makeshift harness, cramping with the effort. The walls were close, but too slimy to use as leverage.

I tried not to think about breathing.

"Sorry," I managed to choke out. We started dropping again, not rapidly, but slowly. We were pulling Richard in with us.

I kicked my legs, hoping to catch on to anything that would take some weight off my slug. The fleshy walls just gave way, offering no easy grip.

"Don't do that," Meredeath snapped. I stopped. "The dungeon will cough or retch. No good can come from it."

Her logic was sound, but it didn't comfort me much as I

watched my stamina bottom out. A muscle spasmed as my health started dropping. We'd stopped falling, but we still weren't progressing up the tunnel.

"I'm not going to be able to hang on much longer." My voice sounded hollow as a muscle slowly tore in my shoulder.

"Adventuring is about trusting your team. Just hang on a moment while Richard's working on his end. Tandy?" Meredeath yelled up. "Can you hear me? Can you *weave* Cole into my harness?"

The dungeon shook, and we dropped another span. I let out a harsh scream as tendrils started wrapping around my body.

"It's Tandy, you ninny. Stop fighting it."

The rope wound its way through my legs, gripping my butt. Meredeath grabbed my collar and hauled me up. I gasped as the pressure released. My stamina and health ticked up as the rope end pinned me to Meredeath.

It was uncomfortable, body to body, face to face. Her breath smelled oddly of mint as her sizable chest pressed against mine.

It was impossible not to look at her, but I tried nonetheless.

How strong was she? I was twice her size, and she lifted me like a rag doll.

"How?" I wasn't proud of the first word that came out of my mouth. Meredeath wasn't either.

"We're [Adventurers] Cole. Did you think I was a useless waif because I looked it?"

I blushed, fully deserving of the mockery in her tone. I didn't respond because, even after watching her tear into the ribbons of hunger, that's exactly what I'd assumed. My inner embarrassment was cut short as we slid back down the shaft. Whoever was anchoring us was losing their battle against gravity.

I'm losing my [Glue] skill, and Leo won't be much use.

I was about to respond when Meredeath beat me to it.

"Damn it, Richard, we were almost there." She could hear Richard? Before I could ask, Meredeath started wriggling her body to free her arms and legs from the tangle. She reached for the wall, muttering a skill in an unidentifiable language. "[Schrödinger's Feline]."

"Can you hear him?" I didn't bother hiding the outrage in my voice. If we were about to fall, so be it, but had they been talking behind my back this whole time?

Meredeath opened her eyes, but they weren't hers. Alien purple slitted eyes stared at me with a glassy flatness. Weren't her eyes green? Even across this alteration, I could tell she wasn't amused.

"Do you want to survive or grill me about my relationship to your slug?" Her voice hissed like water on a hot pan. Her skin changed, and fine, dark hair grew rapidly on her face. "Hold on, Cole. This isn't easy."

Meredeath reached for the fleshy wall behind me. I craned my neck to see that her long fingernails had become claws. Her claws dug into the walls, gaining traction immediately. Meredeath kicked her legs out, her feet earning a hold as well. Our weight came off the rigged line as she clung to the dungeon's throat like a cat on curtains.

As I watched, her face continued to transform. Her eyes shifted into almond shapes, purple swirling around her vertical pupils. Her ears grew pointy and tufted. Not completely a cat, not entirely human.

Was this an [Adventurer] class? I'd never heard of shapeshifting skills. I felt useless as I dangled from Tandy's weave. Meredeath was holding both our weight, seemingly effortlessly.

The dungeon revolted as she climbed. The walls shook violently, trying to remove us, as though we were a fishbone stuck in its throat.

It coughed, covering us in wet droplets of spit and mucus. Meredeath kept climbing, slow but steady. I tried to wipe the sticky mucus out of my eyes, but it wasn't easy with all the coils of rope around us.

"Stop it, or I'll have to drop you," Meredeath snarled.

I dropped my arms, reduced to dead weight.

Meredeath climbed undeterred. Our bodies rose steadily. The rope harness helped. Although they weren't pulling us up anymore, someone started bringing in the slack. On the few times she'd lost her grip in a violent shudder, the rope held.

I tried and failed to fight my inner [Self Critic].

When we breached the mouth of the dungeon, it was chaos incarnate.

Tandy bounced on the tip of the dungeon's tongue. Leo stuck to the roof. Richard was glued in place, hauling in the slack.

No one noticed us at first. The dungeon was rumbling and tossing everyone around. As soon as we'd started pulling over the top, Meredeath's face began returning to normal.

Her eyes shifted green. The fur vanished like a fading illusion.

I was still pasted to the front of Meredeath in a rope and slime-fueled mess. She stood before the team as I hung in a hunched mess as though trapped in a baby sling.

"Sorry, not sure how to get us unstuck," Meredeath said out of the side of her mouth.

"That's what she said!" Leo yelled.

Meredeath rolled her eyes.

[Skill Acquired: You have gained a new [Error - Class Not Located] skill, [Minor Slime Manipulation]. You have bonded in slime. This skill gives you minor control over your [Companion's] slime.]

Took you long enough.

Did I get that because I've been cocooned in banana slug glue for the ascent? Gross.

All that struggle, and all I get is a [Slime Manipulation] skill? It didn't even help get me untangled from Meredeath.

My mind drifted back to my dreams of a dire wolf companion with a frosty breath.

Meredeath jiggled up and down, snapping me back to the present.

"Damn, I can't just shake you off. Thanks for the assist, Richard. Tandy, please tell me you can unweave us?" Meredeath called to our teammate, shifting her body so I could see everyone out of the corner of my eye. "No offense, but I like to get to know a guy first."

"None taken," I whispered back, craning my neck to see a thoroughly disheveled Tandy slowly walk over. She looked like she'd made out with a dragon. Dizzy, she carefully picked her way to us.

"You okay?" I asked.

Tandy's glazed eyes focused on me slowly before she spoke. "Yes? I've got a concussion from getting knocked around. Give me a moment to decide what skill would be best."

"A concussion? Aren't weaving skills mind ba—?"

"[Unintended Weave]," Tandy called her skill with an unsteady voice, collapsing in a heap. The ropes that bound us dropped away, along with every stitch in my shirt.

Meredeath shook her foot, releasing the last coil as she stepped away. Leo gave a loud wolf whistle as I stood topless.

Tandy waved at me. "Sorry. Want me to fix it?"

"No, that's okay. I'll just... grab something out of my pack over there." I carefully stepped around Tandy, not wanting more of her undressing magic. I didn't have much left to lose.

I pulled out one of my older shirts, an off-white number with a lace-up chest.

"Don't you [Adventurer] types always defeat dungeons bare-chested?" Meredeath teased as I threw the shirt over my head.

I do!

I tugged my head through the collar only to be granted a

vision of Richard with his chest proudly puffed out in all its naked, slime-coated glory.

Meredeath laughed as I wondered if Richard was an exhibitionist.

Unseeing a foot-long, fanged banana slug in a bodybuilder pose is tough. But I was going to spend the rest of my life trying.

"What's next?" I asked, every bit of me resigned to the next horror.

Tandy chuckled darkly. "The only way out is through." She pointed to the throat. I was questioning my life choices.

"Hey, guys," Leo called down. "First, can someone get me down?"

Chapter 19

YOU CAN'T POLISH THIS

One might ask how I ended up back between Meredeath's thighs so soon.

"How much time's on our dungeon quest?" Meredeath asked as she used a dagger to cut at the glue pinning Leo to the ceiling. Richard's glue hadn't mixed well with the dungeon's saliva.

The only person who could reach Leo was Meredeath, sitting on my shoulders.

I brought up the text. "It says 10 hours."

"Not long enough." Tandy was working on Richard, who was also glued to the floor.

I stumbled a little as the floor rippled. It was almost as though the dungeon was as unhappy at our slowness as the [System]. Meredeath sitting on my shoulders didn't bother to comment. She kept prying at the glue. So far, she'd freed his right arm.

"What's our plan?" Meredeath asked as though we weren't relying on her for a plan. I thought it was rich for her, this overpowered feline-human, to ask *us*.

"We should discuss the tools we have available," I said, curious about her capabilities. The team needed to know the range of possibilities. I also had questions for Richard.

The dull sound of blades sawing at toughened glue filled the cavern. Looked like they were going to ignore me.

I opened my mouth to push, but Meredeath pulled at my hair. Looking up, she mouthed, *You owe me*. I jerked my head down.

Did I owe her? She'd saved my life, but we were in a dungeon together, so how much did that count?

Determined, I opened my mouth only to have her jerk my head again. Irritated, I looked up.

Her panic softened into desperation. Eyes pleading, she mouthed, *Please don't*.

Shame burned in my chest. Was I really willing to override her wishes?

I amended my original statement: "Did anyone else pick up any new skills?"

She squeezed my shoulder with a silent *Thank you*.

I'd save my questions for her until later. What *was* her class? *Could* she talk to Richard? We'd talk some place more private. Hopefully, survival and privacy were something I'd experience again.

"I didn't think we'd get any new skills until we finished the trial." Leo sounded tired. He mimicked the [System] in a stiff, fake voice. "*Further details and rewards will be aggregated and awarded upon [Trial Dungeon] completion.*"

"Well, I'm not sure mine's much of a 'reward.' I got [Minor Slime Manipulation]." I demonstrated by flicking a small bit of slime off my shoulder. Instead of flicking, it jerked to the side and oozed down my arm.

"Wow, that'll save us in a pinch." Meredeath said what we were all thinking.

"This is the stupidest test I've heard of, and I've been having my grandmother test me my whole life!" Tandy grunted, slicing through an entire section. Richard was almost free.

"We've got two more chances. I already told them about the intestines, but Meredeath, what made you and Richard turn around?" Leo asked as he scratched his nose with his free hand.

"Leo, you saved us. I have a [Breathe] skill that made me immune to the spores, but everything else fell asleep once the tunnels were saturated. First, Richard passed out. Then the tentacles and finally, as I was watching, the floor boss. I killed it with one swipe, cradling a snoring Richard."

I shifted my weight to the other foot, wondering what she'd used to slit its throat.

"Believe it or not, it dropped loot."

"I thought we couldn't get loot in the [Trial Dungeon]?" Leo's left hand snapped free. He began to pull at the glue around his chest.

Meredeath dug in her bra. At first, I thought a flake of glue had fallen in, but she retrieved something much better: an oversized brass key that shimmered with magic.

With a crack, Leo freed his torso. I helped Meredeath slide off my shoulders as Leo finished extricating himself. He landed smartly on his feet.

The tumble didn't dampen his enthusiasm. In fact, Leo vibrated with excitement. "Is that what I think it is?"

"Well, the key activates a bypass mechanism. So, if that's what you think it is...?" Meredeath trailed off, unsure what to do with his sudden enthusiasm.

"It's a [Progress Key]!" Leo exclaimed.

Tandy looked at him as if he'd grown a third eye. "Sorry, Leo, I'm not up on dungeon lore as much as you are." I could tell it was hard for Tandy to admit. "But what the hell is a [Progress Key]?"

Leo grabbed the key from Meredeath and danced a little jig. "Cole, do you remember? Those old timers at the Ram's Horn? We can bypass any section of the dungeon we've already completed. I'm surprised, though. I thought they were only in the elite dungeons."

These keys were supposed to save the team the grind, if I remembered correctly.

"Weren't they only available in the dungeons that gave you more than one life?" I asked, the memory coming back to me.

"Maybe it's here because it gave us three chances?" Tandy said as she stood up, holding a free Richard. He looked exhausted.

Tandy handed him over. Richard curled around my neck as usual. It was funny, the things I was getting used to.

"No, there's a catch. I remember that night, that old [Brawler]..."

Ram's Horn had been slow, so they'd released me early for the night, and Leo and I shared a table that night. We sat for two hours, just listening.

"You can use a [Progress Key] alright, but you should be careful," the grizzled [Brawler] had said. He took a long swig of his ale, drawing out his story. Wiping his beard, he continued. "You know why, right?"

"Oh, come on, Dian. You're a slow-boiling teakettle tonight, ain't you?" One of his teammates rolled his eyes. "If you're not going to tell her, I will, and it'll be much faster."

The [Brawler] Dain grinned. A nasty scar sat across his lips. "You never did know how to tell a story. Anyway, [Progress Keys] are a boon if you're trying to solve a dungeon, but if you're trying to level, they will hold you up—no levels or skills earned from what you bypass. The [System] only counts the last run. The final product of the team."

Their young teammate looked between the two warriors,

awe in her voice. "Is that how Cerlon Hammerstrike finished the Labyrinth without loot?"

The old man grinned. "I told you she'd do. A smart one we've got here. Aye, that's the supposition. Although no one knows what really happened. He lost his team, and he said little after that."

"Any progress we've had so far in the dungeon won't be counted toward our final loot totals." I said at last. "Something like that?"

We looked at each other briefly before Meredeath spoke, "I don't know you all too well, but loot isn't any good if you're dead. I say we use it."

"Honestly, I'm willing to do anything that doesn't force me to take another acid bath," Tandy chimed in.

I looked at Leo. Tandy was never loot-focused. It'd always been Leo and me hoarding over our childhood treasures.

Even knowing all of that, his vote still surprised me. "I vote we save it. We've got *two* more chances. Why not use one of them to try again? I've waited my whole life for this chance, and I want to step into an [Adventurer] class with as much collective experience as possible."

Leo looked at me, his last hope. I had the power to throw us into a tie or move us forward. Richard was notably quiet. Leo was tense. I could tell he wanted this desperately. He had felt insignificant for so long that he would do anything to grasp this opportunity.

I empathized. I wanted this too. But it wasn't worth it if we didn't survive.

"I hate to say this, Leo." He sighed, knowing my vote. "But I will have to go with Tandy on this one. You're almost untouchable, and you still died in the intestines. What if we need both our attempts to defeat whatever's next? Look, brother." I grabbed his arm, waiting for him to look at me. "You'll have the rest of your life to accumulate all the levels, classes, and skills you can dream up. I want to be there to see you do it."

The words, the promise, sat between us. I held my breath, willing Tandy to stay quiet. Leo had to come to this conclusion himself instead of being harshly overruled.

"I've been dreaming for a long time." His mouth twitched into a sad smile, accepting my logic. "You all are going to owe me a lot of levels, classes, and skills after we get through this dungeon. I've got twenty-five years to catch up on."

"I promise I will help you get *all* the skills." I said. I meant it, too. He deserved it.

Tension left his body upon his acquiescence. "Fine. We use it. Now tell us about this final boss of yours, Meredeath."

All eyes returned to Meredeath. She nervously fiddled with her amulet. I hadn't looked closely at it before, but the ivory top was carved into a delicate skull. She was such an odd individual.

"I've heard tales of this monster, and saw a moving illusion of it once. The stench is unbearable, and it has a gas attack that can hit swaths of [Adventurers] at once. I'm honestly shocked it's in a [Trial Dungeon]..." She trailed off.

My mind raced. What was waiting for us at the end of the road? How much did she know about dungeons? Could it be a dragon? One of the legendary Gawools? Nothing high-level had made it to Woodsten yet, not since the Ursine Wall blocked the Wilds. Not with the magical guardians patrolling the mountains.

This [Trial Dungeon] threw out the rulebook. We had a [Progress Key], something [Adventurers] could go their entire careers without earning once.

"What is it?" Tandy asked, impatient for the truth.

Meredeath hesitated before saying, "It's a Golgothan."

"Wh-what the hell is that?" Leo asked what we were all thinking. A Golgothan sounded terrible. Was it a miniature version of the leviathan we were stuck in?

Meredeath turned the key over in her hands, a smile tugging at the corners of her mouth. It was apparent she would not give us more. I tapped Richard on the head.

It's a shit demon, Richard translated dryly. He was tired and unimpressed.

"Crap," I said, then slapped my hand across my mouth trying to hold in a chortle. Everyone looked at me. "That's a load of crap."

Meredeath's eyes twinkled as she nodded. "I couldn't have said it better."

Tandy and Leo looked at us as if we were lunatics.

"We're about to step in it." I grinned as Meredeath snorted.

She answered with her own joke, saluting Tandy as she spoke. "But it's our doo-ty to finish this dungeon."

Tandy looked at the two of us making poop jokes and shook her head. "It's a shit monster, isn't it? Why does it always have to be such a shit-show with the two of you?"

Meredeath and I looked at her as she looked at us. We held it together for a few seconds before absolutely losing it. Wailing with laughter, I bent over, my sides hurting.

Even Richard chuckled to himself.

Chapter 20

BLOCKAGE

"Tandy, a little help with these?" Meredeath was ineffectively trying to carve up one of my old shirts with her dagger.

Digging through her pack furtively, Tandy pulled out a *legendary* item I never thought would leave her studio.

"Are those your *fabric scissors*?! You brought them *here*?" I scrambled forward to get a better look. I'd heard the story. Leo had *borrowed* her scissors to go mushroom hunting. The two didn't speak to each other for a month after the tongue-lashing Tandy gave him.

Looking at them, I couldn't see what the fuss was. They were metal scissors with shiny black handles. Sure, they looked sharp, but worth the security locked [Enchanted] pouch she kept them in?

"If I catch either of you with these in your hands. I will end you." I watched her cut through my shirt like butter. They were sharp; I'd give her that.

I could tell Leo had already accepted the challenge of swiping her scissors. He could never resist poking her when she got wound up about something.

"Tie these tight. I can't explain just how bad it smells down there." Meredeath handed me a strip of cloth to use as a mask. "Double, triple the fabric. Fold it as many times as you can still breathe through."

I'm so jealous right now.

"Can't we make some masks for you?" I asked, my voice muffled as I tied the mask off.

I smell through my top tentacles, which also help me see. Richard's body quivered, his mental voice dry. *I will never unsmell this place.*

The more I learned about slug biology, the less I understood it.

"Is your sense of smell that powerful?" All I could smell was the foul breath that'd lingered around us since I'd entered the [Trial Dungeon].

Richard bobbed a tentacle in the universal sign for *yes.*

"This whole place must be a slug nightmare." I expected dungeons to be gross, but I hoped this one was an outlier.

It makes one wonder if someone purposely made it to piss me off.

"Are we ready to go?" Meredeath's voice pulled us out of our private chat. Tandy was putting her scissors away in the [Enchanted] pouch worth more than a year's rent.

I looked at [Your Mom's Party] like an outsider, trying to measure if we were up to the challenge.

Tandy's braids had returned to their impeccable norm. Everything else was spotted with saliva and stains. She held daggers awkwardly in both hands. The glint in her eyes told me she was ready, even if she was clearly unprepared.

Meredeath was weaponless, holding the [Progress Key] in one hand. The black of her outfit somehow stayed unmarred by the dungeon. The straps, chains, and tears all looked somehow sexier for the general dishevelment. She touched the amulet on her chest, checking to ensure it was still there.

Leo held his double-bladed axe in front of him, a grin on his face. He'd cut the top of the pink sweater, claiming it was choking him in combat. So now it had a rugged V-neck with some of his chest hair sticking out. Even in Tandy's sweater, he looked like a veteran [Adventurer].

And finally, me... and Richard. Can't forget the slug. I held my hammer with both hands to hide my shaking. Slime had gotten into my boots, and I wondered if I'd packed extra socks. Richard, well, Richard sat like a slug on my shoulders: all confidence, no consequence.

"Let's go." Meredeath held the [Progress Key] in the air.

Nothing happened.

Leo and I exchanged smiles as Tandy went over to help. The two women conversed in low tones.

Tell them to hold it in the air and do a jig.

"I will not," I whispered, trying not to laugh.

"You've got to twist it," Meredeath exclaimed as a shimmering gold portal appeared.

Richard dry-heaved as we stepped through, and I agreed. None of Meredeath's descriptions of the cavern prepared me for the landscape.

It *smelled.* It smelled not just of shit, but of every type of decay. Like the wet, earthy compost at work, the sheep manure on a damp spring day, and a carcass rotting in the sun.

"You'll get used to it," Meredeath said with a grimace. "Sort of."

This creature needs to rethink its diet.

The walls exuded the magical light the rest of the dungeon had, but these pulsed, brightening and dimming. It made the space lighten into a pink. More than any other space, I felt that this place was alive.

Piles of unidentifiable food remnants littered the floor. A

burbly orifice blooped and squelched in one corner, releasing sulfurous gas.

A wet slurp sounded ahead of us. We stepped forward as a group, each footstep chosen carefully between piles of decay and the slick, glistening floor.

"I saw the demon in the next fold," Meredeath whispered.

I realized she'd described what I hadn't grasped. The cavern we were in tapered to a fold, turning so sharply that we couldn't see what was next. This really was the rear end of the creature's digestive tract.

One by one, we took turns peeking into the next cavern. I was last, patiently trying to glean some hint from each person's expression after they saw it. Leo'd been downright giddy, while Tandy had looked thoughtful.

I tipped my head slowly around the crease. The next cavern was similar. Nothing stood out except what I assumed was the Golgothan. It was so much smaller than I expected. Almost cute, if that word could ever be used to describe a mobile pile of poo.

The creature was the size of a dog. It slithered between two different orifices, collecting gas.

I ducked back, joining the huddle.

"I can take *that* out with one swing of my axe." Leo was probably right. The pile of excrement may have come up to my hip.

"This shit stinks of a trap." Tandy turned to Meredeath. "Is that creature what you thought was a boss?"

"Well, I didn't explore further than this chamber. It's a shit monster. Just because it's small doesn't mean it's not deadly." Watching her rip through the stomach parasites, I agreed. "Hey Cole, does Richard have anything to say?"

I agree with them. There's more to this than Leo killing that sentient ooze.

I guess they were done with talking to each other directly. I relayed his message back to the team.

We debated various ideas, but ultimately settled on Leo's original plan.

He charged in, axe swinging, and smacked the poo pile with the side of his blade. The axe went straight through the creature as it exploded in a splatter.

Leo started coughing hard as the thick smell of sulfur hit our nostrils. Otherwise, nothing happened. The room didn't shudder in protest, no giant granddaddy poo exploded from the floor. The orifices just burbled and popped.

Leo held his axe ready as we walked forward. A distant slurp sounded.

"I hate to admit it, but it looks like I was wrong? I guess?" Tandy said wearily as she scanned the room for danger.

"This is going to be ea—"

"Shut up, Leo," Meredeath snapped. "Just keep that thought to yourself."

The second chamber was much like the first. Nothing stood out on the floor, it was full of decay, slime, and more orifices. The walls still pulsed eerily, as though beckoning us to continue.

I snuck forward to look first this time. A slightly larger brown ooze slowly glurped along.

This one absorbed all sticky, decaying matter in its path. Each collection caused it to swell, adding to its overall mass.

I brought back my nugget of wisdom. "Assuming this isn't a trap, we should move quickly on this monster. The longer we wait, the bigger it's going to get."

The three went together to peek. Richard had curled up, stuffing his head into my collar. The increase in smell caused him to tap out of this room.

I could have predicted what came next.

"Leo, no!"

"This'll be no problem!" Leo disappeared into the next chamber, followed by a loud *smack.*

Silence.

The lack of a catastrophe almost made it worse. I joined Meredeath and Tandy in examining the room.

Leo was proudly shaking off his axe. The walls pulsed at seemingly the same rate. The floor was a little shinier with a little more squelch to each step, but otherwise fine.

Richard popped a tentacle out to look around. *I've got a bad feeling about this.*

"You and me both, buddy." I muttered.

The fourth room held long, slimy strands hanging from the ceiling. With no discernible monster, we sent Leo first. I told myself he wanted the job.

The curtains of mucus almost parted for him until he reached the middle of the chamber, when they collapsed on him like he'd triggered a bear trap.

Tandy and Meredeath leaped into action, cutting through the mucus. Leo looked frantic, but I could tell through [Partial Rapport] that although he was losing life, it wasn't rapid. I kept my hammer out, on guard for an ambush.

The promised Golgothan sat in the fifth room. I looked around the fold to find a creature resembling a stack of the biggest cow patties to disgrace a pasture. A yellow miasma of sulfurous gas billowed out from several small blowholes on its back. The floor was covered in sludge and debris, which pulsed at the same tempo as the walls.

Is that slime from the last room? Richard was piecing together what we were missing.

I watched as the slime we'd cut away pooled around the creature's base, creeping up and coating it like a gelatinous armor.

Oh shit, we just gave it weapons, and mass, and armor.

Of course, we made it with our hubris. In a dungeon, overconfidence was a deadly sin.

"It wasn't that hard to kill the mini-creatures. This guy is just a collection of everything I already defeated." Leo insisted, twisting his axe in his hand so the blades spun.

"Yeah, but you're the only one who damaged those things. What are the rest of us going to do?"

He shrugged as if to say, *Do I really need your help?*

In the end, we formulated a basic plan.

Meredeath stepped into the room first. She'd slipped on what she claimed were bracers. They looked like long beaded black lace gloves that went from the base of her fingers up her forearm.

"Hey, turd!" she shouted at it. "You ready to go down the drain?"

The Golgothan didn't reply, but the floor rippled as though insulted on the demon's behalf.

Wham! A geyser of filth erupted under Meredeath's feet, throwing her across the room.

"I've got Meredeath!" Tandy shouted.

Leo twirled his axe. "It's my turn." He charged forward with his [Enchanted] axe singing.

He carved into the creature's flank, the blade sinking halfway in with a squelch.

Straining, he pulled at the axe, trying to dislodge it. His tugs were futile. The axe kept sinking into the monster's body.

"Leo, move!" I called, swinging hard through the center.

No resistance. My hammer hit nothing but jelly.

Completely overextended, I couldn't stop the counter as a surge of putrid waste slammed into my face.

Richard went flying. I hit the ground hard, vision doubling as I rolled. My hammer vanished into the muck.

Bulbous growths appeared on the Golgothan's chest. Several grew rapidly, threatening to burst.

Leo's weapon began to shake loose.

Leo tugged harder.

Meredeath was up, knife in hand. She threw it.

The knife hit right in the chest, exploding a bubble.

Sulfurous gas enveloped Leo. Blinded, he staggered away.

"Cole, grab Leo's axe!" Tandy yelled. The axe was two-thirds gone. We were going to lose it if I didn't do *something.*

I ran forward. Unarmed. Desperate.

My foot slipped. I smacked onto the ground hard. The Golgothan loomed over me.

That's my hero!

"Richard, don't be a—"

Splat.

Something landed on my head. Heavy. Wet.

Everything faded.

[You, Cole Thornfield, are [Dead].]

Chapter 21

TEAMWORK MAKES THE SPLAT WORK

Splat. My body bounced off taste buds slick with saliva. The room shuddered with pleasure because this dungeon could taste us.

I had one life left and was positive the dungeon wanted to finish its meal.

I was now in the dungeon's holding tank, waiting for the rest of the party to wipe or succeed and leave without me. Respawning wasn't painful, exactly, but I felt distant. Removed from the world. And as my senses and thoughts returned, I was more demoralized than ever.

I'd died again, and now I was on my last chance. My last life.

This time, the consequences were real.

Head hanging, I checked the quest status.

[Quest Update: [Trial Dungeon]. This is the final test to receive your [Adventurer] status. You have one attempt left in the [2 hours] remaining. Your continued choices will influence final classes and skills achieved, assuming you survive. Adventure Onward.]

Well, crap, that didn't help. I peeled myself off the floor.

This might be my last two hours, ever.

Maybe less, I *was* the first one to die.

Seconds later, a death notification for Tandy saved my pride.

I ducked out of the way as the portal opened again.

A ball of shit appeared in the portal window. I thought the [System] had made a mistake for a second, but as the ball got closer, Tandy's form was taking shape. The shit fell off into the ether, and she was clean and whole two seconds before she hit the floor face first. It looked like neither of our deaths had been glorious.

For all my grousing, I thought we would survive the trial. I had this impenetrable belief that Tandy, Leo, and I could survive anything. Richard and Meredeath only added to my confidence.

But this was our last attempt, and it wasn't looking great.

Tandy sat across from me. We'd been dumped and dragged through so many body fluids that the stink didn't bother either of us anymore.

"Cole, we've got a problem," she said. No kidding. Are a sheep's tits cold after a shearing?

Too tired to sass her, I just gave a nod.

The last leg of the dungeon was a doozy. It would have been impossible without the progress key, but none of us had seemed to do any substantial damage to the giant Golgothan.

Tandy continued, ignoring my lack of engagement. "Let's discuss this pragmatically. Leo's brute force didn't work. He just lost his axe in the effort. Even as I died, he was trying to pull it loose. That goo blocked your hammer strike. I tried to lay down a trap with what's left of my rope, but it was taking too long. It killed me while I was placing it. Meredeath tried to protect me, but she kept getting bogged down in the muck." She shook her head. "Who knows where Richard ended up? I lost track of him when you took that first hit. Do you see the same problem I do?"

I raised my head to find two brown eyes boring into me. Reason number 145 why Tandy was our [Party Leader]: she wouldn't accept lackluster head bobs as a legitimate answer to a question. Also, her eyes could bore holes in lead.

I tried to duck out of committing verbally. "It depends." *Tandy and I were dead weight.* Saying it out loud to Tandy, however, made it too real. "On what you see is the problem." I finished with a 'cute smile' trying to get out of the question. It hadn't worked on my last girlfriend, and it didn't look like it was working on Tandy.

She just sat unblinking, waiting for me to continue. The soft oozing sounds of the dungeon mouth salivating at its anticipatory snack were our only companion. I hadn't been dead for two minutes, and she wanted answers from me?

Self-pity wasn't good to indulge, so I started rambling every word trying to avoid what I didn't want to admit. "Well, this time, we didn't know what to expect from the boss. The longer the others hold out, the more they can learn. Meredeath and Leo are a deadly one-two punch."

There, that seemed reasonable enough. Maybe she'd turn off her soul-baring stare.

"You're right." She said it in a way that I knew there was a 'but' coming. I patted myself on the back for outmaneuvering her quest for truth. "But the *real* problem isn't defeating the Golgothan, is it?"

I let out an explosive sigh. We sat silently for a few seconds before I caved. "No, it isn't. The real problem is us." Every ounce of defeat I felt came out in the tone of those words.

"Yeah." She sounded as dejected as I felt, which somehow was comforting. If the most put-together person I'd ever known was lost, then it wasn't just me.

"It's the splat factor," I heard myself saying.

"The splat factor?" she asked with a raised eyebrow.

I held my two hands out, connected by strands of saliva. "Yeah, we're too easy to kill." I clapped my hands together with a wet smack. "We have a high splat factor. No armor, no health, we're way too squishy."

"Ah, yes, exactly. Maybe the three of them could defeat the monster if they didn't have to worry about keeping us alive. We're holding them back. And neither of us has the damage output or any real utility to make up for our 'splat factor'..." Tandy trailed off, losing herself in thought.

Splat factor. I absentmindedly wondered if it was a behind-the-scenes mechanic that the [System] tracked. We'd been the first to die in both our dungeon encounters, and I only survived the root canal uprising because I ran.

I was a little more death-resistant than Tandy, with 25 hit points to her 10, but I made up for it by thinking I could follow Leo onto the beast's maw. She was right. The question was, what do we do about it?

We could sit out the fight. Let the heartier half of our party deal with the monster. Then waltz in afterwards and collect the reward. It was a lovely daydream, but I was sure the dungeon's mechanics prevented it.

Just like the bogquackers, raiders, and widowmaker sent to hurry us along, it'd been clear from the beginning the [System] had an agenda and a schedule. The [Adventurer's] contract was tight. We gave up our [Mundane] existence to join the elite, and the cost of entry was risking our lives in a [Trial Dungeon].

"What if...?" Tandy spoke quieter this time, as though she didn't want to say what she was thinking. "What if I let you all go ahead without me?"

"I'm not sure what you mean," I asked, making my confusion clear.

"What if I just died in the final battle? Once I died, I'd fail the [Trial Dungeon] and you all would pass. You're all in this mess because of me. You and Leo always dreamed of being [Adventurers] when we were kids... I just..." The words caught in her throat as the reality of our situation took hold. "I just didn't want to be a [Weaver]."

It wasn't any consolation that I'd considered doing the same thing. Even if we'd taken her up on it, her offering to sacrifice cemented in my mind why we wouldn't allow it.

"Nope."

"No?"

"Correct. We walked into this challenge as a team, and we'll walk out of here or die trying as a *team*." I said it confidently, ignoring the twinge in my heart that just wanted to return to my mediocre life in Woodsten.

"That's just a useless platitude, Cole. We're talking about life or death." Tandy's voice had an edge to it. She didn't want us to sacrifice our lives for her either.

"Maybe, but it's one I believe in. No one is sacrificing their life for mine. We're in this together. Besides, you're always the one who says that our attitude limits our choices. If you're determined to sacrifice yourself, you'll never think of a solution where we all walk out of here [Adventurers]. We're not that *desperate* yet. Let's think."

So we sat in the warm, damp spawning ground for the dungeon, thinking and waiting for the rest of our party to die.

"We need to split its attention. It can't target us both if it has too many targets to focus on." Tandy wasn't wrong, but her logic had a critical flaw.

"But the monster targeted the two of us, like it knew we were vulnerable. It's too difficult to protect both of us at the same time."

The problem is we can't split our protection. I wish we were more advanced or had some real combat-based [Adventurer] skills. Back home, we'd talk about getting illusion or protection skills. Hell, I'd give almost anything for a breath-related skill, something like Meredeath's.

[Your [Party Member] Leo Patch is [Dead].]

[Your [Party Member] Meredith Steele is [Dead].]

The portal runes began glowing, announcing the failure of our other companions. Meredeath and Leo fell towards the portal in four pieces. They'd been entirely sliced in half. I swallowed my bile as their bodies stitched back together, as they shimmered through the portal in a tangle.

The portal went dark. I watched Leo and Meredeath untangle themselves, seeing no telltale flash of yellow.

I'd forgotten about Richard. And now he was gone.

He was missing.

Frantically, I checked our bond only to find a cold echo where his presence should be.

And Meredeath's name was Meredith? What in the frozen hells was going on?

Chapter 22

PLANNING SOMETHING STUPID

"Where's Richard?" My voice was tight.

Meredeath gave me a flat stare. "Calm down, he'll join us soon. Unless you got a [System Notification] that he died?"

I shook my head.

"It'll just take him some time to get back to us." She wasn't here during my panic. Bags under her eyes belied the perfectly crafted makeup. She looked like she'd entered the dungeon a decade ago.

He's not dead. I said the words to myself. The [System] hadn't given us a death notice, but the bond felt cold. Lifeless, as if something vital was missing from the air. What if he stayed gone?

My heart spasmed. Not for the first time, I had to admit I was getting attached to the jerk.

As though sensing my heartache, a warm thrum twanged

through our bond. Richard was alive, but busy? Distant? And a little annoyed at my doubts.

"Okay, but did you read the death notifications?" Leo asked with a grin, "Meredith?"

He was full of the energy the rest of us were missing.

"It was a [System] error. Look at our Party interface." She shrugged off the comment. The [Party] interface still had her listed as Meredeath.

Leo's grin dropped as he confirmed as well. I hadn't heard of that type of error before, but Leo and I could intimately attest to the [System's] brokenness.

"So, how'd it chop the two of you in half?" Tandy brought everyone to our situation at hand.

"It sliced through us with a high-speed torrent of sewage. Did you see its eyes glow? I didn't even know it had eyes." Leo addressed Meredeath, the only person in the room who had an inkling of what he was talking about.

However, I was getting a clue.

Meredeath propped herself up against a tooth, using it as a backrest. She shook her head. "Yeah, that was creepy as hell. The stream was thin but powerful. I'm guessing it has some emergency [Cornered Rat] skill when it takes significant damage."

Meredeath's words seemed to inflame Leo, rather than calm him down. "We almost had it! I could see its death coming! I just needed one more strike, and it would have been down!"

"Woah, you guys almost killed it?" I hadn't lasted more than a couple of minutes, and the two of them almost killed it. Impressive. "What was your trick? Last I saw, your axe stuck to the creature, and my hammer did nothing to it."

Meredeath waved at Leo to answer.

"I figured it out," he said. "My slices weren't working. Either it did minimal damage, or my axe would get stuck and I'd be open to a counterattack." He looked at me, serious for a moment. "Cole, you've got to stop trying to save me. I can take a hit or two. You're only going to get yourself killed."

"Yeah, fine, I'll let *you* get killed next time." Leo wasn't wrong. I just didn't want to hear it. "Message received. How'd you almost kill it?"

"Well, the next time I swung, I saw it tense up. It was making its body denser to grab the axe blade, so I twisted my blade in the last second. The head smacked into it like I'd done with the oozes. The blunt damage worked as long as I tricked it."

"He was awesome," Meredeath said, patting Leo on the back. "Leo hit it like a freight train, and a chunk of the guy's shoulder blew right off."

I squashed my jealousy. The battle had brought the two of them together. We were a stronger team because of it. It was good, right?

"What's a *freight train*?" Tandy asked.

Meredeath shook her head. "Not important. He hit the thing like a battering ram."

Leo mimicked his overpowered swing in the background. It sounded epic.

So the monster braces for slashes, allowing a smash to deal tons of damage. But if you just flat-out try to hit it with a bash, it'll give way and let you through with no damage. I looked down at my hammer, feeling useless. I had no way to 'trick' it like Leo had.

"It takes more than one hit to kill a monster." I glanced at Tandy, then asked, "How'd you stay alive long enough to figure all of this out?"

Leo pointed at Meredeath. "It's her. She's been holding out on us. Meredeath can absorb sooo much damage. She was everywhere, taking hit after hit. I've never seen anything like it."

"Yeah, I have an heirloom from my mother." Her voice dipped as her fingers brushed the amulet, like the memory of it burned. "Ironically, she was the only person who saw me for who I really am. Said the amulet *fit my aesthetic.* Never tried to make me into someone I wasn't."

Meredeath shook her head, as though banishing the past. She said 'was' like her mom was gone. I wasn't going to press now, but if Meredeath stayed with us and we survived this, I'd ask about her family later.

"Anyway, when she gave it to me, I didn't know it was [Enchanted]. But yeah, it absorbs a considerable amount of damage. It takes and stores 50% of any inflicted damage aimed at me. I have to... I have to release the damage later. This place is all about balance. But it's a convenient tool in a fight."

Her eyes had grown hard as she talked about "releasing the damage later." I couldn't help but wonder how that was accomplished.

"Why'd you die? Is there a limit to what it can absorb?" Tandy asked, I'm sure she wanted to file its capabilities away in her team's list of tools.

"Not that I know of, or at least I haven't hit the limit yet. But—" She paused and tried to hide it, but her body had begun to shake. She was afraid of pushing it too far. Her voice was flat as she finished. "The price is high. My [Analyze] skill is still low, so it hasn't told me much about the enchantment."

"Then why did you die with Leo? It sounds like you were close to beating the Golgothan." Tandy was insistent. She never could read a room.

"He died first, and there's no reason to go on without the rest of you. This exercise is a party pass or fail. My surviving the fight alone wouldn't help any of us. I already did that, and it got me here."

Malyc promised us she would be motivated to help [Your Mom's Party] survive. Turned out he was right.

"So this isn't the first time you've attempted a [Trial Dungeon]?" Tandy asked quietly.

Meredeath's voice dropped to an icy note. "Yeah. My original team died. The benevolent [System]," her words thick with sarcasm, "gave me a month to try again with a different group. Malyc didn't tell me the Ursine Wall portal wasn't heavily trafficked. I'd almost given up hope of trying again. If you hadn't come along, I would have failed on my contract."

We all winced. The contract we'd signed was clear: failure to attempt the [Trial Dungeon] was an 'abandonment of duty.' And as a magical contract, it punished those with a gruesome form of death. It's why none of us had tried running away.

"My timer is just about out. There are no more [Trial Dungeon] attempts for me if we don't win collectively. This is it."

I leaned back, trying to grasp the ramifications of her revelation. On one hand, I was glad that, if we failed and Leo survived, he'd theoretically get another chance with another team.

However, the stakes had grown higher. If Tandy and I didn't make it out alive, Meredeath would end up losing her life, too.

"I've always thought it wrong, the penalty for not succeeding," I said. At least, they didn't consider dying in here as 'abandonment of duty.'

In the end, the [System] didn't tolerate dropouts. Fail the [Trial Dungeon] and you die. Try and fail, you die. Don't try at all? You die slower. Uglier.

Meredeath nodded. "It's twisted. I don't understand it either. On my last team, we had a weaker member. He wanted to be a [Mage], like you, Tandy."

I glanced at Tandy as we shared a look. Meredeath must have assumed that since her mana was so high.

"[Mages] are at such a disadvantage, so we tried to protect him by leaving him behind in the run. I found only a few pieces of him left when I went back to escort him out."

I imagined the root canals popping out on an unsuspecting Tandy and fighting over her body. No thank you, we would not tempt that fate.

The [System] had internal rules about how it wanted parties to progress and wasn't above violently enforcing them.

My eyes glazed over as they continued bantering back and forth about tactics. I already knew the truth: we were doomed. Or rather, I was doomed. I began hoping that I would die first, so I wouldn't have to see Tandy go down. Or watch Meredeath become a walking undead husk.

"Cole, how are your acting skills? Do you think you could... pretend to be dead? Meredeath, what do you think the average intelligence of a shit demon is?" Tandy's voice made me lift my head. She had an idea.

"Pretend to fail? Please, I can do that any day of the week." I'd been pretending to be a successful [Adventurer] all day. That hadn't gone so well. But pretending to fail? Failing would be easy. It was pretending that was hard.

My mind checked the [Party] list, Richard still hadn't returned. I couldn't shake the feeling that something was desperately wrong with him.

I sent another mental note into the abyss. *Richard, you'd better come back soon. We're planning something stupid.*

Chapter 23

FREIGHT TRAIN DIPLOMACY

Tandy's dagger felt strange in my hand.

I stabbed the Golgothan hard in the belly. Too hard. To my horror, I watched my hand and forearm sink into the creature. The cloth wrapped around my face blocked out most of the smell, but I couldn't block out the feeling of my hand being coated in sludge.

Stuck fast, I crouched over and waited for retribution. Out of the corner of my eye, I saw the appendage coming. Springing to the side as it hit, I forced my body to go limp. In a flash, half of my health bar vanished as I smacked into the wall of the cavern. Sliding down into a heap, face down, I held my breath.

"You killed Cole!!" Meredeath screamed, charging at the beast. It was an impressive yell. I almost believed she cared about me.

If things were going as planned, Leo'd be right behind her, drawing his share of the demon's attention.

I'd fallen carefully so that my arm cradled my head, keeping it out of the muck coating the floor. I tried not to breathe as my heart thumped loudly in my veins.

Counting silently, I imagined the team performing their pre-planned actions.

It didn't seem like the boss knew I was still alive. Thank the Ever Bear. Prone and vulnerable like this, it'd have taken one geyser, one aimed hit, to finish me off.

The fight was going better than last time. Meredeath and Leo were grunting as they knocked health off the demon.

"Watch out, short-range breath attack!" Tandy shouted. I could hear the creature inhale.

Fear lodged in my chest. This was the weakest part of our plan. This area attack would have killed me if they hadn't drawn it far enough away.

I could hear Leo and Meredeath increase their hits, trying to push it further. They weren't sure they'd gotten it far enough away from me. Each step they took was difficult because of the swampy septic runoff pulling at their feet.

The creature exhaled through orifices scattered throughout its body. A thick, noxious yellow gas emitted from the holes like splattering geysers filled with rotten eggs, and the sulfurous miasma enveloped anyone within ten feet of the beast.

Thankfully, it wasn't close enough to decrease my health. However, the smell made my nose twitch. I hadn't practiced my death feint for ten minutes for nothing. I squeezed my watering eyes shut, willing myself not to cough, move, or react. I waited for the end...

That didn't come.

I kept my attention on my health bar, which slowly increased.

Leo let loose a battle cry, and I heard a *thunk* as the back end of his axe struck. Gloop rained down from the ceiling. I cringed as two hit me, taking off five more points of damage.

"Leo, look out!" Tandy yelled as the Golgothan let out a battle cry of its own. A sickening thwack sent Leo careening towards me. As his staggered footsteps got louder, I braced.

He knocked into me, causing my 'dead' body to roll. I suppressed a groan. My job of pretending to be dead just got infinitely more complicated, as my face rolled towards the fight.

Leo scrambled to get up. Tandy threw a woven net at the monster. The net landed on the beast's head.

"[Tighten the Weave]!" Nothing happened. "Oh, for the love of wool, [TIGHTEN THE WEAVE]!" she roared.

The net sat unimpressively on the Golgothan's face. Tandy let loose another string of invective insults.

Meredeath sprang into action before the monster targeted Tandy. Her hands shifted into claws as she leaped forward, slashing rapidly. Clods of Golgothan flew. Leo slipped as he tried to stand up, elbowing me in the gut. He was a bit woozy from the last hit.

The Golgothan was missing an arm. Leo's hit had been massive. The creature looked down at Meredeath's tiny frame and was unimpressed. It slammed the remaining arm down on her head. Her amulet glowed red, absorbing the damage as she staggered back.

The boss inhaled. I closed my eyes, knowing what was next. It was going to activate another breath attack. This time, I was too close.

Leo realized it too, and he charged, ramming the creature in the gut. The hit worked, expelling the deadly gas out of its mouth in one whoosh. Leo and Meredeath were covered, but the toxicity stayed localized. Tandy and I were still safe.

Leo bent down, coughing, as Meredeath used him to pull herself up. Her amulet glowed ominously red as it absorbed more damage. She looked pale in the red light.

With the beast's attention elsewhere, I blinked to clear my eyes. Had her makeup changed? I couldn't tell if it'd gotten smudged, but it looked like dark streaks bled from her eyes. She looked like vengeance incarnate, ready to drag the Golgothan back to hell.

The shit demon slowly recompiled, using its mass to reform appendages and seal gaping holes. This time, it stood bulky but much smaller. Only slightly larger than Leo. If I had to guess, they'd taken off more than half of its health. The creature had deep-set eyes, pinpoints of red sunken in a featureless face.

The eyes started to glow.

Oh shit. This was the moment that wiped out the team last time. The mysterious skill that sliced Leo and Meredeath cleanly in half.

Tandy was distracted, still trying to trigger her weave skill. I willed her to pay attention. To look up and realize what was going on. She looked down at her training cloth, trying to troubleshoot [Tighten the Weave]. *Look up!!*

Leo must have heard my telepathic urging, because he'd finally cleared his throat and realized what was happening.

"Tandy!" he roared, moving towards the demon. The mud pulled at his feet. Leo wouldn't make it.

The monster opened its mouth, and a thin stream of water shot straight at Tandy. Our adventure was over before it even began.

Suddenly, Meredeath was there. She came out of nowhere, jumping in front of the beam. I watched the shock and… acceptance?… cross her face. The amulet glowed deep red as the attack hit. Then it flickered and snuffed out.

The liquid stream etched through the midsection of Meredeath's body. She fell to the floor, her dull amulet sinking into the slop. Her bisected body sat for a moment as her health bottomed out. Then she shimmered and disappeared.

[Your [Party Member] Meredith Steele is [Dead].]

I didn't see if it hit Tandy, but the lack of death notification was telling.

Meredeath was gone.

We'd failed. I replayed Meredeath telling me this was her final attempt, this was it.

And she'd lost. She'd gambled on us. On our misfit trio. And we'd let her down.

The Golgothan didn't give a shit about our tragedy. The creature swung its head around, the cutting stream of liquid arcing across the room, headed straight for Leo. I was safely below the cutting zone, and it still wasn't aware of me.

Leo ducked the initial spray and then ran. Dodging and ducking as the demon tried to target him. The attack must have had a time limit, as the arc of sludge fell slowly. The monster looked even further deflated.

Sensing his moment, Leo sprang up and charged. His axe, however, had been left sitting next to my body. It was a casualty he'd dropped as he tried to stay out of the death zone of the slicing attack.

Leo arrived at the base of the Golgothan, staring it down eye to shit-covered eye, weaponless. Without flinching, he balled his fist and punched the creature in the face. His hand hit with a thunderous smack, sinking into the creature's chin.

Leo's fist was stuck.

"What the hell?" Leo tried pulling it out, but anything he tried to use as leverage also got stuck. In moments, his hands and one foot were glued to the creature as it used some unseen skill.

With glee, the Golgothan picked Leo up and ran at the wall. It slammed Leo against the cavern. Feces splattered everywhere.

I started to move. My hand reached for the [Enchanted] axe. The monster peeled itself off Leo, who was physically glued in place. He'd been effectively trapped. The monster stood over Leo's helpless form, gloating.

Thankfully, its back was still turned to me.

I gripped the axe with both hands. It felt right, like my hammer in the forge. My muscles tensed. I almost felt warm, as if I were working in front of a fire, hitting strike after strike to hammer metal into shape. I raised my axe/hammer. It was my turn.

The Gogothan turned, hearing my squishy footsteps. I raised the axe and swung. I could see the beast tense. The skin oozed as it firmed, bracing for the hit. In the last second, I twisted the blade instinctively, triggering [Pound]. My muscles bulged as the axe came down.

I imagined the head of the demon as the flat surface of a nail. A nail I was going to strike perfectly. A nail I was going to [Pound].

"This is for MEREDEATH!" Then, as the axe whistled, coming down like a hammer, I shouted my skill. "[Nailed It]!"

This time I *willed* the skill to work.

As Meredeath said, it hit like a freight train. Slamming with the might of two skills and the [Enchanted] weapon, the Golgothan ripped in two from forehead to crotch. It rained shit.

My hands shook as I filled with awe. The axe glowed with power. I did this.

Stepping over the remnants of the boss, I pelted what was left of it with some rapid-fire strikes.

With the job finished, I stood over the Golgothan's ruined body. The axe hummed in my hands. It was dead. I avenged Meredeath. We'd won, but it tasted like shit.

[Dunglord defeated. You have earned experience. All experience and rewards are deferred until the exit of the [Trial Dungeon] by all party members.]

"Cole, you killed it. Cole, are you okay? Put down my axe, buddy, and help get me off this wall." Leo's voice finally cut through the fog.

I turned to him, my forearm still flexed. His face held an

expression I'd never seen him make at me. Awe. I drank in the moment. I'd never caught him admiring something *I'd* done. Shaking my head, I stepped towards him, only to find his expression changing quickly to worry.

I looked down, and I was holding an... axe? Wasn't it a hammer? I was covered in Dunglord. Dropping the axe, I focused on Leo. His hair plastered to his face, beard streaked with brown muck.

I grinned. "You look like shit."

"Haha, very funny. Now help me get down."

I pulled at Leo's hand and his arm. My boots slid in the sludge as I tried to get leverage.

"Let me help," Tandy's voice cut through my mechanical fog. I surveyed the chamber, and there she was. Alive!

Leo pulled free, one slimy appendage at a time.

"I can't believe we won," Tandy said, scraping shit off her hands.

"But we didn't, Meredeath died." The plain statement sliced through her like the Golgothan's [Cornered Rat] attack. It was harsh, but I couldn't feel good about our victory. "And I still don't know where Richard is."

We stood there silently for a second. Tandy, with shoulders slumped in guilt, while Leo wiped at his eyes, smearing more 'mud' across his face.

The cavern shook, giving us no more time to grieve. Whatever was next, none of us wanted to find out in the dungeon's colon. Walls quivering, we walked towards the next chamber.

Leo slipped, his foot coming free of his boot. He kept going. The cavern was starting to fill with a noxious gas. Turning the last corner, the final cavern was small in comparison. A wall had opened to reveal an exit portal. Another rumble rocked the room.

"What's going to happen next?" Leo asked, pulling us up at the last moment.

I shrugged, thinking about our missing companions. "Does it matter?"

Tandy slapped me on the back, drawing my eyes to hers. "Of course it matters."

I looked at my shit-coated friends. Leo was no longer blond, covered head to toe in crap. He stood slouched sideways with one shoe missing, holding his double-bladed axe.

Tandy stood next to him, half of her face smeared with goop. Her braids were matted down. Pack clutched resolutely, her brown eyes had a steely glint.

Whatever came next, we would do it together.

As I opened my mouth to give a platitude, the dungeon undulated. Tandy clutched at our arms as we stumbled through the portal together.

Chapter 24

MEASURING CONTEST

The three of us floated in the incorporeal ether of the portal. Tandy and Leo were sucked forward to an exit gate, but I was drawn in a different direction. Richard's thread tugged me somewhere else.

With no fanfare, I appeared tucked behind a large bookcase, an unwilling audience to an argument.

I won! Richard mentally shouted as he sat on a crumbling marble bookstand.

A glowing orb spun before him. The blue orb spun faster with tinges of red, seemingly annoyed at Richard. I could sympathize.

I floated, tucked behind shelves in the oldest library I'd ever seen. Rows upon rows of books and scrolls, all covered in an eon of dust.

[You cheated.]

I gasped soundlessly in my incorporeal form. The orb was *the [System]*?

I cheated?! Richard's voice raised in fake outrage. *Me?! You're the one who pulled me out of my team's [Trial Dungeon]. A trial specifically chosen to piss me off. You pulled me out just as they attempted to take on an overpowered boss. You have no right to accuse* ***me*** *of cheating.*

The orb spun quietly.

Richard's eye tentacles stretched forward, glaring.

[I hate you.]

The feeling is mutual.

The orb turned back to a mollifying green.

[A compromise. You stay here. Help in holding the Ursine Wall. Your [Cole Thornfield] and his friends get [Adventurer] status.]

How is that a compromise? Richard shook his tentacles. *My team gets what they earned, and I'm stuck here with you? I noticed you didn't mention Meredeath either. No deal. What do you give up in that 'compromise'?*

Richard's voice dropped into the smallest earworm, meant only for me. *Look around you, idiot. I can't stall it forever.*

I jumped. Richard knew I was here. I started looking around.

The library was hard to conceive. Row upon row of shelves filled with books took up more space than probably all of Woodsten. Giant columns held up fragile arches made of marble. The stone had metal filigree twining along the joints in intricate weaves. Even in my nonphysical state, I could see that they thrummed with power.

The roof was full of holes where parts of the framework had fallen in from age, from attack. I could see the holes still covered by a glimmering magical shield that flashed every few moments as though defending against a magic spell.

Looking at the shelves near me, I started examining the books.

Many were in languages I didn't understand. In letters I'd never seen before.

[What do you propose?] The [System's] voice boomed in the library. Much louder than the notifications I received in my everyday life.

I moved along the shelves quickly, floating along the ground. Being incorporeal had advantages, as I didn't disturb the dust. Richard was giving some reply I couldn't hear, but I finally reached a section I could read.

Basic Magical Weaves, The Anatomy of Dragons, Methodologies for Removing Corruption, A Proposed System for Progression, Magic for Magi, Magic for Warriors, A Merit Proposal for a Division of Power.

The list went on, and my research was interrupted by the [System's] booming reply.

[Absolutely not. Do you know how much power that would take? The barrier would be down within a month!]

Richard was muttering some response. What did he want me to find?

I tried to pull out a book, but my hand passed right through, which was probably good. I wasn't sure these tomes would survive being pulled out of their centuries-long resting place.

A mental tug pushed me on. There was something here I needed to see.

Desks were set up against the far wall. Well away from the spinning orb that controlled my world. I went to investigate. The desks were probably once at the height of opulence. That they were even standing was a testament to their original quality.

Now, however, they looked wormy and fragile. Two I could see had collapsed under their weight. The other eight against this inner wall looked a breath away from joining their kin.

One desk, however, was not only the most stable-looking but also had two books open on top of it.

One book had an obvious slug-induced slime trail on it. *On Immortality and Death* by Magus Reaver.

Everything in me burned to turn the page. If I could just, my hand passed straight through the pages. The book was open to just the title page. My hand passed uselessly through the page over and over. Not even Richard's slime stuck to my fingers.

A spark went off in my head. I triggered [Minor Slime Manipulation], willing the slime to turn the page over.

It shifted, and the pages shifted in a goopy slurp that would cause most librarians to cry.

There are seven classifications that contain the skill [Immortality]. Please see the attending chapters for details on each:

Chapter 1: Veil Walker

Chapter 2: Lich

Chapter 3: Remnant

Chapter 4: Ascendant

Chapter 5: Flicker

Chapter 6: Fanged Banana Slugs

Chapter 7: Cursed

What the hell? Fanged Banana Slugs were an [Immortal] class? The pages were handwritten. This one had a significant amount of slime on it. I wondered whether Richard had forged it.

Before flipping to Chapter 6, I read the rest of the page.

Equally, four classifications contain the skill [Manipulate Death], and three that contain the skill [Dodge Death]. All of these classes and skills are closely related to [Immortality] and thus a subject of this book:

Chapter 8: Hollow Heart

Chapter 9: Scythe

Chapter 10: Last Vestige

Chapter 11: Death Warden

Chapter 12: Death Dodger

Chapter 13: Slip Soul

Chapter 14: Oathless

I flipped the page, eager to learn about [Immortality], dealing death, or the truth about fanged banana slugs.

The pages flipped with a slurp of slime. My shaky control over [Minor Slime Manipulation] caused a chunk of pages to stick together.

Chapter 12: Death Dodger

Oh, for fuck's sake. The pages wouldn't turn to any other chapter, no matter how hard I tried. Resigned, I started reading.

Death Dodger is unique in the classification of powers. Initially theorized, it has only been attempted by a few willing to admit, and even fewer have professed attaining a deep understanding of the classification. This book has few details because of these limitations.

I rolled my ghostly eyes. Of course, it doesn't have any helpful information about the class.

Those who attain Dead Dodger generally stumble upon their greatness. These individuals are slippery in history's annals, not cheating death through force but through the subtle manipulation of events. They sit in the shadows, testing [System] integrity, slipping through loopholes, and challenging the odds of fate.

The most famous to pursue the Death Dodger power classification was Leara Flamecraft. While known primarily for her mastery of flamecraft, Leara alternatively pursued the higher levels of death magic. It is rumored that she attained high levels due to her successful pursuit of her primary class. It is well known that flamecraft is not for the weak of heart.

Individuals in this power classification can attain a mastery of death, becoming inappropriately [Immortal] through conventional and magical means. Variations of power enable odd acts of salvation, healing, evasion, trickery, and paradigm-shifting leaps in logic. Beware, individuals who attain this classification can be power brokers and breakers.

The text continued on the next page, but no effort could make it flip.

I didn't know what to think of this Richard obtained knowledge. Was he suggesting that he was a [Death Dodger]?

Or that I should become one? Was this an elaborate prank that showed me that [Fanged Banana Slugs] were listed under [Immortality]?

No joke was above my little slug.

The other book, *A Discussion on Power Dynamics,* presented an argument for power management, establishing a system to distribute skills and control magical classes. I leaned in.

This author does not intend to take a side in the Great Debate, but to describe a system in which power is shared by merit and equality if it is decided that such a system is necessary to protect the realm.

First, the governing body will establish those skills and classes with a mundane quality. Those progression markers in which the peasants shall excel are insignificant to the greater struggle and are unlikely to cause further imbalance to the Great Scale. These classes and skills shall be open to all and will breed a satisfaction in the populace that will do better than any debate at squashing ambition.

For those that seek greater power, the [Trials of a Hero] should suffice in weeding out the rubbish…

I continued scanning the text as a notification triggered.

[Quest Granted: [Trials of a Hero: Heart]

Congratulations on taking the first step to higher power. You have completed one of three prerequisites to meet the requirements to enter the Trial at the Library of Alta. This path is not for the faint of heart. Completion of the Trial at the Library of Alta will grant the class [Hero]. No time limit given for this quest.]

Great, another insurmountable trial just as I finished the first one. At least this one didn't have a time limit. The last line on the page was a head-scratcher.

These trials will ensure that magic, true power, is kept safe for those who will use it wisely.

I had never heard of the Library of Alta. My mind spun at the idea of ancient and powerful classes and skills. The age before, when legends walked and some of the greatest wonders were built.

[It is settled. You are making a mistake, but my opinion has never stopped you.]

The [System's] shouting interrupted my reading. This time, Richard's voice was louder, fuller. A mental echo vibrating in my mind.

I have faith in my team. They are the key we've been lacking. They will stand against the tide, and it will break.

The [System] laughed. Dust flew up as the library vibrated.

[You have become so small with small ideas. I will let you go only because I have realized you are no longer worthy. The years have eroded your power.]

The years have eroded your soul! Richard shouted back, throwing his mental weight into the argument.

[I bind you to them. The wall cracks. [Corruption] has taken a Guardian. If your team has such promise, they will have no problem with this challenge.]

A [System] message appeared in my notifications:

[Quest Granted: [Clean the Corruption]

The great barrier is failing. A Guardian of the Ursine Wall has been [Corrupted]. Defeat the [Corrupted Guardian]. Reward: [Adventurer] specific [Enchanted Item].]

And Meredeath?

[[Meredith Steele] is not part of this bargain.] The [System] finally said. [But she is not yet claimed.]

But…

[Begone!]

And we were.

PART II

Swamp Mommy

Chapter 25

CORRUPTION

The [System] banished Richard and, consequently, me from the library abruptly.

My heart panged in grief for the knowledge-filled stacks evaporating before my eyes as I was sucked into the portal with Richard.

Before I could worry about our fate, we were both violently ejected from the gate on Bear Ridge.

Richard squeaked as he hit the rocky ground, rolling like a sea cucumber in the tide. I staggered out. My boots were slipping on the smooth slab of granite. My stomach lurched with portal sickness, and I threw up.

You've got to find a better way of greeting me.

It wasn't like I'd aimed at Richard. He just attracted projectile vomit.

Richard slithered out of my blast zone, glowing yellow

with his [Clean] skill as the evidence of my sin melted from his body.

Now that my stomach was satisfied, I looked around to ascertain how much time had passed.

The ruins were as I remembered, granite stairs framed by the stone ribs of buildings. Only low rock outlines remained where a city once stood. This time, however, a green fog snaked out of the portal, shrouding the city in ominous shadows.

The hair on the back of my neck bristled as I saw Leo and Ched standing next to each other, weapons brandished. Leo's pink sweater flapped in the wind. It was ripped in a dozen places with blood oozing into the fabric.

Ched wasn't much better. He held a frying pan and a paring knife, as though he was about to take on a bogquacker.

Blood dribbled down his arm.

Before them was an enormous, magic-infused mechanical bear. It glowed a malevolent pink. Radiating rage and hunger, the bear's head turned to regard me.

It was one of the infamous Guardians of the Wall. 'Was' being the crucial signifier. The once glorious guardian, whose heart-forged bell comforted me as a child, stood before us, rank with corruption.

Every story and painting of the bears in Woodsten described them in blues and greens. The guardians were supposed to be a harmonious match of steel, nature, and magic. Walking blessings from the Everbear.

The monster before us foamed at the mouth like a rabid fox. The heart of the guardians, the wide bell that sounded out warnings across the Ursine Wall, sat frozen. Its clapper laced in a filament of rust and magical decay, bound deep in the metal rib cage of the beast.

It smelled of undeath. Muscle and fur had been replaced by meat and bones. Jagged fusions of biological and mechanical parts screamed of abomination.

This bear was not defending anyone from [Corruption]. It was death incarnate. Metal claws eight inches long dripped red.

Frozen, I stared at the twisted amalgamation of violence and horror. A nightmare come to life.

It roared, hot, fetid breath. The stench of carrion rotting in the sun filled the glade.

Its malice floated in the air. Flashes infiltrated my mind: Fish floating dead on a poisoned lake and flowers snapping closed over honeybees.

I shivered at the creeping hatred of humans and life.

Reaching for my hammer, I found the cold iron of its head reassuring. Unclipping the tool, with the leather-wrapped handle in my hand, I didn't feel quite so helpless.

Ominous red eyes glowed with intelligence, studying its prey. The guardian's jaws flexed, held together with tenuous bands of sinew. My body tensed, ready to react.

"What did you guys do? I was only gone for five minutes," I asked, scooping Richard up as I neatly sidestepped the remains of my lunch.

Notifications blinked in my mind, but I dared not break eye contact with our foe.

"Glad you finally decided to join us. Is Meredeath behind you?" Leo asked between great, gasping breaths as though they'd been fighting for hours. How long *had* it been?

"Why isn't it charging at us yet?" I slowly moved to join them. As for Meredeath? The words stuck in my throat. "Meredeath is dead."

She'd died protecting Tandy. I hadn't had time to think about it, to feel it. But it was as though saying it out loud made it real. My heart ached.

"Oh," Leo said, the syllable low and sad. I kept my eyes on the monstrosity in front of us, wishing I had the luxury to mourn our friend properly.

Leo looked even worse close up. A massive bruise was

forming on the left side of his face. Ched, on the other hand, looked terrified. His hand shook as he held the frying pan. He'd taken several hits too, his leather armor in tatters.

"It doesn't seem to want to attack, as long as we face it," Leo murmured out of the corner of his mouth. "Make yourself big, like I am with my axe, and whatever you do, don't look away."

I squared off against the [Corrupt] guardian, holding its gaze. Pink foam oozed between canines like a dog anticipating a snack. Red eyes shifted back and forth, as though trying to assess who it should target.

"Where's Tandy?" I squinted. Was the blood on its claw Tandy's? Was the pink drool from a recent kill?

Rage and panic warred as I took a step toward the beast. She couldn't be dead. I'd already lost Meredeath. A world without Tandy was unimaginable.

I began bargaining with every god I could name.

Scanning the ruins and countryside, I desperately searched for Tandy. She had to be here, alive.

This was a mistake. The beast had found the weakest target, me, and charged with a roar.

"Cole, run!" Leo shouted, pushing me as he stepped forward, ever the hero.

I heeded his directive and ran.

The ruins surrounding the portal were ancient. Remnants of crumbled walls outlined worn granite foundations. I careened down the stairs and started running through the blueprint of the ruined city.

Looking back, I saw the bear barrel between Leo and Ched. It knocked them aside to focus on me. I slammed my shin into a stone block, catching myself as I returned to fleeing.

The bear roared. I could smell its hot, [Corruption] filled breath. That spurred me on, like flames licking at my heels.

Hurdling a half wall, I landed awkwardly and rolled my ankle. Ignoring the pain, I ran on.

Moments later, the [Corrupt] beast barreled through the wall. Rock and debris peppered my back in warning.

I had to run faster.

Legs pumping, my feet slapped hard on the granite as I focused on the tree line thirty yards away. I took another obstacle, the base of a broken pillar. Hopping atop it, I leaped forward, landing with a roll.

Back on my feet, I resumed my sprint.

I heard a crack as the bear simply ran *through* the pillar.

Run faster!

"Fine words, coming from a slug." I gasped, hurdling another half wall.

Richard bit my ear. I stumbled as he tugged.

To the right, you overgrown monkey! He pulled at my earlobe like an over-correcting auntie.

To the right, tufts of grass parted for a small deer track. It wound down to a glistening alpine lake. Crystal clear water reflected pillowy clouds and a sunny day.

I followed Richard's suggestion and headed down the deer track. If I were going to die, at least, thanks to Richard, I'd have a beautiful view.

Bear claws scraped against rock as the guardian turned to follow, iron-bound paws scrabbling in the loose dirt.

Its bell must have shaken loose on a hit as it rang dissonantly. The unnatural jangle had no resemblance to the guardian's deep tonal promise I'd heard over the years. The clapper stuck, freezing the bell again.

Duck! Richard screamed in my mind.

I dived forward, as the snap of teeth filled the space formerly occupied by my head. The bear stumbled as it missed.

I somersaulted and landed back on my feet.

Looking ahead, I saw what Richard had seen. A brief glimpse of auburn hair.

Tandy sat halfway up a tree. From her perch, I could see the faint glint of a spiderweb crossing the path.

Except it wasn't a spider's web, it was Tandy's. She'd set a version of our 'goblin' traps we'd made as kids.

Renewed with hope, my legs pumped harder. They just had to get me a little further. Sprinting, I gained enough ground to dive between the two large aspens hulking next to the path.

I ducked through, thanking the Everbear for Tandy. The trap filament was almost invisible in the sun, so the unsuspecting bear slammed headfirst into the webbing. It shook the trees as it roared.

Tandy whooped, scrambling down from her spot to join me.

The guardian pawed at the filament, eyes boiling in rage. Sitting back on its haunches, it dug at the netting embedded in its body. The fur on its face pulled back grotesquely. One of its mechanical eyes bulged out of the socket, dangling uselessly. It no longer glowed.

The pink magic fueling its rage pulsed angrily as the beast shook its head.

It'd taken a hit, but even as the magic leaked through the scraps of fur, I could tell it wasn't done. The bear, enraged, suddenly glowed brighter. It roared, muscle and sinew snapping, flesh stretching, as it used an enlarging [Berserker] skill.

Leo appeared out of the fog. His axe whistled as he sliced down…

The [Enchanted] weapon bounced off the bear's back in a shower of sparks, doing minimal damage.

The beast expanded again. I realized in horror that it wasn't trapped in Tandy's net anymore. Flesh dripped off the engorged bear, as its metal frame glistened in the sun. With an expansive maw, it used its elongated canines to bite through the remnants of Tandy's net.

We were completely outclassed. This just wasn't fair.

"We need to get into the forest. I can set more [Invisible Thread]," Tandy said, pulling at my hand.

"Go." I pushed her behind me. "I'll get Leo."

The [Corrupted] guardian turned, bell clanking loudly as it fixed an eye on us. It stood almost twice its initial height. The barrel chest was now broader than the portal itself.

In a show of dominance, the bear roared, blood-soaked spittle flying. I could feel the threat in my very bones. Hatred boiled in the remaining eye. I'd never felt such concentrated emotion. It hated me more than my ex-girlfriend. More than Tandy's grandmother. Maybe even more than myself.

It hated with an intellect that stripped my humanity.

The beast completely ignored Ched and Leo. They banged on its sides inconsequentially, irritable flies to be dealt with later. I, alone, was its mortal enemy and the subject of its ire.

Falling back, my feet slipped on the loose shale of the hillside.

The bear hit Tandy's trap again, rage blinding it to logic. I turned, grabbing at a juniper to regain my balance.

My hammer seemed a pitiful weapon next to the bear's gnashing teeth.

Throw me at it!

This time, I ignored my slug. Instead, I tore across the clearing. Tandy needed time to get another trap set, so I took a wide arc, trying to lead the bear away.

My breath heavy, I responded to Richard. "You can't do anything to a nine-foot-tall, [Corrupt] bear!"

You underestimate me.

Fuck it. I turned and grabbed Richard by the tail. With a grunt, I hurled him like an overripe banana into the nightmare.

I didn't even bother checking whether I had hit. If the idiot was [Immortal], he'd live. I kept running.

You missed! Can't you do anything right? Thankfully, his voice faded as the distance between us increased.

The ruins were back in sight. Tandy had scaled another tree and was waving her hands in the air. She still wasn't ready. Leo had been ineffectual, and Ched was a wallflower. It was up to me to stall for time.

Malyc still stood before the gate, locked into subservience to its magic. The portal pulsed as a cloud of green fog rolled out.

A flicker of a plan entered my head. Could I send the guardian into the [Trial Dungeon]? It might just work.

I bee-lined for the arch and Malyc. I didn't know why the man kept it open, but this may be my only chance.

My feet took the stairs two at a time. Breath came in large gasps. I just had to get the guardian there. My ankle ached, protesting each step. I was almost there. Nothing was going to stop me.

The heat of the bear's hate drove me forward. I imagined its teeth a hair behind me, foaming drool ready to devour me whole.

But I wasn't dead yet.

I sprinted towards Malyc. His eyes unfocused as he kept magic flowing into the arch. The portal shimmered with a liquid green-silver that reflected the peaceful sky.

As I got closer, I could see my reflection. Did I look *that* afraid?

Then the bear came into focus. Teeth snarling at my reflection, at me. My back itched.

Four yards, three. I fought for air as I skidded to a stop, watching the mechanical horror leap. Its chest puffed out, leaking [Corrupt] tendrils of magic.

I should have been afraid, but I wasn't. My legs poised to roll.

I jumped sideways.

The portal shimmered.

Meredeath's weary visage formed as she materialized. Red lips, pale skin, winged eyes. Her skull amulet sat between the leather chest plates.

Oh shit.

The bear towered in the reflection behind her.

She was alive!

But oh, so dead.

Chapter 26

IN HINDSIGHT

My ex-girlfriend, Minvi, would tell you that timing wasn't one of my strong suits. As I watched Meredeath's face change from a warm greeting to horror at the atrocity barreling down on her, I had to agree.

The portal winked closed behind Meredeath as Malyc's sense of timing mirrored my own.

Fuck.

The Guild Administrator blinked slowly, as though coming out of a trance.

The [Corrupted] guardian dropped a clawed paw right in the middle of Meredeath's chest, pinning her to the ground. Unable to stop, the bear's momentum carried right into the archway.

The impact shoved its broad, size-enhanced shoulders through, but jammed the beast between the magical columns. Neither torso nor hips could fit.

I couldn't decide if the bear had expanded that much or, now that the column's magic was dormant, if it'd shrunk. Either way, the bear was stuck.

The ground shook as it frantically tried to free itself. This was temporary. I had no doubt the former guardian would be free soon.

Getting to my feet, I scrambled to where I'd last seen Meredeath.

She was gone.

"Will someone help me?" Meredeath screeched from an improbable position under the haunches of the bear. The guardian's metal claws kicked to either side of her, trying to free itself.

Tentatively, I stepped closer to the beast, trying to figure out how to help.

Rotted fur hung from steel ribs as I tried not to smell it. Dark magic whirled beneath its bones. The ominous, hot-pink tendrils of [Corruption] reached for me as I leaned into the mass, trying to free Meredeath.

I felt around, searching for her, with the [Corruption] burning my hands.

I found one of Meredeath's boots. My hand scrabbled against the leather until I latched onto a dangling chain and *pulled*. With an unheard pop, I was able to get her out from under the beast.

Every one of her defensive enchantments had triggered. Her lace bracers glowed, the skull amulet sparked, and her skin shimmered with magic. She looked sunburnt from the proximity of the [Corruption].

I stared in shock. Despite it all, Meredeath was alive.

She looked at me, unimpressed, as she broke the silence.

"A hello would be nice." Meredeath patted herself, as though checking to make sure she was all there. She looked stunning, with the sun reflecting on her teal hair. Green eyes sparkling under her dark eyeliner. The fishnet bracers and leggings were whole, without a snag. Even the new pinkish-tan looked good.

The [Corrupt] guardian struggled next to us, but I was so grateful Meredeath was whole, everything else melted away.

"You're alive?" I asked it like a question, even though the answer was standing right in front of me. All the emotion I'd boxed up in the dungeon threatened to spill out. She was alive, and I hadn't *completely* failed her.

The bear roared, trying to stand up on its hind legs, and it slammed its back into the top of the arch. Dust choked the air. We didn't have long.

"Well, I am for a few more minutes," Meredeath said, taking a step back from the former guardian. "I survived the Dunglord twice only to get run over by undead taxidermy? What the hell, Cole?"

I looked over to Malyc for help. He was a senior administrator for the Adventurer's Guild, after all.

The mighty guild representative had dropped the portal key and was running away from us. He disappeared into the only modern building on the ridge, a small shack used to house any attending guild representatives. It wouldn't last three seconds against the bear.

"Welcome to [Your Mom's Party]?" I shrugged and gave her my best cheesy grin. She rolled her eyes at me. "Personally, I'm choosing to blame Richard."

You would, you cretin. See if I jump in front of the next deathblow for you.

Meredeath raised an eyebrow. "His mood's improved, I see."

The guardian pushed with its paws, causing the magic runes on the arch to flare in warning. It looked as though the gate was on the verge of breaking. Time was running short.

"We've got a plan. Sort of."

Meredeath's eyes narrowed, and I gave an apologetic wave at the rest of the party. Leo and Ched looked like two marble heroes, all muscle and poise, standing guard over Tandy's tree. She was two-thirds of the way up a fir, fiddling with some rope.

"What about you?" Meredeath's voice had a steely quality, as though if the bear dared to mess with me, there would be consequences from *her*.

"I'm fine. The [Corrupt] guardian is attached to me. Join Tandy and Leo, I've got this covered."

"If the plan doesn't work, we're going to have words," she threatened with a grin.

We both knew if the plan didn't work, it was doubtful any of us would be alive to talk. Meredeath threw one last comment over her shoulder as she started walking toward the rest of the party.

"And Cole? We really need to figure out this odd attachment you have to strange creatures."

I started to protest. They were attached to *me!* But she took off before I could spit out my argument.

Turning back to the bear, I felt good for the first time in the fight. Meredeath was back. The team was whole. We even had a pan-wielding Ched on our side, so things were looking better than ever.

If Leo hadn't been able to do much damage with his [Enchanted] axe, maybe the key was blunt damage? I looked at my trusty hammer and decided it was worth a try.

Winding up, I swung, shouting my skill, "[Hammer Time]!"

Instead of delivering the expected three rapid strikes, my skill fizzled, providing a dull spank to the meaty rear end of the beast.

A notification triggered:

[Skill Failure: [Smith] skill [Hammer Time] delivers a triple hit to a metal medium. The target did not meet the criteria. Cooldown is tripled for this skill failure. You have [1 hour] before [Hammer Time] is available.]

"Spank it harder!" Leo yelled, laughing from across the ridge. No failure went unpunished in [Your Mom's Party].

The bear wasn't metal all the way through, damn it. Why couldn't my skills work when I needed them to?

The creature turned its head, one baleful eye focused on me. With renewed vigor fueled by what I suspected might be indignation, it thrashed at the gate. I backed away as I saw the arch begin to pull up from its foundation.

"Tandy, hurry up!" I called and started running down the stairs toward my friends.

Tandy looked at me, frowning. Her hands looked like she was playing an elaborate game of cat's cradle. Knowing Tandy, this was a good sign. It meant she'd had an idea and was thinking it through. Her crazy plans tended to work.

The bad news bear, in this instance, was that our [Corrupt] guardian would be free and headed toward me before she was ready. I scanned the countryside, noting Richard slowly gliding towards Tandy. He was such a great help.

I took off, deciding a lap around the lake for my health would be worthwhile. I was counting on the bear's continuing rage at *me.*

Defensive skills, such as healing or running, would have been helpful. My ankle burned as I ran. If 'bait' was going to be my role on the team, I needed to expand my utility.

The path down to the lake was steep, and I slowed my descent as my feet threatened to send me face-first down the incline. Roots and loose rock littered the slope.

The lake was glacier-fed, shallow, and cold. It looked serene until a bellow and crack sent ripples through the still water. I glanced back to see that my foe had finally broken free in an explosion of rock and magic.

For a brief moment, I dared to hope the explosion of the portal had taken care of the monster.

My hopes sank as the dust cloud took on an angry pink glow. A gust of wind cleared the air, revealing the bear standing calmly on its hind legs, snout sniffing as though trying to find my scent.

The beast's lip curled in a guttural snarl as its eye focused on me. Prey identified, its claws tore at the ground, kicking up debris as it bounded toward me.

If it caught me, I was *dead.*

At least it wasn't going after Tandy.

Clipping my hammer, I took off, realizing I hadn't gained nearly a sufficient distance from the monster. I wasn't sure there was a safe place in the entire realm from the hate in its face.

The ground was soggy, overgrown with reeds that bounced as I circled to the far side of the lake. Water trickled under the last bit of seasonal glacier that clung to the shadowed side of the bowl. I slid to a halt, my boots digging into the loose ice crystals as I turned to look.

The [Corrupt] guardian was flying down the ravine in perfect unison with the terrain. It reached the edge of the lake in record time and stared at me. This was the moment of decision: did it go around the right side of the lake, closer to the cliff edge, or to the left, where ice still clung to the edges and the ground gave way into a bog?

The bear whuffed, its hot breath visible in the cool mountain air. I was ready to sprint, and my foe realized it.

Every breath, every second, was one more moment Tandy had to get set.

I made as though I was going to run to the right, along the cliff edge and the outflow of the lake. As the bear jerked in that direction, I reversed as though I was going to run towards the bog. It was the most ridiculous fake-out for a game of tag except the player who was 'it' was going to rip my throat out if it caught me.

Finally, the predator made up its mind, and it started wading out into the lake. I hadn't even considered this a valid choice. It moved with slow confidence as it stalked me through the water.

I evaluated my two options.

I started edging towards the cliff-side. The beast's trajectory changed to cut off my escape. I hesitated a moment too long, and the [Corrupt] guardian bounded forward in the water, splashing in my direction. Two more leaps and it'd be on me.

I bolted in pure panic. No plan. Just instinct and a silent prayer to the Everbear.

I danced along the cliff-side, hopping from boulder to boulder. One slip meant a one-way trip down the waterfall into the valley below. My ankle throbbed as a rock bobbled.

I dove under a paw and landed hard. The bear, off-balance from the missed swipe, teetered on the cliff's edge.

I grabbed my hammer, sensing an opportunity. As I swung, I didn't attempt a skill after the last failure.

A meaty smack fulfilled Leo's earlier wish, and the bear's head whipped around. My hit hadn't moved it an inch.

The bear scrambled on the edge of the cliff, slowly regaining its footing. Angry pink magic pulsed through the rips in its hide. Between pulses, I could see through the ribcage, mechanical whirls fueled by a sickly red stain inked along the runes that powered the creature.

The beast pivoted, ready to finish me off. I closed my eyes, resigned to my fate.

The final blow never came. Instead, a wet squelch sounded as the rock the bear stood on gave way. It tumbled backwards, claws flailing.

Not waiting, I turned and ran. I had gained seconds, and I wasn't going to waste them. No part of me believed it was over.

One heartbeat passed. Then two.

I was still alive. A glance confirmed that the undead beast

was fighting for purchase on the cliff-side. It wasn't down, but I might have enough time to make it to Tandy.

Dignity forgotten, I scrambled up the path on all fours. A triumphant bellow echoed from the bear.

I'd run out of time. My heart pounded, counting down the seconds I had left. I had to *move.*

Once I crested the bowl, a welcome sight greeted me. Tandy and Leo waved frantically, beckoning to the tree line.

The new trap was ready. All I had to do was survive the last twenty yards. My lungs wheezed, my legs burned.

Run, you fool! Richard urged.

I was running. Five yards.

I could see Richard sunbathing on a rock between me and Tandy's trap.

Four yards.

His tentacles waved, his slime glistened.

My heart pumped in my ears.

Tandy was shouting.

A wet paw hit the back of my pack, sending me sprawling forward. My face ate gravel as I rolled towards my target.

Twisting, I looked up. The bear stood before me. Fate. Doom. The end.

At least I was an [Adventurer]?

Do I have to do everything? Richard's whiny voice broke through my terror.

You literally have one job: don't die. And you're terrible at it.

Chapter 27

BEAR THE STORM

Whatever Richard had planned, he didn't have time to trigger a skill before Tandy came flying out of the tree.

She jumped *onto* the [Corrupt] guardian's head. The part with the deadly sharp teeth. She clung with her legs on either side of its snout and stabbed with…

Were those her fabric scissors?

Leo ran forward, swinging his axe into the beast's ribs, while Meredeath looked like an untouchable goddess as she activated her fishnet bracers and blocked a clawed swing aimed at Leo.

My view of the bear was unique. I could see *into* its ribcage where an old city bell dangled in a deep miasma of magenta [Corruption]. Magic wrapped around the metal clapper, stifling its movement. The bell had degraded over the years, corrosion freezing it in place, and flakes of rust peeled off its runes.

The bear's body rocked as Leo hit it with a heavy blow.

With a roar, the beast shook its head, knocking Tandy off its face. She'd lodged her fabric scissors in the monster's remaining eye. Tandy clung desperately to a dagger lodged in the bear's back.

The beast clawed at its face, trying to remove the scissors. I'd regained my footing, kneeling between the monster's hindquarters.

Grabbing my hammer, I thrust it into the chest cavity. If I could just hit...

The bear torqued on its haunches, and my hammer slammed into the bell.

A low, mournful, dissonant twang erupted from the bell as it staggered back. I surged forward, clanking the head of my hammer on the bell again.

A [System Notification] popped:

[[Critical Hit]. Weakness identified: [Guardian's Heart].]

As though to emphasize the message, pink lightning erupted, and internal mechanisms in the bear jangled. A burst of energy exploded from its core.

Tandy went flying, landing painfully on the rocky ground, and Leo was by her side in an instant. She waved him off as he tried to pick her up, but settled for leaning against him as they moved towards a large tree.

I focused on them, ignoring the state of my body. Warnings and notifications flashed in my vision as I watched them duck behind an old growth. They were safe for the moment. The breath I'd held expelled as the pain rolled in.

My hands and arms were charred. My clothes were singed. The hammer toppled out of my hands as my fingers refused to hold on to it. I watched, unable to move, as the head of my hammer thumped into the dirt. My skin alternated between red and black, and my hammer glowed, looking molten against the ground.

Unencumbered, the [Corrupt] guardian brought its claws

around. I could see my end coming. Time seemed to slow as the deadly claws inched towards my body. Pain is temporary, death eternal.

I shifted all of my pain into a box I'd evaluate later if I lived. Then, I grabbed the handle of my hammer. With a swift repositioning, I lunged forward. I would put all my strength into one more hit. Ring the bell one last time.

[Peel]!

My foot slipped dramatically, spilling me backwards.

"Dammit, Richard!" Why couldn't he just give me the win?

Two paws clapped together in the space I vacated. The thunderous crack of an executed skill reverberated in my bones.

Electrical discharges forked through the air. The hair on my arms stood on end as a ball of lightning snapped into existence.

You might want to move. Quietly. It can't see anything.

Between an earlier hit and Tandy's scissors, the [Corrupt] guardian was blind. Another bolt of energy zig-zagged, striking the stump a foot to my left.

This wasn't a normal skill. It stank of [Corrupt] magic. Of the ether that broke the natural laws and boundaries of skills.

I moved, crab walking backwards towards the stump. Lightning never strikes twice in the same place, right? My skin was hot and tight, protesting every move.

The guardian shifted its paws further apart, and the ball of energy grew. Electricity crackled in its eye sockets and between its ribs. The sharp smell of lightning and sparks filled the air.

Each movement was a testament to the force of my will. My focus was singular. I'd reach the stump. My mind was fixated on the idea of it being safe. Lightning wouldn't strike twice, the old adage repeated in my mind.

The bear's head slowly tilted down, as though it could see

me. Twin balls of energy sat in each eye socket. It grinned, energy dancing between serrated teeth.

Suddenly, I realized a fundamental truth of the universe: spells and monsters didn't give a fuck about old wives' tales.

A fork shot out as I moved, splitting my legs. The energy hit between my knees in the middle of the stump.

Shit! With my future progeny at risk, I scrambled backwards.

Ched came out of nowhere, giving me a helpful hand up.

He pulled me behind a tree as the former guardian's power output increased. For some reason, it seemed rooted to the spot.

The five of us huddled between two trees on either side of the path. Lightning shot out of the bear indiscriminately, as though it only had rudimentary control of it.

"What do we do now?" Leo's voice was low. His sweater was singed, and sweat dripped from his face.

I looked at Tandy; she always had a plan. I could see the whites of her eyes. Her jump to the bear had been incredibly risky. I think she was still in shock at what she'd done.

"Cole's attack was working. The weak spot is the bell. That's what sparked off whatever this is." Meredeath waved at the bear as a bolt shot through Tandy's webbing, exploding a third of her trap in a split second.

"Yeah, it gave me a [Critical Hit]. One or two more of those would finish it." My mouth raced as fast as my mind. How were we going to get close enough to deliver another hit?

The bear's fur stood on end now, little bolts dancing between bone and cog and clump of flesh. The smell of burnt meat drifted across the ridge.

This was fucked up. There was no way we were going to get closer to the beast.

The fur around its eyes had begun to change from a grizzled brown to white. The energy increased as it widened its paws again.

"Whatever we're going to do, it needs to be soon." I continued as another zap exploded a tree in a shower of splinters. "I don't know why it hasn't just finished us."

Meredeath frowned. "I just assumed the skill couldn't be activated when moving." We looked at each other for a moment. It made sense. It was building up power to *do* something.

"Richard, what do you think?" Where was Richard? I peeked from behind my tree. Nothing.

I kneeled and took a longer look. He wasn't where I'd slipped on him. I didn't see any slime path away from the [Corrupt] guardian.

Squinting at a flash, I scanned the forest floor. Where was my damn slug?

I closed my eyes, willing [Partial Rapport] to *work.* My mind felt a slight tug towards the bear.

"I see him," Meredeath said. She'd joined me behind the tree, pressed tight, trying to squeeze close enough to leave no target for the beast's magic. My breath caught as she shifted, pressing her chest against my back as she tipped her head around my body to look at the bear. Her fingers gripped my wrist, dragging me forward as she pointed.

"Do you see him?" she said in awe.

I winced as her fingers dug into my burnt arm. Confused, I squinted into the harsh light of the spell. Between flashes, I caught a glimpse of yellow in the bear's ribs.

"What the hell?" What was he doing?

Meredeath pulled us both back under cover as a strike shot out in our direction. Her breath was hot against my ear as she answered my unspoken question. "He's going to disrupt the spell."

I shivered, goose bumps running down my back, as I leaned out, trying to confirm her assumption.

A bolt ricocheted within the bear. Richard glowed as he was struck. The lightning burst passed right through his boneless body. My vision burned with the afterimage of a slug imprisoned by lightning-soaked ribs.

I blinked a few times, my eyes watering. Staring at the [Corrupt] guardian, I had to ask, "Is Richard glowing?"

Maybe he was a glowworm after all.

Meredeath didn't answer. I looked back at the empty spot next to me. My arm still ached where she'd squeezed it.

She was gone.

My frantic search ended abruptly as I caught sight of her slinking towards the bear.

Lightning danced on the shiny surface of her boots as I watched her agilely move forward. Her forearm was flexed as she held my hammer, its head still glowing from my original strike.

I fingered the loop where my hammer should have rested.

A fork of lightning struck the tree Ched had been hiding behind. The man shrieked as he fled. Meredeath didn't pause as she crept forward, tracking towards her goal. Richard glowed. I could almost hear his slime bubbling as energy surrounded his body.

Tandy, Leo, and I were frozen watching the scene as our protectors took on the [Corrupt] ancient sentinel.

An arc struck out for Meredeath, missing as she rolled to the right. Her feet moved, froze, and shifted as though she could see lines of energy invisible to us.

Richard climbed higher, towards the bear's heart. His yellow form stood out in golden radiance against the angry pink.

Meredeath was almost within range. The bear tilted its head, and two bolts shot from its eyes. My jaw clenched as I watched. These bolts were unavoidable.

Forearms cross, a magical shield popped up in front of Meredeath, deflecting the attack. The bear shifted, and a paw lashed out, backhanding her.

Meredeath hadn't expected the move, and she went flying.

Her shield shimmered out of existence as one of her fishnet bracers sparked angrily, its [Enchantment] broken.

Grinning maniacally, our teammate got to her feet and moved *faster* towards the towering beast. Her hair stood on end as though she were a vengeful goddess. She ducked below a clawed paw. Meredeath swung my hammer not towards the bell, but towards the glowing ball of energy *in front* of the bear.

"No!" Tandy yelled, starting to run towards Meredeath.

Leo roared as he raised his axe with both hands and *threw it*. The [Enchanted] axe sang as it whipped end over end towards the beast.

Tandy was too late. Leo's axe was too late. Meredeath had already arrived.

Reality exploded.

Chapter 28

HAMMER, SHIELD, OR... SLUG

I woke up. Guess I'll take that win.

Bear Ridge needed a new name. [Corruption] Crater? [Your Mom's Mistake]?

Everything was whiter than it should be. It was still bright out. The sun and clouds resolutely insisted on a lovely day.

Oversized snowflakes drifted in the air. No, not snow. Ash. I held out my hand and caught a flake. Delicate and warm, I wondered what part of the ridge it'd been.

Everything was eerily quiet.

A large paw landed on my shoulder. I froze, ready to fight. My fingers wrapped around a rock as I turned.

The beast was... Leo?

The rock fell, as my foe was my oversized friend. Blood dribbled slowly from a cut on his forehead. Frayed gashes cut through the weave of his singed pink sweater.

After almost dying to a pink [Corrupted] guardian, I'd decided pink was indisputably badass.

He shook me urgently, his eyes worried. Oh, his mouth was moving.

It wasn't quiet. My ears were broken.

"I CAN'T HEAR YOU!" I shouted, rubbing at my ear. Leo stopped shaking me and nodded. Apparently, I'd spoken loud enough for him to hear.

Leo gestured back to a huddled Ched, and a white-faced Meredeath. He pointed to his eyes, then at the clearing, making a scissors-snipping sign that we'd used for Tandy since the great fabric scissor heist. I nodded my understanding and shakily stood up.

"Tandy!" I yelled. "Richard? Where's Tandy?!" By the Everbear, where was *Richard?*

Shut up, you dolt. You don't need to yell, I'm right here. Richard licked my neck to emphasize his point.

"Damnit, Richard, don't be a dick. We need to find Tandy." And I needed my hearing back. As my wits returned, a niggling worry took form. Tandy was alive, right?

The ridge had been blown to hell, but most of the blast went away from our party. The alpine lake drained as a temporary cascading waterfall into the new basin. It was raw in its beauty.

Richard bit my ear, tugging me to the left. I looked up the slope to find Leo waving. His mouth was working hard to say, *I FOUND HER!*

Relieved, I scrambled up the ashen landscape. "You don't have to bite me, you know. You could just tell me Leo had found her."

What would be the fun in that?

I didn't bother responding. I just scrambled back to the top of the crater to find Leo's arm wrapped around Tandy. She looked as good as I felt. Like we'd just survived the angry death of a lightning-obsessed demigod.

A dull pop sounded, and I could hear again. A tinny ringing muted everything. I rubbed my ear, wishing it'd heal faster.

"HEY." Whoops, I really had been talking too loudly. "Hey, guys," I continued, my voice lowered. "Looks like we made it."

Great words, Captain Obvious.

Tandy cradled something in her hands. I squinted, my mind slow to comprehend the silver globe floating in her palms. It flickered like a heartbeat, taking the shape of scissors, a dagger, and a butter knife.

What was it? A tear of grief dripped off her cheek, landing right on the shimmering butter knife. Flicker.

Scissors again. Realization dawned as her face transformed into awe. This was the remnant of her most prized possession—her fabric scissors.

"What *is* that?" I asked. "I've never seen anything like it." It defied my understanding of the world.

Meredeath had joined us, handing me the handle of my hammer. "You should check your notifications, Cole." Shrugging, I brought up the long-ignored notification list.

[Congratulations! You have completed the Quest: [Trial Dungeon]. You have earned the Base Class [Adventurer] that replaces your [Mundane] designation. Please confirm your removal of all classes and skills associated with your Base Class of [Mundane]. Acceptance will remove [Chef], [Smith], and [Meditation] and all related skills.]

[Do you agree to take the earned Base Class of [Adventurer]?]

The message sat waiting for my acceptance or rejection. A void opened in my chest. How did we not know we'd have to give up our [Mundane] classes? Our skills? My eyes flickered to Tandy. Had she given up all her two hundred skills?

[Do you agree to take the earned Base Class of [Adventurer]?]

Was I ready to leave my old life behind? My old friends: [Analyze], [Steady Temperature], and [Monotonous Calm]?

I'd managed to hang onto [Hammer Time] as a young chef by tenderizing meat on a metal counter. The other staff had looked at me like I was crazy, but I'd tried to keep every hard-won skill. They might not have been the best, but they'd been mine.

On a drunken whim, was I really going to leave everything behind?

I could reject the offer. Go back to Woodsten.

I refocused on my friends. Were they going to be offered the same choice? What were they going to pick? Had they already?

Neither of them gave me a hint. Leo poked at the liquid edge of Tandy's scissors, pulling his finger back in pain as it neatly cut into his flesh. Leo sucked on his sliced finger as Tandy looked at him like he was an idiot.

I could feel Richard's tentacles boring a hole in the side of my brain. I knew what he wanted me to do, but I also appreciated that he had said nothing. This was my choice. The only person I could blame for whatever came next was me.

"I accept," I whispered.

An immediate rush of energy cycled through my body. I stood a little straighter, and the ringing in my ears stopped. It was as if my body had re-knit itself to the boundless energy levels I had as a child.

"Woah." I felt like I could climb a mountain, take on another Dunglord, or spank a giant glowing bear.

"Well, are you all ready to go back home?" Leo's voice rumbled. "I can't wait to get back to chopping wood."

What?! Had they not chosen [Adventurer]? Was I now stuck fighting monsters alone?

My head snapped up to find my three friends stifling laughter, eyes shining. I realized I'd been played.

"I told you he hadn't looked at his [Notifications]," Meredeath said, shaking her head.

"Man, how'd you even survive that fight as a [Mundane]?" Leo laughed. "And you call *me* the dumb one."

"Your face, Cole." Whether it was the joke or relief that we'd survived, Tandy gave a rare uncontrolled giggle ending in a snort. It felt good.

"You all suck." I said with a smile, blinking with watery eyes. A piece of ash must have gotten into them. Yeah, that was it.

Keep reading. Richard gave me a gentle nudge.

The [System Notification] blinked, still demanding my attention. Now that we were out of combat, it was incessant.

[Congratulations, [Adventurer]! Your performance during the trial periods has been evaluated. You defeated one bogquacker, a raiding party, a widowmaker, two root canals, multiple ribbons of hunger, and a Dunglord boss.]

It left out the [Corrupt] guardian. Irritated, I continued reading.

[Choices matter. Your [Adventurer] methodology included: punting, trapping, setting on fire, kicking, pounding (multiple), and faking death. Additionally, [Companion] actions have weight, which includes: using you as a shield (multiple), heat resistance, self-immolation, self-sacrifice, decorative fangs (multiple), running away (multiple), and licking (multiple).

With these actions, you are being given three choices for an initial [Adventurer] class. Choose wisely, just like [Mundane] classes, [Adventurer] classes influence the types of skills and specializations an [Adventurer] can earn. Choose one of the following:

[Hammer Vanguard] - When diplomacy fails, the brutal strike of a hammer succeeds. This class channels kinetic power into overwhelming, blunt strikes. Each hit builds resonance and, at higher mastery, enables devastating shockwaves and armor-negating impacts. This class can be specialized down multiple paths, most frequently as a [Berserker].

Initially unlocks:

[Echo of Impact]: Passive skill that increases the area of effect of hammer strikes at the cost of some stamina regeneration.

[Boom]: Strike that initially has a [30%] chance to ignore armor and a [15%] chance to critical hit for 3x damage. Costs stamina and has a 5-minute cooldown.

[Brickhouse]: Defensive skill initially lasting [2] minutes that negates [25%] of damage.]

The class sounded more suited to Leo than to me, but I did like to smash. I evaluated my next option:

[[Meatshield Martyr] - Protect your friends at any cost. This class uses a wide range of defensive techniques to minimize damage to a party at the expense of its wielder. It routinely intercepts blows, absorbs magical damage, and loudly motivates teammates to get out of their way. This class can specialize in multiple paths. The most frequently chosen are [Bulwark] and [Lastwall].

Initially unlocks:

[You Looking At Me?]: Passive skill that draws foes' attention during combat. Generally leads to focused attacks on you, protecting your party. The higher the skill opponents are using, the more likely it is that it will be directed at you. Costs some mana regeneration.

[Not On My Watch]: This skill allows you to leap in front of a fatal attack meant for a party member within a [6]-foot radius. Grants a [20%] base chance of blocking that stacks with any other weapon, combat, or defensive abilities.

[Rock]: Passive skill that increases resistance to all damage types. Eventual specializations can lead to the complete negation of specific damage types.

[Me First]: This skill grants additional defensive bonuses. These bonuses decrease the more your party drops in health.

This skill costs initial stamina and further stamina regeneration as long as it is active. This skill has a [1 day] cooldown.]

Wow. The name of the class was ugly, but the skills were powerful. I looked at my friends laughing in the aftermath of a battle we shouldn't have survived. I would do anything to keep them safe. This class would help with that. I could be an impenetrable force, blocking and absorbing blows.

Before I picked it, I wanted to see what my last option was.

[[Dead Wrong] - Through trickery, you can thrive like a cockroach hiding in dark corners. This class slips through the cracks, utilizing a variety of off-market skills to avoid and deal damage. The class deals damage by exploiting misdirection, opportunity, and quick reads. Class specialization can take multiple paths; however, there are not enough [Adventurers] who have chosen [Dead Wrong] to identify a common path. Available specializations are [Improvised], [Loophole], and...]

Richard bit me. I swatted at him. "What do you want?"

Nothing, just checking if you're done yet. His voice echoed in my head innocently.

"This isn't a choice to rush." Irritated, I returned to reading. I was pretty sure this class was a joke.

[... [Decorative Fangs].]

Now I knew it was a joke. What the hell?

[Initially unlocks:

[Cheat Death]: Passive that automatically triggers you to cheat fatal damage once per day. The methods of cheating death vary. Use at your own risk.

[Feign Death]: Skill that allows you to convince an opponent of your death. Success relies on various factors, including the foe's intelligence, awareness, and your actions.

[Analyze]: This skill provides detailed information about an entity or object. The information provided varies by level difference, focus, and prior knowledge.

[Improvised Damage]: This skill allows even the most mundane items to be used with deadly intent. Gain a [50%]

damage bonus when attacking with an unconventional object.]

The breadth of the skills on [Dead Wrong] was incredible, but thriving like a 'cockroach' wasn't appealing. It was as though the [System] crafted my options to appeal to my desire to keep everyone safe, specifically so I wouldn't choose this last option. Even the title of the class was ridiculous.

Absentmindedly, I reached up to my shoulder to scratch under Richard's chin. He stretched out in gratitude.

Richard and I hadn't talked about the Library yet or the [Trials of a Hero]. I had the sneaking suspicion we weren't going to either. That he wouldn't, or couldn't, speak of it.

He knew the [System] personally. *They* had history. I still couldn't stretch my mind around the sarcastic asshole on my shoulder going toe-to-toe with *the [System].*

For some unknown reason, Richard had picked me. My heart warmed as I looked at Tandy playing with her scissors, and Leo laughing at his own joke as Meredeath rolled her eyes.

Richard had picked *us.*

"The way it's been going, [Cheat Death] could come in handy," I said to Richard, seeing if he'd react.

Pick that one.

"Why? I mean, it could be dead wrong." I kept scratching. One eye tentacle turned towards me slowly as his body wriggled in pleasure.

Pick something else, then. His words didn't match the serious eye stalk staring me down. Looks like he *couldn't* talk about it.

"I'm going to pick what I want," I said impudently just to tease him.

Both of his eyestalks turned to me, evaluating. Then he gave the slug equivalent of a shrug and started grooming himself with a loud slurp of his tongue. *Yeah, it's guaranteed that whatever you pick will be the wrong choice.*

He was probably right.

Chapter 29

ONE OF US

[You have chosen [Dead Wrong] for your [Adventurer] class. [Cheat Death], [Feign Death], [Analyze], and [Improvised Damage] have been granted. You will retain [Party], [Map], [Stillpoint], [Heartbeat], [Partial Rapport], [Companion], and [Minor Manipulate Slime] as part of your [Adventurer] base class. Legacy skills [Hammer Time], [Nailed It], and [Self Critic] are also available but will no longer progress. Adventure onward.]

No congratulations? The [System] didn't seem pleased with my choice, but at least I was able to retain a couple of my old skills. I looked at [Self Critic], wishing that wasn't one of them.

[Skill Acquired: You have gained a new [Adventurer] skill, [Slug Toss]. You have gained a significant accuracy boost when tossing your companion. Ignore all slime effects. Ignore all taunt effects. This skill can be multiplied by complementary companion skills.]

I joined the rest of [Your Mom's Party]. "So, I'm not one to question luck, but Meredeath..." Green eyes focused on me. My mouth suddenly went dry. "You're dead."

Leo verbally groaned.

Amused, her eyes crinkled along her cat eyeliner. She mimed patting herself down, then looked at Tandy. "Do I seem like a zombie? I feel pretty alive."

Tandy frowned, as though seriously examining Meredeath for zombieism. "No, but I'm not going to rule out vampire."

"No, you know what I mean." I could feel my ears burning. "In that last fight against the Dunglord, you sacrificed yourself for Tandy."

And how many times did she die in total?

Oh. Shit. I wanted to crawl under a rock.

Leo saved me. May the Everbear bless his soul. "It's a good thing you didn't die in the intestines, but what's got me confused is why you didn't come out with the rest of us?"

"Yeah, what he said." I pointed at Leo. Meredeath's gaze told me just how stupid I sounded.

"Well, when you all left *without me*, the Dunglord reset. I had to fight him again while the dungeon fell apart." She said it like it didn't mean anything, that we'd abandoned her in the dungeon, but she wasn't meeting our eyes.

She soloed the boss. She said it with such nonchalance, like it wasn't a big deal. Leo's mouth hung open in astonishment, and his mouth wasn't the only one catching flies.

Meredeath flipped her hair, dismissing our incredulity. "The hard part about that dungeon was keeping you squishies alive."

"What's a squishy?" Leo asked, clueless. I didn't know either, but I knew better than to ask.

Meredeath looked up at my big friend, frowning. "It's a

stuffed animal where I'm from but, in context here, it just means you're easily killed."

"Poke me in the gut, and you'll see how squishy I am," Leo muttered, flexing his abs.

"Are you leaving us then?" Tandy's voice quietly sliced through our banter. "Now that you're an [Adventurer] in name as well as ability?"

Leo and I looked at Meredeath, not having considered *that* particular outcome. I *really* didn't want her to leave. I also wasn't ready to say that out loud.

Meredeath eyed [Your Mom's Party], dancing between Tandy, Leo and me. Finally, her eyes settled on Richard. They stared at each other as though a personal conversation was taking place.

Tandy must have come to the same conclusion.

"You two going to include us in this discussion?" Tandy did not take kindly to being talked over. She received it in abundance from her grandmother growing up.

Meredeath looked at the rest of us again.

You can trust them.

Leo's eyes widened. "Was that *Richard?* My little banana peel, why haven't you been talking to us this whole time?"

"Of course it was Richard, you dolt." Tandy punched him in the shoulder. "But yeah, same question, Richard."

It's a hidden quality of [Partial Rapport]. I refuse to explain further.

Why would he have hidden this from everyone?

Meredeath, tell them or I will.

"Fine, but let's sit down. It's a long story," Meredeath said as she sank to the ground, legs crossed. She sounded defeated.

We were scraped, singed, bleeding, bruised, and covered in ash. My ankle ached, I was pretty sure I was missing my eyebrows, and I looked like I'd spent the day roasting myself in the oven.

We all sat down, as though it was perfectly normal to sit in the crater grave of one of the legendary guardians to have a little chat. Tandy opened her bag and passed out snacks. I brushed off a rock and put Richard down.

Leo handed me my hammer. As my hand wrapped around the shaft, a notification triggered.

[Congratulations! You have completed the Quest: [Clean the Corruption] by defeating a [Corrupted Guardian] and protecting the Ursine Wall. You have earned [Guardian's Promise].]

[[Guardian's Promise] - Soul Bound - This ordinary hammer has been infused with the magic of the Guardians of the Ursine Wall. It is as though a Guardian always has your back, the hammer carries the gratitude of the Guardian [Your Mom's Party], freed from [Corruption]. [Guardian's Promise] is soul bonded with the individual [Cole Thornfield], and all attributes will only work with this individual. The death of [Cole Thornfield] will result in the self-destruction of the [Guardian's Promise].

Abilities: [Target: Dungeon Born] - Grants additional damage against dungeon and dungeon-originating monsters. This scales with user abilities and powers.

[Guardian] - Grants additional damage when used in defense of [Your Mom's Party] or [Mundane] individuals.

[Molten Promise] - Allows the user to alter the hammer head for various purposes. Initial forms are: Hammer, Pick, and Molten.]

[Guardian's Promise] glowed in my hand. Runes like those that had embedded in the guardian's bell glowed along the pitted hammer head. It felt *good*, but I couldn't help but wonder if I'd chosen the wrong class after all. This weapon was meant for a [Hammer Vanguard].

I'd followed my gut about [Dead Wrong]. Time would tell if I was right, but this first puzzle piece was a proverbial gut punch.

I gave the weapon a couple of swings, wondering what the [Molten] form did. The intensity of it glowed brighter, almost with a touch of the [Corrupt Guardian's] lightning. Question answered.

I couldn't believe I'd gotten a soul bound weapon out of the fight.

"Did you guys get the reward for killing the [Corrupt Guardian] too? This hammer is incredible." I sat on the rock, examining my friends.

"You've seen my scissors. They're [Mercurial Scissors] and have several forms." Tandy patted her [Enchanted] bag for her fabric scissors. I could see them shape-shifting through the cloth.

"My axe got an upgrade. Maybe next time it'll actually do some damage against a [Corrupt Guardian]," Leo chimed in.

"I guess you're not giving Ched his axe back?" I couldn't help teasing him. No one was giving Ched his axe back.

Leo laughed. "Nope. I wouldn't feel too bad, though. He ended up getting an [Enchanted Frying Pan]."

"Seriously?" I asked, incredulous.

Leo nodded solemnly. I chuckled. Maybe the [System's] sense of humor wasn't always terrible. I tried, and failed, to imagine Ched using his new pan to make breakfast.

"How about you, Meredeath? Richard?" I really wanted to know what the last two members of our crew got.

"I didn't get an upgrade, as much as my bracers are fixed. And my amulet was discharged, without personal consequence." Meredeath said dryly. I tried not to wince. If she hadn't taken so much damage, she wouldn't have needed a repair reward.

I got a tooth cap.

"A tooth cap? What does that even do?" Richard looked up at me, grinning with his two fangs out. Sure enough, his left fang looked whiter somehow. Maybe even a little bigger?

None of your business.

I rolled my eyes at his antics. I held my hammer for a moment, willing it to its [Molten] form. It glowed brilliantly.

Grinning, I clipped the hammer to my belt, extinguishing the light.

Its description was missing ***torch****. Who's the glowworm now?*

"I *never* called you a glowworm," I hissed. Richard was salty about something he called himself! Typical fanged banana slug behavior.

We were all seated, eyes on Meredeath. It was time for *her* story.

Too bad you don't have popcorn. This is going to be good.

"Okay, I'm only going to explain this once. And you're going to have questions that I either can't or won't answer, so pay attention." Each word was begrudgingly given, as though it was our fault we didn't know what'd happened to her.

"You are from another world?" Tandy blurted out.

I laughed. That was wild. What other world? I realized no one else was laughing. Cutting myself off, I cleared my throat.

"Sorry, I just... You can't... I mean, another *world*?" I said the last word with a squeak. Meredeath's thin eyebrow arched as though daring me to make a bigger fool of myself.

"Yeah," Meredeath looked at Tandy, "I'm not sure how *you* knew. But yeah, I'm from another world. A place called Kansas. My world doesn't have magic, although I think you'd consider a lot of the technology from my world magic, just because you didn't understand how it worked. I'm here, and I received a new quest after the [Trial Dungeon] that I can't avoid. So it plays into this question of whether I go—"

"We'll help." The words were out of my mouth before Meredeath finished her question. I said it, staring right into her green eyes, knowing I'd follow her into hell itself if it would help.

The corners of Meredeath's lips teased a smile, but her eyes flickered to my teammates.

Tandy coughed. Oops.

"I'll help," I said meekly.

"We'll all help, Meredeath. But we *do* need to know what

your new quest is and what this has to do with you being from another world." Tandy's voice was reassuring, and I flicked my eyes to hers. She smiled at me. I looked at Leo, who was grinning from ear to ear.

"Well, the [System] granted me an [Adventurer] base class, but errored out giving me a specific class," Meredeath tried to explain. Seeing our confused expressions, she continued. "It gave some sort of computer error message and told me that it didn't have the mana required to grant my nonstandard class and then triggered a quest."

"Can you share the quest with us?" Tandy asked, ever practical.

Meredeath frowned. "It says the quest isn't shareable. Oh wait, there's an option to share text only."

[Quest Granted: [Find a Sponsor]

Congratulations on passing the [Trial Dungeon] as an [Expeditionary Force]. You have been granted the [Adventurer] base class and have retained your [Adventurer] skills. Since you have not chosen any of the [Adventurer] classes offered, you must now find a [Sponsor] for an appropriate [Adventurer] class. You have [1 month] to complete this task. Failure to do so will result in removal from this realm. Adventure Onward!]

"The thing is…" Meredeath's voice was soft. "It never offered me [Adventurer] classes."

Leo, of all people, was the first to put it together. "You're one of us!" He reached across and slapped her on the back.

Meredeath looked at him like he was crazy, and I must have seemed equally confused. Leo chuckled at our expressions.

"She's one of us, Cole," he said with a widening grin. "She's *broken*."

Chapter 30

TERMS AND DISQUALIFICATIONS

"So now what?" Leo asked the question we were all thinking.

"Now, Richard tells us where we need to go to find Meredeath a [Sponsor]," I said it with more confidence than I felt.

We all looked at Richard. He was very resolute in his study of an ashy leaf on the ground. The slug wouldn't meet our eyes.

"*Richard*!" I was done with it. I *knew* he was more than what he let on.

I'm right here. You don't have to yell.

"Where do we find Meredeath a [Sponsor]?" My patience was thin.

"Can you tell us what a [Sponsor] even is?" Tandy asked, her voice a bit softer.

No.

"No, you won't tell us?" I was about to use my new [Slug Toss] skill to fling him into the horizon.

"Or no, you don't know?" Tandy asked, trying to smooth over the situation.

Richard sat on the stump, the victim of our ire. One of his eyestalks was pointed at me, and the other at Tandy. It had to be the slug equivalent of going cross-eyed. I was sure he was trying to make us laugh, but I wasn't in the mood.

I am abstaining from this conversation. His antenna sank into his body, not completely, but enough to mimic a door slamming in our faces. His skin pulsed, exuding slime that smelled of fuck off.

Tandy and I shared a glance. We were going to revisit this topic with him later. At least the rest of the team could hear him talk, and he wasn't just ganging up on me.

"How about we talk to him?" Our heads swiveled to the small shack Meredeath was pointing at. Ironically, the building I hadn't bothered considering as a good shelter had withstood the fight *and* the blast. It was the only structure on the ridge.

Malyc's eyes were wide as he examined his home. His ceremonial gold-trimmed crimson robes looked out of place in the devastation. My anger at Richard pivoted hard.

"Hey, Administrator Malyc!" I waved, my voice sickeningly upbeat.

His head turned with a look of surprise. I realized he hadn't expected any of us to survive that fight. The man picked his way between rock and upturned tree, holding his robes off the ground in a losing attempt to keep the hem out of the ash.

"Congratulations are in order!" Malyc called as he trundled his way up to us.

I'd never had an opinion of the Guild Administrator. Never thought I'd need a measure of the man. He'd just been an official who visited Woodsten every couple of months.

Now? Now, I low-key hated the guy. I couldn't look at his face without remembering his back disappearing into that little shack. Abandoning me. Abandoning my *team*.

It was hard to change an opinion after that.

We'd all stood up to greet him. Tandy'd elbowed her way next to me and grabbed my arm with the grip of a [Weaver]. I got the message. Say nothing.

Her voice came out smooth as butter. "Administrator, so good to see you. We fought off the bear and survived the [Trial Dungeon]."

"Yes! My region now has four new [Adventurers]! This is fantastic!" he said with a proud father grin, as though he had *anything* to do with our success.

The pot boiled in my head.

"So, you're the Administrator for the region, right?" Tandy asked innocently. It was always nice to see one of her traps working on someone else for a change.

"Yes, I own the Bear Ridge Testing Ground…" He looked around, noticing that the testing portal no longer existed. He cleared his throat. "And the Northeast Mountain District. You're familiar with the Adventurer Guild's district system, correct?"

The way he said it, you knew immediately that only uneducated [Mundanes] didn't know the guild's districting scheme.

Leo and I put our fake smiles on and nodded. I mean, I *knew* what a *district* was. It wasn't hard to figure out that the Northeast Mountain District probably encompassed Woodsten and the area along the Ursine Wall, up north to the sea.

Malyc puffed up at our nods. I shrank the size of the district in my mental map.

"I'm sure you're aware of Meredeath's *special qualities* as an [Adventurer]?" Tandy asked, smiling as though Meredeath's status was as evident as the sky was blue. The words unspoken, only a *[Mundane]* wouldn't inherently understand Meredeath's worth.

"Ah, yes, it appears she managed to integrate into [Your Mom's Party] successfully!" he began. "We're going to have to revisit that party name. We need something that better represents the district."

I could hear my teeth grinding together.

"Meredeath, though, this is excellent!" The man's words didn't match his expression. He was evaluating Meredeath with a skill, trying to figure out what was so special about her.

"Yes, she was very key to…" Tandy waved at the surrounding destruction. The ash had finally stopped falling, but it'd muted everything on the ridge in a gray blanket.

Malyc's eyebrows rose. "That is truly impressive. I'm glad I was able to secure her for your trial."

"Personally, I think we need her for our region." Tandy emphasized the 'our,' leaning into his ego. "We're a new group of [Adventurers], and Meredeath's just got some experience and powers that integrate incredibly well with the team. She gets results, you know?"

Malyc nodded, swallowing the bait, hook, line, and sinker.

"Yes!" He turned to Meredeath. "I hope you're open to staying here with us. This region is remote, but as you can see, it presents numerous challenges. And a lot of opportunities! We have roaming dungeon-born that make it over the wall. You don't get that in the West. We don't regulate our dungeons, so there are no lotteries or lines. Just making your numbers go up, fight after fight."

He spoke as though these were rehearsed lines. Like the frontier was a cult he'd tried selling to urban [Adventurers].

"I could see staying," Meredeath said tentatively. We all watched as Malyc's eyes lit up. Before he could say anything, she continued. "With [Your Mom's Party]. It really depends on where they want to go."

Malyc turned back to Tandy, appraising her. I realized as he looked hopeful that he'd underestimated Tandy. It was a good reminder that [Appraisal] and [Analyze] only gave you skills and numbers, not necessarily an accurate measure of a person.

"I'm sure you three want to stay local?" he said, addressing Leo, deciding he was the one to convince. I'm sure Leo's abs had something to do with it.

That was a mistake. Tandy hated it when someone assumed Leo made the decisions because of his height, muscles, and gender.

Leo grinned, waiting for the hammer to drop.

"That depends," Tandy said with an edge of steel in her voice. Malyc's eyes swung back to her, sensing the impending danger. "On whether you can help us with a few things."

"Well, part of my job is helping new [Adventurers] get on their feet." His voice was guarded, a little less hopeful. "What can I do for you?"

"We need a [Sponsor] for Meredeath, I'm sure if you were to [Sponsor] her...?" Tandy's confident voice trailed off as Malyc blanched.

"H-how long do you have?" His voice had taken on a mournful, nervous quality.

"One month." Meredeath's voice was flat, like she'd been expecting the disappointment we were all feeling.

"I can't [Sponsor] you."

The words were a slap. Meredeath's jaw tightened.

Leo unstrapped his axe. "Can't or won't?"

I stepped in, playing the good guy role. "Leo, I'm sure there's a reasonable explanation. Right, Administrator?"

"I can't. I'm just a [Mundane] Administrator. I'm not even an [Adventurer]." Like a tumbler lock, everything made more sense. Malyc was just a paper pusher.

"If that's true, how'd you open the portal?" Tandy asked.

Malyc's face reddened. "I used an artifact. A portal key. I just slotted it into the arch..." And it just worked for him.

I wondered if they even knew how to replace the [Trial Dungeon] portal at all. The Administrators were caretakers of [Adventurers], artifacts, and systems they didn't even understand.

"But you know who *could* [Sponsor] Meredeath," I said, confident that he did. The power of Administrators was in who and what they knew. Malyc had been afraid when we told him she needed a [Sponsor]. A man like him wouldn't be frightened of something he didn't know.

Yes, you're starting to understand.

"I do, but regrettably, I doubt it's going to do you much good. There were two individuals who had sufficient levels within a month's journey of us." His voice finally rang with honesty.

"Were?" Tandy asked.

Meredeath's face was still downcast. No part of her was expecting a solution.

"Yes, one of our [Sages], Leon Orren, joined the Everbear."

Leo gasped. Leon Orren, *the short king*, was renowned for his short blades and overpowered buffs.

"That's unlikely," Tandy argued. "We'd have heard about it."

When we were kids, Leo had convinced half of us that he'd been named after the famous [Adventurer]. Leon had mostly worked out of Dusridge, a trade hub two weeks south of us. If Leon had fallen, *everyone* would have known about it.

"I would posit that you have the evidence before you. I no longer have a border guardian, and the [Corruption] of the wilds is pressing hard." Malyc waved at the crater we sat in. Point made. "Leon was still in his prime, but [Adventurers] have a dangerous job."

"You said there were two?" Meredeath's voice was quiet.

Malyc looked at her. He let out his breath in a blusterous exhale, his shoulders sank as though he was releasing all his verbal posturing.

"I did, my dear, but the second person isn't so much an option as a legend. And she's a legend you don't want to pursue."

"Let me guess, some mythical forest hag that eats men's livers for a snack?" Meredeath said with a verbal eye roll at our guild Administrator.

An awkward silence hung between us all. It stretched on, making me think Meredeath's joke had been right. But who was he talking about?

Tandy got there first. Her voice was acerbic. "The *bone lady*? You're going to send us into the swamp after *Rhi Voss*?"

Malyc flinched with each syllable.

Abso-fucking-lutely not.

Chapter 31

EARTH AND OTHER ODDITIES

"So, can someone tell me what the big deal about Rhi Voss is? She's a witch?" Meredeath asked as we walked away from the crater of our last adventure.

I beat Tandy to the punch. "We will, if you explain a little more about coming from another world."

"Yeah, is that why you need a [Sponsor] and the rest of us don't?" Tandy chimed in, giving me a fist bump for my proffered trade.

The forest was quietly beautiful. We'd hiked down into the tree line, leaving Malyc to find Ched and pick up the shattered pieces left from our fight with the [Corrupt] guardian.

The hike was peaceful. We were surrounded by the giant firs and cedars common to Woodsten. Moss coated the trunks, and ferns displayed their leaves like offerings to the sun. The damp decay and cedar smells mixed with the chirps of bugs and the occasional knock of a woodpecker.

I was home. A place I wasn't sure I'd ever see again when I was face down in the shitty [Trial Dungeon]. Everything was crystal clear. The sunlight glistened off the dew, highlighting mushrooms and moths alike. My senses were hyperaware of our environment, and, for a moment, I wondered if I was having a stroke.

My focus snapped back to Meredeath as she began talking.

"What do you want to know? Outside of describing my world, I don't know any more than you. I would love to know how I got here and how I could get home." She fingered her pendant, lost in thought. Shaking her head, she returned to the conversation.

"My home doesn't have a [System] and rules." Her voice sounded lost, a stark contrast to the feelings in my heart.

"So you just woke up here?" Tandy pushed, wanting to hear the beginning of the story.

"Yeah, I honestly don't remember anything about the day I woke up. Is this normal? I'm assuming it was some portal? An interdimensional wormhole?" Meredeath shrugged. "Hell, I don't know if this is a multiverse thing, a whole different world, or if I'm just in a coma at Stormont Vail."

"Stormont Vale sounds epic," Leo said.

"It's a hospital."

"Oh."

Each step wound us out of the mountains, towards Woodsten. The route to the swampy domain of the bone lady wasn't so much of a route as a general southeastern direction from Woodsten. No one went into the swamp intentionally.

"Okay, so you don't know how you got here," Tandy said, bringing us back to the conversation. "Why on earth did you become an [Adventurer]? It's *dangerous.*"

"See, you said it again: *Earth.* I can't tell if you're saying my word, or if," Meredeath waved at her head, "there's some magic translating what you call your world to the same thing I call mine."

Was that even possible?

"I didn't pick [Adventurer]. Your [System] informed me that I needed to report to a Guild Administrator within two weeks, or there would be consequences. Your [System] is a... has a lot of charisma, uniqueness, nerve, and talent."

Meredeath's words made little sense. What was nerve?

"The Adventurer's Guild didn't know what to do with me, so they threw me into the trials. The first attempt didn't go well, so they sent me down here to try this portal."

It just didn't make sense. Forcing someone new to a world into a death game was like throwing a perfectly fine carrot into the compost. The Adventurer's Guild had always preyed on the fantasies of youth and promise. No one considered their advertising of adventure anything but scammy recruitment hype. The Leon Orrens of the world were the exception, not the rule.

"So, does your world not have an [Adventurer's] Guild?" Leo asked.

Meredeath gave a self-deprecating chuckle. "No, my world doesn't even have monsters or dungeons. At least not monster-filled labyrinths." She paused for a moment as though questioning if that was true. "Our monsters are people, our dungeons... money and the grind? It's not like this."

We had money too, but the grind sounded awful.

"We have books that talk about different worlds," Meredeath said. "All fiction, of course, none of us has been to another world. Well, except for a couple of old guys who went to the moon. It's just the raving imagination of authors tattooing it on the bones of trees."

My mind shuddered at the thought of trees having *bones*.

"You're talking about books, right?" Tandy said, and at Meredeath's nod, I once again felt like an idiot.

"Do people from your world look like you?" Leo asked, without an ounce of shame.

"Like a woman?" Meredeath responded dryly.

Meredeath's sarcasm went right over Leo's head as he explained, "No, like the chains and... black? The stuff around your eyes and, uh..." His face turned crimson as he tried to explain her chest.

I'd heard of folks dressing with less but, in Woodsten, we were in wool country, and winters were cold. Meredeath was *definitely* going to be identified as an outsider.

"Oh, my clothes? Yeah, this is normal fare where I come from." She looked at me as she finished her thought. "You should see what the *men* dress like."

How hard had that lightning hit me during the fight? Was she *actually* flirting with me?

Are you still in there, or did your brain leak out of your ears?

"He speaks!" I announced, fervently hoping Richard's comment had only been directed at me. He'd been pouting since we'd decided to visit the bone lady.

"Finally!" Meredeath said, rifling around in her bag to pull out a chunk of mushroom. "I've got a treat for you if you're done sulking." She held out a mushroom with a purple head and white base.

Ah, a meal for a king! I love wine cap mushrooms. Cole, I told you we're keeping Meredeath, right?

"If we're keeping Meredeath, that means we're going to have to talk to the bone lady." My life had gotten weird.

Fine. You can talk to Rhi, but I have nothing to say to her.

"First name basis with the scary lady?" I teased my slug. "No one was expecting you to talk. Hell, I'm half expecting to die. I didn't think the bone lady was real, just a nightmare whispered to scare children."

Oh, she's real.

Tandy had handed out more of her dried fruit and nut granola bars. Trail rations were rough, and Tandy had never been known for her cooking. My stomach was happy, but my taste buds yearned for *the Ram's Horn* and Marta's cooking.

Hell, I'd even take my cooking.

"Alright, I've answered your questions. I even got the slug to talk. Now, what is the big deal about this bone lady?"

Not - munch - *it.* Richard opened his slimy mouth and took a gluttonous bite of the purple shroom cap.

"Well, Richard…" I tried, but Richard interrupted me.

CHOMP - CHOMP - CHOMP.

"Isn't willing to share any vital information with us, information he *obviously* knows. But we can fill you in on the rest of it. Rhi Voss is a legend, a monster, and a nightmare all rolled into one. There are a lot of stories. Any mam has their own version passed down. That's why it's hard to believe she's real. If she's the *same* bone lady, she's been alive for hundreds of years."

"I mean, you're being kind of vague. What does she do to people? Can we even find her in a month?" Meredeath asked.

"You don't find her, she finds you," Leo whispered the adage.

Leo and I had explored the edge of the swamp once. A cold, lingering fog enveloped gnarled trees and moss-covered rocks that resembled ancient gravestones rebelling against the earth. I shivered, goosebumps running down my arms. Were we really doing this?

Nonplussed, Tandy began listing some of the stories. She'd never believed in those old fairy tales.

"The bone lady lures people into her swamp to perform experiments. She curses men, causing all sorts of problems from balding to impotence to turning them into worms. She is a cannibal, a dream walker, a necromancer. Some claim she's a blind seer who uses ravens to spy. Or black cats, or cockroaches, or maybe rats. She has three nipples, or none." Each point ticked off during Tandy's recitation had a dozen stories about it. "There are so many stories about her, it's hard to keep them all separate."

"Sounds like she's a real witch," Meredeath said. "I like her already."

Meredeath would. I rescind my approval of Meredeath being on the team. Kick her off, Cole.

Meredeath gave me an amused smile. "You kicking me off the team?"

"I'll note, Richard, you're only having this opinion now that your mushroom is done. Also, I don't have the right to kick anyone off the team; that's Tandy's job." I firmly dodged any and all responsibility.

Wait… you mean I've been sucking up to the wrong teammate this whole time?

"Har har, very funny. But we should think of a plan, maybe over dinner?" I said, my stomach rumbling in emphasis.

"I was thinking of dropping by your parents' place. It's on the way…" Tandy said with a sly smile.

What?! No! I tried to play it cool.

"Why not go into town? We do *not* need to bother my folks on a..." I'd forgotten what day of the week it was.

"On a Sunday?" Leo asked, grinning.

Shit. Was it Sunday? Sunday night dinners were a thing in my family. Tandy and Leo had spent *many* Sunday nights at my house eating and playing games. The Thornfield Sunday dinner was a complete experience.

"I was hoping we'd go into town," I said lamely, knowing I'd already lost the argument.

Leo elbowed me. He pointed at Tandy, whose back was to us. "Not everyone's going to be happy we're [Adventurers]. Give us one last Sunday dinner, man. We're fighting a *nightmare* tomorrow. Enjoy today."

I nodded. Leo was right from his perspective. To a man

with no family, Sunday dinners with mine were always something he cherished.

He'd never had to live in the chaos or the judgment.

He was right, though. Our world was changing, and our life expectancy was dropping rapidly. This might be the last Sunday dinner for me... ever.

Wait, now that *was* a cheery thought.

Chapter 32

RELATIVE CHAOS

I hadn't been home in months.

I had my reasons.

My family homestead had been one of the first successful farms in the early settlement days of Woodsten. Thornfield, my surname, had been earned. My parents had scratched out an existence from the dust and weeds. They'd lived in a sod house with my eldest sister, Floria, for the first couple of years.

Being the third eldest, I'd come along a few years later. By then, they had built an oversized shed from seasoned logs harvested when they'd cleared the land. I didn't remember it and, unlike Floria, I didn't claim I did.

She'd been a *baby*. No one's memory was that long.

I had six siblings and was an uncle twice over. I knew a bit about babies. There wasn't a chance in hell she remembered the old sod house or the hardship. That trophy firmly belonged to our parents.

We walked up the dusty two-track road. The fence posts sat perfectly vertical, separating the pasture from the road. Wild carrots gave their lacy foliage right next to the tall stalks of yellow flowers from the woolly ear plants. Bees buzzed happily.

I closed my eyes and smelled the warm dust and the stillness of the country. I could almost forget why I never came back.

"It's just one night, it'll be okay," Tandy repeated the words I'd been telling myself the whole way here.

I nodded, forcing a smile even as my face tightened. Tandy and Leo had always been my family.

"Don't forget to breathe," she whispered, giving a last bit of advice before we walked up the driveway to the house.

Unclenching my jaw, I took one steady breath.

"Is that COLE?!" Hitch, my youngest brother yelled. He was all of eight, and by far the loudest of my family, which is saying something. Hitch ran across the field with a piece of straw hanging out of his mouth. "It's Cole! Mama, Pop, Flo! Cole's here for Sunday Dinner, and he's got *friends!*"

Meredeath glanced at me. "Is it that surprising you have friends?" she asked.

I shrugged. I hadn't ever brought anyone but Tandy and Leo home and, even then, it'd been a few years.

The old barn stood, red paint faded. It may have developed a small lean, but it still looked solid. Sheep were lined up for their dinner, which was what Hitch had been doing until we walked up. Floria was going to be mad.

The front door squeaked open. Floria stood squinting into the sun. She was bigger than I remembered. A gust of air pushed at her sundress, and I realized she wasn't bigger, she was *pregnant*. I felt guilty because I had no idea she was expecting another. I guess it had been a while.

"Hey, Floria. Hope you don't mind a couple of extra mouths to feed tonight," I said, staring four inches to her left. It was always better not to look my sister in the eyes.

"Oh, for the love of wheat, you know you're the only one that uses my full name, *Cole Moldboard Thornfield*." She sounded worn out.

"I'll stop using your full name when you stop using mine," I said, already tired of her.

I hadn't even used her full name, Floria Beam Hastings. I knew she preferred Flo, but I had to needle her when I had the chance. I was her brother, after all.

Plus, I was the only Thornfield not living on the farm, so I was the only one relatively safe from her retribution.

"Moldboard?" I heard Meredeath's hushed question to Tandy. Ears burning, I let out a resigned sigh. This is precisely what I had feared.

"I'll tell you later," Tandy whispered to Meredeath, grinning.

It wasn't my fault that Dad was such a nerd. Who names their kids after parts of a plow? Who chooses the *moldboard* as one of those parts?

I took one last breath, then walked through the front door.

The house was simple, consisting of a large room that served as a kitchen, dining area, and entertainment space. There were two bedrooms, one for Mom and Dad and the other for Floria and her husband, Jareth. Then the loft with all the kids. I'd moved into the barn for a while until I'd saved up enough to get my own place.

"It's unnnnnnnncle Coooollllleeee!" sang Saphira, her voice horribly off-key. She bounced around me, her dark hair bobbing up and down.

"You're still singing, I see." I smiled as I picked up my favorite niece. She wore a pale green kitchen apron that stood out against her dark skin. The apron told me she'd been on kitchen duty before my interruption.

I twirled her around as she squealed in delight. Floria frowned at us both, which made it even more fun.

I tried to set Saphira down, but her little brown arms clutched me in a hug.

She got right up to my ear. "Am I still your favorite niece?" she whispered in a serious voice.

I squeezed her little body, she smelled of butterbalm and blueberries. "Of course, but let's keep that between us." Then I tickled her. She wailed with laughter and wriggled until I had to put her down before I dropped her.

"Is that a slug on your shoulder?" Share was next. She'd been my closest sibling when we'd been growing up. She was supposed to join me in the city when she came of age, but that dream never manifested.

"It is." I smiled as she made the same face she would when we were little and I'd bring her a frog or a beetle.

"Leave it to my big brother to visit for the first time in months with a *slug*." She wrapped her arms around me, giving a tight hug. "It has been too long, Cole."

I squeezed back.

I like her. She smells like strawberries.

"So, Share, this is Richard. Richard, Share." I lifted Richard from my shoulders and held him out like one of my childhood prizes. She reached out, and a glint caught my eye. "Is that a RING?!"

Share turned tomato red. I dumped Richard onto the table and grabbed her hand. A thin promise ring sat on it, depicting two hands clasped.

"It is," she said shyly.

"Well, congratulations! Who's the lucky person?" Internally, I crossed my fingers. She and Fennel down the street had always seemed like they could be a pair. They'd just both been so damn shy that no amount of matchmaking shenanigans had worked.

"Fennel and I have been dating," she said it with the sweet voice reserved for those in love.

"That's fantastic!" I lifted her and whirled her around like she was Saphira.

The greetings continued. Tandy and Leo took Meredeath to a quieter corner, as she looked overwhelmed. My family was a lot.

I was dog-piled by everyone else. Floria, Flo, stood frowning at the stove. I'd never found it hard to get along with my family, except for Flo.

Lira, Hitch, and Landslide were out doing the evening chores with my dad. And Mom was collecting eggs with Flo's husband, Jareth.

Coulter was talking to Leo about his axe and, before I knew it, Galen, the three-year-old, was plopped in my care as Share and I sat down to talk.

Saphira skipped around us. To Flo's irritation, no amount of cajoling could return Saphira to peeling carrots.

Richard sat in the middle of the table. As a bonus, I'm sure it irritated Flo. He was happy, though, as Share fed him potato peels.

Galen sat on the bench next to me. As a kid who loved to collect shiny things, Richard was mesmerizing. His slime shimmered in the firelight, but he was also a 'worm.' And three-year-olds love worms.

"So, you're back? Or passing through?" Share asked as her hands worked on the potato in front of her.

"Just passing through." I glanced at my friends, my eyes resting on Meredeath as she took in the chaos.

Share followed my gaze and smiled. "So you knew about Fennel? You didn't act surprised." Her hands deftly finished scraping a potato, then used the tip of her knife to dig out an eye.

"I didn't know, I'd just hoped," I said and meant it. Fennel was shy, but dependable. He was a farrier, more skilled with horses than with people. A perfect match.

Saphira picked up on this and started singing. "Fenneeel and Shhharrreee siiittting on a feeennceee." She kept the song going until I shooed her back to work.

"And you, brother mine? You've got a new addition to your group." Share asked the question with such a mischievous grin that I knew she'd been aiming at that information all along.

"I'll introduce Meredeath when Mom gets here." Mom was going to make a fuss. She always did.

"Yes." Share leaned in and dropped to a conspiratorial whisper. "But are you a thing? I can tell you like her."

Did I like Meredeath that way? Yes, but… was it *more* than infatuation? Meredeath was different, and impressive, and hot, and... I stopped myself.

"We're not a thing, it's complicated. We are very different. It's almost like we're from different worlds." I never could lie to Share. My sister always saw right through me.

"I see. Well, she's definitely different from your ex, Minvi, which is good. Things have a way of working out." Share fingered her ring meaningfully.

I smiled, shaking my head. Share was getting married! I watched as Galen got brave and poked Richard. He giggled in delight as Richard gooed his hand.

"Flo's pregnant again, and you're getting married! What other news have I missed?"

Share handed me a potato and a spare knife. "I'll catch you up, but you're going to have to work for it."

We sat peeling and chopping as I got the latest gossip. Mom's health was still rough, and Plow had finally admitted to Share that she liked girls. *Finally.*

Hitch was as spoiled as ever. Share was trying to get

Saphira voice lessons because the girl wouldn't stop singing. Everything was as it should be.

The egg collection crew and the chore crew came inside at the same time. Which started a whole other round of, "*It's Cole!*"

I glanced at Meredeath and couldn't decipher her expression. She just sat in the corner, watching us all. That was until Plow noticed her.

"Who are *you?*" It amused me to no end that my little sister and I had the same taste in women.

The crowd grew silent, all eyes on Meredeath.

"This is Meredeath, everyone! She's from a city out west called Kansas. She's new in town—"

My dad interjected, "Kansas? I've never heard of Kan-sas. Let me get the map!"

Oh shit, what do we do? I looked at Tandy for help.

"Yeah," she spoke up, "Meredeath's an [Adventurer]."

Coulter gasped. He'd always had a not-so-secret desire to be an [Adventurer]. My dad was like a dog with a bone; he'd already disappeared into his bedroom to get his prized possession, an old leather map.

My mom was the warmest person, but she *hated* the thought of anyone being an [Adventurer]. "That's an odd profession for..." She tried to think of a polite way to describe Meredeath's wardrobe. "Someone who's from Kansas."

Meredeath did something I didn't expect from her. She belly-laughed. It was loud and outrageous, and she slapped the table with tears of laughter running down her face. My mom was taken aback, becoming insulted as she thought she was the butt of a joke.

"Oh, Missus Thornfield, I can't tell you how accurate you are! An [Adventurer] from Kansas is the least likely thing in the universe."

Mollified, my mom smiled, wrapping her arms around me in a hug. The conversation moved on.

"We've missed you, Cole," Mom said before releasing me from the hug. "Also, Meredeath's a strange one. Not like you to bring new folks around."

I looked at her, new wrinkles around her face, her hair a solid iron gray neatly braided but without the healthy sheen it'd always had. I hugged her again.

"I know. It's been too long. I've got more things to say, but later." I had Galen clinging to a leg, and Saphira had started singing again.

Dad appeared with his map. "First, can you help me with Dad? Meredeath's an orphan," it wasn't really a lie, and I knew Mom would respond, "and she doesn't enjoy talking about her home."

This had the exact effect I'd hoped. My mom's face melted in sympathy, and she grabbed my dad's hand before he rolled out the map.

"Honey, let's do that later. Dinner's ready, and we don't want to get it dirty."

My dad grumbled and took his prize back into their bedroom.

"Cole's a what?!" Plow shouted.

The family near my friends stared at me as though I'd grown a third eye. Leo looked guilty as Tandy punched him in the arm. Whispers circulated as I tried to think of what to say.

My mom and dad came back from their room, finding their family silently staring at me. Flo was by their side in an instant, catching my mom up.

"Cole, is it true?" Mom's wavering voice cut to the bone. Expectations in our family were always clear, and being an [Adventurer] wasn't part of it. Hell, being "Cole" wasn't acceptable either.

"Guess my secret is out. Yep, it's true. I'm an [Adventurer]. So are Tandy, Leo, and our party member, Meredeath." The words stuck like glue in my mouth as my mom's expression noticeably darkened.

She was *disappointed*.

I never got used to disappointing my mom. Or my dad. The hurt burned in my chest.

You forgot someone.

"Oh, and one more." I pointed to Richard sitting, belly sticking out, full of potato peels. His exaggerated pose saved me, and I smiled at my slug in the middle of the dining table. "And that's Richard. He's my Companion."

"That's not a dire wolf!" Hitch blurted.

What is it with you and dire wolves?

An awkward silence settled on everyone as they looked at Richard.

"No," I said to Hitch, "but he's got decorative fangs, so he's close."

Appropriately, they all stared at me like I was insane while Richard chuckled in my head.

Chapter 33

TABLE MANNERS

[Your Mom's Party] huddled in the corner, trying to formulate a plan while the 'dungeon monsters' ignored us.

"Why did you have to tell them?" I whined.

"Sorry, man, but it just slipped out. He was eyeing my axe and, well, you were going to have to tell them sooner or later." Leo was right, the idiot.

One of the 'bosses' clanked a skillet loudly against the stove. My mom and Flo had long ago mastered the art of cooking angry. I think it was a skill that moms automatically gained when they had their first child. My dad cooked too, but he almost always did it angrily since he was always messing something up when he cooked. They never let him cook on Sundays, not for *family* dinner.

"I don't see what the big deal is," Meredeath said. "It's not like you were sucked away to another world or something."

"You're right, but it's my mom. Her parents were killed in

a dungeon breakout in one of the Western cities. She was raised by her older brother, whose passion was to become an [Adventurer] to avenge her parents. You can guess what happened to him."

It was a sad story, one we'd been told time and time again as kids. I think she chose Dad because he was only interested in farming.

Of course, this meant she had a kid named Moldboard, so there were trade-offs. Well, that and his map.

I looked over at Share, but she wouldn't meet my eyes. That hurt. She was my first friend and closest family member. I absentmindedly petted Richard, who was snoring next to me in a food coma.

"Cole's in troooooouuuubbbbllee! Trouble! Trouble, grouble, trouble!" Saphira wasn't old enough to know why, but she was enjoying singing about my toils. As pots clanked much louder than needed in the kitchen, Saphira pranced around, inventing words that rhymed with trouble.

"Do you think we could look at your dad's map after dinner? I haven't been able to get a good understanding of the land," Meredeath's voice dropped, "since I was dumped here."

"Yeah, I'll see what I can do." I knew I didn't sound hopeful, but I'd already been on the outs with my family. And now this.

"It can't be that bad," Meredeath said. "Your mom seems nice. She cares about you way more than my mom cared about me and my sister."

Tandy's eyebrows went up, and I stored that bit of information away for later. It was the first time Meredeath had mentioned anything about *her* home without being prodded.

"Yeah, Mom and Flo are two peas in a pod. If they're not at the wheel, they're not happy. And so far, I'm the only one that's truly left the preordained path of farming and family."

I'd *never* wanted to be a farmer. Not that I particularly

wanted to be a [Smith] or [Chef] or [Adventurer] for that matter. I just didn't want to be *here.* I wanted to be on my own, have my own space, my own thoughts, be able to tinker in my workshop without someone poking me.

Meredeath looked pointedly at Coulter and Plow. "I think you're just paving the way for the future."

"That's exactly what they're afraid of," I said quietly.

Dinner was served family-style. Giant bowls piled with steaming food. I missed their cooking.

I grabbed a roll and skipped the chicken. I never liked our chickens alive or roasted. Plus, they were making sure we got served first as guests, and there wasn't enough meat to go around. Leo and Tandy followed suit, but Meredeath had grabbed a chunk of the breast meat, which was fine.

Stuffing and potatoes, greens and a rich gravy piled on my plate. Flo had even used her [Cool] skill to cool down a pitcher of blueberry and mint juice. It tasted like home, even though the table conversation was minimal.

"The stuffing is delicious," Leo said, mouth too full to talk politely. His table manners were atrocious.

"Thank you, Leo," Flo replied, polite but curt.

It was up to me to make this right. It was just like my family to make me do all the work.

"Mom, I'm sorry, okay? I didn't intend to become an [Adventurer]." The words came out choppy, as though each one were forced through the knot in my throat.

"I didn't know they'd started conscripting. Has the Adventurer's Guild gotten that desperate? Is this just like you 'happened' to become a [Smith] during harvest?" Flo's 'innocent' question floated over our meal like a horsefly.

My face burned with shame. That'd been different. I'd been so young and needed to escape the farm.

Or maybe it wasn't so different, after all.

I felt defeated. "No, they're not conscripting. I signed up by accident."

"By accident? I didn't know one could just stumble into a pen and sign a contract with the guild. I'll be careful next time I'm in town. Can't have that happen to me." For the love of the Everbear, I wish my sister would just shut up.

"We got drunk on my birthday," Leo explained, beating me to it.

Tandy elbowed him. Leo's cluelessness knew no bounds.

"That explains so much," Meredeath whispered, not helping.

Flo rolled her eyes, as though Leo had confirmed every expectation she'd contrived over the years.

There wasn't anything I could say. I didn't have a 'good' excuse. Nothing I could say would make this better for her. I tried anyway.

"I passed the [Trial Dungeon]. We're full [Adventurers], so you don't have to worry about the trial."

Mom's face raised as I spoke. For a second, I had a brief spark of hope. Maybe this would be all right after all.

Richard burbled. I looked down at him as he adjusted and flopped his tail off the bench.

"Randat had passed his test, too." My mom's voice was low, and her words tight, snuffing out the spark. Even Galen had stopped making noises as she talked about her brother. "He'd survived several quests, was so proud of his polished armor, his overpowered skills," her voice hissed as she finished the sentence, "and his giant [Enchanted] sword. He'd trained for a decade before becoming an [Adventurer]."

She looked at me, steel eyes continuing, "He was *cut down* by one of those *monsters*. None of it saved him. We buried the parts of him that were left."

Her words hung in the room. I couldn't meet her gaze.

They'd buried *parts*. I couldn't help but think that's what would have happened if the [Corrupt] guardian or the ribbons of hunger or the root canals had gotten their way.

"We've put up with a lot from you, Cole, including moving

to the city and chasing job after job. Now an [Adventurer]? You're going to die. Did you ever think of Mom? Of us?" Floria always finished an argument.

You're going to die. Her words echoed in my head. Floria never holds back.

There were many excuses I could have made. But I'd sat in that ashen crater after we'd beaten the [Corrupt] guardian, and I'd *chosen* to move forward as an [Adventurer]. Suppressed anger boiled up in me; my choice wasn't *wrong*. Being an [Adventurer] was just as good as being a [Farmer]. Not better, but equal. And it was better for *me*.

"Mom, I love you." All eyes were fixed on me. "I love all of you." I looked at Share, whose eyes were glistening. "But I've got to live my own life."

"You've made that very apparent." Mom's words bit me deeper than any sword.

She returned to her dinner; the discussion was over. I sat back down, hot tears running down my face. Meredeath put an arm around my back, drawing me close.

"It'll be okay," she whispered, handing me her napkin.

I just nodded, numb. I wanted to crawl under the table and vanish. But I couldn't. If I left now, that would be the end of it.

Eventually, the kids started talking, their capacity to be silent severely hampered by their age. Conversations wrapped around us about the mundane things—weather, which chicken we were eating, and the state of the cattle pond.

No one dared talk to us, and that was okay. I wasn't in the mood.

"I see where his [Self Critic] skill comes from," Meredeath whispered a little too loudly to Tandy.

"Yeah, it's a good thing Cole has us." Tandy reached across the table and squeezed my hand.

"I'm really grateful for all of you." I poked Leo, including him in the statement.

He brought his eyes up for the first time, glad his mistakes weren't unforgivable. The problem wasn't his honesty; it was the rigidity of my family.

When the table was cleared, Share came to take our plates.

"You know I love you, Cole. I've always admired your ability to stand up to the two of them," she murmured low so only I could hear. "I never did have that strength." She took my plate and Meredeath's damp napkin, squeezing my hand. I wondered if she really wanted to marry Fennel after all.

With the table clear, I stood up. Now that propriety was satisfied, it was time to go. I grabbed Richard, who sluggishly moved to my shoulder.

Yawning, he looked around. *Dinner's over?* Richard whined, squirming on my shoulder. The glutton's disappointment was so over-the-top it tugged a smile out of me.

Thank the Everbear for Richard. He saved me from more tears as we walked out.

I didn't want to stay in the house, and they didn't have the room for us, anyway. I walked out, not looking at anyone's faces. The raw wound was too fresh for anyone's sympathy.

Outside was better. The night had arrived while we'd been eating, and fireflies danced in the thicket.

"Hold up, son." Dad's gruff voice stopped us. He stepped outside, closing the door behind him. "What's done is done. It wasn't my choice for you, but you've got to live your own life. Come back this fall." His voice choked a bit as we both had the same thought: *if you're still alive.* "Come back to see us. Things will be different."

I nodded, a fresh wave of tears blurring my vision.

"Take this," he said, handing me an old leather map that had carried him east, all the way to Woodsten. "It served me well. I hope it's as good to you as it was to me. Sleep in the barn tonight. I'll keep the kids inside."

He stood before me, his dark hair sprinkled with salt and

pepper. His face was leathery from a lifetime in the sun and dirt.

"Thanks, Dad," I managed to say.

He nodded, then held out an old, calloused hand. I blinked, then shook it firmly.

"Good luck, son. Try not to die."

I like your dad. That's good advice. You told him we were taking on the bone lady tomorrow, right?

Chapter 34

MAPPING IT OUT

"So, this is your childhood bedroom?" Meredeath asked, as we sat stretched out in the loft of the barn. The gambrel roof sat above us with several murals sketched out in grease and paint. "It's not what I would have imagined."

I blushed. Meredeath struck me as a refined city girl. She probably couldn't imagine growing up in a hayloft.

"Don't feel too bad for him." Tandy stretched out on her back between Meredeath and me, her hands crisscrossed behind her head with elbows poking out. "Share always complained that she got twice as many indoor chores because Cole wasn't in line of sight every day."

Share had many reasons to complain about me over the years.

Can we look at your dad's map?

I didn't want to. As a kid, it was known that if any of us took the map outside, we'd be on latrine duty for months.

Opening it up in the loft seemed like a profane sin in a barn smelling lightly of dung, on top of a rough wood floor covered in straw.

Unfortunately, Richard had used his newly discovered [Party Speak] ability, and so I couldn't just ignore the question.

"Yeah, I guess." I took the roll out of my bag. The leather fiber had become thin after many years of being rolled and unrolled. I untied the leather strap and unrolled the masterpiece for everyone.

Meredeath's gasp was gratifying. Black ink outlined cities, mountains, and roads. Gold filigree highlighted varying details, and light colors shaded many places.

A notification popped up on my interface.

[Skill Acquired: You have gained a new heirloom [Adventurer] skill, [Cartographer]. Your map interface now has multiple new options for viewing world, regional, and local maps. You have gained a [+25%] accuracy bonus when examining other maps, and when creating or updating your own. Note: Experience is the best [Cartographer]. Additions to the map through absorbing external sources may not be accurate. Use at your own risk.]

"Holy shit, I just got a [Cartographer] skill. Did anyone else?" I asked in a hushed tone.

Use your [Map] skill. Richard advised.

I did and got a second notification.

[Skill Upgrade: [Map] has upgraded to [Adventurer's Map]. Your interface map can now update through absorption of external maps and verbal directions. Additional options are available for dungeon environments. Note: External sources can be unreliable and may not be accurate. Use at your own risk.]

"Oh, this is so cool, we just got a skill upgrade from looking at your dad's map!" Leo's eyes were unfocused as he flipped through his settings.

I knew my dad's map was exceptional, but I never expected *this*. It had to be [Enchanted].

Tandy frowned. "I got the [Adventurer's Map] upgrade as well, but nothing about [Cartographer]."

Did you get an heirloom notification?

"I did. Which probably means it has something to do with Dad giving the map to *me*."

Something like that. Richard didn't bother to elaborate.

"Well, I'm glad we're better equipped. Who knew Sunday Dinner would turn out so well?" Tandy said, distracted by her interface.

It made me wonder where Dad had gotten the map, and what he'd been doing with an heirloom skill. I'd never even heard of such a skill.

Dad had always claimed the base of the [Enchanted] map was done by an artist in Filidelfya. Some old friend of his that he'd known when they lived out west.

Dad added bits to it over the years, like the city of Woodsten, etched in a less practiced hand. I unrolled the last bit to show the local map that Dad had added. If he'd had another passion besides farming, it would have been his interest in cartography.

Meredeath ran her hand across the leather, just above the ink, as though she was afraid to touch it. She traced the line of the Ursine Wall south, the mountain range extending all the way to the southern sea labeled Yaris.

"Your world is so big," Meredeath whispered.

Make sure you all absorb it into your personal [Map]. Tandy, make sure you take it into your [Party Map] too.

I triggered the skill again.

[Would you like to absorb the [Enchanted Adventurer's Map]?]

Bringing up the interface, I could see we'd uncovered a clear path from Woodsten to Bear Ridge to my family home.

"Yes," I whispered to the [System] as everyone followed suit.

My interface filled out majestically, including trade routes, rivers, cities, and roads. The interface shaded the new information in a dull gray. A pop-up informed me that the information was several decades old, and data may have changed in the last thirty years.

It was a giant leap forward for us. The map included almost all our district, and it detailed the winding path my folks had taken when they immigrated from the west. However, it also incorporated the general attributes of the map as a whole.

"Does this mean we can just... look at people's maps to fill in the blanks?" Meredeath asked.

It seemed like a cheat to me.

No.

"Just no?" Meredeath asked. She was getting as tired of Richard as I was.

Richard eyed her with his stalks, and Meredeath stared him down, her eyebrow raised in judgment.

The banana slug eventually shrunk, relenting, he gave us a bit more. *It's [Enchanted]. An [Adventurer's Map]. Cole may be able to absorb something more mundane, but generally you're going to want to use an [Adventurer's Map].*

Before our eyes, my dad's map updated with a title: [Your Mom's Party Map]. I watched in stunned silence as it transformed to show the crater on Bear Ridge, and moved the dot labeled 'Woodsten' to the right a quarter of an inch.

"He gave us a bigger treasure than he knew," Tandy murmured.

Perhaps.

I traced a path from Woodsten to the Bear Ridge Crater, seeing but not believing.

You can touch it. It's [Enchanted] against dirt and water.

I did something I'd never dared—I let my finger drop and

touch the old leather. It was smooth, silky almost, as I ran my hand across it.

"Do you see this?" Tandy asked, pointing at the localized section. Her finger touched a landscape labeled 'The Bone Lady Swamp.' "Well, this confirms what we'd already thought."

A skull and crossbones sat at the entrance, the universal sign for 'keep out.'

We all stared at it.

"My uncle once got drunk and told me a story about the swamp," Leo said. It was unusual for him to volunteer information from his family, so neither Tandy nor I interrupted him. "He and my dad had gone to check it out on a full moon. We've all heard the stories, right? But who's actually seen the bone lady?"

He shrugged. "I'm not sure why Uncle Artie told me this story, but he never repeated it. He said the moonlight made the forest glow, but as they drew closer to the swamp's border, everything grew darker. It'd been spring, but the trees had lost their leaves. Clouds crept over the moon, and they both began second-guessing their desire to continue, as swamp water soaked their boots. Artie took out a torch and lit it. The soft glow was enough to push them forward. That's when they saw the lights dancing above the swamp."

"The ghost lights?" I whispered.

"They didn't know. Uncle Artie said that he wanted to turn around, but that my dad had his head stuffed with wool. Dad insisted on going forward, on catching a light. So he walked in deeper, while Artie stood watching. The swamp got wetter, with great sucking steps trying to pull my dad's boots off his feet. Uncle Artie picked a tree to stand by, high ground."

"The further Dad got away, the more Artie noticed the ground. It sloped towards the dancing lights, pulsing like it breathed. He tried calling out, but the words stuck in his throat. His feet were locked, and he couldn't move or yell. He tried to pull his hand away from the tree. It was covered in black sap that glued to the tree."

"Growing more frantic, he pulled harder on his hand. The dark sap pulsed in time with the swamp, climbing higher to his wrist."

"Artie twisted, getting leverage with his feet on a rock he *pulled*. But it only made it worse. Each tug forced the sap higher on his hand."

"He yelled for my dad, but the fog was getting denser, muffling the sounds."

Leo stopped his narration, leaning back against the barn wall. His face was white. I'd never heard this story from him.

Richard sat across from me, his head lying against the floor as though in a torpor.

"What happened?" Meredeath asked, sounding more curious than afraid. Maybe her world didn't have ghosts and bone ladies.

"He had the torch." My mind clicked into understanding.

Artie Patch had always existed on the fringes of the village. The nicest thing anyone'd ever been able to say about him was that he'd taken Leo on after his parents passed.

Taking him on had been a generous description. Leo had a roof over his head and sometimes food but mostly, Artie had ignored his nephew, leaving him to fend for himself.

No one would own up to why he was the town drunk, but I'd always assumed it had to do with the scars that covered the right side of his body. Long, gnarled ropes that ran down his arm and what was left of his hand.

"My dad ran back to him once he heard the screams. The lights followed him, chasing him to the tree. Roots tripped his feet, trying to drag him back."

"Artie said my dad saved him. Dragged him out of the swamp screaming for mercy. After that, neither of them was the same."

Tandy and I looked at each other. *This* is why our adventurous friend had never had much interest in going into the bone lady's domain. It was an unspoken rite of passage to dare the fringe of the swamp in Woodsten, but Leo'd always talked us out of it, never letting us go deeper than the surrounding forest.

Leo looked at the rest of us in the faint glow of my hammer. "Artie said that Dad also had an experience. That the lights were ghosts that spoke to him of an early death..."

That was not Rhi Voss. It sounds like you've got a tidemaw in your swamp.

"How do you know it's not the bone lady?" I asked, not willing to call the horror of our childhood by her first name.

Richard lifted his eyestalks for the first time since we sat down in the barn. He looked straight into my soul.

Because they'd be dead.

We were all silent at his proclamation. What was there to say? Leo's story was messed up, but *Richard,* the self-proclaimed [Immortal], deciding we were doomed? That gave us something to think about.

"What's my alternative?" Meredeath asked, her voice angrily breaking the silence that'd settled on us all.

Richard's eyestalks swung to her, his brow downcast. *There isn't one. That's the stupidity of it. If you're going to survive your initiation into this world, you need a [Sponsor]. The only one within reach is Rhi.*

Meredeath voiced the thought I hadn't dared say. "Then I should go, everyone else stay. I'm the only one who needs a [Sponsor]. It makes little sense for you to risk yourselves."

The platitude of 'sticking together' gummed in my throat before the likelihood of death. I searched for the words to reassure her or to back out of the deal.

"None of that," Leo said, his voice clear, the ghosts of his uncle's story leaving his face. "You saved us how many times in the leviathan? I don't think I want to be an [Adventurer] without you protecting my back."

I found myself nodding. "Yeah, plus imagine how powerful you'll be once she does [Sponsor] you."

They all nodded, buying my glib platitude. My stomach clenched, though, noting my insincerity. I was scared.

"I wonder why none of the rest of us needed a [Sponsor]," Tandy asked, thankfully changing the subject. It was a good question.

"Could it be because I'm from another world?"

It's not.

We all looked at Richard as he innocently began grooming himself. We hadn't shared notes on our classes, still held back by courtesy, but if [Your Mom's Party] was going to survive, we needed to trust each other. My heart still ached that I hadn't spoken up sooner in Meredeath's support, so I decided to make amends by doing something brave.

"My class is [Dead Wrong] and somehow seems to be related to Richard. I think if I needed a [Sponsor], it was probably him." As I said the words out loud, I knew they were right. Richard was my [Sponsor]. Another piece of the puzzle snapped into place.

"That's an odd class name," Tandy said thoughtfully. "I've got [Magic Weaver] which, as far as I can tell, has nothing to do with magic *or* weaving. But, since I was such a high-level [Weaver], I'm getting the impression that I might qualify as my own [Sponsor]."

It made sense if the purpose of a [Sponsor] was to somehow ground us in progression and knowledge. Tandy obviously knew how to progress a class.

All of our eyes swung to Leo.

"I'm just a [Fighter]." He shrugged. "Nothing special, but it's a class." It was a class. Generic, but solid. We needed someone capable of dealing damage. My class was specialized, but I wasn't sure it was helpful.

Maybe Leo didn't need a [Sponsor] because his class was so basic?

"I'm just [Adventurer] until I get a [Sponsor]," Meredeath added glumly. I wondered if the [System] had let her keep any of her cat-like skills.

Richard continued to groom himself. His only contribution was the sound of his sandpapery tongue as it was applied to his body. Eventually, I turned off the molten quality of my hammer. The barn was stuffy, but we'd gathered some hay to pad under our bedrolls. It was comfortable enough.

Exhausted, I dozed off.

I woke to screaming.

Chapter 35

TREE'S COMPANY

"It bit me! Oh my god, I'm going to die."

I don't know what I'd been dreaming, but Meredeath's panicked voice pumped adrenaline through my veins. I grabbed my hammer, triggering the [Molten] effect. The loft flared with light, blinding us all. Shit.

"What is it? I can't see anything." Leo's voice was loud, and I could see him clutching his axe. What I couldn't find were any monsters.

"It's a *rat!*"

Oh. Just a rat? What was the big deal? My muscles relaxed. Did they not have rats on Meredeath's world?

"It's got rabies." Her voice was frantic. "It's foaming at the mouth."

What was the big deal? Barns had critters, and rats weren't uncommon. Sure, it wasn't great that they'd gotten [Diseased], but no one died of rat bites.

"Found it," Leo called out and, with a meaty thunk, the rat was finished.

As my vision slowly returned, Tandy was kneeling, looking at the bite on Meredeath's ankle. Two thin lines of blood dribbled from the wound.

"I don't see what the big deal is. It was probably just after the food in our packs." I'd learned a long time ago that it wasn't worth the hassle to hide a snack in my room. There were too many hungry mouths in the wild.

"It was *foaming at the mouth.* [Diseased]. It had rabies," Meredeath said, choking the words out. "I don't imagine you have rabies shots? A lab to test it?"

Remind me never to foam at the mouth.

I had no idea what rabies was, but I agreed with Richard. No foaming at the mouth.

"No," I said, the word carefully. "But if you've got a [Diseased] state, we can get a [Cure Disease] potion for you. They don't cost much."

Meredeath looked up at me, eyes streaked with tears. Her hair was tangled, and she looked miserable.

"[Cure Disease] potion?" The word came out snuffled.

I kneeled next to her, handing over a handkerchief Leo'd dug out of his pack. "Yeah, check your status. Do you need one? We always have a few on hand out here."

Meredeath got a distant look as she checked her stat sheet. The three of us shared a look.

Tandy went over to inspect the rat.

"I don't think I'm [Diseased]," Meredeath delivered the news we were all expecting.

"Can you die from a rat bite in your world?" I asked quietly. Her world sounded awful.

"Yeah, rats have been responsible for a lot of disease. A lot of death. How many children has your mom had?" Meredeath asked quietly.

"Six." Was this a trick question? She'd met all my siblings

last night. Morning had broken over the farm, and the first notes of dawn could be heard out the window.

"No one died in childhood?" Meredeath's voice was shocked.

Leo, Tandy, and I looked at each other. What kind of world did Meredeath come from? Any thought I had about wanting to visit her world evaporated with the thought of dead children taken down by an errant rat bite.

After the shock of waking, getting ready to go happened quickly. I wanted to get out of the barn before my family finished breakfast. As we climbed down from the loft, a basket of food sat undisturbed on the stairs. A brief note from Share was pinned to it.

Come back safe. The wedding is on the fall equinox.

I tucked the note into my bag as we divvied up the supplies. I would do anything to make her wedding. We'd had a long, cold spring so far. Coming back in five months for it should be manageable. Maybe Mom and Flo would calm down by then.

It was time to go.

No one wished us farewell, not wanting to dare Flo's wrath. I'd deal with that trauma when I came back for the equinox.

My first problem was going to be the swamp and the bone lady. I'd handle my family *later*.

Tall fence posts followed us to the edge of the property. Each one was set by hand. I paused for a moment, wishing my family well. My mom may have disowned me, but I was going to be back. I had a map to find the way and a wedding to give me a reason.

It didn't take us long to backtrack along the two-track to get to the main road south. If we followed it south, it'd take us all the way down to Dusridge. I'd only been down there a couple of times for the regional fair.

"It's time to cut east," Tandy said. The mid-morning sun hit her auburn hair, highlighting the red in her braids.

The finger of dread in my gut spiked.

"Are you sure?" Leo asked, white-faced.

We all pulled out our mental maps. Sure enough, we'd gone as far south as needed. Any further, and we'd have to backtrack north to get to the bone lady's swamp. My dad's map didn't have any details, just a loose blob marked with the skull and crossbones. Everyone knew where the swamp was, even if no one went there.

We all started off the road. Bramble had taken over the understory of the forest. It was going to be a hard push with no trails.

"I'll go first," Leo stated, as though trying to affirm that he *wanted* to do this. None of us wanted this.

Leo swung his axe, slicing through the bramble in an arc. The elderberry and creeper parted from his blade, almost leaning away as it sang. Meredeath stood behind him, and I took the rear position with Richard watching our backs.

Meredeath and Tandy both held bare blades. I kept a hand on my hammer and scanned the brush with my eyes. None of us really knew what to expect, but we were determined not to be surprised.

"Any words of advice, Richard?" I murmured to my companion.

Go without me? For all his bluster, he was terrified of the bone lady. His little body scrunched closer to my neck, and he quaked like an aspen in the breeze.

"I can just leave you right here." I gestured to one of the low-hanging branches covered in moss. "If that's what you really want."

No, I go where you go.

A glob of anxiety-induced slime slithered down my back. I almost wish he'd agreed to stay.

The ground was wet, even this far west. On the map, it

showed the swamp starting a few more miles in, but it was obviously wrong. The dampness pointed to changes in the landscape that didn't bode well for our quest.

The sun was high in the sky, which was perfect. We didn't need to be doing this at night.

An hour of brush clearing and careful steps through the growing mud got us to the true edge of the swamp.

The forest gave way to a waterlogged landscape. The trees were fewer and less healthy, and reeds dominated the landscape with pools of water lilies bobbing in the sun. It looked like a swamp, if I was being honest. It didn't look particularly haunted or deadly, as bugs buzzed us in the heat.

Leo smacked his bicep, squishing one of the innumerable mosquitoes.

"Alright, where to next?" Leo asked. The swamp was vast, extending east into a large valley between two ridges that descended from the mountains. It was a fair question, but I had no idea.

She lives at the apex of the valley.

"And how do you know that?" Tandy's question was sharp. She was done with Richard pussyfooting around the quest, and Richard sensed it.

We knew each other.

"No shit, tell me something I don't already know." Tandy's tone sent Richard scrunching up further behind my neck.

How about I tell you later?

"I think now is a good time." Tandy was determined.

"I agree with Richard on this one. Let's deal with this first," I said as lights started dancing in the marsh behind Tandy. She turned to see what I was staring at when the water by my feet began to move.

We'd found the tidemaw.

"Okay, don't touch any of the trees," I said, as I stopped myself from reaching out to a trunk for balance. "What other tips do we have on defeating this creature?"

I'd suggest running away.

The ground yanked at my feet, and a tree branch swept by my head, catapulting Richard into the swamp. All of us were thrown to the ground, as I watched an almost magically enhanced airborne Richard.

I take it baaaack! His mental shout echoed in our heads as he flew tail over antenna. *Fight the monster! It's a giant water bladder with teeth!*

The splut of his landing must have knocked him out as his mental voice went silent.

Well, shit.

If I could climb a tree and get a better look at the maw, I could [Analyze] it.

I triggered [Analyze] on one of the trees within reach.

[Velcroak tree - This vine-covered tree has fast-drying sap that traps insects and small animals. This tree is hungry. Larger mammals should be wary, as they may also be deemed prey.]

Nope, that one wouldn't work.

[Gloomsap - A cursed tree grown only at the base of a tombstone. This semi-sentient tree hungers for the world of the living. Anyone unfortunate enough to fall for its wiles will find themselves eternally entombed.]

"Guys, we definitely want to stay away from the trees," I called out, just as Tandy pulled herself up on a small island. A velcroak stood next to her as she carefully leaned away from it. The tree looked *hungry*.

I saw another tree, shorter, that was looking healthier. I triggered [Analyze].

[Mawthorn - Typically grows near tidemaws. This bark-skinned mimic masquerades as a tree. Its sap is a digestive lure that numbs and dulls the screams.]

It wasn't Rhi Voss we had to worry about, it's the fucking trees. None of the trees in the swamp were friendly. I looked back towards the forest we'd left.

[Sickened Cedar - This cedar has been subjected to a flood or a change in landscape. It is sickly and will succumb to death if environmental factors are not changed.]

That would work. I stood up, covered in mud, and slogged against the deadly current. Tandy and Leo had grabbed onto clumps of reeds, holding themselves in place. Meredeath stood with her feet apart, a dagger in hand.

I moved, each step hard won as the swamp sucked at my boots. Finally, my feet came out of the mud, and I started climbing the gnarled bark of the cedar. It twisted up, branches extending out like a ladder. The tree was made for climbing.

I scrambled, the sweet scent of cedar enveloping me, as though the horror of the swamp didn't lie a few feet below.

I climbed twenty, then thirty feet. The tree waved in the air under my weight. Wedging in place, I hugged the trunk like it was my lifeline and peered out over the swamp.

The boggy landscape spanned miles towards the Ursine Wall, with clumps of trees forming small islands, while reeds and lilies bobbed in the deeper water. What hadn't been evident was the bone-colored ruins of an ancient town strewn across the valley.

Not a town. I squinted hard, trying to decipher the pattern. Square sets of blocks sat silently, a testament to what? A graveyard? An ancient, expansive graveyard? My mind reeled at the scale of the place. How many died here?

The tidemaw was evident from my position. The mouth gaped open like the ground itself had grown teeth. A notably empty pool of water sat at the heart of the beast. Its body sank low into the ground as though it'd carved a giant sinkhole as a home. I could see Richard, a speck of yellow trapped between a set of reeds.

Triggering [Analyze], I got the following:

[[Corrupt] Tidemaw - Normally at home in ocean-based marshes, this tidemaw is far from home. These creatures typically use and control local tides to draw larvae and other small biological life to their maw, filtering through the creatures like a whale. [Corruption] has led to a shift in the maw's diet to larger wildlife, including humans. The ancient maw's appetite is insatiable. Extending several stories deep, the ravenous beast contains enough water to hold the local swamp in its thrall.]

I tried imagining the shape of the tidemaw. Large, bloated, full of water. The monster sat stationary below the waterline and used its skills to control water levels, currents, and tides to draw prey towards its maw.

It was nothing but a ballooned stomach, full of hunger. Ready to pop.

"Leo, I'm going to need to borrow your axe," I called out as I climbed down the cedar.

I had a terrible idea. It was time to burst some expectations.

Chapter 36

MISSED CHOPPORTUNITY

"I'm not giving you Miss Chopportunity unless you tell me what you're going to do with her." Leo held his [Superior Enchanted Axe of Singing] close, petting it lovingly.

Damn it. There was no way he'd give me his axe if I told him what I was *actually* planning on doing with it. I had to come up with an alternative plan.

"You're calling your axe Miss Chopportunity?" Tandy asked.

"It *works*. She's Choppy for short." Leo held the double-bladed axe as though it'd saved his life. I guess that wasn't far off from the truth. It made me wonder what Ched had named her.

I needed them to stay distracted while I came up with another solution.

"You could have gone with Miss Cleava," I said with a grin. Leo's penchant for cleavage was well known.

Leo looked at Choppy, considering.

Meredeath smacked my arm. "What about a *guy's* name? Jack the Ripper has a nice ring to it."

"Why Jack?" Leo asked, confused.

Meredeath was distracting everyone with descriptions of a rather gruesome part of her world's history while I was free to cast about for another option. Her world really did sound scary.

My hammer wasn't the right tool for the job. I concentrated, and the hammer shifted to its [Pick] form. It was pointy, but not great for slicing. I needed a pointy, edged weapon that could puncture and rip through flesh.

I eyed Meredeath's daggers and Tandy's glowing scissors. Either might work, but I wasn't sure I'd survive an attempt to swipe them. Looking for inspiration, I scanned the ground.

A suspiciously pointy stick sat a few feet away from me. The bark was rough, curling up as though it wanted to slice into an unsuspecting hand or foot. I triggered [Analyze]. The description of the stick popped into my vision:

[Cutwood - This branch is from a cutwood tree, known for its razor-sharp tendencies. This tree can cut a hole right through a person or just as easily cut them in half. Cutwood splinters can be deadly if they enter the bloodstream and take root.]

This was precisely what I needed—something sharp and cutting.

"Meredeath, can you hold this?" I handed her [Guardian's Promise]. I'd have to think of a snappier name for it if I survived.

"Sure?" She took the hammer and promptly dropped it. Her hands kept slipping from the handle. The hammer's soul bound nature repelled her.

I bent low and picked up the cutwood carefully, immediately regretting the decision as the thick base bit into my hand. Damn, these trees didn't mess around. I dug through my bag, finding a strip of cloth to wrap around the base for grip. It was already bloody.

Leaving my pack on the ground, I took off towards the tidemaw.

My sprint quickly aborted as the mud sucked at my feet. I slowly made my escape one heavy footstep at a time.

I imagined Richard's voice taunting me: *You really thought that through, champ.*

"Shut up," I muttered to my [Self Critic].

I had been banking on the race to my death being a quick, ill-thought-out decision. Instead, I slogged forward, muck sluicing into my boots. Plenty of time to doubt. Plenty of time for everyone to figure out what I was attempting.

"Cole, where are you going?" Tandy called. I could hear her soggy footsteps behind me.

"It's pretty obvious," I said, glancing back. She was having a worse time than I was. Leo stood looking dumbfounded, and Meredeath looked pissed as she awkwardly held my hammer.

Blood dripped from my injured hand. This caused malformed trees to reach for me. They leaned in, circling like sharks smelling blood in the water.

"Go back, Tandy. I'm going to take care of the tidemaw." She was going to get herself killed. I was barely staying out of the trees' reach.

"With a stick?" Tandy's incredulity hurt. She thought I was going to get myself killed.

"Well, I could have used Miss Chopportunity, but yes," I said, taking two more squishy steps.

The trees leaned down, branches reaching for a juicy snack. I swung the cutwood overhead like an axe, and each questing branch danced away. Maybe the cutwood *could* do the job.

"You don't have to do this. You can't take on the tidemaw by yourself." Tandy's voice was distant.

I looked back, surprised to find that she'd actually stopped following. A cut on her forehead dripped blood down her face.

Leo took a few steps towards us, leaning away from a Velcroak. He was already stuck, his heavy frame sinking even further in the morass. Tandy stood halfway between us, wiping at her brow, frowning in disapproval. Meredeath blew me a kiss, waving one pointed finger at me in salute.

This was my shot. Slow or not, none of them were going to catch me. I turned my eyes ahead.

Anxiety threatened to freeze me in place, and I could feel [Self Critic] triggering. It was my turn to contribute, to show my value. If I really had any.

I looked ahead at the dark pool of water. My plan could work. It would work. I took another step, building my resolve.

It was my turn to be useful, even if I was [Dead Wrong].

The air was thicker, ripe with the heated exhale of the tidemaw. Humidity slithered into my lungs and clung like the last gasp of winter flu. The trees leaked sap as if they were ready for harvest.

The pull of the beast was drawing at my feet. Everything—the mud, the trees, the ancient tombstones strewn across the landscape—pulled towards the dark heart of the swamp.

The mud was losing the battle, sliding into the maw. Soon, I'd be at the point of no return. My feet slowly took me near Richard's prone form. I grabbed him by the tail with my free hand and used [Slug Toss] to chuck him towards the team.

"Is that Richard?" Leo yelled as the skill sent Richard whipping through the air.

I blocked him out. I was on a mission to prove I wasn't *just* deadweight on the team. Hopefully, Richard would stick with them even if I wasn't around.

I tried to pull up to slow my descent into the maw. But my feet couldn't gain purchase. The tidemaw's suction was too great. I fell back, trying to use my hands to gain traction in the mud.

My efforts were fruitless. The ground gave way underneath the water, sloping towards the beast. I'd hit the point of no return.

The trees, the fallen logs, the rectangular stones in the bog, everything, was falling *inward.* My eyes were drawn to the faded inscriptions in an unknown language. What had killed so many people?

A large sarcophagus sat stuck in the mud, right at the aperture of the tidemaw's mouth. I tried aiming my slide towards the stone box, using my cutwood stick as leverage.

The sarcophagus was open, the top plate missing, but the base was stubbornly wedged as though it protested giving its charge to the beast. I hit the edge and tumbled straight into the coffin, landing face-to-face with a papery corpse.

Her sunken eyes stared sightlessly at me. The woman lay with a pearl cord wrapped around her head, keeping shimmering blue hair from her leathery face. She must have been royalty, a princess deserving of a full tomb. She smelled of brine, lavender, and dust. A crushed velvet dress covered her body even as it decayed.

It would be my luck to survive the tidemaw only to gain an eternal curse from a pissed-off princess from a long-forgotten country. But I wasn't afraid. Her face held peace, not horror.

No time to think of the impropriety of disturbing the grave. I sent a silent wish for forgiveness to the Everbear as I tried to change position to view the tidemaw's vortex.

The mud and water rushed around us as the tidemaw began swallowing the swamp. It was as though the beast could smell mortals in its territory and was eager for souls. It wanted me. Hungered for my friends. I could feel it in my bones.

Thankfully, I still clutched the cutwood. Blood ran freely from the slices in my hand. It was part of me and, by the slivers, I could feel worming their way into my palm. I was part of it.

The sarcophagus had tipped almost forty-five degrees, so I

got a good view of the fate awaiting anyone who fell in. Three rows of serrated teeth were full of debris. In the center was a dark pool of water with chunks of trees and meat bobbing. Each inhale of the beast sent ripples through the swamp. It was hungry, starving.

The tidemaw's mouth was almost thirty yards across. Its body was set deep in the ground. Teeth sat like breakers filtering out debris and mud. In the center, the pool sat dark and clear, as though all the muck had been filtered out.

I could jump past the teeth if I had a little more leverage. A stump struck hard against the sarcophagus, tilting it further towards the teeth.

I looked over at the mummy. Two gaping holes sat in an ancient face framed with tendrils of shimmering blue hair.

"I'm sorry," I told her as I stepped over the mummified body, trying to angle myself for the jump.

My instincts shouted at me that this was suicide. My heart pounded in my chest, answering the fear. I thought of Tandy and Leo here, trying to take down the beast, and of Meredeath with two tiny daggers.

Clenching the cutwood, I laughed as it looked like a mere toothpick to the beast. I would sacrifice myself any day to save my friends, and it looked like today was the day.

I went to leap, but five bony fingers wrapped around my forearm. In horror, I looked back. The mummy lay out, looking as dead as ever, but gripped my arm hard. The other hand held a silver ring with an aquamarine stone. It shimmered, beckoned.

Was this really happening? Was I robbing the dead? Or was she gifting it to me? It looked like a gift. Maybe I'd finally lost it under all the pressure.

I reached for the proffered gift. As my hand touched the ring, a spark shot through my arm. Jerking, my fingers spasmed, grabbing it without another thought. The silver ring slipped onto my finger as the ground heaved.

A gushing spout of water sent the mummy, sarcophagus, and me soaring through the air.

The bony hand broke free, as though it'd used its last bit of life to give me the gift. The woman's papery face began disintegrating before my eyes.

I took a couple of deep breaths, ignoring the urge to cough out the suddenly dusty air.

And as my body flew, I got one last glimpse of my friends in the distance. Leo's pink sweater stood out against the browns and greens of the swamp. He was cradling Richard like a baby. Meredeath and Tandy shaded their eyes as they watched me cartwheel into the tidemaw.

I hit the water with a splash, the ring on a finger, mummy dust in my lungs, and cutwood firmly grasped. The sarcophagus hit the water above me, which was exactly what I needed. I wedged my body under the stone as it sank. The rest of the mummy was lost in bubbles.

I sent silent thanks as I used its final resting place to facilitate my plan.

The sarcophagus's weight helped me sink fast. The mouth of the monster was a whirlwind of debris and bubbles. Bits of monstrous trees bit, struck, sapped me as everything sank.

It was hard to see anything or even keep track of which way was up, except for the weight of the stone above my body.

It was getting harder to hold my breath, harder to hold on. I refused to inhale.

A log rammed into my gut, knocking the remaining air out of me.

It must have been a gloomsap because the log stuck to me and dragged me *down* as I struggled to breathe. My ears popped, and I couldn't stop myself from inhaling. Water filled my throat and lungs as I started coughing. My health bar dropped rapidly as I drowned.

The log took any escape I had in mind out of my hands.

As I kept sinking, my only thought was to hold the cutwood tight. I was only going to get one chance.

What in the ever-living sea slug are you doing?

Bubbles left my mouth as I smiled. Richard was finally awake.

It was right that he witnessed my heroism *and* my stupidity.

Water filled my lungs.

Chapter 37

[DEAD WRONG]

The thing about a skill that triggers on death is that there's no great way to test it.

The real problem is that the description of the skill was pretty frustrating.

[[Cheat Death]: is a passive skill that automatically triggers you to cheat fatal damage once per day. The methods of cheating death vary. Use at your own risk.]

On the positive side, it was passive. So, if death snuck up on me, it still would have saved my life. On the other hand, 'use at your own risk' was kind of a dick move. What did that even mean?

You're a moronic sea slug! Richard was letting me know just how stupid he thought I was as I drowned.

Each health point drop came with the panicky sensation of choking on swamp water.

Congratulations, Cole, you've been outsmarted by a sentient puddle.

I'm sure it didn't take that long for me to die but, from my perspective, it was an eternity punctuated by a particularly annoying slug.

Finally, the notification triggered:

[You, Cole Thornfield, are [Dead].]

This time, instead of being deposited out of a dungeon portal, I materialized in a room. The room had no door, just a straw bed and an empty desk with an uncomfortable looking wooden chair. It didn't shout 'prison cell,' but it didn't scream 'comfortable eternity' either.

I examined the walls. They weren't made of brick or wood, nothing I recognized. They were just there, smooth, as if someone had created the idea of a room without thinking through the details.

[You're Richard's pet, are you not?]

"I guess? He is my [Companion]." The words stuck dry in my throat. Was I talking to the all-knowing [System] itself?

[Would you give up your class [Dead Wrong] for another one? The options I will present to you will be personally advantageous, I guarantee it.]

I didn't need Richard on my shoulder to tell me that whatever the [System] was going to offer me was likely going to be a terrible deal. No one giving a good deal had to tell you it was good.

"I like my class," I said as confidently as I could manage, considering I was still technically dead.

[How about Richard? What if I offered you a [Heroic] class? Would you give up Richard?]

The [System] sounded annoyed, but tired. There was nothing in the world that would make me give up my friends and, unfortunately, I counted Richard a friend.

"Sorry, can't do that either."

Silence. I stood up, stretching. My clothes were dry, if a bit tattered. The whirlpool had taken its toll. I still had the princess's ring on my finger, and a good-sized aquamarine sparkled at me. I tried to use [Analyze], but none of my skills seemed available.

"How long is this going to take?" I didn't bother hiding my irritation.

[How long is it going to take for you to be reasonable?]

I laughed, bluffing through my teeth. "My last name isn't Thornfield for nothing."

The [System] didn't seem impressed.

"Look, I deal with Richard every day." I sat down and picked at my fingernails. I could almost hear the cussing at my nonchalance. Maybe Richard had been rubbing off on me.

[I will return to you as soon as the changes are complete.]

"What changes? I didn't agree—" My words cut off as I started screaming. It felt like razor blades had been applied to my neck and tiny splinters poked at my lungs. I could feel tissue slithering around in my chest.

Thankfully, I lost consciousness pretty quickly.

When I woke up, a notification blinked in my vision, red and urgent. Floating on a cloud, with only a couple of health points down, I decided to read it.

[Cheat Death] has triggered.

[Blessing of the Waters] has triggered.

[Skill Acquired: You have gained a new [Dead Wrong] skill, [Gills]. This skill was acquired through a combination of [Cheat Death] and [Blessing of the Waters]. You have a permanent body augment that allows you to breathe underwater while retaining your ability to breathe out of water. The cost, however, is a decrease in stamina as one lung is dedicated to each activity. Additionally, you have gained a preference for moist environments.]

I opened my eyes to find what my body already claimed: that I was underwater. Deep underwater.

I took a breath. Cool water slithered into my neck, the sensation tickling my throat. The liquid air filled my lung, giving me a sense of rightness even as my mind revolted at its alienness. The air tasted smoky, dirty, as though I was breathing in the smoke from a fire.

It *was* swamp water. And the gloom pressed in on me, the world dark, cold. It was new, but I was comfortable. I could execute my plan.

My hand no longer held the cutwood, but instead it'd barbed itself to my palm. I noted a [Bleeding] status. My health should have been slowly ticking down but, in my status bar, it held steady. Then my eye caught the dim sparkle of my ring. This time [Analyze] worked.

[[Blessings of the Waters] - This ring belonged to the most powerful [Water Mage] in an age, Leal Voss. It is imbued with magical properties including [Error], [Error], and [Error]. You do not have the correct class to utilize this ring fully. [Blessings of the Waters] is soul bound. A facet of this ring has been used by [Cheat Death] as a boon granted to [Cole Thornfield].]

Haunted by [Error] notifications, I could only imagine what they'd have said. Probably something useful like [Explode Swamp] or [Breathe Underwater without Gills]. Hell, I'd even settle for a [Summon Swamp Mommy]. Couldn't a guy catch a break?

The water shook as though triggered by my audacity.

My fingers wrapped around the cutwood. I still had a job to do.

I'd come awake exactly where I wanted to be, at the bottom of the tidemaw's stomach. I twisted my body, still breathing without actually taking a breath. I took my hungry stick and pressed it into the spongy bottom of the pool.

For a second, I thought my plan was going to fail. I felt [Self Critic] activating. I was really going to die in a puddle, wasn't I?

My hand loosened on the stick. I couldn't force it through the thick hide of the leviathan. What was I thinking? I closed my eyes in regret. This was it.

A swirl of water brushed my arms. The ring on my finger had started to glow. *Someone* had believed in me. My [Self Critic] fell away as I gripped the cutwood, driving it deeper.

Two feet of the stick disappeared into the monster's skin before everything changed.

Pop!

Water started rushing past me, rushing *out.* My cutwood ripped out of my hand, slicing its way towards freedom. Apparently, the wood believed the tidemaw worthier prey than me. The hole I'd made grew bigger, and I quickly had a different problem as I started to get sucked through.

I kicked off the bottom, trying to gain distance from the hole. My feet kicked hard as I swam against the ever-growing current.

Shit. My stamina was draining, and I had little to begin with. In all my grand scheming, I hadn't made a plan to survive, and now that I had, I wasn't ready to die. Panic clawed at my chest the way the water should have.

The sarcophagus had been thrown up in the turmoil. I grabbed its sides, pushing myself up, as it fell.

The thing saved me. It wedged right in the hole, stopping the flood of water. At least temporarily. I swam hard. My [Cheat Death] skill was on cooldown for the day, so I didn't have another free pass.

Legs kicking, I gained feet, then yards. I could see the sparkling sunlight through the debris. My stamina was tanking. I was so close.

An illogical eddy pulled at me. Swirling in the water, I caught a glimpse of a ghostly blue-haired nymph before I shot up.

My hands broke the surface, and suddenly I was choking on air. The gills on my neck spasmed as they dried out, then closed. The air was hot and humid, and thick in my working lung.

The sun shone brightly. It was a welcome sight. The

swamp hovered around the mouth of the maw, waiting for what was next.

I heard a distant shout. "Look, there he is!"

Shading my eyes, I saw Leo, Tandy, and Meredeath standing on a small island with a downed tree. I waved.

Then the sarcophagus must have burst through because the tidemaw spasmed again, and a great whirlpool formed. Helpless in its rotation, I started circling down the drain.

Each rotation brought me close to my friends for a few seconds as I sank lower in the water. I could hear them yelling, but couldn't make out any of the words.

My 'very detailed' plan to poke the tidemaw in the stomach ended right after I poked. I hadn't considered how it would play out. I think part of my brain imagined a dungeon creature disappearing and leaving its loot behind.

We weren't in a dungeon, though. This was real.

Something attacked my head. I flailed for a moment, dunking into the water. Trapped beneath the monster's sticky grip. It pulled at me, tugging me through the water like a sinker on a fishing line. I realized, after swallowing more than a bit of the swamp water that it was a sticky net that I was trapped in.

"Cole, we're going to try to pull you up," Leo shouted above the sounds of the tidemaw.

I just gave a thumbs-up. Their net solution would have drowned me without the [Gills]. Win? I guess.

The net pulled me up out of the water, against the spongy dark blue gums of the beast. Another pull and I'd be right on top of the first ridge of teeth. I suddenly wasn't too sure of their plan.

"Uh, guys... It's going to shred me!" I yelled as they pulled me closer. I was surprised the teeth did not fray the rope as it rubbed against them. The line glistened with a substance, or maybe magic? A skill of Tandy's?

"Just hold on, try to get your feet against the side of the mouth," Tandy called.

I twisted, sticking my arms through the net, trying to get as firm a grip as I could. It wasn't hard. The sticky, blue substance in the net helped hold me in place. With my feet braced, I had a better view as Tandy unrolled her bedroll across the teeth.

Tandy must have kept some of her weaving skills as the blanket tripled in length. With a firm yank, I was walking up the gums of the beast. As my foot hit the blanket, it fluffed up and hardened, almost like a wooden plank. I danced over the teeth, holding onto the net as my friends hauled me out of the maw.

For the second time in a week, I survived being swallowed by a leviathan.

As they pulled, I stepped over one set of teeth, then the next, and was almost vertical in my ascent. The tidemaw seemed to be closing its mouth more and more as the inner pool drained. By the time I was on the thin, bulbous skin that had to be its lips, I was ten feet in the air.

Below me stood my friends, sweaty and covered in mud. Leo anchored the rope I was climbing by tying it around his waist. He dug his heels in the mud, having slid in the endeavor to rescue me.

Tandy's eyes looked to be rolled up in her head as her hands stretched out, sending waves of skill power into the rope and bedroll. Meredeath hovered between the two, ready to leap into action if either faltered. Richard sat on her shoulders, looking woozy but alert. My friends had saved me.

Get down here before it snaps shut and you become its last meal.

Leave it to Richard to bring me back to reality.

I glanced back. The whirlpool had expanded and was furious. Down in the center stood a figure. My eyes squinted. It was the blue-haired mummy, except she was brought back to life. Her hair and dress tossed in the wind as she spun in time with the whirlpool. It was as though she stood vigil, overseeing the last moments of the tidemaw's life.

I touched the ring on my finger. She looked up at me and gave a nod. It may have been my imagination, but it felt like she was giving thanks.

Then with a pearly grin she waved a hand. A splash of water rose, hitting me square in the chest, sending me flying over the lip of the maw. Tumbling down, I fell ten feet, hitting the ground with a dull splut, sinking up to my waist in the muck.

I give that landing a 7 out of 10.

"I hate you, too, Richard."

Chapter 38

I'M NOT CRYING, YOU'RE CRYING

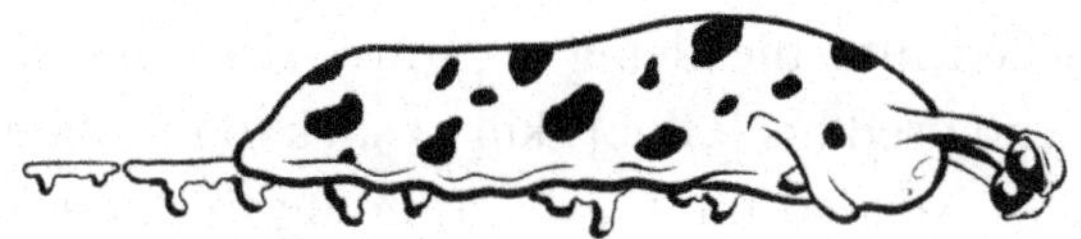

Tidemaws are giant leviathans who sit in river deltas and salt marshes. They slowly burrow into the ground, expanding their bodies and control over the local water. The creatures get their names because they can influence the tides, drawing prey in or pushing potential predators out.

Our tidemaw was a giant among leviathans, controlling almost the entirety of the swamp with its moist breath, drawing more than one curious explorer towards its mouth with dancing lights.

Tidemaws, while classified as monsters, mostly preyed on bugs, small animals, and water creatures. They existed much like the brushcomb whales of the deep ocean. My stashed monster compendium backed up my [Analyze] skill.

This one had been different, influenced by the [Corruption] spilling over the Ursine Wall. It was twisted, reveling in human flesh, in the draw and trap of sentient life. I wasn't sad to see its life end, but as I fingered the now-closed slits along my neck, I knew that killing a legend didn't leave me unscathed.

The tidemaw's death throes were long and violent. It opened and closed its mouth, as though snapping for the life draining from it.

I had a front seat to the tidal forces, as no one was able to pull me out of the muck. Waves of water gushed out of the beast, followed by moments the ground almost tilted as suction drew moisture down.

Everyone else had to retreat to higher ground or risk getting sucked into the dying creature. Everyone that is, but Richard, who used his [Glue] skill to stick to my shoulders.

At first, I worried the maw was going to drain the swamp with it, but it died with its jaws clenched shut. A tall wall of warty skin shut tight, leaving a giant green mound where the dark pool of death had been.

[[Corrupt] Tidemaw defeated. You have earned experience.]

[Quest Granted: [Legacy of Lael Voss]

You have defeated the [Corrupt] [Companion] of Lael Voss, earning her undying gratitude. This completes the first half of the [Legacy of Lael Voss] quest. To complete Lael's legacy, talk to Rhi Voss. If you are successful in obtaining [Lael's Key], return to her workshop and clear out the [Corruption] to complete the quest. Adventure Onward!]

Great, another quest. If that was Lael's [Companion], I didn't want to know what waited in her workshop.

If I have to get covered in muck one more time, I'll quit.

We'd been through several rounds of water receding, then flooding over us, then receding. Richard had kept using his [Clean] skill to wipe the muck off every time. He refused to use it on me, however, insisting I deserved to be covered in swamp much. So, I looked like a bog monster out for revenge.

"You could have left. I'm sure Meredeath would have

taken good care of you." I said the words calmly, refusing to bite the bait. Richard was fine.

Every time I let you out of my sight, you die.

I didn't have a rebuttal of that. He was right.

"At least I don't stay dead?" I wiped muck from my eyes. I was tired of the smell of half-rotten vegetation and the mud in my boots. Of being dirty. There was grit in my gills.

Yes, but [Gills]? What are you, a sea slug? Richard shuddered, as though nothing in the world was worse than a sea slug. He had his hang-ups.

I didn't know what I was anymore. Was I human? I had *gills*. Sure, it was associated with a skill, but skills rarely altered a person's physical appearance. Maybe I *was* becoming a swamp monster.

"Richard, can you explain to me why I have [Gills]? Skills aren't supposed to work like that, are they?" I was proud that my voice quavered only a little. I was alive, for which I *should* be grateful, but I wasn't sure [Cheat Death] was something I wanted to use if it was going to change me like this.

I was hoping we could avoid this question for a while. What do you say? Could you refrain from dying in the immediate future? Are you even capable of that?

"You planned for me to have [Gills]?" Everything I thought I'd pieced together about Richard was falling apart.

No, the body augment. [Cheat Death] is an obnoxious skill if you are not careful with it. And you've been anything but cautious.

"It's going to be a bit before the rest of them join us, and I'm stuck. So let's have the conversation now."

Richard undulated, moving from his shoulder perch. The swamp was still wet, but it was drier than it had been with the tidemaw dead. The muck around my body had dried, cementing me in place. Once everyone was back, they would have to help dig me out.

Richard oozed his way onto the wet mud and perched himself across from me on a bit of bark.

His yellow skin stood out in bright contrast to the rest of the grays and browns of the landscape. Richard's tentacles extended towards me, as though asking for patience. This conversation was long overdue.

What do you want to know first?

I had a hundred questions that had piled up. It was rare that I got any alone time with my slug.

"Am I *your* pet?" The question I was most afraid of bubbled out of me. When the [System] said it, I thought it was making fun of me. I'm sure it was, but I was afraid there was truth in its taunting.

That's a strange idea. Where'd you come up with that?

He dodged the question. Was I the pet of a slug?

"The [System] and I had a little chat after [Cheat Death] triggered." My words were tight.

Richard stood before me, his foot-long body glistening. His skin rippled, something I'd come to associate with discomfort.

The [System] is a world-class dick.

"Takes one to know one."

I don't know why the idea bothered me so much. It'd become apparent that while his powers weren't terribly helpful, Richard was somehow much more powerful than any of us. He'd been around for a *long* time. Hell, he claimed to *know* the bone lady. He called the *[System]* a jerk. Who did that?

But I was hoping that in becoming an [Adventurer] and surviving the [Trial Dungeon] that I'd finally step out into my own. I wasn't broken, I wasn't weak, I wasn't the tag-along. I was Cole, the [Adventurer]!

That's why the truth hurt. I was still just an extra, an add-on to Richard. Survived by chance, mainly because Richard and Meredeath protected me.

I looked at the fanged banana slug coldly. The slug's antenna drooped. The dark spots on his hide were dull and washed out.

So we're linked. We're [Companions]. Does it matter who's 'in charge?' We're both entities with agency, wants, and dreams.

He was my owner. I'd been relegated to the role of a pet.

The realization was like a boulder hitting a lake. Ripples of change raced across my mind, reassigning meaning to our interactions, to my class choices, to my role on the team.

"Are you [Immortal]?" I asked, chickening out on the question I needed answered. My guts quivered as I tried to build up the nerve to ask what I truly needed to know.

I'm not dead yet.

"That's not an answer."

It's remarkably hard to prove [Immortality]. I haven't died yet, that's the best answer I can give.

I hadn't died either, but it didn't mean I was [Immortal].

"Why me?" I wasn't proud that I'd asked. I wasn't proud of how much I needed the answer to be something special. Something that set me apart. Made me unique.

You said yes.

Had I? I don't remember the [System] *asking* me if I wanted a yellow asshole following me around. Or me following him around.

"Does that mean I could say no now?"

You always have the right to say no.

[Please confirm: You wish to terminate [Companion] and [Sponsor] relationships with [Richard, the Fanged Banana Slug]?]

The pop-up notification hung in my vision. I thought about it and made a choice.

[Your relationship with [Richard, the Fanged Banana Slug] has been terminated. You have lost the class [Dead Wrong] and associated skills, you have lost the effect [Weak], you have lost the skill [Companion], you are no longer in [Your Mom's Party], you have lost [Partial Rapport], [Slug Toss] and [Minor Manipulate Slime].]

[Quest Granted: [Find a Sponsor]

Congratulations on passing the [Trial Dungeon] as an [Expeditionary Force]. You have lost the [Sponsor] for your specialized [Adventurer] class. You must find an appropriate sponsor for an [Adventurer] class that you are qualified for. You have [1 month] to complete this task. Failure to do so will result in a return to a [Mundane] status. Adventure Onward!]

I watched as my health, stamina, and mana bars ticked up a hair. I flexed my arm muscles, feeling powerful, and stronger than I'd felt in a long time.

"Had you been holding me back this whole time with a [Weakness] debuff?" I was angry and embarrassed. Betrayed.

Richard stared at me, his tentacles drooping.

Slugs don't win by might. We're tenacious. Survivors.

Tenacious liars.

If I could have walked away, I would have. But I was cemented in dried mud.

The voices of my friends filtered through the forest, it'd been a bit since the last dying spasm from the tidemaw.

Richard's head drooped, and I resisted the instinct to make a consolatory joke. To make him feel better about the role he'd put me in. This wasn't my story. It was his.

Half sunk into the ground, I didn't have a great view of the forest, but I heard Tandy laugh. That'd been rare these last few years. She'd been pulled further and further into her family's plans for domination of the weaver trade. Their family dynasty. It was good to hear her laugh.

I needed to figure out whether that was enough for me.

Meredeath rounded the corner first. When she saw me, her face lit up with a smile.

"Looks like you're still stuck," Leo said, teasing me.

"I could use some help," I admitted, plastering on a fake grin. "Turns out a slug [Companion] isn't so helpful at mud removal." I wondered vaguely whether [Companion] was even an appropriate word. *Master? Owner? [Sponsor]?* He was nothing now. Just a slug sitting on the log. "Also, Tandy, could you re-invite me to [Your Mom's Party]?"

I watched her expression as she frowned at the interface. "Sure, Cole. Did you do something? You're not showing up under R—the party drop-down anymore." She'd stuttered. Tandy almost said *under Richard.* She'd known this whole time I was Richard's pet?

A nugget of anger simmered in my chest. Had they all known?

I smothered the rage, pretending I hadn't heard her slip. I needed their help to get free of the mud.

As it turned out, no one was good at mud removal. Not without a shovel. It took the rest of the afternoon for us to free me, and by the end of it we all looked like bog monsters.

That night, we camped at the divide between the swamp and the forest. Richard clung to Meredeath, and she said something about him not feeling good. I couldn't hear him for once. There was no incessant commentary about how I was screwing it all up.

I turned my back to the fire, contemplating how I was going to get a new [Sponsor] and possibly some new friends.

Chapter 39

UNTIL YOU BELIEVE IT

Silence.

I didn't realize until that moment how much noise Richard created in my head. Like his slime, his thoughts tended to get in everything.

I'd fought my whole life for silence.

When I was a kid, I cherished every scrap of time I managed to get for myself. Even my loft space was rarely my own with Coulter, Hitch, or the animals taking up space. I'd go out into the woods trying to escape. Flo accused me of dodging chores, but that was only half of it.

When I left home, seeking that solitude, I realized silence was overrated. My mind filled the quiet for me.

I'm not sure if other people are like this. Never really talked to Tandy or Leo about it. Or Share, for that matter. But when I was alone, my brain took over. It's why I tried so hard to pick up [Meditation] to quiet the voices in my head.

That's when I picked up [Self Critic]. It was like my own personalized Flo took over.

Another reason why I had to leave Richard.

I sat in the chilly morning fog, looking out across the swamp. I'd agreed to take the early watch because I wanted this time alone.

Before the questions started.

To sit with my thoughts.

Meredeath moaned, caught in a nightmare. She'd done it every night she'd slept. I asked her whether she wanted me to wake her up. Her response still gave me a shiver.

"If you woke me up every time I have a nightmare, I'd never get any sleep," she said it dead-eyed, as though this was normal.

I ran my fingers across my neck, feeling the scaly gills on my skin. Maybe walking nightmares were the new normal.

The gills were now a permanent part of my body. A nightmare I couldn't escape. The gills fought my normal lungs. Everything worked, sure, but only just. Breathing felt like slipping air through a straw reed.

When the [System] notified me I was losing [Dead Wrong] and all the attributed skills, I'd hoped that [Gills] would go too. [Cheat Death], [Feign Death] and [Improvised Damage] had.

A cough wracked my body. I spat a wad of phlegm onto the dirt. My stamina was halved. It made sense with only half the lung capacity. But it making sense didn't make breathing easier.

The problem with becoming an [Adventurer] is that I'd lost most of my [Mundane] skills. So [Meditation] wasn't something I could trigger with a thought. I went back to my first lessons, sitting calmly. One eye scanned the swamp for threats, the other trying to find the inner peace I desperately needed.

"Hey."

I almost jumped out of my skin as Tandy sat down next to me on the log.

"You're supposed to be sleeping," I said, wondering why she was up.

Tandy ignored my question and started her first morning chore, unbraiding her hair. Unbraided, her hair sat in wild waves. I think her hair was as straight as a board, like mine, but a lifetime of weaving made it wild.

"Did you sleep much?" she asked as she too watched the swamp.

I hadn't, as I found it hard to get comfortable. I'd taken breathing for granted my entire life, and now that I couldn't seem to get a full breath, it was impossible not to think about.

"Not really," I admitted. We sat like that for a while, waiting for the other to continue.

A dull rumble rippled across the swamp.

"Does that still happen often?" Tandy asked.

"Yep," I replied. Ever since the tidemaw had died, the swamp seemed to be adapting to its new reality, or it was taking note of us, plotting our death. I wasn't sure what was going on, but I certainly didn't feel like talking about it.

Morning came late this close to the Ursine Wall. I stared off into the distance at the looming peaks, dark against the predawn light.

"Why'd you go off and fight the tidemaw alone?" Tandy's question wasn't the one I expected or wanted.

I played with a reed, bending the fibers back and forth, daring it to crack. "I wanted to prove to myself that I wasn't just a tag-along. That I belonged on a team with you, Leo, and Meredeath." I left Richard off, I wasn't sure any of us belonged on a team with him.

Tandy shook her head, running fingers through her hair. Bits of leaf and twig fell out. Once satisfied, she started her daily task of rebraiding the strands together.

"I think *I'm* the useless one," she said, surprising me

again. Before I could argue, she cut me off with a glance. "I have no real combat capabilities. And I've almost died a dozen times. I don't know what I'm doing most of the time, and I've lost most of the skills I'd earned as a [Weaver]. Objectively, I am the most useless in the party. You've at least killed a few monsters. I haven't even done that."

I thought back through the fights and realized she was technically right, but not really. Tandy hadn't earned a kill per se, but she'd saved my life more than a couple of times.

"You've pulled me out of death's jaws more times than Leo's stolen your scissors." I wheezed at the joke, my debuff deflating my laugh. "It just doesn't tally up the same way."

The crickets chirped. An owl hooted a farewell to the night.

"My value came from Richard," I said, my throat closing on his name. The truth was, I'd never had Richard. I was his. My dream of having a dire wolf someday seemed so childish. So out of the realm of possibility. I couldn't even be trusted with the charge of a slug.

"I'm sorry about that. I—we should have told you, but..." Tandy stopped braiding and turned to me. "The longer we waited, the more it was going to hurt. Cole, I love you like a brother. I know that means something different to you, you've got six actual siblings."

I tried to protest, but she stopped me.

"What I'm trying to say is that I don't have any siblings. You and Leo are it. You're my family. So, I'm going to say this as kindly as I can, because I think you need the truth."

I braced as she took a steadying breath.

"The problem isn't us. None of us has viewed you as a tag-along. Richard didn't seem to treat you like a pet. I mean, he's a jerk, but he treats us all like that." I forced my eyes to meet hers. "You're the one who needs to decide you belong here. You need to believe it."

That was it? I needed to believe in myself? If only I had thought of that.

"If only that were true." My self-deprecating laugh was thin as I looked back over the bog. A red-winged blackbird flew overhead, perching on a cattail. It let out a shrill call.

"It's true, and I'll be by your side until you figure out what you need to do to believe in yourself. But taking on crazy risks isn't it. You can't tell me you feel better about yourself now." I couldn't argue. She stood up, saving me the embarrassment of trying to hide my tears. "Come on, let's cook some breakfast. If we're going to face the bone lady, we might as well do it with a full stomach."

I stood, my knees creaking, quickly wiping away the evidence of our chat. "Thanks, Tandy."

"No problem. If we survive this, we need to sit down and have a real talk. I need to do something I should have done a long time ago."

"What's that?" I threw my reed into the grass, brushing off my pants.

"I'm going to tell you my family's progression secrets," she said confidently.

My breath hitched, and this time it wasn't the damn gills. Was she really going to tell us her secrets?

Over the years, both Leo and I had noticed how she watched us struggle with our broken builds. We never held her secrets against her. She'd wanted to tell us, that'd been obvious, but we knew her family wouldn't have forgiven her.

Leo snored as I got the fire going, and Tandy sliced up a couple of apples to add to the oatmeal.

"Do you think we'll find her today?" Meredeath asked as she sat up and stretched on her bedroll.

I blocked out Richard's voice. I could hear him now through the [Partial Rapport] since I was back at the party, but I didn't have to. The glory of it was that now I could choose to lock his voice out and, so far, I had.

"That's good," Tandy said. Which I surmised meant we'd make it. No one wanted to be in this swamp longer than a day.

"It'll be fine, Richard. If you want, we can leave you here. I can find Rhi Voss on my own." Meredeath looked up at the rest of us. "Honestly, that's true for all of you. You don't have to be here." She looked straight at me when she said it.

"I belong with the party as much as anyone." The words bubbled out of me. Why did she want to leave *me* behind?

"That's not what I meant. Damn it, Cole, you almost died in the tidemaw for me. This is *my* quest. *My* problem." I could tell Meredeath was angry, but I didn't understand why. She was clutching the pendant at her neck, and I realized it was glowing red under her hand.

"I didn't die, and going after the tidemaw was *my* choice, not yours," I said, trying to calm her down. I stepped closer, my hands out. Richard was still lying on the log next to her. "Everything's okay."

Meredeath's knuckles were turning white as she clutched at the skull pendant, her eyes had gained a red haze. I could see her jaw clenched, as though trying to prevent herself from saying something. Or...

"Are you taking damage?" I brought up our party interface to confirm. Yes, she'd dipped below 50%.

"I am," she said between clenched teeth. "Got to work off the Dunglord still, much less that damn bear."

I nodded, meeting her red eyes. "What I did with the tidemaw wasn't any different. You're not the only one who can sacrifice for the team."

Her eyes flashed, slitting vertically as she repressed a snarl. I backed away.

Maybe my [Gills] weren't so bad. It seemed like the [Adventurer] gig extracted a price.

Meredeath shook, trembling, until the haze in her eyes

dulled, and her hand released the pendant. Meredeath turned away, her teal hair glowing in the morning light.

I made myself busy by walking off to find some dry wood for the fire. She seemed like she needed a moment as much as I did.

Why did everyone feel like they needed to protect me? I kicked a rotten log, reveling in the splintering of wood. Meredeath was literally torturing herself to protect us. Some small part of my brain knew I was being whiny and, if Richard were still in my head, I'm sure he would have told me.

I picked up a barkless stick that had worm tracks across the wood. Using it, I poked at a wine-capped mushroom. It was Richard's favorite. I mauled it with the stick.

Did I want to be an [Adventurer] without a safety net like Richard? Did I have enough guts to tell Tandy and Leo that I wanted out?

"Cole, we need you back here!" Leo called frantically, his voice echoing in the woods. I dropped my stick and started running.

They needed me.

Chapter 40

COMMUNICATION ISSUES

I never expected to survive the [Trial Dungeon], but I was still surprised when I realized we were all about to die. To be fair, Richard had warned us about Rhi Voss. As much as I wanted to, I couldn't really blame him this time.

"Uh, guys, what are we going to do?" I asked, proud that my voice wasn't shaking.

Leo, Tandy, and Meredeath stood with weapons drawn before two dozen animated skeletons. I focused on the one in front, trying to trigger [Analyze] until I realized it was one of the many skills that I'd lost.

"We're going to go with them," Meredeath said calmly. Richard trembled on Meredeath's shoulders, his tentacles pulled tight. "This is our escort."

The lead skeleton stood regally. He looked at me, green orbs glowing in empty eye sockets. His armor was rusty and old, like that of his companions, but it was more ornate in design. Etchings of falcons were outlined in moss and grit. He'd been the one in charge in life, and that seemingly extended through undeath.

"Is this your entire party?" The skeleton lord stepped forward. The voice was *hers*, Rhi's, but the body was still his. It made every word feel dissonant in my ears.

"It is," Meredeath responded coolly, as though talking to a yellow boned undead puppet was a typical Tuesday. Maybe it was now.

"Very well. Know that my swamp will take care of anyone you've omitted." The bone lady's tone made it clear exactly *how* any stragglers would be dealt with. "Follow Ter Lance and his escort."

The light in presumably Ter Lance's head flickered from a flame to a spark. The skeleton lord mechanically turned towards the swamp, not bothering to monitor our compliance.

We hurried, shoving camp supplies into our packs. I quickly rolled my mom's old quilt, stuffing it into the top of my bag. My lucky nails clinked at the bottom of my pack.

Our escort encircled us, weapons on display. Some held spears, while others wielded rusted swords with round shields made of rotten wood. A few held ancient bows with unfletched arrows notched on them. I wasn't sure what damage they could do, but at this range, it wouldn't take much.

We set off. The undead moved in a precise cadence that was hard to mimic in humanity. Each step was taken in unison as they turned to face the swamp.

The soldiers marched eerily silent, faces pointed towards the swampy horizon. I held my hammer, contemplating how many I could take out before they killed me. The answer was simply not enough. The skeletal warriors didn't seem to care whether we had or held our weapons. They were rightly confident in their ability to handle any threat we posed.

The water of the swamp rippled. A line of disturbance

seemed to race towards our position. I braced, ready to fight whatever new foe this was.

"Is it a snake?" Tandy asked. She hated snakes.

"Too fast," Meredeath whispered.

"How fast does a skeletal snake move?" I asked, watching the approaching gush of water. I wasn't willing to negate any possibility.

The skeletons stood ramrod straight as we were showered in muddy water. A ball of green energy crackled in the air. Wisps of magic reached out and danced along the flaking edges of the escort's armor. The skeleton lord stepped forward as though he'd been given an unheard command.

It was no snake, but Rhi's magic.

"That's incredible," Tandy murmured, eyes fixed on the ball of energy. "It's going to part the waters for us."

I'm not sure how in the corrupt hells she knew what the spell was going to do, but sure enough, as the skeleton lord stepped forward, the swamp peeled away from his feet. The escort began a steady march onto the dry strip the magic created. Their intention was apparent. We were to follow him to their mistress.

This time, I didn't bother blocking out Richard's voice.

We are so fucked.

For once, he spoke nothing but the truth.

We got a unique view of the swamp. Water and mud parted in a ten-foot-wide corridor.

Meredeath was in awe, as though this were a miracle of miracles. I guess water magic like this wasn't much of a thing in her world. Richard sat coiled tightly around her neck. His skin glistened with anxiety slime. I didn't miss that.

I stepped into the corridor first, and the swamp water stood three feet high, held back by an invisible curtain. We were really outclassed. I imagined the water straining at the barrier so that it could break through and devour us.

The bone lady's magic was powerful. Even the tree roots

had parted with the water. My boots hit solidly. The ground was dry, packed earth with rectangular brown bricks peeking through. It was as though I stood on an ancient road.

I looked past the ornate lord, noting the path led straight towards the heart of the valley and the ancient ruins I'd spotted from my tree perch. Maybe it *was* a road.

The skeletons moved forward in unison, their bone heels clicking on the brick. We had little choice but to follow. Being left behind wasn't an option with the sharp spears of our rear guard pointed toward us.

The skeletons weren't protecting us from the swamp. They were here to ensure we followed directions.

I was just glad I didn't have to slog through miles of mud. For the first time in days, I started to dry out. It should have felt good, but my gills *itched*.

As we moved down the corridor, the magic holding back the swamp folded in on itself, sealing our fate. Water rushed in, closing any hope of a quick escape. The barrier protecting us sat only six feet away from the rear guard.

The skeleton escort walked without fear through the deadly swamp. Trees that would have ripped the skin off our faces leaned back away from the magic. They lashed their branches in displeasure, but none dared cross into our bubble.

The undead minions had no time for our awe as they set a brisk pace. They didn't pity us as we tried to keep the flies and mosquitoes from their feast. They didn't care that I was having trouble catching my breath.

"How far is it?" Leo's voice broke the silent march.

The skeleton lord turned its head 180 degrees to face Leo as he marched forward. His mouth clacked but, without the green magic of the bone lady, no distinguishable words came. The unnaturalness of it all didn't encourage follow-up questions.

I dropped back in the pack, letting Meredeath take the lead. This was her quest, and I wasn't suited for the vanguard role. Richard clung, a glistening mess of slime, to her shoulders. He kept his tentacles forward, actively avoiding looking at me.

I didn't blame him. I didn't want to talk to him either.

The miles passed quietly. Our guards kept an untiring pace. I'd begun to really struggle. My stamina and health bars had started a slow but steady decline. Each breath was a sharp attempt to grab as much air as I could. Every time I slowed a little too much, trying to catch the next breath, the butt of a spear poked me in a kidney.

"Cole, you okay?" Tandy's voice quietly cut through my suffering.

"Yeah," gasp, "I just," gasp, "can't catch..." For the love of the Everbear, I couldn't even form a complete sentence.

Tandy stopped walking, dropping behind me as she stared down the rearguard. Grateful, I stopped, bending over with my hands on my knees. I just needed a couple of good breaths.

"Stand up, Cole. Hands on your head. It'll help open up your breathing," Meredeath said, pulling me up.

I glared at her as I complied, resting my hands on my head like an idiot. I just wanted to be left alone. Couldn't we just be there already?

Our guards were not amused. They'd come to a stop and faced us with raised weapons.

"Hey, I can keep going," I lied. I mean, I could keep going, but it was becoming plain that I wasn't going to keep going all the way to Rhi Voss.

My companions formed a ring around me, facing out with their weapons handy.

The skeleton lord stood impassive for a moment. The dim spark of magic in the back of his skull flared as his mouth started moving.

"I am surprised you're choosing to sacrifice yourselves to the swamp." The skeleton's jaw clacked like a puppet with

Rhi's voice floating through its mouth. "Although the energy donation will not go unused."

"We are not sacrificing ourselves, we are resting. *Humans* need to rest," Meredeath said, pointing at me.

The lord stepped forward, the edge of his sword threatening violence. The spark in his skull grew larger, backlighting his eyes.

"Weakness should be plucked like a weed. I could do you a favor," Rhi purred.

I couldn't keep my eyes off the pitted longsword pointed at my face. The edge looked sharp enough to do the job.

Meredeath's fingernails elongated into claws as she crouched, ready to defend me. As dangerous as she looked, claws weren't going to be much use against that sword.

ENOUGH! Richard's voice thundered in all our heads. One of the more deteriorated skeletons' heads popped off with the pressure of Richard's mental shout. The pile of bones crumbled to the ground with the soldier's corroded sabre hitting tip down like a martial grave marker.

Are you blind, old woman? Do you see his ring? Richard's mental voice hissed, like water on a hot pan.

The skeleton didn't have eyes, but its head tilted towards me. Expressionless and still, it was hard to gauge a reaction.

"Graverobber?! You bring me a graverobber?!" she roared. The undead stepped forward, ready to finish us.

Technically, she wasn't wrong. My panicked mind remembered the blue-haired mummy, hand extended. But she wasn't right either.

He has her blessing, you bag of dust! Have your eyes rotted completely out of your head?

The advance of the skeletal guards stopped. She eyed me through her bony puppet.

"I must verify this trickery personally. Carry him if you must." The skeleton lord twisted abruptly, and they set off at the same untiring pace. I was quickly gasping again, this time a stitch formed in my abdomen.

Step after step. I focused on Richard's slimy form. The jerk had saved us yet again. Maybe I *should* just go back to being his pet.

My vision blurred as my health and stamina started to sink. My lungs burned, and the gills on the side of my neck flexed ineffectually.

I stepped on Leo's heel and tripped.

"I'm sorry," I blurted, as I failed to catch myself, my knee slamming into the ground, followed by the slap of my hands trying to cushion the fall. Leo caught himself before he joined me.

I braced for the expected jab from the rearguard. My knee throbbed, and my hands stung. I wasn't sure I could stand, much less get back to marching.

Nothing happened. The entire retinue had stopped, and the guards behind us stood, their eyes fixed on the ground. Tandy kneeled, helping me up. Her eyes glued to the guards, waiting for a reaction.

I stood slowly, wincing as my muscles protested. Our escort waited silently.

I limped forward, my knee was already swelling. Nothing happened—no threats, no spear butts.

This is why we never worked out! The silent treatment isn't healthy communication.

Chapter 41

SOUL BOUND AND SINKING

We started moving again, this time much slower.

I eyed Richard on his perch. He avoided my look, not because he was ashamed of us, but because he didn't want to answer any questions about his relationship with Rhi. Instead, he sat indignantly, head forward, tentacles stretched out as though he were leading us himself.

What a poser.

With the pace slowed, my health and stamina bars had recovered. I could breathe. I could think. The ring gifted to me by Rhi's sister sat heavy on my hand. I tugged at it, but it stubbornly refused to move.

"I think it's stuck," I said out loud, tugging at the gold band.

Tandy, who hadn't left my side, frowned. She grabbed my hand, examining the ring. It was fit for a queen, gold threads twisting together to hold the aquamarine stone. Tandy gave a couple of gentle tugs, but although it shifted, the ring refused to move off past the first knuckle.

"[Detect Weave]," she murmured, gripping my wrist tightly as she held my hand up in the air. "Cole, I think you're going to regret putting this on your ring finger."

"How so? I just slipped it on in the middle of the fight."

"It's soul bound, isn't it?" Tandy still held my hand up as she examined the ring.

Was it? I scrolled back through my notifications. Sure enough, [Blessings of the Waters] was soul bound.

"Looks like it," I said, staring at the [Error] messages in the description.

"Well, now you have an excuse for your inability to get a girlfriend," Leo chimed in, chuckling. Tandy even had a bemused twinkle in her eye.

It was on my left ring finger, right where a promise ring would go. Was I engaged to a blue-haired undead mummy?

I imagined a possessive ghost haunting any potential match. Leo was right. I would never find a girlfriend.

"You can't make this stuff up," I said dejectedly as Tandy gave the ring a couple more tugs.

With our pace slowed, I'd finally been able to pick up my head and look around. The water level had doubled in this area of the swamp, and we walked in a corridor with six-foot-tall walls. The deeper water had gotten clearer, and I could see through it.

My assumptions about the ancient graveyard had been mostly correct. It appeared as though we were walking through a ruined metropolis.

Half walls stood crumbled or flattened, only giving the vague footprint of a foundation. We passed a ruined town square with an ornate fountain made of marble with three bronze horse heads held high. People repurposed the sides of the road, the dirt surrounding the fountain, and the floors of the collapsed buildings for a darker reason.

Gravestones sat in neat lines along the road, surrounding the fountain, and even in the middle of the building's foundations. Some markers had script, some were ornate, but a horrifying majority were simply blank, with just a year of death noted.

"Does anyone know what happened in the Fifth Age, 743?" I'd taken the village classes, all youth did, but history had always been a weak point. Who cared what happened before? We lived in the present.

I was seeing the shortsightedness of my youthful philosophy.

"I think the Fifth Age ended in 750?" Tandy said. She was always the bookworm in our group. She blamed her grandmother's intolerance of imperfection, but I think she just liked school. "So, whatever happened here was probably a precursor to the rise of the Ursine Wall. I know our classes didn't cover this. I would have remembered an ancient city on the doorstep to Woodsten."

Bobbing my head, I agreed. Even my inattentive teenage brain would have held onto an ancient burial in our backyard like a dog with a bone.

I watched as a water viper followed us. The venomous snake was swimming across the top of the water, its tongue whipping as it tasted the air.

"They probably didn't want to tell you for fear you'd go investigate," Meredeath said, her head turning towards us. "How about you, Richard? You obviously know Rhi. Do you know the history of the place before she took up residence?"

We all focused on Richard as his tentacles drooped. *They once called this the Niyatgra, which translates roughly to Blessed Waters.*

"Like my ring?" I asked, confused. The Fifth Age ended over six hundred years ago. Were Rhi Voss and Lael, her sister, really that old?

Yes, like your ring. Rhi and Lael were the ruling sisters of the city before it fell.

"How is she still alive?"

"How did you know her?" I blurted over Meredeath's question.

Richard's skin was almost dry, his head downcast, tentacles retracted.

The snake that had been tracking us made its move, jumping from the water straight at Leo's face. One guard moved smoothly, chopping the viper in two midair. The warrior kneeled quickly as the head of the snake bit ineffectually at its fleshless hand and stabbed through the head of the snake.

I was suddenly glad I hadn't tried to take on these ancient warriors.

Richard carried on as though my heart thumping in my chest was overdramatic.

It's a long story, but it comes down to [Immortality]. Rhi is a [Lich], which you probably could have guessed.

"What's a [Lich]?" I asked, unfamiliar with the term.

Meredeath turned to look at me, almost tripping. "How do you not know what a [Lich] is? Even *I* know what a [Lich] is and..." She glanced at our silent sentinels, worried they might be listening. We'd agreed to keep her otherworldly background a secret. No good could come from Rhi understanding *that* little quirk about her before she was ready.

The world has forgotten so much. Richard's mental voice sounded so tired. I almost felt for the little slug. *A [Lich] is a class, and Rhi is above a [Sage] in mastery. One specialization available to [Liches] is [Necromancy]. As you can see, she has this specialization. [Lich] is also one of the few paths to [Immortality].*

A memory triggered. The slime-covered book in the Library of Alta and *On Immortality and Death* by Magus Reaver. Lich was one classification that contained the skill [Immortality]. Then again, so did [Fanged Banana Slugs]. I did not know it was a necromantic class, and wrapped up in the walking dead that surrounded us.

"And you know her?" Tandy repeated my question, not wanting it to be dropped.

We dated for a while.

Meredeath gagged, weakly speaking, "Maybe someone else can carry Richard for a while."

No one volunteered. How did a slug and a presumably undead human date? I had to shut down that line of thinking before it went too far.

I could just picture… Nope, wasn't going to do it.

Richard ignored our collective horror. *And then I was her prisoner for a decade. Let's just say my presence isn't going to help your cause.*

Richard fell silent, and his words had a finality that prevented any of us from asking more questions.

Had Richard been around for the fall of Niyatgra?

The path sank lower as we walked, and now the water surrounding us rose to fifteen feet. It was as though the swamp had given way to a real lake.

We're getting close. This was the reflecting lake in front of the palace.

Looking around, the ruins had given way to what looked like an actual lake bottom. Long strands of lily pad roots dangled while toothy fish zipped in and out of the tangle. Strips of seaweed waved as they reached towards the sun.

A four-foot-long predator with an elongated snout full of teeth deftly swam through the weeds. I found myself grateful we hadn't tried to complete our original plan by slogging through here ourselves.

"What was the tidemaw's home?" Leo asked. My confusion must have been clear as he coughed and added to his question. "If it's deeper here because of the reflecting lake, and the tidemaw sat three times deeper into the ground, it had to be sitting in something, right?"

My eyes swiveled to Richard. It was a decent question.

The tidemaw wasn't always that big. It was a pet of Lael's, and when she came home to fight the war, it rested here.

It probably grew bigger in the ensuing 500 years. How long did tidemaws live?

I think it ended up at the old marble quarry. Although I'm not intimately familiar with tidemaw biology, it's possible the beast could burrow out its own nest with magic. Or maybe Lael and Rhi blasted a place for it in the earth?

We'd hit the middle of the lake, towering walls of water extending twenty-five feet above us. If Rhi wanted us dead, this would be an easy way to kill us. My hand rose to touch my gills, thinking of it. I might have a slight survival advantage, but the vindictive wildlife would make a snack of me.

"What do you think our chances are of leaving this place alive?" Tandy asked as we finally passed the halfway point.

Very low.

Most days, I just wished Richard would shut up.

No one argued with him. It pissed me off even more when he was probably right.

With each step, we were gaining elevation. The undead seemed lighter, as though they were relieved to be home.

As we neared the shore of the lake, an unimpressive expanse of more swamp sat before us. It proved to be a mirage as the air began shimmering.

The illusion of wilderness dropped to reveal an unseen wonder. A palace's spires rose out of the wilderness. Nothing in my rough-hewn experience of the [Outpost] of Woodsten prepared me for the scale and magnificence. It made Woodsten look like an outhouse.

White columns extended, holding up a dome of shimmering marble. The building continued to the right and left, towering over the swamp. Gold accents sat highlighting reliefs of great heroes and heroines fighting monsters and traveling the world. A boggy lawn of waist-high reeds floated between us and a swath of gray steps that led to a huge doorless entrance.

"Hush," the giant skeleton lord spoke in a deep voice. His

head turned to us, and at once, I realized he was no longer an animated puppet, but an independent sentient being. "We must tread carefully. [Corruption] has infiltrated Niyatgra, and not all who tread the palace grounds are friends."

For telling us to be quiet, the warrior was awfully wordy. The skeletons around us all watched the waist-high reeds as though expecting an attack at any moment.

As we stepped forward, I pulled [Guardian's Promise] off my hip. Whatever magic had parted the swamp, it didn't touch the reed covered pond. We took tentative steps onto the onto waterlogged ground. The magic that had provided us a path to the palace dissipated, water rushing to fill the last trace of our journey.

I looked back out across the swamp. Water lilies, reeds, and bog trees dominated the landscape. An errant call of a bird was the only interruption of the buzz of insects and deep throated tone of toads. Nothing spoke of the ancient head-stones and ruins of the once-thriving city. Niyatgra rested in its watery grave, forgotten.

The hair on my arms raised as I repressed a shiver.

I returned my attention forward, almost missing having a slug to watch my back. The reedy grass mat bobbed under our feet as we spread out, trying to distribute our weight. Each step forward rippled through the woven reeds. It reminded me of a fly caught in a spider's web.

Leo was having a tough time keeping his feet. His weighty frame had a distinct disadvantage when attempting to move stealthily through the matted reeds. One heavy stumble and his foot went straight through the mat. He sunk to mid thigh in the water.

Swearing loudly, Leo tried pulling himself out of the bog, but only bust his other foot into the soupy undercarriage of the reeds. He had a reed mat wrapped around him like a giant diaper.

Leo mocked me for my ring placement, and now he was

getting swallowed by swamp diapers. Cosmic payback is quick sometimes.

Flailing, my giant friend looked about to throw a tantrum.

"A little help here?" he grunted, trying to pull himself up on the quickly disintegrating weeds around him.

A howl went up in the distance, it was long and mournful. Several howls and barks joined the call.

Ter Lance swore. "You've done it now. The water hounds are going to be on us. They were the first to fall to [Corruption]. Prepare for battle."

The squad of soldiers snapped into formation, weapons pointed down at the reeds themselves. I kneeled next to Leo, helping him scramble back on top of the mat. I had the sickening impression we were going to need his singing axe momentarily.

Meredeath must have agreed as she joined me. We shared tight smiles as Leo continued to struggle.

Chapter 42

I'VE GOT 99 PROBLEMS AND THE [LICH] IS JUST ONE OF THEM

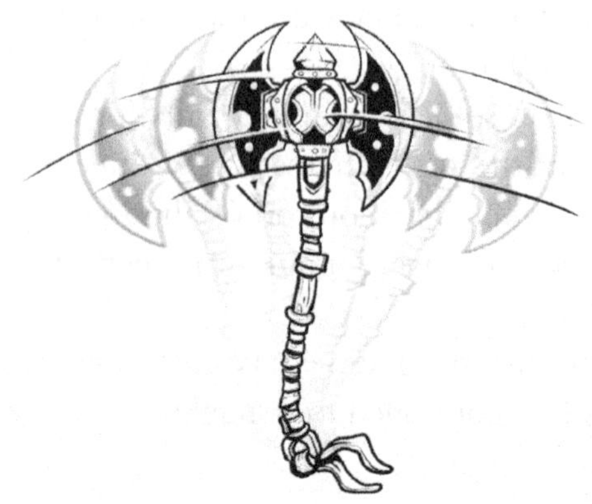

The howling grew louder, but I didn't see any hounds.

Meredeath and I struggled to pull Leo out of the reeds. Finally, we had him jump butt first onto the mat, effectively distributing his weight.

"Where are they? I can't see any of them." Tandy sounded frantic, as the [Corrupt] water hounds sounded like they were right on top of us.

Ter Lance opened his mouth to reply when a dog jumped through the matted reeds and latched onto his leg. In one swift movement, the dog pulled off the skeleton lord's tibia, as another skeleton cleaved the monster in half with a sword.

A jaw full of teeth latched onto my ankle. It was some sort of aquatic-dog zombie, with otter-like tufts of fur surrounded by pale blue skin. The dog's teeth tore through my boot, sinking into my skin as it used powerful hind legs to pull me into the water.

My last glimpse of the team was of Leo drawing his axe and Meredeath's glowing pendant as she blocked an attack on Tandy. Then I was gone, dragged beneath the water.

The dog must have had webbed feet, as powerful strokes pulled me down. The weight of my hammer helped sink us to the bottom of the lake. I struggled to hold my breath, not ready to die.

Unable to hold it any longer, I took a long gasp of the murky water. My gills kicked in, and my second lung took over, giving me sweet, sweet air. I didn't need Richard to call me an idiot. I knew it.

My body went limp as I marveled at my gills working, the sensation of water entering my neck, and my water-lung providing me with air.

This was fortunate because my body going limp was what the [Corrupted] water hound was waiting for. It let me go, assuming I was already dead. The dog took off towards the surface to capture more prey.

My ankle burned as I kicked off the floor, launching myself towards the surface. My aim was off, and I slammed into the underbelly of the reedy mat. I hit hard, as though one of the skeletons had been standing above me.

My head throbbed and my ears rang as my fingernails scrabbled to break the matting. My two lungs, for once, worked in unison, providing enough air as I struggled.

It was only a matter of time before the dogs noticed I wasn't dead and dragged me off. Finally, my frantic efforts rewarded me as my fingers tore through the reeds.

The high-pitched whining in my head worsened as I breached the floor like a beached whale, throwing my body across the weeds. Immediately, my breathing grew ragged as my gills disengaged.

I blinked at the scene. Meredeath stood in front of Tandy,

hair wild with her claws out. Her pendant glowed ominously as she crouched in her platform boots. Leo stood spinning his axe in the air as though he was trying to ward off evil spirits. It whistled as it whirled above his head like a dog whistle from hell.

Sitting around him like he was about to dole out treats were five [Corrupt] water hounds.

The skeletal warriors had been wrecked. Several lay on the ground, missing leg bones, while others clung to the edge of the mat with their remaining hand.

As I stood, I pulled my hammer free. It was time to join the fight. I limped towards the mesmerized dogs.

"Can you hurry up?" Leo asked, his voice strained. "I don't know how much longer I can keep their attention."

I glanced at Meredeath. She was breathing heavily with wild eyes dancing around the battleground. I wasn't sure she understood Leo's request. Tandy looked to be in a trance, lost in some skill.

It was up to me.

"I've got you, brother," I said, stepping forward and swinging my hammer at the first dog.

My swing obliterated the water dog's head in a magical flash and spray of viscera. Multiple notifications blinked. [Guardian's Promise] *did not* approve of the [Corrupt] hounds.

The other dogs still sat complacently transfixed by Leo's axe. One of them licked the spray off its snout. I rampaged through the rest of the dogs, my hammer absolutely wrecking the pack.

Panting, I stood covered in blood and guts, looking like a vengeful god.

They just wanted to play fetch.

I looked over at Richard, still clinging to Meredeath's shoulders. "I've got a yellow chew toy I could give the next set of dogs that show up," I growled.

I was not in the mood. My ankle *hurt*, and I was soaked,

chilled, I'd been threatened, almost killed a half dozen times, fried, drowned, en-fucking-gaged to a swamp mummy. I was done.

I marched towards the palace, ignoring the bony carnage. Ter Lance's head followed my path as he worked on reattaching his tibia. The reeds bounced under my feet as I stomped towards our goal.

Quickly, my boots hit dirt, then gray granite stairs. My ankle throbbed with each step as I climbed all hundred steps to the grand entrance. Giant pillars six feet across towered above me. The grand doorway stood open, its wooden door rotted away centuries ago. The inside of the palace sat in dark shadows, ominously daring me to enter.

It was all huge. Grandiose. Made to make people like me feel *small.*

I was done feeling small.

"Rhi Voss, the all-powerful [Lich] of the palace, who can't be bothered to protect her soldiers and guests from a herd of [Corrupt] zombie dogs, show yourself!" My voice thundered as I channeled the most asinine version of Floria I could come up with. "You have violated the basic rules of hospitality. I have a grievance with you!"

The ground rattled. Dust and pebbles fell from the stacks of giant stone blocks. The colonnade bounced dangerously, angrily. It was as though the very building spurned my taunt.

One of the distant pillars toppled, great circles of stacked granite falling. The whole facade shook with the impact, showering me in dust.

In front of me, shadows were given form as they reached out of the crumbling doorway. Like claws of a behemoth, they dug into the walls and *pulled.*

Walls groaned as they resisted folding under the pressure. The sharp grinding of rock sliding over rock was my only clue. The shadows weren't pulling the doorway down but using it as leverage to pull something *forward.*

Out of the darkness came a throne. But to call it that was an understatement. No, an otherworldly platform inched into view. The stairs appeared to be made of black stone but were hollowed out in an interlocking lacy depiction of an epic battlefield of monsters fighting soldiers, stacks of skulls, and a city burning.

An angry flame ignited in the heart of the staircase, sharpening the scenes of warfare in a harsh light. My eyes traveled up to the pinnacle of the platform, where skulls were stacked to form a grotesque throne.

Fire flickered in eye sockets, through hollowed noses, and gaping mouths—a parody of life sat cruelly posed in judgment of the living.

Upon the throne sat a monster that wore the skin of a woman. Her stringy, bone-white hair hung off her skull, doing little to hide her sunken face. No hint of beauty was found in the [Lich's] features, sharpened by desiccation and age.

I thought she was grinning at me until I realized her lips had receded too far to change expression. Was she grimacing? Smiling? Who could say? She was all teeth.

The macabre scene was so grossly over the top, I should have been afraid. It was all uniquely sculpted to strike terror.

She opened her mouth, but I spoke first. "Are you done?"

Her words caught in her throat. It was probably dry.

I waited, foot tapping impatiently.

The rational mind that I'd shoved into a deep corner of my brain quivered and blubbered in the small crevice it was regulated. The new idiot in charge of my mouth, the fearless fool who wouldn't shut up, couldn't resist egging her on.

"Dust in your throat?" I asked, eyebrows high.

She stood, her moth-eaten gray rags crumbling with the movement. Her chest cavity was sunken with ribs barely covered by a thin layer of stretched skin.

My companions had arrived, standing behind me. I didn't need to look to imagine the shock on their faces.

Ter Lance, the imprisoned officer, walked around me. He positioned himself between me and Rhi Voss. His sword was up as though daring my impudence.

"Who put you up to this?" The woman's voice was thin, aristocratic, and outraged. "Was it *Richard?*"

I looked over my shoulder at the quivering slug clinging to Meredeath. Why was it always the god-damned slug?

I stepped forward. Ter Lance raised his sword threateningly.

"Why," I bit the words through clenched teeth, "does everything have to revolve around *that* asshole?"

Her eye muscles twitched as though she tried to blink, then her cheeks rose infinitesimally, "So his charms have improved, have they?"

I stared at the remnants of the queens of Niyatgra as she looked at me, eyes wide.

We filled her ancient antechamber with gales of laughter. Mine full-throated, deep, and alive. Hers was high-pitched and oddly girlish.

Chapter 43

WHAT REMAINS

Richard was not amused.

Which made the laughter all the more satisfying. Rhi must have thought so as well, as she hadn't killed me yet. The fires of her throne danced with each chortle. I wiped the gritty tears from my eyes, glancing at the rest of my companions. Meredeath and Tandy grimaced, as though watching a wagon accident, that they couldn't stop staring at.

Leo, however, arched his eyebrows as he whispered. "Good sign, hitting it off with the in-laws." He grinned as I choked on an errant bit of saliva, giving me two thumbs up.

Coughing, I turned back to the [Lich] to find her mood had flipped. She sat on her throne, long fingernails tapping on the stone armrest.

It was as though my courage had evaporated with my laughter. I couldn't bring myself to say anything. I just stood there dumbly staring at her.

Meredeath stepped forward, her boots and corset jangling. She must have handed Richard off to Leo or Tandy, because he was no longer wrapped around her neck. She looked up at Rhi, her pendant still glowing from the [Corrupt] water hound fight.

"I seek your assistance," Meredeath said. Her words echoed in the silence.

Rhi Voss sighed. She moved inhumanly, as though time passed differently for her. She was sitting and then standing before her throne in a blink. Her hands were out, with blackened nails angled towards us as though she was going to attack. Face bare, she looked every bit the swamp terror of my childhood.

Meredeath matched her energy, dropping into a crouch. With her claws coming out, she was prepared to meet an attack, no matter how outclassed. Purple lightning crackled between Rhi's fingers as though energy built for a strike.

I was frozen by some sort of [Fear] skill, unable to do anything but watch.

S-T-O-P! You unregulated [Lich]! Richard yelled in our heads, leaving no doubt he'd considered an alternative to [Lich]. My eyes danced around until I saw him sitting on a broken pillar, looking for all the world like a throne made for a slug.

His shout did nothing. No self-respecting goddess of the undead listened to a banana slug, fanged or not. Chest puffed out on a fake throne or not.

"He's engaged to your sister!" Leo shouted, pointing at me.

The purple lightning dimmed. The wisps that were Rhi's remaining eyebrows knitted together.

"Wh-what? The graverobber is a gold-digger?" Her confusion was unmistakable.

I guess it was my turn. The blue ring sat heavy on my ring finger.

"I'm not really engaged to Lael." I opted for the truth

despite the anxiety-laden look Tandy gave me. "But she did give me her ring."

I held my hand out. In the blink of an eye, Rhi was before me. I bit back a shriek.

Everything about her was worse up close. Her skin was a collection of flaky layers that were too stubborn to fall off. Her teeth were yellow and sharper than they should be. She smelled of vinegar and ash like she'd soured with age. My expression must have given away my thoughts as she moved even closer.

"See if you look half as good at my age," she said with a raspy voice. "Tell me again, boy, why do you wear my sister's ring?"

"She gave it to me—"

"I don't sense falsehood in your statement; however, I don't see how this can be true. She's been dead for over," her hand moved, and she booped me in the nose with each word, "six-hundred-years."

She looked at me as though she could see my soul. Fear had me pinned in place. Her eyes were dark, fathomless pools. Her body might have faded over the centuries, but her eyes held her soul. It was like looking down into a deep well and having something in the darkness look back.

"You are not nearly old enough," she said with finality. In a blink, she was halfway up the stairs.

My mind raced, knowing what was going to happen once she got back to her throne, when she assumed a position to pass judgment on us.

"I may be young, but she gave it to me to help me kill her [Companion]." At my words, the [Lich] froze. It was as though I'd reflected her own [Fear] skill back.

"She's dead?" Rhi whispered, her tall back ramrod straight. "I'd sensed the water levels were lower, but I figured it was just a beaver dam breaking."

I prayed to the Everbear that I was reading her correctly.

"Yes, she's finally at peace." My words had the effect I was hoping for.

The stiff-backed woman hunched as though the air had been released from her body. She kept her back to us as she walked slowly, like an ancient human, up the stairs.

The tension in the room released. The flickering fires of her throne muted their promised threat by softening. Ter Lance, her skeletal lord, lowered his sword, responding to an unspoken command.

As she turned around to face us, the world twisted.

The darkness faded. The flames blinked out. We stood in the palace, but it wasn't the conjured nightmare. It was old, bleached with age, ruined. The ceiling of the palace was missing. The room was hollowed out except for a few empty stone tables and the throne itself. It held reliefs decorated with scenes of battle, but the throne was made of solid granite. The battles celebrated glorious victories.

The room smelled not of death and ash, but of dust and age. A faint breeze whistled through a crack in the wall.

Ter Lance stood before us, not the bone minion of an undead queen, but a commander in shining armor with a greased mustache. He gave me a slight nod of recognition, as though acknowledging he was still him.

Rhi, herself, had changed. She looked not much older than any of us. Her hair was glossy and black, her skin human, her teeth hidden behind thin but functioning lips. The only thing that hadn't changed was her eyes. They were still dark orbs that whirled with intelligence.

"Behold the truth." She waved at the empty room. "I know not what assistance you come seeking, but my power is not what it was. The Incursion comes for us all. Even me."

I gazed at the once-ominous, once-beautiful palace. Rhi Voss sat alone on her throne, the undying queen of a dead civilization. My heart ached for this stranger at the understanding she'd granted us.

The Incursion is here? The Ursine Wall no longer holds? Richard sounded concerned, but I wasn't sure about what. What was this Incursion?

"Have you been asleep for so many years?" Her eyes shifted to Richard. "It presses near. [Corruption] in my dogs. They ate through most of my remaining kin. It's gotten older and hungrier." Her voice caught on the word as though this hunger scared her. "It won't be long now."

"Is there something we can do to help?" Tandy surprised me by asking.

"You, child?" Rhi said, her voice not unkind. "You are talking to one of the [Immortal Legends] of the fifth age, and you're asking what *you* can do to help? I appreciate the gesture, but I think I'll be two ages too old before long. No, I don't think there's anything—" She paused as though using [Analyze] on us. "[Your Mom's Party], really? I don't think there's anything [Your Mom's Party] can do to assist me."

"Cole slew the [Corrupt] tidemaw." Tandy's statement sat heavy in the silence. Tandy always had a way about her. She'd just state the truth, not caring about the ego-crushing consequences.

"Yes, he slew an ancient, nearly toothless tidemaw. I'd give him a trophy, but my sister beat me to it." Rhi looked at us again. Her head was shaking.

"I've got a quest, [Legacy of Lael Voss]. Do you have Lael's Key?" I blurted the words out before common sense stopped me. Rhi's hand dropped to her side, where a leather pouch sat.

"I have her key, and that ring gives you the right to it," Rhi said slowly. Before she continued, Ter Lance cleared his throat and spoke.

"Mistress, surely you will not send these children to the workshop. We have claimed too many for the ranks of the dead." Ter Lance spoke calmly, as though he could tame Rhi's nature.

"Lance, after all this time, do we really have a right to go against Lael's judgment?" The two undead clothed in illusion stared at each other. The proud, haughty lines of their posture shifted. It was as though the weight of age and grief gave them a frailty they could no longer shrug off. Rhi turned to me and continued, "I will give you her key, but it comes with a warning. You are not ready."

Her bony fingers rifled through the pouch, and with a flick of her wrist a golden key flew towards me. I caught it, examining the key. An aquamarine sat in the head, with gold filigree etched into the steel frame. It sat heavy and hummed with magic.

I gave her a solemn nod, putting the key into my backpack as I read my new notification.

[Quest Updated: [Legacy of Lael Voss]

You have obtained Lael's Key from her sister Rhi. Journey to her coastal workshop and clear out the [Corruption] to complete the quest. Adventure Onward!]

I finished reading the update, only to realize Rhi was speaking again.

"… And if I find out you've told them of the location before they're ready, I will cage you again." Rhi's threat seemed directed at Richard.

As though I want them dead any more than you.

"We both know death is a tool." Rhi laughed, a high pitched thin laugh on the edge of hysteria. It cut off abruptly, as though she remembered her audience.

Then she looked at Richard. It was as though she couldn't marry the fact that we were [Your Mom's Party], newly minted [Adventurers], and yet had defeated a [Corrupt] tidemaw. Or that we had Richard in our group.

It pained me to admit it, but it *did* seem like Richard was someone important and possibly [Immortal]. Stupid banana slug.

"What are *you* doing with *them*? Last I knew of you…" She

frowned as though trying to remember where in her cellar she'd left the potatoes. "Last I remember, I had you trapped. When I felt you wake up, I trapped every banana slug within ten miles of your resting place."

I escaped and bonded with Cole.

She studied Richard and me, likely using another [Examination] skill.

"I suppose I should let the other slugs go. Hmm... You're not bonded now. Did he get fed up with you that quickly? That's a new record. A new low for you, Richard, trying to bond with someone so young and still failing. Almost like Randal, isn't it? You remember how that ended. I hope you get a different outcome here. Why *were* you here again?" Rhi's words danced around almost too hard to follow. I wasn't sure which question to answer or who should answer it.

I looked at Richard, and he looked chastened, tentacles down. He wasn't going to respond.

"I am here seeking you as a [Sponsor]," Meredeath said, her back straight and her voice strong.

Rhi's eyes narrowed as they snapped back to Meredeath, as though she was reevaluating the woman she'd dismissed out of hand.

"*You* need a [Sponsor]? The algorithmic windbag valued *you* that high with his imaginary rubric?" She looked at us as if we were a puzzle she hadn't figured out.

To be honest, I empathized.

"Can you explain that? I'm not from this world, dimension, whatever it is. I'm not from here, and I'm not sure why I need a [Sponsor]. Why was I even required to be an [Adventurer]?"

I was shocked Meredeath had just casually told the bone lady she was an off-worlder, like this was just a common occurrence. However, it had a magical effect on Rhi. Her haughtiness drained from her face as she looked at Meredeath. It was replaced by compassion? Pity? It was hard to tell.

"[Sponsor] requirements come from a very old philosophy. It predates the [System] in fact. In the past, high-potential individuals entering one of the colleges had to be sponsored by an elder. It was a way to mentor and control. They did love control. Now it is the [System's] way of attempting to increase the survivability of high-potential [Adventurers]. Survival has become increasingly difficult in the Fifth Age..." Rhi's voice trailed off as she studied Meredeath.

As though she'd made a decision, she continued. "Come here, child. Let me take a look at you."

Meredeath started climbing the stairs, her boots jangling.

"An off-worlder." Rhi's voice whispered in wonder.

Meredeath kept climbing until she was on the platform with Rhi. Considering the [Lich] we'd just been face-to-face with, I found this very brave.

The two talked on the dais, but their words were garbled. Rhi had used some sort of [Privacy] skill to keep her words secret. What *wasn't* secret was the outcome. We watched as Rhi reached out and touched Meredeath's forehead with her thumb.

As Meredeath turned to us, I saw a glowing imprint where Rhi's thumb had touched. Meredeath's face had changed. Her features had grown less cat-like, her eyes and face rounder, her nails less sharp. She had let go of something she'd been and tethered herself to Rhi Voss. Tears traced down her pale cheeks, as though a cost had been paid.

I wondered what class she'd been offered.

"And you, Cole. Do you need a [Sponsor] as well?" Rhi's voice whispered in my ear, even though her lips hadn't moved. Her words were meant for me alone. "You have earned it. I couldn't bring myself to kill Tilly after Lael's death."

I looked at Rhi. She looked sad, sure, but beautiful. The long-forgotten queen could grant powers beyond death itself. She had hundreds of years of wisdom to bring to bear. Her offer was tempting.

Richard's yellow skin had an unhealthy, dry look to it. His tentacles drooped in the way they had since I broke our bond. He sensed me looking at him, two eye stalks lifting.

We looked at each other with different motives. I was trying to make a decision critical to the course of my life. He was trying to figure out why I was suddenly staring at him.

I saw the moment he figured it out. His tentacles dropped in a way I associated with a forfeiture of hope.

I looked up at the sister of the blue-haired Lael, Rhi Voss, the undying [Lich], queen of Niyatgra, and gave my answer.

PART III

Wayfinding

Chapter 44

THE HUSTLE AND BUSTLE

"Once we're in Eddie's Mill, we need to grab some rooms and look at the quest board." Tandy was doing what she normally did, which was ordering us around. I shared a smile with Meredeath. It was her turn to poke our fearless leader.

"I was planning on shopping first. I need to get my boots resoled, and that last leaf slime left a stain I can't get out," Meredeath said nonchalantly, knowing each word was going to irritate Tandy. She reached up to pet Richard. "Besides, the slug wants to check out the produce stalls. From what we've heard, Eddie's Mill is big enough to have a full market. Got to take advantage of it."

Persimmons are in season.

He played along, making lip-smacking sounds at us all.

"Seriously, guys, we don't have *that* much coin left. We need to pay for our rooms first before we start spending it." Tandy never picked up when we were teasing her.

Usually, Leo joined in on the banter, but he hadn't been himself since we left Rhi. A lot had changed for all of us, but Leo's unnatural silence felt heavier. If I didn't know better, I'd think my friend had been cursed.

I was going to talk to Tandy. See what she thought. But I just couldn't find a moment alone with her.

"I *guess* we can check out the hotel first. But I have to get my boots resoled. It's an equipment issue, and those take priority," Meredeath said, parroting back Tandy's reasoning when she denied Meredeath's request to get a [Mundane] onyx ring. In her defense, we couldn't afford the [Enchanted] ring that would have been useful.

Tandy eyed Meredeath as though she expected to be pushed harder. Meredeath just innocently scratched Richard under the chin. It wasn't that we weren't on the same page regarding expenses. None of us wanted to sleep on the ground again. It was just—it would be nice to *pretend* for once that we were doing better than we were.

High potential or not, [Your Mom's Party] was just another [Adventurer Party] looking for the next quest that wouldn't get us killed. We'd hit the road after meeting with Rhi Voss, and it'd been just run-of-the-mill leaf slimes, bogquackers, rats of unusual dispositions, and escort quests.

I didn't mind the lack of life-threatening situations. It was a nice change.

It'd given me time to get used to my gills. I still felt like I was breathing through a straw on dry days but, for the most part, I could keep up with everyone. Tandy told me the gasping was just in my head, and she'd been mostly right. Turns out, almost anything becomes normal if you experience it enough. You get a lot of practice breathing over a month.

Rhi had given the best suggestion before we left, to wear a wet bandana around my neck. My gills weren't nearly as angry when they were damp.

Eddie's Mill was the next major city west of Dusridge. We'd stopped at all the little villages and hamlets along the way, making sure to clear out their quest boards. Most of the quests hadn't given us more than a few coppers and a night in a barn. The people were kind and hospitable, but they had country problems that didn't even trigger [System] rewards.

None of us minded those, after the constant terror of the [Trial Dungeon] and Meredeath's quest for a [Sponsor]. We were country folk ourselves and understood that some quests were just worth doing, even if the payout was low.

What wasn't happening, however, was progression. No one had earned new skills. It was time to get serious about being an [Adventurer], and Eddie's Mill was the place to do it.

We crested a hill and got a view of the town. The eastern edge of the city butted up against the Niyat River, which was at this point thirty feet wide. Two bridges spanned the river, one wide with a line of wagons waiting to be admitted. The other was narrow, meant for foot and single-horse traffic. The buildings along the Niyat looked muddy. A few small docks peppered the shore. Wagons lined up on the cargo bridge.

From what I could see, Eddie's Mill seemed to be thriving.

Across the river sat one of the city's namesakes. A mill sat with a wheel rhythmically dipping into the river. The city rose before us, topped by a giant windmill at the center of town. Multicolored tents surrounded it, likely the aforementioned marketplace. Idly, I wondered which mill came first.

Otherwise, buildings in varying sizes and opulence showed a patchwork of roofs from straw to the eastern-style tile to the northern slate. Eddie's Mill seemed to have a cauldron of aesthetic influences, most of which I'd only read about.

"You done gawking, country boy?" Meredeath said, slapping me on the back. "Can you take the slug for a while? I hate getting all the looks." She batted her eyes in what I'd come to realize was a fake flirtation. It was just how she was, but even knowing this, I wasn't completely immune to her charms.

"Sure, hand him over," I said. Meredeath attracted a lot of attention *without* the slug. I could see him being an added burden.

I'm not a piece of luggage to be bandied about!

"You are until you grow legs, big guy." I rolled my eyes at his outrage.

If someone is carrying this team, it's ***me****.*

I didn't bother responding to that one. Even if he was right, and I'm not sure he had the evidence, I would die multiple times before I'd admit it.

Tandy marched us right up to the pedestrian gate. The bridge guard looked at us bored.

"State your business. It's a copper each to enter the city." The guard spoke in the monotone of someone on the verge of a yawn.

"[Adventurers], and why do we need to pay a copper each?" Tandy cut to the chase, putting words to what we were all thinking.

The guard looked at us, eyebrows raised.

"[Adventurers]? Well then, it's a silver each for such accomplished folk. An extra for the slug too." He stood a little straighter, excited at the payout. The guard was outfitted in what I assumed was an official uniform. A silver pin depicted two swords crossed over a windmill. His puffed chest prominently displayed his badge over his worn leather armor.

I guess the windmill came first. Mystery solved.

We didn't have five silver coins. We hadn't seen that type of money offered on any quest board.

"Sorry about my cousin here," Meredeath interjected. The guard looked between Tandy and Meredeath, who didn't look remotely related. "She's got dreams, a bit muddled from falling out of the neighbor's apple tree, if you know what I mean."

I didn't know what she meant, but the guard smiled like he understood.

"We're here visiting our auntie down in the water district. My mum told us we needed to take these two farm boys to 'protect' us." Meredeath rolled her eyes, communicating clearly what she thought of our 'protection.'

"Ah, visiting relatives. Can I get your names and the name of your auntie?" The man held a clipboard with a ledger of entrants. "It'll still be a copper each for using the bridge," he eyed Richard, "so five total." We had six coppers on our persons.

We could afford four, but it wouldn't leave us anything for room and board.

"Tandy, can you hand the man the four coppers your momma gave you? And our aunt is Millie, that's M-I-L-L-I-E." Meredeath spoke the lie so smoothly, I almost believed her. She leaned into the guard conspiratorially as she dropped into a loud whisper. "The slug's dinner. Aunt Millie's favorite. You're not going to charge us extra for dinner? Tandy here is a sensitive soul. She wanted to treat the slug to a view before he gets the axe."

The guard eyed Richard for a moment, then nodded. "Four coppers. I'm sure a slug that big would make a good meal."

Tandy, still shocked by the prices, opened up the coin pouch and started fishing for the fee.

"But we've already crossed the bridge," Leo piped up. He was as irritated as Tandy. "What would you do if we couldn't pay? We'd have to use the bridge again."

The guard looked at him, eyeing the axe strapped to his back.

"It's a tax to pay for the bridge construction. If you don't have the fee, then I won't let you in. Do we have a problem?"

Meredeath stepped between the guard and Leo. "No problem. Don't mind him. A lot of cotton up in Woodsten."

The guard held out his hand, collecting Tandy's coins. He waved us through, dropping three of the coins into a collection bin. I watched as he didn't even try to hide pocketing the fourth copper.

I opened my mouth to object when I got a sharp elbow to my ribs. Message received.

We walked into Eddie's Mill, three country bumpkins who didn't know the first thing about a city and Meredeath. Who, for once, seemed to know more about our world than we did.

As first impressions go, the guard gave us an accurate one. Eddie's Mill was loud, muddy, and hard to navigate. Even Tandy was intimidated by the strangeness of it all. People hollered in a variety of accents and languages. At first, we wandered aimlessly, awestruck by the noise, sights, and godawful smells of the city.

Meredeath eventually took charge, leading us away from the river. I was pretty sure she had no more of an idea of where to go than us, but I was more than willing to let her make navigational decisions. Even Tandy gave up when she almost got run over at a cross street.

The fishy smell of the docks district gave way to the smell of bakeries and roasted nuts. None of which we could afford. That didn't stop me from eyeing the nut-covered croissants and cream horns dusted with powdered sugar.

A cart sold roasted nuts dusted in cinnamon and sugar. I'd take on another tidemaw for some nuts.

Richard drooled a bit, leaning off my shoulder to sniff at the air. The thick glob fell right on my boot.

I'd pawn Richard for a good pastry. Too bad his slime was worthless.

Meredeath marched us up to higher ground, angling us away from the towering mill and associated market, tracing along the river district as though she were on a mission.

"You three stay here," Meredeath said, pushing us into a little alley. "I'll be right back."

The street she'd taken us to was lined with buildings that supported a type of business I didn't even know existed.

Each bar had a distinct style, made plain in garish murals on the front of the windowless establishments. As though that wasn't enough of a clue as to our whereabouts, the eaves were all painted red, indicating exactly what part of town we were in.

Leo, Tandy, and I looked like sheep that had wandered into a bear den. None of us could stop gawking at the women and men who called out to each passerby.

Leo stood wide-eyed at the flagrant display of wares happening around us. Tandy, face as scarlet as the eaves, pretended to root around in her pack. Richard leaned forward, tentacles high, so he had the best angle to watch people.

The people were caricatures, painted to draw the eye and show off their assets. Heavy floral perfume warred with the musky scent of cologne. Red lips, large tits, bejeweled codpieces, curly flamboyant hair, dresses that clung or draped loosely—every bit of artifice was built to entice and tantalize.

I'd always considered myself experienced. I didn't have Leo's popularity, but I wasn't an innocent. But I was beginning to understand my worldliness had limits. I tried to find a safe place to let my eyes linger, unwilling to follow Tandy's example. I settled for staring at the red eaves, hoping Meredeath didn't take too long.

Hopefully, the Adventurer's Guild quest board had something better than rat duty listed. If not, we might have to take up jobs scrubbing codpieces.

A balcony door flew open, right in my line of vision. An oiled man stood with a giggling, nearly topless woman with mussed hair. I decided the cobblestones might be a safer view.

This is my kind of entertainment! Richard said it with the right snark that indicated he was talking about our discomfort, not the people selling their bodies around us.

"I regret picking you," I told the self-important slug.

Richard smugly preened on my shoulder. I refused to let him see me smile.

Chapter 45

THE THINGS WE CARRY

"I don't understand why we're here," Tandy said, as she sat on a bottom bunk bed in what could only be described as an attic hallway to nowhere.

"We are here because this room is a copper a night. And the mistress of the house was willing to take us in, even though we had no one to vouch for our character," Meredeath explained slowly, as though Tandy were an idiot.

I'd vouch for you.

"Like your opinion is worth anything." Sometimes, I just wish Richard would shut up.

"Look, I know this isn't your scene, but the rent is cheap. We'll be treated fairly and left alone." Meredeath looked at the three of us, an eyebrow raised. "Unless you want to explore?"

Her voice rose hopefully, eyeing Tandy and me. I chuckled, imagining trying to navigate the clubs we'd walked by. No part of me was prepared to explore. It'd been a long day.

"Maybe later," Tandy lied for us. "It's been a long month. Tonight, I just want to get some sleep."

Meredeath nodded, kindly taking her words at face value.

"Anyone got any food?" Leo asked.

My stomach rumbled. It was still angry that I hadn't sold Richard for some spiced nuts.

"I've still got a bit of granola left," Tandy said, as she began digging in her bag. The three of us looked at each other over our friend. We'd all independently concluded that if we had to have *one more day* of her granola...

We ate the granola anyway. Even Richard, who had mainly been subsisting on weeds. We had one copper left, which wasn't enough to buy much of anything, and we decided to keep it just in case we couldn't find work the next day. Everything hinged on the quest board and what was available.

When I'd imagined the [Adventurer's] life, I hadn't envisioned straw cots and barn lofts. It'd been swinging swords and slaying monsters. I never considered the cost of feeding and housing four people.

The attic was on the fourth story of a bar and theater. I had the impression that "theater" might be a generous term for the type of shows that went on. Part of the deal Meredeath got on the room included being seen as little as possible around the clientele. Apparently, three country bumpkins and a slug might be bad for business. I think everyone but Richard was relieved.

It meant, however, that for the first time in weeks, I could empty my bag and get comfortable. It'd been constant movement since we'd left Rhi's dusty palace.

The [Lich] had tried to be a good host, but she didn't have a great understanding of the needs of the living anymore. Leaving us to sleep on the granite floors as her remaining warriors endlessly clacked around. We'd stayed a couple of days as the [Lich] trained Meredeath in her new [Sponsor] given class and skills. Ter Lance and Richard had spent countless hours reviewing what they called the frontier defense against the Incursion.

I'd been relieved when we left, but it'd been an exhausting march to Eddie's Mill.

I pulled out my rolled-up quilt first. It'd held up remarkably well, thanks to Richard's [Clean] skill and a [Reinforce] skill that Tandy still had. My mom had made the geometric design with my favorite colors. The green fabric had mostly faded, and the blue had turned a purple hue.

Even though it was worn, it reminded me that someone cared.

Things had become a little more complicated in recent years with my mom. I was working on letting go of her disappointment and trying to keep the love. Our relationship was a work in progress.

Next was my untouched toolkit. I'd thought about selling it, but a part of me still hoped we'd need it.

Finally, I brought out a couple of books I'd been lugging around. I just hadn't brought myself to let them go yet. When I'd gotten a chance, I'd wrapped them in wax paper, which saved all three from a constant dunking in various liquids.

I had *Tinkering for Beginners,* which was a gem of a book. It'd walked me through making each tool in my toolbox, but not much further.

I also had *Monsters of the Frontier.* I picked up this book with a faint hope that it would prove helpful. Flipping it open, a faded picture of a bogquacker stared back at me. The description was nonsense: "*a hellacious quacker from the fifth circle of hell.*"

Leafing through it quickly, I confirmed what I already knew: no mentions of bone warriors, cutwood, or dunglords. The tidemaw description had been way out of touch. We'd already outgrown *Monsters of the Frontier*. I tossed both books into the 'sell' pile.

"I'm going to go downstairs." Meredeath paused, looking

at the collection of items strewn over my bed. "You sure you don't want to join me?"

A part of me yearned to say yes, to be the guy cool enough to go with her, but I shook my head. I just needed a moment to get my pack under control, and recenter myself on who I had been.

"Thanks for the offer, but I'm exhausted," I heard myself say. Out of the corner of my eye, I saw her sweep her eyes to Tandy and Leo, then shrug. The door closed behind her with an audible click.

"You don't need a girlfriend, you're already engaged," Leo said with a wide smile. It'd been the first rib he'd given me since Niyatgra.

My face was hot as I went back to my pack. I took out my dad's map, holding it gingerly. Richard had insisted it was almost indestructible, but I'd had twenty-five years of parental-enforced fear over ruining the artifact.

I unrolled it. I could bring the map up in my interface, but there was something about the feeling of the magical vellum. I carefully traced our journey so far, from Woodsten to Bear Ridge to the ruins of Niyatgra and our slower trek to Eddie's Mill. The world to the west of the Ursine Wall was pretty detailed. The east was blank.

Richard sat on my pillow, slowly crunching through a pile of granola. I wasn't sure how he was even grinding the bits of oats and nuts up.

"Richard, where is the Library of Alta?" I asked. I had unrolled the map a few times, trying to memorize the foreign city names and trade routes. The world was a lot bigger than I'd ever imagined.

Richard cracked a nut in his mouth. *It's not on your map?*

"No, that's why I'm asking."

It's on the eastern side of the Ursine Wall, north by the sea, nestled in the mountains.

I frowned. The eastern side of the Ursine Wall was relegated to the wastelands. We'd been taught nothing survived in the monster-infested desolation. The Ursine Wall had been raised in the cataclysm to protect the civilized world from unchecked [Corruption]. How could the library survive unprotected?

"Is the library still standing?" Tandy asked. I hadn't told anyone about the extra stop Richard and I had upon exiting the dungeon.

It stands for now. As ever, the Incursion threatens all human civilization. The Library of Alta has withstood much, but I've lived long enough to understand that nothing lasts forever.

"That's rich, coming from someone who claims to be [Immortal]," Leo muttered.

Before Richard could respond, I asked a question I'd been dying to ask, "What exactly is the Incursion? Rhi wouldn't answer my questions."

Richard's head came up, his tentacles waving away from each other. *Despite having lost touch with reality, Rhi was remarkably insightful. I'll fill you in once you complete your first official [Veteran] level quest.*

"Why? Why make us wait?" I was tired of Richard's haughty superiority. What was he holding back?

Honestly? I don't want you running off and dying. As Rhi indicated, there's nothing you can do right now to help.

"Oh."

Suddenly, the room seemed way too small for the four of us. I threw my empty pack at Richard, watching as he tumbled off of the bed.

"I'm going to go get some air." I pulled the door shut, harder than intended. It slammed behind me. I stood on the dim landing, taking a couple of deep breaths.

My heartbeat whooshed in my ears as I carefully navigated the narrow stairs. They used the magical glowmoss as a light source here, too, but the moss hadn't been recharged in a long time. The establishment didn't seem to rent out its attic rooms too often.

As I got down to the second story, I opted to keep walking. I didn't want to think too hard about the activity on this floor. I stood at the base of the stairs to the first floor.

Music and voices spilled into the stairwell. The bar sounded full. For a moment, I could imagine it being *The Ram's Horn* with one of the traveling bards set up in the corner.

It was louder, maybe a festival weekend where everyone's family came in to visit, drink, and dance. I stood leaning against the wall with my hand on the handle. The servant's stairs were empty at this time of night. The ebb and flow of music and murmurs and the uneven thump of dancers sounded so *normal.*

The doorknob suddenly flew out of my hand as someone opened the door. Before me stood the mistress of the house, the woman who'd led us to the attic. She wore exotic silks, smelling of lavender and spice. Her red lips and rosy cheeks were loud in their artifice.

"What do we have here?" Her voice was deep and full. Painted eyebrows raised as she waited for an answer.

I glanced out past her, dashing all the illusions that this was home. Dancers stood on a stage decked out in bright feathers and little else. People sat at tables in fancy gold-threaded waistcoats and dresses that hugged the body. This place would be an absolute scandal in Woodsten.

"Sorry," I mumbled, trying to think of an excuse. "I just needed some air."

The mistress's eyes narrowed as she smiled warmly.

"Not much air in the stairwell. I was about to bring some dinner up to your group. It looks like it has been a long journey." She held up a metal rack that held four bowls of stew, with rolls balancing on each bowl. It smelled divine—a rich, meaty brown sauce with potatoes and carrots.

"Wow, that's... *thank you.*" It didn't take a genius to be grateful. This woman had no reason to treat us kindly. I scrambled to stand. "I can take that up, if you want. Save you the trip."

"That would be lovely, dear boy. My knees are not what they used to be." She handed the rack over. I balanced it carefully.

"Why are you doing this?" The question came out before I could stop myself.

"Doing what?" she said, her smile widening, as though daring me to be more specific.

"Helping us." I gestured at the stew in my right hand. "No one has been... nice like this. Not since we've been on the road."

"Do I need a reason to be kind?" She'd read between the lines. I couldn't believe *she'd* cared, here in *this* place. My face was already red, so I went for it.

"I just never would have thought—here," I stuttered, realizing how insulting it sounded halfway through.

"You never thought to find help *here?* Among my kind? It's okay, I get that a lot. You're new and a bit out of place, so I'll take that question out of ignorance, not hate."

I nodded, grateful.

"My people," she waved at the dancers, "have received little love in the world. Not unlike, I would imagine, your little group. Kindness hurts no one, and it can make all the difference to a soul."

Underneath a shimmering rainbow of eye shadow and long fake eyelashes sat a sincerity and compassion I'd seen before. Her eyes held the same warmth as Marta's.

"I think I understand."

"Good boy. Now run upstairs. There isn't anything for you here tonight." I knew a dismissal when I heard one.

"Thank you, Mistress."

"Mistress Del, to you. Meredeath told me you were

[Adventurers], right?" She kept speaking, not waiting for an answer. "You look a little shiny to be [Veterans], but I've got a little job that needs doing. Do you think your crew is up for a challenge?"

"Yes!" I didn't hesitate with my answer. We needed a challenge, and we needed someone who believed in us.

"Such confidence, young one. Let's talk over breakfast in the morning."

The door, not unkindly, clicked shut in front of me.

Chapter 46

PROGRESSION FOR A PRICE

With a full stomach and aching feet from the day, I should have been asleep immediately.

I envied Richard. He was curled up on his half of the pillow in a wet spot of slime and drool. He even breathed in time with Leo's log-cutting snore.

Rrriiiiiip.

And then there was Tandy. Every night, she fell asleep *practicing*. She'd rip or cut her practice cloth, then mend it with a faint shimmer of golden light. Remarkably, she'd retained more than a couple of her old [Weaver] skills.

I'd cursed her with longer cooldowns so I could get to sleep, but the gods weren't listening.

She needed spells. We were going to buy her one at Eddie's Mill. Unfortunately, I suspected we wouldn't be able to afford it, even if we found one.

It might take *years* for us to buy a single spell.

Rrriiiiip.

Between Leo's bear snore and Tandy's endless tear-and-weave loop, sleep was a lost cause.

Meredeath had found another bed, probably just to avoid these two. My mind refused to think of other reasons.

Tandy's face was a study in concentration as she poked at the different threads of fabric, then triggered a skill.

"Why are you doing that?"

She started, her skill fizzling as she looked at me, annoyed. My whispered question came out harsher than planned.

"I'm practicing to figure the skill out," Tandy said, as though this was the most obvious thing in the world.

"Why practice a *skill*? You've already learned it. And what are you trying to figure out?" It didn't make sense. Skills just *worked*. There was nothing to figure out.

She turned her head to look at me, eyes flicking to the loudly snoring Leo.

"Tomorrow, I can go over it with both of you. Right now, I just need to do this one more time," Tandy lied. It wasn't going to be one more time, but fifty more times, a hundred.

Her skill triggered, knitting the weave back together like it had a thousand times. I watched as the skill worked, the golden magic connecting each thread and pulling the fabric together.

She glanced at me guiltily as she ripped the cloth again.

"I have a theory about skills," she whispered as though the explanation was her apology. Maybe it was. "I think all skills—martial, magical, crafting, [Mundane], and [Adventurer]—are magic."

Her words made no sense. Everyone knew that [Mundane] and [Adventurer] skills were completely different, and that [Mages] like her, or Lael Voss, were few and far between.

It took a special type of [Adventurer] to wield true magic. The wonders of the world had all been done with greater magic than modern [Mages] could even imagine. It was a class in decline, peaking during the last age.

"That's ridiculous." The words were out of my mouth before I could stop them.

Tandy's expression darkened. "And *that's* why I hadn't told you." She dismissed me and returned to her fabric. "[Detect Weave], [Seamless Fix]."

Eventually, sleep found me in the hot, stuffy attic. I dreamed of muttered skills and a hibernating bear.

Meredeath shook me awake.

"Is it really morning?" I asked groggily.

"Yep, and breakfast is waiting. Get dressed. I'll meet you in the dining hall." Meredeath made sure we were all awake before skipping downstairs like a ray of sunshine. I refused to imagine why she was in such a good mood.

"I hate mornings," I said, carefully stretching so that I didn't boop Richard. He was awake, but ill-tempered until he ate.

Tandy looked at me bleary-eyed.

We made an odd group sitting in a booth. Meredeath and Leo cheerily made small talk with the one waitress on duty, while Tandy and I slumped over cups of coffee. Richard sat in the middle of the table, glaring at anyone who talked too loudly.

Breakfast was ordered and put on a tab we couldn't pay.

Meredeath unwrapped her silverware from the neatly folded cloth napkin. She placed the cloth in her lap and picked up her mug of coffee, blowing on it gently.

"How'd you all sleep?" she asked, taking a small sip.

"Good, and you?" Tandy responded, mirroring Meredeath's actions.

"Very good," Meredeath said with a smile that made my stomach turn. I should have explored with her last night.

Leo reached across the table to grab the canister of sugar.

He spooned a heavy amount into his coffee before offering it up to the table. I shook my head, preferring black coffee.

"So, we've got our first real [Quest]."

"I need to tell you about my family's progression strategy."

Meredeath and Tandy talked over each other.

"[Quest] first, then strategy," I said, making the call. I needed food in me before I heard the secret that Leo and I had wanted our entire lives.

"Yes, well, I talked to Mistress Del last night. She gave me some details about a problem they've been having. We managed to get the [System] to trigger a formal [Quest], let me share it across the party." Meredeath's eyes went unfocused, and a [System] notification pinged.

[Quest Granted: [Missing]

Mistress Del is worried as several of the ladies of the community have gone missing. Further, a couple of the local street urchins haven't been seen in weeks. She suspects the underground delivery staff. Investigate the tunnels, identify the issue, and fix the problem. This is a non-Adventurer's Guild quest and is not rated.

Base reward: Mistress Del will grant free room and board for a month upon the identification of the problem. Additional rewards may be available if all criteria are completed. Adventure Onward!]

"Not very specific, is it? I wonder why she didn't get a more experienced [Adventurer] group to take it." Tandy said as the waitress plunked down a family-style feast including a mess of scrambled eggs, crispy hash browns, and roasted rosemary tomatoes.

"I suspect no 'real' [Adventurers] give Mistress Del the time of day unless it is for other reasons," Meredeath said dryly.

She had a point. We wouldn't be here if we could afford different accommodations.

"If this is what free room and board looks like, I'm in," I

said, directing the conversation to the food piled in front of us. I grabbed a serving spoon and started scraping potatoes and eggs onto my plate.

Save some for me.

"We should still hit up the Adventurer's Guild. There might be some easier [Quests] to work in parallel."

No one argued with Tandy.

"So, Tandy, about that progression strategy…?" Leo said around a mouthful of eggs.

Tandy nodded, holding her coffee cup with both hands. Her leg was jittering nervously next to mine.

"Yeah, so we're a team." She spoke the words carefully as though not believing what she was about to do. "And it is dumb to hold back information that I know would make us stronger. But…"

Her pause extended uncomfortably.

"But it's your family's secrets and, if we blab to everyone, it will look really bad," I finished for her, taking pity on my friend.

She gave me a grateful nod. "Yes, but it's not only that. We paid a pretty high price to the," her voice dropped, "*Null*—"

Leo gasped, cutting her off. Meredeath looked at us like we were crazy, but we knew what she was going to say. The *Nullwrights* were a rumored organization that was a power broker across the continent. They made soul-rending back-alley deals to grant fame, money, and political power. Admitting to a deal meant a death sentence if the *Nullwrights* found out.

Tandy's family had sold their souls to the shadows.

I remembered her parents' sudden divorce. It'd been wild because her parents had always seemed happy together. Now I knew why. Her dad would never have agreed to working with the *Nullwrights*. Tandy's grandmother must have been behind it all.

Tandy's face was white, her hands shaking.

What price had they paid?

"I'll explain later," I told Meredeath, not wanting Tandy to chicken out. "Go on, Tandy. We got it. Won't tell a soul."

She took a deep breath, her voice shaking only slightly as she continued. "If you do tell anyone and *they* find out, I'm dead, and likely my family as well."

We nodded solemnly, agreeing to the unspoken oath. This was serious.

Suddenly, her secretiveness made sense. If Leo or I had made any huge strides in progress, they would have noticed immediately. It all clicked together.

Richard sat on the table, chewing a potato with all his tentacles attuned to Tandy.

"I was the first generation in my family to use the shared progression method. It's a simple truth, but when utilized as a strategy, you can build a strong enough base to make it to [Sage]." She paused again. I could see her willing the courage to spill the secret.

"The trick is—"

Stop.

Four pairs of eyes swiveled to Richard. He sat, mouth mashing a potato, looking for all the world like an overgrown pet slug. His yellow skin glistened with a healthy amount of slime. Swallowing, he looked at us, each tentacle focused on a party member.

The Nullwrights magically track breaches of contracts.

Tandy swore using a word I'd never heard out of her. She'd been seconds away from dooming herself and her family.

Besides, I suspect I know what Tandy was going to reveal. She knows one of the three tenets of progression.

Now, *that* I hadn't predicted. Richard preened under our scrutiny.

"And? Go on already, Richard," Leo pushed. His hands

clenched his coffee cup as though it was the only thing preventing him from slug murder.

Practice makes perfect.

I watched Tandy trying to gauge her reaction. She closed her eyes, giving a faint smile as a tear traced down her cheek.

"That's it?" Leo said, unable to control his anger. He slammed his mug down on the table inches away from Richard.

Richard's head swung around, his dark eyes almost glowing. *Did you know that the main reason people lose a skill is due to disuse? Skill failure is a product of the size of an attempt and lack of practice.* His head swung toward me. *That specializations are earned through rote? The [Trial Dungeon] kept threatening that your choices matter. Why is it so surprising for you to learn now that they do?*

I shook my head. Sure, I'd practiced creating nails over and over. I just wanted to master the twist and pull of metal. And Marta had me on breakfasts the first three months I'd been a [Chef], which put me in charge of the morning gruel. I'd always focused on the details, knowing the importance of a foundation.

Realization shook me, Tandy, and I had shared that passion. I'd been unintelligent in my focus. Otherwise, I might have had [Sage] potential too.

She'd just gone about it a lot smarter. In a way that bent the [System] to her family's will.

I looked at Leo. He was pissed.

"That explains nothing. I wasn't even able to get a class." His words were angry. I didn't blame him. I was mad at myself, the echoes of [Self Flagellation] kicking in. I realized my whole [Self Critic] skill set was because I *practiced* doubting myself.

"How long have you ever tried to master a skill? Staying at a job?" Tandy's voice cut across Leo's anger like fabric scissors across a yard.

"I didn't have a *choice*. Artie put me to work to make rent."

The panic, the heartbreak over years wasted, came through in Leo's voice. I reached for my friend, but he was already standing.

"This is *bullshit.* I'm going for a walk. I'll meet you at the Adventurer's Guild in an hour." He left before I managed to find the words to reach him.

Silence hung in the air around the table.

"So, practicing with your cloth wasn't just your neurosis?" Tandy didn't respond to my comment as I unwound our childhood. "We made fun of you that whole time, and it was all wrapped around your progression strategy?"

The food lost its flavor; it was just texture and regret. How foolish we'd been. I understood Leo's need to flee.

And that's just the first tenet.

"I spent so many years blaming the [System]... and it was my own fault the whole time," I said, despondently as I moved cold scrambled eggs around my plate.

There's a lot to put at the [System's] feet, don't feel too bad.

I raised my eyes to Richard's. For the first time, I really saw him. He was a theoretical [Immortal] in the confines of a banana slug's body. A shiver of fear traveled up my spine.

"I'm afraid of what else you know," I whispered, glancing at white-faced Tandy.

Richard's tentacles looked out into space as he absentmindedly reached for a tomato skin. Red juice sluiced down his chin, and his eyes swung creepily towards me.

You should be afraid.

Chapter 47

ONE MORE DEMON

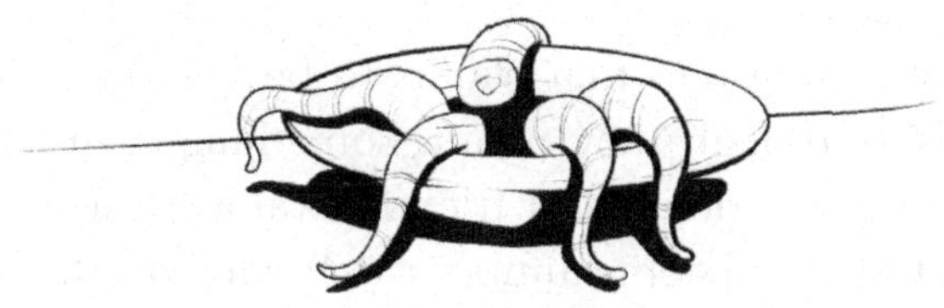

[Heartbeat] tugged at me. I *had* to find Leo. He was spiraling out of control.

Fortunately, Eddie's Mill was less intimidating with a full stomach.

The city was divided into four areas: the docks, the shops, the residential district, and the professional district. There were smaller, specialized subdistricts. *The Velvet Box* was in the slums between the docks and the shopping districts, called the Red Eaves neighborhood. The Adventure's Guild sat firmly in the professional district, wedged between an apothecary and an accountant. This should have been the first clue that Eddie's Mill [Adventurers] were built differently.

The door to the Guild was set like a saloon, swinging open as we entered. The entrance dumped us into a parlor of sorts, with an uninterested clerk shuffling papers on a heavy wooden desk. Three doors sat behind him—one painted green, one painted red, and an ornate door of wood with gold accents.

"Welcome to the Adventurer's Guild. How can I help you?" came a dull monotone greeting as the guy looked at us curiously.

"Uh, we're new in town. Looking for the Quest Board," Tandy said.

"And we're meeting a friend. Tall guy, blonde hair, and he's got a double-bladed axe," I added. I was anxious to check in on Leo. I didn't need [Party Rapport] to know that he was hurting.

"Ah yes, the group that claims to be [Marked]." He said the words as though they meant something to us. "Proceed through the green door. Your friend is waiting inside."

"What's behind door number two?" Meredeath asked. She was as bad as a cat with a closed door.

The clerk stood slowly. Sitting, he wasn't intimidating, but standing, he towered over all of us, matching Leo for size. Muscles flexed under the robes.

"Entrance through those doors is earned through rank." His voice was cool, brooking no argument.

Rank? This guy wouldn't know what to do with a truly powerful [Adventurer]. Wake me when something interesting happens. Richard curled his tentacles inward, a sure sign he was going to nap.

Meredeath shrugged off the threat and casually walked over to the green door. Tandy and I gave the man a wide berth as we followed.

The green door opened onto a stairwell *down.* The stairs were wide and well lit, with polished handrails. Even so, the message was clear: everyone started in the basement.

The room opened up into a tavern of sorts. A bar sat against the far wall. A bartender polished glasses with a long, oiled mustache turned up at the ends. He watched us neutrally.

A scattering of mismatched tables peppered the dining

hall. Some stained [Adventurers] sat at a central table eating breakfast. They smelled of blood and body odor. The two ate, heads down. A pile of gray noodles sat untouched next to them on a platter. I could almost see flies buzzing over their heads.

Leo was against a wall in a booth, sitting by himself. On the far side of the room, a board sat with presumable [Quests] available, and a clerk sat in a cubby, reading.

[Heartbeat] tugging at me, I joined Leo at the table. Meredeath and Tandy went to examine the board.

"Hey, man," I said, scooting across from my friend.

Leo muttered something unintelligible, his eyes down, tracing a crack in the wood with a finger.

"Hey, I'm mad too. That..." I looked around, seeing several eyes on us. "That thing that Richard told us? It could have made all the difference growing up. Complete bullshit."

Leo's eyes raised and, for an instant, I saw behind the curtain. Hurt and rage warred for prominence. The curtain fell, and his eyes shifted to the side, almost blank.

"We're here together. That's what counts." His voice was flat, emotionless, just like his platitudes.

I shifted, picking up a now-sleeping Richard and placing him on the table. "It's going to get better, you're an [Adventurer] now."

"Yes, and unlike you, I'm not burdened with needing a [Sponsor]." He said the words through clenched teeth as he stood. "And I don't have to be the pet of a slug." Leo's hard eyes stared down at me for a second. I felt like an ant.

"Sorry, Cole, I need to use the privy," he said, walking off. We both knew he hadn't needed to use the restroom. He just needed space. Space from *me*, his best friend.

His back was rigid as he walked away, and he looked naked without Tandy's pink sweater. My heart ached.

Leo left his axe in the seat, an unspoken promise he'd return. At least I didn't have to worry about that.

You sure fucked that up.

I didn't have a comeback for Richard. He was right. I put my head down on the table, ready to crawl under a rock and take a nap. The table's aroma of maple syrup and beer seemed fitting. An optimistic start to a day, mixed with the need to accept what happened.

Raised voices came from the quest board, and I tilted my head to watch Tandy argue with the clerk. I should probably intervene, but I just didn't have it in me. Tandy was raising her voice as she pointed at the pieces of paper pinned to the board.

The clerk looked irritated, like she'd dealt with this complaint before and knew the outcome.

Meredeath pulled at Tandy, trying to get her to walk away.

I sat, my mouth dry. I didn't even have the coins to order a beer and watch the show. [Adventurers] were supposed to be wealthy, full of loot, and have a lust for life. Not stuck in a basement arguing with a paper pusher.

I twisted my head to face the table, blocking out Tandy and brought up my stat sheet.

When Richard and I had rebonded, I received my [Dead Wrong] class back, along with all the inherent skills it granted. At least this time, I knew what I was signing up for.

I could feel [Self Critic] trigger, but I didn't care. I deserved some criticism.

How can I apply the first tenet of progression to my skills? The list was hardly noteworthy, with a few exceptions: [Cheat Death], [Alive, For Once], [Gills], [Analyze], [Improvised Damage], [Party], [Stillpoint], [Heartbeat], [Partial Rapport], [Companion], [Minor Manipulate Slime], [Hammer Time], [Nailed It], [Cartographer], [Slug Toss] and [Self Critic].

My most valuable skill was the one I vowed never to use—[Cheat Death]. The skill would keep me alive, but the cost...

I could practice [Gills] by jumping in a river. Triggering [Analyze] on the table, I waved away the resulting message.

Raising a finger, I triggered [Minor Manipulate Slime]. Concentrating on the pool of slime that'd formed around Richard, and folded it up over his prone body. It slipped, so I folded it again and again.

[Skill Upgrade: [Minor Slime Manipulation] has been upgraded to [Slime Manipulation]. You now have the ability to control and move larger piles of slime. Congratulations!]

Was this all there was to it? Just practicing the skills? I could do this. So could Leo.

The big man had returned, propping his axe against the wall.

I started to share my skill upgrade, but squashed the instinct.

*Good to know you have **some** sense.*

"Leo, I'm sorry that things haven't worked out differently. But we've got this knowledge now, we can figure it out."

"Sure, Cole. We'll figure it out," Leo muttered flatly, not meeting my gaze. I mentally switched off [Self Critic], deciding to take his response as a win.

"If you want Richard, you can have him." We both looked at the slug who glistened in the slime I'd folded over him.

"He's too slippery, hard to pin him down to commit," Leo joked.

I smiled, almost feeling my [Heartbeat] skill level. I'd broken through!

"Yeah, I had to trap him in a compost bin, poor fellow. Plus, he's given me a [Weakened] debuff. Probably not worth it."

"Is that why you die so much? I thought it was just you," Leo ribbed and, for a moment, we were back to our usual selves.

"Fucking Malyc and those sheep-loving bureaucrats." Tandy sat down heavily, her words hanging in the air. Meredeath waited as Leo made room for her.

"What's the word?" I asked, unenthusiastic about her reply.

"Malyc hasn't submitted paperwork on our passing the [Trial Dungeon]. So they've got us listed as [Sworn Adventurers] instead of [Marked Adventurers]." Tandy sounded resigned, as though this difference ruined us.

"Can't they just [Examine] or [Analyze] us?" I asked quietly.

"They did." Meredeath's words were bitter, as though she was ready to gut the clerk herself. "The clerk said our classes sounded fake. Apparently, faking a class is something you can do. She didn't believe us."

"So, what does this mean?" Leo asked quietly.

"It means shit training [Quests] meant for part-timers working up to the [Trial Dungeon]," Tandy explained.

It didn't sound *that* bad. As though reading my thoughts, Meredeath filled in the blanks.

"We're still only allowed the low-pay 'rats in the cellar' jobs. And because they expect [Sworn Adventurers] to have a day job, it's not going to be enough."

Ah, that was the rub. If we were being honest, we probably should still be working low-level jobs, but we needed money.

"I grabbed these since they'll align with Mistress Del's [Quest], but we're going to have to move on if her charity runs out." Tandy threw two slips of paper onto the table. The [Quests] triggered in my vision.

[Quest Granted: [Rats in the Tunnels]

The city of Eddie's Mill has a rat problem. There is a .1 copper bounty per rat. Rewards will be granted per tail.]

I glanced over at the two downtrodden [Adventurers], realizing in horror the platter of 'noodles' on their table was dozens of rat tails. Something odd was going on in the city if they'd caught that many rats.

The second [Quest Notification] popped:

[Quest Granted: [Guard Duty]

The port of entry has experienced theft lately. The Merchant's Guild has offered 1 copper per guard to watch the stores overnight. Bonuses are available for any thief caught in the act.]

"Not thrilling, but better than nothing, I guess." It was hard to work up more enthusiasm than that.

We talked, making plans as we eyed the bartender thirstily. I decided to go back to Mistress Del's and get an afternoon nap. Sleeping was free, and we were about to pull the graveyard shift. The girls went window shopping, presumably so they could get a sense of the cost of items.

I think they just enjoyed torturing themselves with the things they couldn't have.

Leo waved us off, opting to stay at the bar. It was going to be a long night, so I didn't bother arguing.

Leo'd been fighting his demons his whole life. He never gave us credit for having stood by him.

Now I couldn't help but feel I'd joined the ranks of demons. Just another disappointment he had to fight off.

Chapter 48

FLIRTING WITH DISASTER

"We never should have split the party," Meredeath muttered for the tenth time. I didn't see what the big deal was.

Tandy wanted to investigate the sewer junction, looking for rats. I thought observing the warehouse operations for the night would be beneficial.

It didn't hurt that I ended up pairing with Meredeath. Or that Richard went with Tandy because he had a *nose* for rats. Whatever that meant.

It was a win for me, and honestly, I needed a win.

Too bad I couldn't capitalize.

"So, what is your new class?" I tried to change the subject and, like some dumbass, I decided chatting about stats was the way to go.

I could hear Richard's imaginary taunts. *What are you going to do next, Cole? Ask her about her shoe size?*

I had an inner demon, and his name was Richard.

"Did you even know my original class?" She was still irritated, but at least she was talking about something else.

We were crouched behind a pile of crates in the underground warehouse. In the end, we didn't join the guards huddled around torches. It was pretty obvious after five minutes why the pay was so low and why they hadn't caught any thieves.

"Point taken, but I've been curious. It's important to know your capabilities," I pushed, not needing Richard's help to triple down on my stupidity.

Meredeath's secrecy bothered me. When she'd admitted to being from another world, I thought that was it, that she'd start opening up. But since she gained Rhi Voss as her [Sponsor], she'd become even more secretive.

We already knew Rhi was a [Lich]. I wasn't sure how much worse Meredeath's secrets could get.

"I'll make you a trade: you give me the details of your class, and I'll give you mine."

Well, fuck. I didn't want to talk about being Richard's pet. Or that my class relied on me dying or pretending to die. It wasn't sexy. I didn't have a hero's class.

"Uh..." I scrambled for an excuse.

"Exactly." Meredeath read my hesitation accurately. Tandy never made being smart look so sexy, but Meredeath did it effortlessly.

Shifting my weight, my boot squelched in the mud. For a city sophisticated enough to have an underground goods delivery network, they sure hadn't thought through the logistics of having the port of entry so close to a river.

It was wet, cold, and as dark as Richard's soul.

Meredeath had insisted I not use the torch function on my hammer, maintaining it'd ruin our night vision. Personally, I didn't have any vision to ruin.

Maybe her eyeliner was [Enchanted] with night vision?

"How about a counter? A guessing game. We share our

theories, and promise to admit if the other person is right?" I asked.

I'd spun theory after theory in my head about what Meredeath's true build was, before and after her [Sponsorship]. This seemed like a no-lose gamble.

She turned her head towards me. The faint smell of patchouli and mint hung in the air. She was close enough to kiss. My heart thundered in my ears.

"Deal, but I go first. You've got a skill that allows you to come back from the dead. It's not an [Undead] skill, but it lets you cheat." Her words slapped the imagined intimacy right out of my head. She continued with her cold analysis. "You died fighting the tidemaw. I saw the notification pop before it vanished."

"I—Uh..."

"I already know I'm right, so just out with it." Her voice rose with a grin. Damn it. Every time I thought I had the upper hand, she proved me wrong.

"Yeah, the skill is called [Cheat Death]." Resigned, I admitted the truth. "But it's less of a cheat and more of a trade. The [System] doesn't give handouts."

I shuddered, my mind reliving the undulating skin and tissues as my lungs realigned. It was a trade from hell. A tiny part of my humanity had vanished. I'd spent weeks trying to get a full breath before my senses adapted.

Reaching out, she ran her fingers lightly against my gills, acknowledging the price.

The touch was sensual, on the verge of ticklish.

Maybe gills weren't so bad after all.

"There's always a cost," Meredeath whispered, touching her amulet. Her eyes rose to mine, faintly glowing green. Her voice caught as she finished her thought. "Even when you stand still."

The words cut, especially after Richard's revelations about skill use. I don't know how close I was to losing [Cheat

Death], but I was going to have to figure out some way to practice it.

What price had she paid for standing still?

Shadows danced in our corner of the warehouse, forestalling my questions.

A delivery wagon rumbled out of the southern tunnel. Wood creaked as a lone horse and driver plodded along. A small, dimmed lantern hung from the driver's seat. The whole outfit was painted black, as though a reaper from the land of the dead had made an appearance.

Delivery and operations had shut down hours ago. A delivery from an all-black wagon at the witching hour? *This* was exactly what we'd been waiting for.

"Your turn," I whispered as we watched the slow-moving wagon. "I know you've got some sort of night vision skill. But you've refused to use any other new skill since we left the swamp."

"It's [Dark Vision], and it's a passive that I can't turn off, which is irritating..." *for someone who likes to hide in the shadows.* She left it unsaid, but I got her point.

"And the rest of your skills?" I pushed.

Her eyes flared, angry. "The rest of my skills haunt me," she said as the air chilled around us. It was so cold my breath fogged, and my lungs ached. Then it was gone the next instant. "Did you see the stain on the tailgate?"

"No, I don't have [Dark Vision]," I said calmly, willing the icicles from my lungs.

"I think we've got our first clue. Let's follow the driver. I'd like to look at that cargo." Meredeath stood, mapping out a path to follow the wagon.

She'd gone from threat to business in an instant, not unlike her [Lich] of a [Sponsor]. She might have more reason than me to be cautious.

"What color was the stain?"

"Red," she whispered, her voice wavering.

The wagon wove through boxes and crates, steadily aimed at the riverside exit while avoiding the posted guards. It moved with the slow confidence of routine. No one challenged the driver.

The river entrance was tucked under the southern bridge. We'd completely missed it while getting ripped off entering the city.

Meredeath and I watched as the wagon rolled unimpeded out onto the boardwalk connecting the docks. We stood in the shadow of the bridge pylons, silent witnesses to the exchange.

With the help of the moon, we had a perfect view as the uncovered wagon pulled up not thirty yards from the bridge.

A figure popped out of one of the river runners, not bothering with a lamp. The driver and boat owner exchanged words. This was a planned rendezvous.

Moving to the tailgate, the two looked at the wagon's only cargo, a long, narrow box.

"They're unloading her." Meredeath was standing, with anger and outrage pulsing through her voice. "She's alive, I can *feel* it. We've got to do something."

Before I could respond, she ran down the dock, glowing daggers in hand, like a vengeful spirit.

That escalated quickly.

Of course, she charged. Why ask questions when you can kick ass first?

"Unhand her!" Meredeath shouted, her voice carrying over the docks.

As I caught up, lights were coming on in the surrounding boats. The driver faced Meredeath's anger, hands out unthreateningly. He looked rough, with a greasy beard and several white scars across his face.

"On whose authority? We're conducting legitimate business." He sounded tired, as though he were used to being accused. It wasn't what I expected from someone smuggling a girl out of the city in the middle of the night.

Meredeath, all five-foot-one of her, stood pointing her ominously glowing dagger at the man.

"I'm an [Adventurer], and I will not let you kidnap her. I don't need formal authority to stop human trafficking." Her teeth were clenched.

"Oh, Tad, another one of *those*?" someone called from one of the boats. "Everyone, go back to bed, it's just Tad delivering another body."

Groans and complaints issued from the boats around us as lights flickered off.

"Well, Miss [Adventurer], my name's Tad, and I'm the undertaker for the city. This young woman," he gestured to the feet he'd begun to pull from the back of the wagon, "is an Unfortunate. No one claimed her at the morgue, and no one has reported her missing. So, unless you have the burial fee, I'm going to hand her off to Lennie here and be on my way."

I put a hand on Meredeath's shoulder, trying to will her to calm down.

Instead, she whirled, her daggers up. Sharp green malevolent eyes saw only an obstacle to cut down.

"It's okay," I said calmly, lowering my hammer to the ground. Trusting Meredeath not to stab me, I talked to the undertaker. "Sorry, sir. Just an honest mistake."

"I saw her move," Meredeath hissed between gritted teeth. I stepped back, no longer certain I was safe.

For the first time all night, I wished Richard were here. He'd defuse Meredeath with some witty joke.

"Well, we can check," Tad said, possibly saving both our lives. "But she's been dead three days. Kept her in the cooling caves, but that still does a number on the body."

He pulled the woman out of the wagon, laying her on the ground. A stained linen shroud wrapped her body. The woman, the body, was limp and lifeless.

Meredeath and I stepped forward, and I was immediately overcome by the sweet smell of rot.

I coughed and stepped back, but Meredeath was undeterred. She used a dagger to pull back the linen.

The woman was dead. What had been a youthful face was marred by the discoloration and bloat from decomposition. Clouded eyes stared sightlessly at the night.

Meredeath sheathed her daggers, bending down to touch the girl's face. "How'd she die?"

"Stabbed in the kidney. One of the delivery drivers found her bled out in the tunnels near the spice district." Tad's voice was softer, kinder, speaking of the dead. He sounded as though this was not an uncommon occurrence. "The rats had already gotten to her, or I'd have kept her longer, but times being as they are… Thank the Everbear for Lennie here, and his soft heart."

Lennie, the boat captain, had joined us. He walked with the arthritic gait of an old man.

"I'll take her. It does her soul no good to gaze upon the stars." Lennie bent next to Meredeath. "You carry that pain deep, don't you? May you honor your loss."

Squeezing her shoulder, he covered the nameless woman and motioned to Tad to grab her feet. Meredeath stood, joining me as they loaded the body into a protective cradle, cushioning it from the rocking of the boat.

The two men shook hands, then Tad unwound the mooring lines. Lennie used a long pole to push off from the dock, gliding into the current.

A soft glow of a skill lit the boat as it moved upstream. Lennie stood at the aft, glowing with magic like a mythical ferryman for the dead.

"Lennie's a good man," Tad said, joining us as we watched. "He lost his daughter years ago. He takes all the unclaimed women and gives them a proper burial on his family land. It's a kindness in the world. Even death is expensive these days; the city only pays for a mass grave. This is better."

Silent rivulets of tears ran down Meredeath's usually stoic face.

Here was one of her secrets, laid uncomfortably bare. I wanted to reach for her, to say something clever. But grief wasn't a monster I knew how to fight.

Instead, I turned to Tad, trying to give her a moment. "You said rats got at her body? Is the rat problem particularly bad in any one spot?"

[Partial Rapport] gave a distant tug. I ignored it, hoping to get a lead.

Tad studied me, white scars reflecting in the moonlight. "You're both a bit green to be taking on a problem like that, aren't you?"

"I think we can handle some rats," I said, my pride stung.

He leaned in, his breath heavy with garlic. I tried not to gag. "They're heaviest in the southern sewer junction. Down by the restaurants." He grabbed my shoulder. "There's more'n rats in the sewers. They're fleeing something."

His hand squeezed, emphasizing his last words. "Do you know what rats fear, son?"

I wordlessly shook my head.

"Neither do I," Tad said, as he let go of me.

The undertaker turned back towards his wagon, pulling a toothpick out of his pocket. He set himself stiffly on the bench, the toothpick between his teeth. With a nod, he shook the reins.

"That's where Tandy and Leo are," I said to the night air.

The itching in the back of my mind that I'd associated with [Partial Rapport] vanished. Leo, Tandy, and Richard were gone.

"I told you we shouldn't have split the party."

Chapter 49

NOT YOUR AVERAGE SEWER RAT

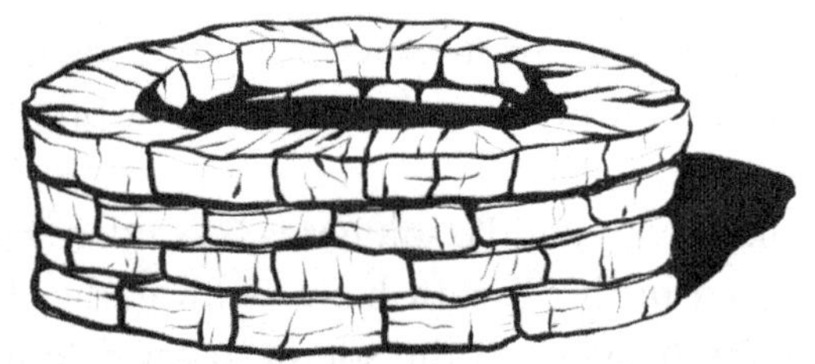

"Richaaard! Tandy? Leeee-oooo!!!!"

We'd been wandering under the southern restaurant district for an hour. Back and forth, calling. I'd triggered [Molten Promise] on my hammer, turning it into an oversized torch. No crack or crevasse was left in the dark. We'd looked at our party [Map], and they'd crisscrossed the area so much it was hard to tell where they'd disappeared.

The empty spot in my mind that they inhabited was a raw, sharp wound. It was as though they'd been excised from my psyche with an obsidian knife, and all I could feel was their absence.

The red-hot panic started to turn into resignation. [Self Critic] had me doubting it was even possible for me to find them. The city was *so* much bigger than Woodsten. I was out of my depth. They were gone.

I knew I needed to keep searching. Keep looking.

But I felt helpless.

"They didn't die," I said, primarily for my own benefit. If I spoke it, it had to be true.

"No, we would have gotten a death notice. They're *still* in [Your Mom's Party], just not *here*." Meredeath backed me up with the confidence of someone who believed in the [System's] rules.

I knew better.

We sat back against the sides of the tunnel. [Guardian's Promise] sat next to me, illuminating the walls like a certain glowworm.

Even if I were going to allow myself to believe Meredeath, I had no idea what to do next.

The delivery tunnels were a fairly straightforward web that followed the roads of the city. We'd searched *everywhere* they were supposed to explore. Not only had we not found them, but the place was empty. No rats. No deliveries. Nothing suspicious.

"Let's go back to the sewer juncture." Meredeath suggested. "If Tad is right, and that's where the rats are congregating, then that's where they *should* have ended up."

Her words were calm, logical, and made sense. And that, irrationally, pissed me off.

"We already checked. They're not there!" We couldn't find them, and she didn't seem that upset by it. Worse, she'd been *right*. Splitting the party had been a bad idea, but I'd been so excited to get some time alone with her.

Meredeath stood, patting the dust off her legs.

No part of me wanted to imagine being [Adventurers] without Tandy and Leo. I tried triggering [Heartbeat] again, but all I got was heartburn. It was all my fault.

"COLE! Snap out of it! Look at me." Meredeath snapped her fingers. I refused to look. "I don't know what's got you stuck, but sitting here in an empty tunnel isn't going to save *our friends'* lives. Now get off your ass and start doing something useful."

"But it's *my fault.*" The truth I'd been clutching came out in a whisper.

"Has your [Self Critic] leveled or something? Even if I agreed it was somehow your fault, which I don't, how are you fixing it?"

I looked up at her. She had a hand extended to help me up. I took a deep breath, trying to will the tension from my body. I took her hand, and she pulled me to my feet. [Guardian's Promise] flared when I grabbed it, as though it sensed my resolve.

Without another word, Meredeath headed back to the main junction for the district. The leather of her black corset armor reflected the glow of my hammer.

"You should take your own advice," I called after her as I willed my feet to move. Her back stiffened. She didn't turn to look at me, so I continued. "Whatever it was in your previous life? It's not your fault either."

Meredeath kept walking, ignoring my comment.

I knew why. It wasn't easy advice to follow.

Fifteen minutes of silence, and we were back where our investigation had started.

The sewer junction sat in the middle of a wide roundabout. Tunnels exited the chamber like spokes on a wagon wheel. The delivery tunnels in this section of the city all sloped down to here.

This sewer was larger than the other junctions we'd seen. Not only were there grates for runoff but also a waist-high giant drain positioned in the center. Presumably so restaurants could bring their frying grease and dump it.

The whole place reeked of old cooking oil. It was a sewer rat's paradise.

I leaned over the drain, holding [Guardian's Promise]

above it. The pit continued well beyond the light of my hammer.

"I don't understand how they made these tunnels. This wouldn't be easy to build, even in my world. And you're a lot more…" Meredeath caught herself. I knew what she was going to say. Our world is a lot more 'primitive.'

"They likely used magic. Back when Eddie's Mill was built, we had true [Geomancers] who handled most of the underlying build of these old cities. That's why the new districts are always crappier. A lot of skill and spells were lost in the cataclysm that ended the last age." I wasn't about to admit that I, too, was impressed by the city's design.

Meredeath peered into the darkness. Light wasn't a limiting resource for her eyes anymore.

"Do you see anything?" I asked.

She leaned further still, squinting into the abyss.

"Best lean back," came a low, gruff voice. I nearly jumped out of my skin.

Clutching [Guardian's Promise], I turned to face the newcomer.

"No harm intended," he said as he stepped into the light, palms up.

Meredeath's eyes were glowing as she crouched, ready to jump into action.

The guy was short and stocky. He wore flexible scaly armor with joints made of chainmail and a midnight black double-bladed axe. Bushy eyebrows and a pair of brown eyes peeked over a thick green bandana. A long tangle of rope coiled around his arm as he stepped into the center of the roundabout.

I hoped he was a fellow [Adventurer], because if he was the person causing issues in Eddie's Mill, we were about to become his next victims.

He stepped past Meredeath, looking down into the drain.

With a grunt, he threw the coiled rope into the hole. He held a grappling hook in his hand as he watched the rest fall.

"You with the glowing hammer. Find an anchor for me, will you?" His nonchalance disarmed me as much as anything. This was a man at work.

I cast about, looking for anything that could be considered an 'anchor.'

"It's over here," Meredeath beckoned. The man's eyebrows raised as he walked around the drain. Sure enough, she'd found a steel anchor poking out of the concrete.

He latched his rope to the steel rung and walked back to the drain, looking into it.

"Are you going down there?" I asked the obvious. I could imagine what Richard would say.

"Yes, people to rescue and all that." He hopped onto the rim of the drain and, without another word, jumped into the abyss.

Meredeath and I ran up to the rim and watched as he rappelled down. The drain was just wide enough for him to kick off and drop in three-to-five-foot increments. The walls were slick with grease and threatened to cause him to slip at any moment.

Ten feet, then fifteen. He kicked off and disappeared. A faint shimmer flickered in the drain as a cool breeze blew up from the hole. The air smelled of grease, but felt heavy, like a storm was brewing.

"Can you see him?" I asked, grabbing Meredeath's arm. Was this a trick of the light? I held [Guardian's Promise] over the hole, squinting to see the guy.

"No, he's just gone."

The rope suddenly went slack, bouncing flat against the wall. I had a sinking feeling I knew where the rest of our party was.

"Do you think it's a portal?" Meredeath asked.

I looked down again. As far as my eyes could tell, the drain was a bottomless pit. Except it wasn't. It felt like the pit was watching me back.

"I have no idea, but he must have hit the bottom, right?" I pulled at the loose rope.

"Either that or dropped to his death," Meredeath countered. We stared at the brown twisted rope a bit longer.

My mind raced, evaluating all the possibilities. "That guy seemed too knowledgeable to just jump to his death. He had to be an [Adventurer], right?"

Meredeath tugged at the rope, testing the grappling hook.

"It seems sturdy enough." She looked at me, her eyes pensive. I wasn't thrilled about going into a grease trap, but if Tandy and Leo were down there, what choice did we have?

"I've never heard an [Adventurer] story about climbing into a sewer," I muttered, unhappy with the task before us.

Meredeath looked at me as though evaluating whether I was serious. She started chuckling, one of those insane little uncontrollable laughs. Before I knew it, she was bent over, grabbing her stomach.

"You obviously haven't played Dungeons and Dragons," she wheezed, wiping tears from her face.

Dungeons and Dragons? What kind of world did Meredeath come from?

"Who would play with dungeons *or* dragons, much less together?"

Meredeath lost control again.

I had a sneaking suspicion we were going to find more than rats down here. I just hoped it wasn't dragons *or* dungeons.

Turned out the joke was on me.

Chapter 50

DUNEGONS AND …

Meredeath demanded to go first, because of course she did.

Which meant as she dipped down into the shimmering hole, my last connection with [Your Mom's Party] disappeared.

[Heartbeat] echoed endlessly, waiting for a response.

Silence.

Meredeath was supposed to poke her head back through and let me know it was okay.

Nothing.

Then, the rope suddenly jerked before going completely slack.

Fuck.

Did I go after her?

If she needed help, I couldn't just stand around.

I slung a leg over the lip of the well, rope in hand. The greasy pit smelled repulsive.

Time to be the hero.

If this was *really* a mistake, at least I had [Cheat Death] off cooldown.

I rappelled down, three feet at a time. It was going well until I hit the shimmering portal, my foot slipped, and the sudden weight on my hands snapped my grip. I fell uncontrolled headfirst into the...

[Quest Granted: [First Run]

You have discovered the [Basic Wild] [Unnamed] dungeon beneath Eddie's Mill. This undiscovered dungeon has had [0] successful completed attempts. Complete the dungeon to earn naming rights, faction association, and a [Dungeon Treasure Chest]. Adventure Onward!]

...dungeon.

I somersaulted, landing *hard* on my ass.

"Glad you could join me." Meredeath looked down at me. "Good thing I didn't need any help."

"Why didn't you—?" I said, then looked at the rope dangling ten feet off the ground.

"Once I fell, I couldn't reach it." Meredeath explained. "You figured it out. No harm, no foul. You know anything about this [First Run]?"

"Not a clue. I barely qualify as an [Adventurer]." The truth hurt, even when I said it.

"Might as well be from Kansas, huh?" Meredeath offered me a hand up. My bruised backside protested.

Standing, I looked around at what was apparently a dungeon in the sewer beneath Eddie's Mill. I'd never heard of an [Unnamed] dungeon.

I could sense the rest of the party vaguely. It felt muted, like they were distant, but at least we were in the right place.

Concentrating, I brought up the party map to see if [Partial Rapport] showed any details on Tandy and Leo's location. For the first time in weeks, I grinned.

"Looks like Tandy and Leo are doing just fine." My [Cartographer] skill came in handy, as it showed, in detail, what they'd explored so far. Also, three blinking marks indicated the location of our absent party members.

We headed south, towards a maze of tunnels with branching junctures and dead ends.

I expected sewers to match the leviathan's colon in terms of grossness, but the sewer was oddly clean. Except for some leaf litter in a few corners, nothing stuck out. It was as though something had eaten everything that didn't belong.

A low hum came from the dungeon's ambient light source, an embedded magical filament running along the ceiling.

The dank tunnel was rather dull for a real dungeon. No monster ambushes, no acidic moss, not even a distant growl. We found small glistening piles of slime once in a while, but I just assumed they were from Richard.

"Do we have to worry about traps?" Meredeath asked, breaking the monotony.

"We're just retracing their steps. They should be disarmed or already triggered, right?" I paused as Meredeath grabbed my arm. "Why are you asking?"

We were a dozen feet away from a junction. From the map, it looks like Leo and Tandy continued forward.

"People have died here," she said.

"How do you know?"

"It's a skill, okay? [Detect Death]." Her voice lowered, as though she didn't want to admit the skill. "I turned it on after the docks."

The skill certainly would have saved us some embarrassment.

We approached the junction cautiously. She was the first one to see the trap. An inconspicuous plate sticking up marginally higher than the others.

Throwing a rock at it, we were rewarded by an audible click, followed by a high-velocity burst of water. The streams would easily flay flesh from bone as they crisscrossed the trigger plate.

"Damn, that would have hurt," I said, impressed. My [Gills] would have done nothing to prevent *that* death.

"Yeah, be careful," Meredeath said blandly. "There's probably more."

We sidestepped the trigger carefully.

"I'm surprised Leo hasn't stepped onto one of these," Meredeath commented as we avoided several more suspicious-looking stones. Her [Detect Death] skill hadn't gone off again.

"Oh, that's Tandy's fault. She's always looking out for him… us. With the clout of her family, she could have done much better than us for friends." I'd long ago stopped questioning the illogic of our friendship. Her presence was as immutable as the mountains.

The quiet of this god-forsaken dungeon freaked me out. Where were the monsters? Giant sewer rats? Goblins with poor hygiene and sticks? Even [Basic] dungeons should have had some martial challenge beyond traps, right?

"Is that blood on the wall over there?" Meredeath knocked me out of my thoughts as she pointed to one of the oozing walls. A splash of red stood chest high, looking for all the world like the spray off an axe.

"Do dungeon monsters bleed like that?" I asked.

Meredeath looked at me like I were a world-class dumbass. "How the hell would I know? I'm from Kansas, remember?"

"Well, I'm just a loser with an [Immortal] sentient slug," I threw back at her.

"G-reat," someone moaned down the split to the left. "And here I was hoping you'd be able to help me."

Meredeath and I exchanged a look. Had we just spilled the beans on our most important secrets to a stranger? She unsheathed her daggers, and I gripped my hammer as we turned down the tunnel, finding an old friend.

The guy who jumped into the dungeon sat against the tunnel wall, axe on the ground before him, holding a wad of cloth against his shoulder. It was soaked in blood.

"Uh, hello again. Happy to help, that looks bad," I said, clipping my hammer as I kneeled next to the guy. He wasn't going to be a threat in this shape.

Meredeath stayed on guard, daggers in hand.

"What got you?" Meredeath asked, braced for an attack from him or his assailants.

The man groaned as I took over, holding the compression in place. The rag was covered with sticky blood.

"I'm embarrassed to admit that they were oversized raccoons. Damn bandit-faced jerks came at me with knives. I didn't expect that in a [Basic Wild] dungeon. The one that got me had some sort of anti-coagulant on its blades." He must have picked up on my blank expression. "You an [Adventurer], son?"

I nodded, his blood oozing between my fingers.

A squeak echoed down the tunnel. Meredeath and I exchanged looks.

"We're new at this." I waved down the hallway. I moved his rag to take a look and gagged. The wound was deep, cutting muscle down to the bone. His arm hung limply.

"I see. Well, let's get me patched up, and we can talk. Do you have any [First Aid] skills? I've got some, but I can't use them on myself. I'm Andrew, by the way. What's your name?" His voice was a lot calmer than mine would have been if the circumstances had been reversed.

"Gods-damn-it, you're whiter than I am." He snapped his fingers in front of my face. "Focus on me, boy."

I took a couple of breaths, holding the cloth against the wound, and focused on the guy's face. He was a little older, with some gray streaks in his beard. An old scar ran across his face from cheek to chin.

This guy had seen a few fights. If he wasn't panicking, I

could hold it together. Even if I didn't know what to do, he did.

"Okay, open up my pack. There's a red tin, grab that. Every [Adventuring] party should have its first aid kit, regardless of whether anyone has [Healing] capabilities," Andrew lectured. The man reminded me of Marta. That calm explanation of how things should work. "Remind me what your name was?"

A faint scratching of claws on stone echoed ahead.

"Cole."

"Right, Cole. Did you find the red tin? Yes, I see it. Great, now pop it open. There should be a jar of powdered herbs, yes, that's it—"

That's when the raccoon bandits attacked.

Three bounded down the hallway, three-foot-tall armed bundles of fury. Their eyes glowed blue with magic as they clutched knives in their hands. I turned to meet the attack, but Meredeath stood tall, defending us in leather and lace.

"I've got this, Cole," Meredeath said calmly. She didn't even glance back at us. Instead, she spoke her first skill. "[Death's Kiss]."

Green flames erupted along her daggers as Meredeath crouched, ready to take on the monsters.

The raccoons didn't hesitate as they surged forward, eyes glowing red in the eerie light. My hand went for my hammer, but Andrew stopped me.

"She's got this," he murmured, eyes plastered to my teammate.

Just as they closed the final distance, knives gleaming, Meredeath called another skill. "[Whirlwind of Death]."

Her body spun, and the unsuspecting raccoons paid for their stupidity. Meredeath's daggers cut through the creatures like butter. Arms, viscera, and blood went flying. Not once did her protection amulet flare as she danced through any resistance.

When the skill ended, Meredeath staggered to the wall. She retched, dizzy and disgusted, covered in blood. The flames cut out on her blades, but her eyes still blazed green, the internal fire almost hinting at the skull under her skin. It was a stark change compared to her slitted cat-eyes.

"A [Death Knight]?" Andrew whispered next to me in awe of Meredeath's destruction. "That's a harsh road. Maybe your team *can* survive down here."

I squatted next to the guy, fumbling in his tin of healing supplies. [Death Knight]. He'd revealed the secret Meredeath had been holding on to in just one example of her skills. That's what the [Lich] had offered her… or one of her options. She *chose* this.

The gills along my neck flapped uselessly in the air. I wondered whose [Sponsorship] ultimately cost more. Rhi Voss, [Lich] Queen of Niyatra, or Richard, the [Immortal] fanged banana slug.

I suspected that neither of us had paid the ultimate price. Yet.

My hands shook as I poured the powdered yarrow and plantain into Andrew's wound. The mixture stopped the oozing.

"Alright, now clean it out, then we'll get to stitching and making the poultice. If we can get it closed enough, I've got a minor [Regeneration] skill that should take care of the rest."

I nodded numbly at the man's words as he talked me through each step. Focusing on his wound, I tried to block out everything else. I was afraid to look at Meredeath and the carnage she'd caused. She hadn't just fought the creatures, she'd *dismembered* them.

[Skill Acquired: You have gained a new [Adventurer] skill, [First Aid]. Your efforts to heal injury will now be [10%] more effective, and attributed regeneration will be [20%] more effective. This skill is bolstered or hindered by your knowledge of treatment for wounds.]

"You get the [System] notification?"

"Yes, how'd yo—?"

"Good, now we can get moving." Andrew stood up, using both arms to leverage himself off the wall. "It seems like you'll be useful after all. I've been tracking a lost kid. Join me and I'll share the [Quest]."

[You have been invited to the [Two Angels Party]. To join this party, you must leave [Your Mom's Party]. Do you wish to join?]

Chapter 51

[DETECT TRAP]

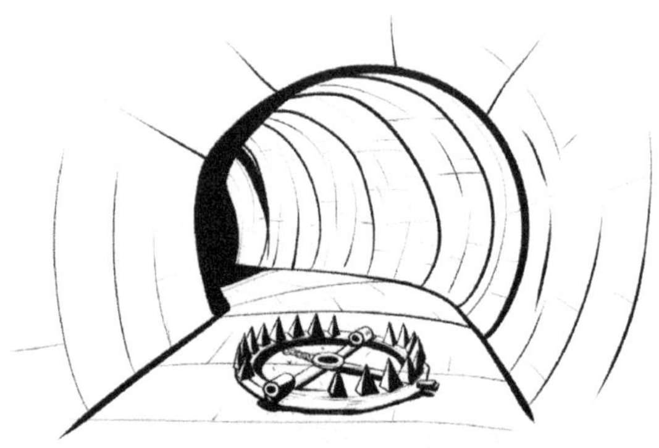

Before I could reject the guy's offer, Meredeath smoothly interjected, giving me a green-eyed side-eye to shut up.

"You're looking for a child?" Her eyebrows raised.

"Yes, I'm a [Wayfinder]." Andrew lifted his chin, as though being a [Wayfinder] meant something. Meredeath looked at me, and I shrugged. Andrew looked between the two of us incredulously. "A finder of the lost? Protector of children?"

"Someone give the man a gold star. *Why does that matter?*" Meredeath was not hiding her loss of patience.

Andrew's eyes grew sharp at Meredeath's rudeness. She just picked at her fingernails, ignoring his look.

Andrew lost the battle of wills. "[Wayfinder] is a specialization for [Adventurer] — I find the lost, not just kill monsters for experience."

"And this [Quest] to find a child?" Meredeath asked, unimpressed.

The man deflated. "Yes, I work with orphanages. The Ashlight Haven requested assistance. Once I have the kid, I'll be out of here."

I realized something in that moment. It was some combo of body language, insight from [Heartbeat], and intuition. Andrew'd been on a quest to find a missing child and was ill-prepared to take on a dungeon. He needed us as much as we needed him.

This time, I cut Meredeath off.

"Look, we need to work together. Meredeath and I are not joining your [Party]." I held up my hand, forestalling his protest. "We're already in a [Party], and we're using our [Party] functionality to find our teammates. So how about you join us?"

Meredeath looked at me like I'd gone crazy, but I was pretty sure we weren't going to beat this dungeon without Andrew's help. I sent over the mental command, inviting Andrew into [Your Mom's Party].

He looked at me, considering. I could feel his hesitation, so I sweetened the offer.

"We'll help you find the missing child." That offer was easy. None of us would leave a child down here. "No need to share the quest with us, you can keep the reward for yourself."

Andrews' bushy eyebrows raised. Meredeath again looked at me like I'd lost my mind. Maybe I had. I had a good feeling about this guy, and a bad feeling about the dungeon. We needed each other.

[Andrew Ashborn has joined [Your Mom's Party]].

I could almost hear Tandy yelling, '*Who the hell is Andrew Ashborn?*' from here. A little chaos was good for her.

[Heartbeat] triggered as Andrew joined, and he felt, safe. I closed my eyes momentarily, letting the skill pull me toward the connection. I got the impression of him covered in a pile of kids pulling at his gear.

Then a wall appeared, blocking my vision. Opening my eyes, I found Andrew staring at me.

"It's not polite to pry," he said gruffly, more from embarrassment of what I might have seen than any true irritation.

"Welcome to the party, Andrew," I said, more confident in my words than I had been moments before. Examining his general attributes in our team interface made it pretty clear that he was a [Veteran], and we were babies. Thankfully, Tandy was still listed as the [Party Leader]. "If you bring up your party map, you can see that we've got a way to go."

The map revealed a maze of connected sewer pipes the team had already traversed, with pink, yellow, and green blinking dots at the outer edge of the revealed territory. Black, blue, and gray dots represented us.

"They're going in the wrong direction," Andrew said, frowning with the distant expression of someone who was looking at their interface. "Are you all…?" He paused as though searching for a kind way of saying it.

"Complete idiots when it comes to being [Adventurers]?" Meredeath chimed in with her natural charm. "Yes."

"Well, I was going to say 'inexperienced,' but yeah, okay. Well, let's go get your friends before they get killed."

Andrew started moving back towards the junction we'd come from. His legs ate up the ground quickly.

Meredeath and I exchanged a look. She was angry with me, and I just shrugged. Andrew might have been a mistake, but we weren't prepared for a dungeon either. I'd rather die trusting my gut on someone than get eviscerated by a trap I hadn't seen.

Andrew pointed down at a trigger at the next junction, one of the plates we'd caught moving through it the last time. Once he was sure we'd seen him point out the trigger mechanism, he turned left towards the rest of our [Party].

"Okay, he's growing on me," Meredeath murmured, following Andrew a little closer. The guy had his double-bladed axe slung across his back. The dark axe's edges gleamed in the dim light of the tunnels.

Andrew kept walking, pointing out more traps that we would have likely caught. If it weren't for our interface map, I'd have gotten lost. Each juncture and tunnel looked remarkably similar.

Meanwhile, Leo, Tandy, and Richard's positions had changed. They were in a large room and hadn't moved for a good ten minutes. This wasn't a good sign.

"You two ready for some action?" Andrew had paused at the next juncture, as though he'd spotted something we hadn't. I peered over his shoulder, trying to spot what he'd seen.

"I don't hear any raccoon bandits, and nobody's died right here. What are you seeing that we're not?" Meredeath asked, studying the juncture herself.

"Normally you'd have to pay a [Dungeon Guide] big bucks for this, but since we're a team," he smiled, taking the bite out of the words, "we'll call this a teachable moment. Do you see any difference between the tunnel we're standing in and the one on the other side of this juncture?"

I looked, and it had the same brown, rusty floor. The walls and ceiling were made of concrete, with moss and cobwebs clinging to them. The recessed light strip ran across the middle of the ceiling. Everything looked the same to me.

"It's wetter," Meredeath pointed out.

I squinted at the floor. It didn't look *that much* wetter than our tunnel, but she was right. The floor looked damp. The leaf detritus that had haphazardly littered the floor behind us was completely absent ahead.

"Good, and do you see the trigger mechanism in this juncture?" he asked, with the patience of a born teacher.

Meredeath stepped forward, examining the ground. She

started to lean into the juncture to get a better look, and Andrew pulled her back, giving us our first clue.

I kneeled to get a better look, spotting just a few cobwebs trailing from the ceiling.

"Is it the cobwebs? Is a spider going to drop on us?" I was not too keen on meeting the widowmaker's sewer cousin.

"Yes, good job, Cole." It was hard not to beam at his praise. Maybe I could excel at trap finding? "It's common knowledge that dungeons can be tricky like this. They'll give you trap after monotonous trap, then," he clapped his hands together, making both of us jump, "you'll die to a sophisticated switch-up. It's one of the most commonly made arguments for dungeon sentience."

Eyeing the two of us critically, he didn't bother holding back his final thought. "It's also why you shouldn't be trying a dungeon without a guide."

"Good thing we've got you," I said cheerily.

"I just hope your friends are still breathing by the time we reach them."

"They're still on our map, aren't they?" Meredeath was less amused by the situation.

"Sure, but they could be suspended above a pit of alligators or hiding in a hole while a boss monster waits for them to pop out. There are a million ways a dungeon might trap you or stretch out a kill." He spoke not unkindly, but with a blunt cynicism that Tandy would appreciate. It gave his words an emphasis of experience.

"Alright, duck here. Be careful not to touch any of the elements in the environment we're in. *Anything* can and will be used against you. The threat isn't just a monster."

We moved more slowly, and my perspective on the environment changed. Andrew pointed out a moss trigger, more cobwebs, and suspicious patches of dirt. At some point, fake rungs were leading up to a painted maintenance hole, all built to cause someone to back up and fall through a false wall into an acid pit.

We were getting close to Tandy, Leo, and Richard. They hadn't moved in the last hour, and I tried not to think about what it meant. Eyes on the environment, I tried to stay focused.

"Stop!" I called, freezing everyone. "Andrew, step back."

I'd seen the carefully spaced moss that indicated recessed water jets of death, so there *was* a trap here. But I hadn't found the trigger mechanism. No mysterious plate, no cobwebs or draping moss. No wobbly stone that sent an errant hand into a wall panel. Nothing in line with the water jets. Maybe it was a delayed trigger?

I began examining Andrew. His hair was pulled back in a warrior's knot, free of any filaments that would have indicated disaster. His leather armor creaked as he stood doing his own study of the hall, his pack secured tightly with his axe hanging free. The metal of his boot glistened, reflecting off *something.*

One of the first rules of trap finding is to look for differences in the environment or patterns that are too regular, Andrew's wisdom echoed in my head.

"There's a spot of light on your boot, that's got to be it." I traced the spot of light back to a pinhole in the wall. I was getting the hang of finding traps.

The [System] agreed:

[Skills Acquired: You have gained new skills.

[Dungeon Diver] - This [Adventurer] skill acknowledges a rudimentary understanding of dungeons and grants the user a passive bonus to awareness within such environments. Further associated skills and specializations may become available.

[Detect Trap] - This [Dead Wrong] skill is a passive that increases the chance of identifying traps by [25%].

[Detect Trap - Dungeons] - This [Dead Wrong] skill is a passive that increases the chance of identifying traps within dungeons by [25%]. This stacks with other non-environmental skills.]

"Ah, yes. A light trigger." Andrew's voice was taut as he took a step back. The beam of light kissed a pinhole on the far wall. Seven jets of water screamed across the tunnel, cutting deep grooves into the stone like knives through butter. Instant death for a mortal, [Wayfinder] or not.

"Good job, Cole. I've only heard rumors of these, never seen one up close." Andrew's voice shook as his facade of calmness broke. I'd caught something he'd missed, and it unnerved him.

This highlighted more than the [System's] recognition of the progress I'd made. Maybe I wasn't just stumbling along anymore; I finally had a chance to catch myself before I fell.

"Wasn't this supposed to be a white bread dungeon? Not a five-course death trap?" Meredeath's voice cut through my ego stroking. She kneeled, waving her hand through the light, causing the trap to go off multiple times.

"I agree, it's too sophisticated for a [Basic] dungeon. Most of these traps would be at home in a [Challenge] dungeon. I haven't been in an [Unnamed] dungeon before, so it could mess with the classification..." Andrew stood thinking, as Meredeath kept triggering the water spouts. I tried to follow as he continued to ramble about the different types of dungeons. "We've only seen the raccoons and, even for a [Basic] dungeon, they're meant to overwhelm rather than kill. By the Ashborn! I bet this is an [Unclassified] [Trap] dungeon."

"Is someone going to tell me what that means?" Meredeath was unimpressed.

"This dungeon might be [Basic], but it's not new. If it's been feeding on the underbelly of Eddie's Mill, then it's developed an appetite. Dungeons are predators. This one's laid a trap, and your friends are the bait."

I checked the map. The team still hadn't moved.

The hair on the back of my neck stood up. For once, it wasn't Richard creeping me out.

I couldn't shake the feeling that the dungeon was watching us, waiting for the right moment to strike.

Chapter 52

DEWER STAKES

Took you losers long enough. I would advise not coming into the room.

"What's that voice?"

"That's Cole's little Richard," Meredeath explained *oh so* helpfully. Andrew looked at me with bushy eyebrows raised.

"He's my sentient [Immortal] slug," I elaborated.

Andrew's eyes flashed downward. "That's a new one," he muttered.

"No, he's a fanged banana slug." I was done with this conversation. Andrew would figure it out when he met Richard.

Peering into the room, the team was suspended from a cage above a giant bubbling vat of green liquid. The concoction looked deadly. Oily bubbles formed and popped with a sizzle, making me think it was an acid. Tandy sat, dejected with a yellow slug on her shoulders. Up on his tail, Richard waved his tentacles at us.

"There she is. I knew she was still alive," Andrew whispered, pointing. Adjusting my gaze, I saw on the opposite side of the room another cage, dangling above what appeared to be a vat of normal water. In that cage sat a young girl. She crouched, little hands holding tight to the bars. Behind her sat two decomposing skeletons.

This was not a good look.

"What is this, some sort of Bond movie?" Meredeath whispered. "Where's the villain?"

"I don't see anyone, do you?" A raspy voice came from behind us, hot breath on my neck.

Meredeath whipped around, and the green flare in her eyes dimmed as horror took hold.

[Stillpoint] caused everything to happen in slow motion for me. Andrew reached for his axe as he slowly spun. Four giant claws burst from my chest as my body lifted off the ground. They were yellow and bloody as they poked through my torso.

Meredeath dodged, rolling into the room to avoid the claws aimed at her.

I was dimly aware that my body was feeling pain. I could feel blood pumping uselessly out of my wounds. That vital organs had been punctured. But my awareness was floating away. The creature, which I still couldn't see, shook its paw, flinging my limp body over Meredeath's head.

I caught a glimpse of her shocked expression as my blood speckled her pale face. My body twisted, giving me a quick view of the giant raccoon standing behind us.

The bandit-faced creature squinted as it grinned at my demise. It stood ten feet tall, clad in a giant trench coat with thick arms and foot-long claws. Sunken eyes, missing whiskers, and sagging lips gave it an unnatural appearance.

My spine had been severed, so I hit the ground in a boneless heap. My mind was trapped in jelly as my health plummeted to 0.

[You, Cole Thornfield, are [Dead].]

[[Cheat Death] has triggered. You are incapacitated until the analysis of the situation is complete. This may take some time. I hate this skill.]

Later, I'm sure, my team will ask me what it feels like to be dead. I floated above my body this time, watching my team lose to the amorphous beast. Dying feels helpless.

At least the [System] hadn't sequestered me in the room that wasn't a room.

The beast barreled forward, knocking Andrew down and trampling Meredeath. Green daggers flashed forward, aimed at its underbelly. The creature didn't flinch, its body almost bending away from the blades.

A horde of smaller raccoons flowed in behind it, filling the corners of the room. An audience for the spectacle. They chittered, watching their god take on the two [Adventurers].

Something about the boss bothered me. I tried triggering [Analyze].

[Your skill [Analyze] has failed. You are [Dead].]

A glob of fat shot out of the sleeve of the creature, pinning Meredeath to the floor. The green on her daggers snuffed out as she struggled to keep her mouth free of the goo.

Andrew roared a skill as his double-bladed axe sliced neatly through the monster. The two halves of the creature split. Tandy and Leo cheered, but the watching ringtails seemed unconcerned.

Don't stop, it's still alive! I tried shouting, uselessly. No lungs pushed air through my incorporeal throat.

The two halves of the creature slapped back together with a wet smack. The monster's skin sloughed off as it relinquished the disguise. Underneath, the beast looked like a collection of all the fat and grease dumped into the sewers over the years.

A congealed arm whipped out, slamming Andrew into a vat, acid sloshing over the rim. The [Wayfinder] spun, his face bloody and bubbling. I fully expected him to be joining me in the afterlife.

Instead, he flashed a grin, knuckles white on the handle of his axe.

Flecks of red fury danced in his eyes as he spat two skills, "[Bloodlust], [Mirror Weapon]."

I wouldn't have considered Andrew small; his shoulders were too broad to be petite. Short? Yes, but small? Never.

Now the [Wayfinder] towered over the boss menacingly, as he'd tripled in size. Stepping forward, his axe had magically split so he could dual-wield mirror copies. He looked ready to kick ass.

Sensing their master's unease, the audience bounded into the fray. Little knife-wielding furry hands stabbed Andrew as they crawled up his body. The [Wayfinder] laughed at their little toothpicks, tossing the raccoons bodily into the waiting vats.

Enraged, the boss spat a glob of fat at Andrew. The man deflected the goo with the swipe of an axe.

Andrew triggered another skill. He spun as the raccoons flew like debris in a tornado. His axes arced, spraying congealed chunks across the arena.

Not even Leo would dare challenge *that guy* to a fight.

As the skill wore off, Andrew staggered back, dizzy but self-satisfied. A giant wedge had been chewed out of the beast's body. He watched as the creature toppled sideways.

"Mira, I'm going to get you down. Don't worry!" Andrew called to the girl, who was watching him wide-eyed.

I focused on the body of the boss, presumably dead, on the floor—the goo of its body leaking through the holes in its coat. The goo started congealing with intelligence that could only mean one thing. It wasn't done yet.

I yelled, the words stuck in my psyche. There had to be some way to get their attention. I closed my vision, mimicking taking a deep breath to center my mind and gather my will.

This time, instead of screaming at Andrew, I mentally shouted.

THE BOSS LIVES!

Andrew heard none of it. Meredeath, on the other hand, started shouting.

"Behind you!" she screamed, trying to get the shrinking brute's attention. Meredeath threw a dagger across the expanse, and it hit the creature with a dull slurk.

Andrew's [Bloodlust] skill had worn off now that his attention was focused on Mira. His body shrank down to his normal size, the axes combining into one.

The creature rose, no longer trying to be sly, with a dagger hilt sticking out of its head. Within its gelatinous body, a raccoon skull floated like a berry stuck in gelatin. The creature was smaller than it'd been before, but not by nearly enough to make a difference in the fight's outcome.

Andrew turned, finally getting the message. The monster wasn't taking any chances this time, raising both its arms. A giant glob rocketed towards the [Wayfinder], catching him full force in the face.

The fight had ended.

The raccoons still alive skittered out from the darkness, surrounding the boss with chitters of adoration and praise. The monster used a skill to pop Meredeath into the cage holding [Your Mom's Party], and Andrew into the cage holding the girl. Gelatinous fat dripped off them both into the vats below. Angry fins appeared in the water as sharks fought for a chance morsel.

[Analysis complete. Here are the skills you and your slug deserve.

You have gained the skill [Gelatinous]. This is a permanent body augment that allows you to resist physical damage. You have decreased resistance to [Heat] and [Cold]. [Moist] environment needs have increased.

You have gained the skill [Gelatinous Regeneration]. This

is a permanent body augment that gives you increased regeneration from physical attacks. You have a decreased resistance to [Poison], including chemical mind-altering effects.]

My consciousness slammed back into my body. I lay using [Feign Death] to pretend to be dead. I clenched my teeth, trying not to moan, as things shifted around my wounds. It felt like my skin slithered over the gashes in my chest. Imagined worms burrowed in my body, slithering things into place to fix the damage.

I concentrated on my health bar, which showed 4/25 and began ticking up rapidly. Although the new skills were uncomfortable, they seemed effective. I could feel my guts seal into place. Mentally, I curled in on myself, trying to resist the need to move into a fetal position. I knew I'd lost another chunk of my humanity. This wasn't healing; this was *something else.*

Richard brought me back to reality. *Be careful, you're our only hope now.*

Richard always cut to the heart of it. If humanity was the price to pay for my friend's lives, then so be it.

Triggering [Analyze], I finally had a name for the creature.

[The Fat Berg takes on characteristics of its last kill. Gelatinous, it's resistant to most physical damage.]

The dungeon had seemed to go into a resting state. Raccoons had scattered, running down the dim corridors to their natural hiding spots. The gelatinous monster had followed them, as if he were going to review the traps and placement of his maze. Maybe he was.

The boss chamber was quiet, just the low hiss of the bubbling cauldron and the silent sobs of the girl clinging to Andrew.

I sat up slowly, dismissing [Feign Death]. Eyes on the dark corners, I moved slowly. The room appeared to be empty.

The control mechanism for the cages is on the wall behind the vats.

Carefully, I followed the wall. Even the girl had stopped

sobbing, eyes glued to me. The chains holding up the cages ran along several pulleys down to a magically enhanced crank. Buttons sat on the panel to lower the cages, to raise them, and to swivel the hook holding them in place. Another set for each vat to empty and fill them, and an emergency release.

The labels seemed straightforward, assuming they were labeled correctly. One wrong button punch could drop everyone I cared about into an acid pit.

I slowly approached the control mechanism to get a better look. Andrew's training kicked in as I looked for a potential trap. This was too obvious to be a simple hit of a button. I spotted recessed nozzles pointed around the panel. My health had ticked up at a supernatural speed to 20/25.

I didn't see a trigger plate. The buttons themselves must be the trigger mechanism. Taking a step closer, a plate clicked. Shit, I hadn't thought to look out here.

An alarm started blaring, the inset lights in the dungeon's ceiling flashed red, alerting *everyone* to the intruder. Fuck.

"Cole, he's coming!" Leo shouted. No kidding.

My mind raced. Which button to hit? I noticed several spouts on the floor. The panel was trapped, and I was running out of time.

An audible *splut* drew my attention. The trench-coated blob turned the corner, its face morphing into a wild raccoon grinning at me with sharpened teeth.

An arm pointed at me, ready to cover me in goo.

I lunged for the buttons.

Water jets tore through my body as I slammed into the panel, hitting several buttons at once. I flew into the air, hearing the girl scream as her cage dropped an inch, and the acid began sloshing out of its vat.

The Fat Berg was overdue for a bath.

Chapter 53

BATH TIME

I can't describe the pain of having your body bored into by highly pressurized water. Thankfully, my [Gelatinous] skill was worth its weight in gold. I managed to survive the event. Now I just needed to stop screaming.

As my body flew, the chaos of the dungeon room was everything I'd hoped for. I button-mashed the controls so that both vats split open, spilling acid *and* sharks across the floor. Clinging to the pipes above the button panel, I had a magnificent view of the devastation.

The [System] picked that moment to trigger a notification.

[Skill Acquired: You have gained a new [Dead Wrong] skill, [Mind the Gap]. When triggered, you can jump up to 10 feet. You must focus to use this skill successfully, and it is limited to once per day.]

I'll take it.

The Fat Berg bubbled as the sharks devoured it one toothy

chomp at a time. Raccoons uselessly scratched at the walls trying to escape.

The room was one giant shark tank. Blood, fur, and Fat Berg flew in the air. Maybe they should have done a better job of feeding their sharks regularly.

The whole thing was gross and satisfying. I watched my health slowly tick up. It'd bottomed out at 3 points, much too close a call.

As the last remnants of the boss monster died within the crunch of a shark's jaws, I finally got the message I'd been waiting for.

[Quest Complete: [First Run]

You have completed the [Trap] [Unnamed] dungeon beneath Eddie's Mill. This undiscovered dungeon has now had [1] successful completed attempts. You have earned 1000 Faction Points and the right to name the [Unnamed] dungeon. You have earned a [Dungeon Treasure Chest].

[Cole Moldboard Thornfield] is responsible for the death of the dungeon boss [Fat Berg]. You can now assign 1000 Faction Points to one of the following Factions: [System] Faction, Rhi Voss Faction, Tandy Selvedge Faction, or Richard the Fanged Banana Slug Faction. You have [ten minutes] to make your decision.]

The sludge in the boss chamber drained, and the monsters disappeared, replaced by a large wooden chest wrapped in brass. It was our [Dungeon Treasure Chest]!

A brass key glimmered into existence in my hand. I pocketed it into the remains of my tattered pants. This lifestyle was hard on clothes. It's a good thing I had Tandy.

My health was back up to 20 thanks to [Gelatinous Regeneration], so I risked climbing down without fear of dying from a slip. My shredded boots did little to protect my tender feet. I winced as my toes clung to the pipes during the descent.

Richard was probably loving it.

My feet hit the wet concrete with a bounce. I walked over

to the real honest to god *treasure chest.* Our financial woes were over!

"Hey, you loot goblin, you going to get us down?" Tandy called from her cage.

Did you get Faction Points?

"Cole, how about we name this dungeon [Your Mom's Dungeon]? Has a nice sound to it, doesn't it?" Leo suggested.

I went to the panel and pushed the descend buttons, listening to the cages crank down to the floor. I felt for the little girl. She clutched the bars of her cage as tears ran down her face. Richard, on the other hand, looked like he was about to lunge out of Meredeath's hand to get to me.

What are your options?

"Your Mom's Dungeon? Really, Leo?" I said to myself.

[[Your Mom's Dungeon] has been named by Cole Moldboard Thornfield of [Your Mom's Party].]

Oh, for fuck's sake. The [System] really just wanted to make me miserable, didn't it?

"Really, Cole? You went along with *Leo?*" Meredeath complained as she stepped out of the cage. Richard was sitting on her outstretched hand. Admitting it'd been an accident seemed almost a worse sin, so I kept my mouth shut.

The [System] dropped some more information about the newly named dungeon.

[[Your Mom's Dungeon] has now been [Claimed]. It is now [Classified] as a [Basic Trap Dungeon].]

Interesting, I still didn't know what it all meant. I'd have to ask Andrew.

[Freeze Moment].

The world stopped.

My eyeballs froze in their sockets, focused on Richard, who sat, slime glistening, tentacles outstretched before him like a child reaching for their favorite blankie.

What are your options?

Honestly, I would have told him at this point, but my lips wouldn't move.

WHAT ARE YOUR OPTIONS?!

My eyeballs itched as they dried out in the frozen moment.

For the love of slime, this god-awful [System]-cursed skill.

Time unfroze, and everyone acted as if nothing strange had happened. Tandy and Leo went for the treasure chest. Meredeath joined them after handing me Richard. He undulated up my arm so fast that I didn't have time to react to the trail of goo on my neck.

Let's take this conversation to the corner while they're trying to pry open the loot box. First, under NO circumstances mention the Faction Points to anyone else.

I watched as Andrew kneeled down, wiping the tears off of Mira's face. My teammates were standing over the [Dungeon Treasure Chest] like it was a wedding ring. As Leo got out his [Enchanted Axe of Singing] to try to fit it into the seam of the lid, I stepped back into the corner of the room. Meredeath's daggers glowed green as she attempted to get one into the lock. Tandy stood muttering, as though trying to dispel the locking mechanism entirely.

"Why not?"

Please, for the love of slime, just trust me on this one for now. You will get to tell them eventually, I promise. But right now, the time isn't right. ***Now, what are your options?***

"I have four."

Four? Are you sure? [System], Rhi, me, and…? Richard asked as though the fate of the world hung in the balance.

"Tandy Selvedge, although I don't know why. I figured it was just a vote for [Your Mom's—" I stopped mid-sentence. Richard's body was vibrating so hard he could have qualified as a marital aid. I'd never seen him so excited.

"I guess you want me to pick Tandy?"

Fuck no, I want you to pick Rhi.

"Not even you?" I was *very* confused. I knew Richard had

no love for the [System]. They had history. I was hoping they hadn't dated. But to pick Rhi, the undead, possibly maniacal [Lich] that doubled as an ex-lover to a fanged slug? No way.

No! Give it to Rhi Voss. She and Ter Lance need the support.

Richard had used the mental voice that brokered no argument. It was the same voice my mom used when I was about to touch something hot. I selected the Rhi Voss Faction, opting just to go with it.

"Why?" I asked, not able to resist an attempt to fuck with him. It's a bonus if he actually gives me some helpful information.

[Congratulations, [Adventurer], you have joined the Faction War. You have permanently assigned Your Mom's Dungeon to Rhi Voss's Faction. All earned benefits, awards, and Faction Points will benefit the Rhi Voss Faction.]

My mind clouded over, and I was back in Rhi's swamp. It was dark, but less gloomy. The palace of Niyatgra stood proud, white columns extending to the heavens like an ancient hand reaching for the gods. Rhi sat on her throne, Ter Lance at her side, armor gleaming. She looked up at me.

"Faction points?" Her disbelief was as subtle as Leo's axe. "Lance, the infants send us Faction Points." She stood from her throne, green fire blazing in her eyes.

"It's been a long time," her commander said, standing with her. His sword rose in salute.

The two proud, ancient warriors from a forgotten queendom had transformed into a hint of their former selves. Green flames shot around her hands and down Ter Lance's sword. They looked ready for a fight.

From my vantage point, I could see a horde of [Corrupt] monsters burrowing through the mountain, ready to break through. A thin green magic held the line. It flared with renewed vigor.

"Tell Richard he's still a dick!" she shouted as she turned to her antechamber, towards the horde invading Niyatgra.

Skeletons began rising from the floor, dust falling off bones. Rhi Voss, [Lich], was summoning her army. Green lights danced in the bone lady's swamp for the first time in a hundred years.

"This isn't from him," the words spilled out, whispered across the wind.

Rhi turned her head as though listening to my words. Her quiet response returned on the wind, caressing my ears. "It's good to see a new generation stand up. Hope is dangerous, but maybe Lael was onto something. My thanks, child. Watch your back."

[Quest Updated: [Trials of a Hero: Heart]

Congratulations on the second step to higher power. You have completed two of three prerequisites to meet the requirements to enter the Trial at the Library of Alta. This path is not for the faint of heart. Completion of the Trial at the Library of Alta will grant the class [Hero]. No time limit given for this quest.]

I can't use the points. I have nothing that could truly help in the fight against the [Incursion]. The [System] has most of the dungeon Faction points in our territory. Rhi needs it. She's barely holding on, and I don't think the [System] can plug that hole.

"You're not trying to get back together with her, are you?" I teased him. I couldn't help it. He might be a key player on some cosmic chessboard, but he also deserved teasing.

She'll never take me back. She picked Ter Lance. Cole, you've got to do this; you must have only minutes left.

"Oh, oops. Looks like time elapsed—"

WHAT THE FUCK?!

"G—good thing I already chose Rhi's Faction."

Fuck you. Two pinpricks of fangs bit the side of my neck as Richard showed his displeasure. With my [Gelatinous] skill, I didn't even lose a health point. *Why the hell do you taste so strange?*

"Better be careful or you'll get stuck. I want to see what's in this [Dungeon Treasure Chest]." I ignored his mutterings as I rejoined the party.

Leo had raised his axe above his head, ready to strike the chest from above, determined to smash through and get his just rewards.

"Leo, hold up, man. I think this key might help." I brandished the key. Three angry eyes swung towards me.

Chapter 54

DREAMS IN A BOX

"You had a key this whole time?" Tandy looked at me like I was a total dumbass. I guess I deserved that.

What was I going to say? I was busy taking advice from a talking slug on picking sides in a continental Faction War against the [Corruption] that ended the last age.

"Yeah, I was having fun watching you all problem solve." Wow, I was starting to sound like Richard. The little twerp was rubbing off on me.

Meredeath gave me a dirty look as she snatched the key from me. She marched over to the trunk. With a sharp twist and an audible click, the lid popped open.

Our money problems? Solved. The top of the chest overflowed with silver and copper coins. Leo was digging through the money when Andrew and Mira came to look.

"I've never seen so many coins in my life," Mira whispered in awe. Same here, kid.

The coins were shiny too, untouched by grubby hands.

"If you dig into the top, there should be a handle. The real treasure is underneath the coin layer," Andrew said, using his teaching voice. He really knew a considerable amount about dungeons.

Leo dug around and pulled out the top compartment of the chest, spilling copper and silver coins everywhere. They rolled across the floor, and Mira started chasing them down.

Below sat, well, I wasn't exactly sure *what* it was. It looked like an assortment of junk.

My persimmon! Richard moved down my arm to the edge of the chest. Tandy reached in and handed the golden piece of fruit to the slug.

"That's a small reward for beating a dungeon. A persimmon?" Tandy, annoyed, reached for the tarnished thimble at the bottom of the chest.

"Dungeons put rewards in the completion chests that match the thoughts of an individual when they enter for the first time. You should always school your thoughts before stepping into a dungeon portal."

I thought of our first encounter with the [Trial Dungeon], and how the magic warped the whole challenge around some of my thoughts. I needed to think about this more carefully next time. Of course, it would have helped to *know* I was stepping into a dungeon.

"Cole, who is this guy?" Leo asked, frowning as he picked up a scroll.

"This is, Andrew. He's a [Wayfinder]," I said, as though that meant something.

"He's *the* [Wayfinder] and the very best Ashborn in Eddie's Mill!" Mira added, giving me a dark look at the injustice I'd done her hero. "Andrew helps the orphanage and teaches us things."

"Like, *don't go wandering in the tunnels*. What *were* you doing down here?" Andrew asked sternly as the girl tried to look away.

"I know, I know, but..." Her small voice trailed off for a second. Then she looked at us, full of resolve. "But with the refugees, we need *more*. And you can't do it all."

Andrew sighed wearily. "While I appreciate the desire to help, perhaps getting caged in a hidden dungeon is not the best way. I've taken two days off from [Quests] to find you." He gave us all the apologetic look of an overtired caretaker.

I didn't want to ask. No one else had shown that they'd even really heard the exchange between the two, but it tugged at my heart.

"There are refugees? What's going on with the orphanage?" My question lingered between us, my companions refusing to look at me. Richard perched on the edge of the chest, sweet sticky juice running down his chin.

"I didn't want to involve you, but we had an influx of children from Terny. The town was leveled in some sort of dungeon outbreak. Might have happened here, too, if we hadn't completed this one. Anyway, they sent the children out of the city, while the adults fought the horde. A lot of orphans were created that way."

"The den mothers say that we're going to have to send some of the new ones away if we don't figure out *something,*" Mira added in her tiny voice. "So Andrew always tells us that if something needs doing, you're the one who should do it. So I was hunting rats!"

She'd been hunting rats so her friends could keep a roof over their heads. Life sure had a way of putting our problems into perspective.

"By the claws of the Everbear, I'm never going to have a full coin purse, am I?" Tandy looked morosely at the pile of money sitting on the floor. She'd come to the same conclusion I had. We weren't going to keep the coins.

I'd never been prouder of her in my life.

I looked in the chest and saw a small coin pouch. It was surely meant for Mira. I picked it up, feeling its light heft. The girl was definitely someone to watch.

"I think this was meant for you, little one." I handed her the small pouch. She opened it, squealing in glee to find three gold coins. She held it tight to her chest as though it were the greatest treasure in the world.

I looked at the rest of the coins, feeling a pang of guilt in the face of her need.

Here Mira was, doing what I kept failing to do. Actually making a difference.

She looks like Rhi Voss with her Faction Points. Hopeful—ultimately doomed, but hopeful. Like a cold moth headed to a candle. If only a pouch full of coins could save the world. Could Richard read minds now?

"I'm assuming this is yours?" Meredeath handed Andrew a green scale that matched his armor. I hadn't noticed it before, but his scale armor only extended halfway down his chest; the rest was normal enough chain mail below his shirt.

"Ah, yes, another leaf in my mantle, although I don't feel like I did anything to deserve it. Young Cole here took out the boss." Nonetheless, the [Wayfinder] snagged the scale from Meredeath, and the armor shimmered as it clipped into the mail.

"So, it's like a Boy Scout patch?" Meredeath asked. She looked at our blank expressions with exasperation. "Like a rank? The more of these scales, the grander the hoo-ha of [Wayfinding] you are?"

"Ah, yes, something like that." Andrew smiled uneasily, lost in translation.

The bottom of the chest contained a dark onyx ring and a pin with a lizard. I didn't want to admit that the aesthetics matched those of certain group members who hadn't received their share of the loot.

"Why do I have a lizard pin?" I asked, trying to trigger

[Analyze]. Andrew gets an armor promotion, and I get a gecko pin?

It's not a lizard, it's a chameleon. Well, chameleons are lizards. It's not just any lizard, it's a chameleon!

What was in that persimmon?

"Are you drunk?"

Do I look like I've eaten a hot pepper?

Richard looked up at me, half of his persimmon falling into the chest. Bits of honey-yellow flesh stuck in his teeth as juice ran down his entire face. This is what the world needed: more slugs drunk on persimmons.

I shook my head, reached down for the persimmon, and handed it back to him.

Thank you, kind sir.

Now I *knew* he was drunk. He was never polite. My hand touched the pin.

[[Pin of the Chameleon] - Got something to hide? Pin this on and [Camouflage] as a 'human.' Cost: 1 MP per hour. Warning: prolonged use has side effects.]

Interesting pin. I wonder what anxiety ***that's*** *solving?*

Was that what I'd been thinking when I entered the dungeon? That I needed to hide?

"What does your ring do?" I asked. Did it hold a death ray? Or some source of magical eyeliner? Another [Protection] barrier?

Meredeath jumped, her focus broken. She slid the ring onto her finger quickly.

"It's just the ring I was looking at in the store, the one we couldn't afford. I never could get it out of my mind; apparently, now I have." She gave me one of those smiles that didn't reach her eyes. Neither of us seemed happy with the implications of our prizes.

"Holy shit! I can't believe it!" Except for Leo, who was jumping up and down with excitement. "Do you know what I've got here?"

Tandy and I looked at each other. "No, you haven't told us," I said.

"I've got, right here, in my hand, an invitation to the Ceaparean Drift Hunt!" Leo was vibrating with excitement.

Even Andrew and Richard, coming from their respective focuses, looked at Leo. Each had the look of someone triggering an [Analyze] skill just to verify his claim.

Legends were born during the Ceaparean Drift Hunt. It was a twice-a-decade celebrity monster hunt with every [Adventurer], noble, and merchant on the continent. Fancy people hunting fancy monsters.

And we had a ticket. Great. We were going to look like country bumpkins with sticks.

Leo grinned like he'd won the strength contest at the county fair.

"I guess we know where we're going next," Meredeath said, her tone a counterbalance to Leo's radiance.

We were going *hunting*.

Chapter 55

ONE LAST QUESTION

Mira giggled as she helped chase down coins that'd rolled away as they scooped the money into bags that Andrew had provided.

Meredeath had walked over to the cages, examining the skeletons that had kept Mira company.

"See anything interesting?" I asked.

Her eyes turned to me, flashing green. I could see the outline of her cheekbones through her skin. I tried not to react, but it was becoming increasingly obvious that she was using her skills and powers almost constantly.

"We still haven't found Mistress Del's missing ladies." Meredeath's words echoed my own thoughts. "These remains might give us some clues."

I nodded. "Do you [Detect Death] or are these just dungeon constructs?"

"It definitely feels like these skeletons are real. I got a new skill, too." She leaned in closer, whispering. "[Speak with the Dead]."

A shiver ran up my back. Meredeath's class was treading in a direction that was dangerous. I wasn't sure how close [Death Knight] was to [Necromancer], but it seemed close enough. General society didn't look kindly on the necromantic arts, and the Adventurer's Guild put out bounties on anyone found practicing, dubbing them heretics to the order.

Andrew already knew, but we couldn't trust Mira. She was too young.

I needed a reason to split the party again. As I turned, I realized everyone was staring at us.

Andrew spoke first. "Lesson #432 of adventuring. If you want to keep a secret, you shouldn't say it out loud. Too many people have skills associated with [Listening], including our Mira here." He patted her on the shoulder.

That's why I use my head, Richard said wisely as a glob of persimmon drool slid down his face.

I covered my embarrassment by walking over to the treasure chest and picking up my snarky 'owner.' He was limp in my arms, so I draped him across my shoulders.

"Okay, well," I said, wiping Richard's slime from my arm, "Meredeath can [Detect Death] and has a new [Speak with the Dead] skill. I'm going to suggest she use it on the skeletons. We might be able to close out Mistress Del's quest."

"Are you a [Necromancer]?" Leo asked, shifting his weight. What the hell, man? You don't just ask someone that.

I opened my mouth to respond, but Andrew cut in. "No, she's a [Death Knight]." His eyes flickered to mine, a subtle hint of unease. I wondered how safe [Death Knights] were from allegations of necromancy.

Was this secret truly safe even with Andrew?

"A [Death Knight]? That's so *cool*!" Mira added her two cents, breaking the tension. She would not be turning us in.

"Great, Meredeath's going to create an entire fleet of

[Death Magic] users," Leo grumbled. "If you guys don't mind, I'm going to head out. I want to get some rest before we leave for the Hunt."

Leo turned towards the dungeon exit, now clearly marked on our party maps. I could feel a tug at my heart. Whatever the invitation had granted him, he was still struggling with his role in our party.

He didn't look back. That hurt more than I wanted to admit.

No one else noticed Leo's state of mind. Instead, they were examining the skeletons that'd been in Mira's cage.

I joined them, apprehensive as the shadows in the room elongated. Meredeath's glowing eyes flared. Tandy also seemed to use a skill, her eyes gaining a passive golden color.

Looks like Meredeath's not the only one with new skills. Richard yawned, nestling his head into my shoulder as though we weren't about to rip open the veil between life and death.

I'd quiz Tandy on it later, when there weren't so many curious ears.

Andrew held Mira tight, but they were leaning forward with curiosity. Was I the only one left nervous about speaking to the dead?

The bones were dry, with tiny bite marks. One was even missing an entire leg. Both remnants had curled fingers holding them upright, as though sheer stubbornness could fight off death.

"[Speak with the Dead]," Meredeath spoke her skill, invoking a magic that I'd hoped never to encounter.

The shadows in the dungeon pulsed. The bones in the cage stood out white in the darkness. I took an involuntary step back as the skeletons began to glow, bones outlined in a thin flickering green fire that mirrored Meredeath's eyes. Sweat beaded on the [Death Knight's] forehead as she tried to hold the spell.

"I think it's failing." Meredeath's voice was strained, taut.

I put a hand on her back, attempting to infuse her with my own resolve. Richard lifted his head, slithering over to her shoulders. I closed my eyes, trying to will the skill to work.

"Ow! Richard, stop biting me!" Meredeath said angrily, her magic flaring. Clever little slug, leveraging anger for her magic.

Mira gasped as the skeleton shambled up, bony fingers clenching the cage's bars. As the body straightened, its head swiveled to face Meredeath. The jaw opened wordlessly, clacking its teeth together.

Magic flared again, faintly outlining a young woman in a low-cut dress superimposed over the skeleton. She wore a lacy hat pinned to a pile of curls. The ghost's eyes pierced my soul as it raised a hand, pointing.

Before I could glean more, the skill ran out, plunging us into complete darkness. The world fell away, trapping us in the abyss. My breath caught in my throat as I reached out, grabbing Meredeath's arm. Her warm skin battled the sensation of undeath surrounding us, and slowly the shadows and terror receded. The room snapped into focus.

"Holy shit." The words clawed out of my throat before I could stop them. I staggered sideways, gripping Tandy's arm. Meredeath had saved us multiple times, but these new skills were a lot. I couldn't help but think of Rhi's mummified [Lich] form and her bone warrior army. Meredeath's class was a dangerous one.

Tandy's voice shook as she spoke. "Were you able to get anything from her? We couldn't hear anything."

Meredeath turned. As the magic drained from her eyes, it seemed to be replaced by a mix of exhaustion and fear. Her face was thin and drawn, with the whites of her eyes clearly visible. Meredeath shook her head as though trying to dispel the magic quicker. I don't think she'll be using this skill often.

"She's the one. The lady's ring is the proof we needed." Meredeath's voice was distant, as though still under otherworldly influence. She sounded like she'd lost part of herself in the magic.

"It's probably where she was pointing," I said, moving towards the corner of the room.

A pile of wet debris sat on the floor. I bent down, separating the leaves and gunk to find a dainty jade ring. The tarnished silver was full of corrosion, and the jade wobbled in its setting, but it was definitely a lady's ring.

"The skeleton pointed? I didn't see that." Tandy looked at me, concerned.

"Yeah," I stood up, handing the ring to Meredeath. The [Death Knight] took it gingerly. Richard coiled around her neck as her earlobe bled a little from a tiny bite mark.

[Quest Updated: [Missing] - You have obtained an artifact of Mistress Del's missing ladies. Return the ring to Mistress Del for a reward.]

"We've at least met the quest criteria." Meredeath was right, but I couldn't help but wish we hadn't just solved the case. The woman was dead. I dreaded seeing the pain on Mistress Del's face.

The [Death Knight] clutched the ring, like it was a lifeline to the living. I don't think she was looking forward to explaining what happened either.

"Well, we should leave," Andrew said for Mira's benefit. The girl seemed caught between awe and fear, clutching his hand with white knuckles.

Tandy and I looked between the two, coming to the same conclusion.

"I want to see the orphanage, if that's okay? We don't have any in Woodsten, and I want to see where Mira lives." Tandy's lies were more convincing than anything I could have come up with. We really just wanted to give them the money in a way that Andrew couldn't refuse.

I nodded sagely, going along with Tandy's ruse.

Tandy's excuse was enough for Andrew. Mira even ran up to me, grabbing my hand.

I looked down at her wide eyes. Instantly I regretted making eye contact, as she took as an invitation to talk. She began babbling.

"I can't wait to introduce you to the mothers! And show you my rock collection! Boni's going to be so jealous. Do you think you can do that thing? Where you fly? I think the other kids would *love it*, and it's been so boring. Everyone's so sad, but I think they'd laugh if they saw you cartwheel through the air!" Once she started talking, she did not shut up.

I'll stick with Meredeath. Altruism isn't my thing. ***Kids*** *aren't my thing.*

For once, Richard and I shared an opinion.

The Hunt was calling, but first, apparently, a rock collection.

Chapter 56

REFUGEES

Exiting the dungeon turned out to be a lot simpler than entering. Now that we had defeated the creature controlling it, our mapping interface unlocked, showing the true extent of the maze. Traps were shown as disabled, and the exit portal clearly marked.

The exit dumped us into an alleyway in the professional district, skipping the whole underground tunnel network. I can't describe how relieved I felt to breathe in fresh air and feel the heat of the morning sun on my face. The dungeon had a wet-blanket closeness that my gills loved but that had kept me on edge the entire dive.

Also, I didn't miss the stench of the Fat Berg.

Meredeath handed a sleeping Richard back to me. The joke was on him. She didn't want to babysit *him*.

She peeled off to go back to *The Velvet Box*. I wasn't going to think too hard about why she was in such a hurry.

Richard had moved from messy drunk to sleepy drunk. He curled around my neck, filling my ear with soft snores.

Andrew led us away from the city center and business district. Foot traffic had picked up in the city as commerce began. Little did they know, a dungeon had been boiling beneath their feet, on the verge of an outbreak.

Andrew held Mira's hand as they wove between kids on their way to school and servants on the way to the market. We walked right past the giant windmill at the heart of the town. Giant sails creaked as they slowly rotated.

"Fish! Fresh fish!" a stall owner cried.

"Dried fish! Nothing fresh comes from the Niyat River!" the neighbor stall shouted.

"Ah, for fuck's sake, who the hell put their stalls next to each other?"

Andrew and Mira were unfazed by the noise and the bustle of the market. They took us further north into a residential district. Homes started off grand, with staircases framing a second-story entrance. Butlers stood on the balconies silently judging all those who walked by.

We kept going past the squares with fountains touting war heroes and politicians. The buildings got taller but less grand. Paint chipped, the soffit sagged, and overgrown bushes decorated small front gardens.

"We almost there?" Tandy asked. We'd split the loot between our bags, but it was getting heavier with every step.

"Almost." Andrew sounded tired. We walked past a couple of burned-out buildings, the brick garden walls the only reminder of the home. The wealth and the business of the central city gave way to quiet, unkempt gardens and weedy walkways.

I bumped into Andrew's back as we arrived at the orphanage without announcement. Before us, a high rock wall loomed, separating the neighboring properties. A loud screech pierced my ears as Mira wrenched the heavy gate open with all her might.

Where the hell am I?

"Orphanage," I whispered.

Meredeath! The betrayal. He tucked his tail tight against my neck, a sure sign he was pouting.

The front garden resembled a tent city, with canvas draped over almost every inch. Hungry little eyes poked out to look at the newcomers. A stone pathway between tents wound its way to the front entrance of a modest-looking two-story row house.

Oddly, the front door was the same color as Andrew's armor. It had the traditional deep blue trim that showed all were welcome. Whispers surrounded us as we walked the path.

Any doubts I'd had about donating our dungeon run's wealth had evaporated with the hungry look of little grubby faces.

This is shameful, Richard said. All drunkenness and betrayal forgotten as he extended his tentacles to look at the tents.

Mira marched right up to the front door and threw it open. "Mother! We've got guests!"

"I don't need any more guests," came a grumbling response from the kitchen.

The house was old styled with tall wooden baseboards and a cramped stairwell that hugged the wall. Normally, the room would have been a living room wrapped around the central fireplace. Here, a giant wooden table sat with enough seating for at least two dozen. A teenager stood trying to wrangle two toddlers into highchairs.

"I think you'll want to meet these two," Andrew said, moving to help the struggling teen. It was incredible to watch his warrior ways fade as he gently grabbed one toddler and slotted their legs effortlessly into the wooden holes.

The kid began crying, having lost her game of 'I don't fit'

in one smooth motion. Having both watched and experienced that challenge with my younger siblings, I wondered if Andrew had a skill he'd used.

"Do you know how many mouths I have to feed, Mira? Wait. Mira, is that you?" A matronly woman came out of the kitchen. She was thin in an oversized food-splattered apron. Brown and gray frizzy curls haloed her head, giving an unkempt appearance. She held a wooden spoon in one hand as though she were used to wielding it on food and misbehaving children alike.

"Andrew, you found her?" The relief in the woman's voice was easy to spot. She rushed forward, giving Mira a teary hug. My estimation of her immediately jumped; she loved these children.

Mira hugged her back, squeezing with all her might. The woman's face transformed from plain to beautiful, all smile lines and bright teeth as she lifted Mira up, returning the squeeze.

"Is that gruel you're cooking?" I asked, spotting a bit of mush stuck to the spoon. "If so, why don't you let me take over in the kitchen so you can have a reunion?"

The woman looked at my ratty appearance on the verge of declining when Andrew stepped in. "Eryn, it's okay. This is Cole, Tandy, and the slug is Richard. They're [Adventurers] that helped me find Mira."

With a frown, Eryn handed over the spoon. "Just don't burn it. I can't listen to them complain about a burned breakfast all day."

I grinned. "It's been a long time since I burned any gruel. Richard, can you give me a [Clean] to start?"

Richard obliged, my hands glowing a golden yellow as all traces of the day melted away.

"Oooh! Can you do that to *meeee*?" Mira ran forward, hopping up and down.

What am I now, a child washing station? Put me on the table. He sighed as though he'd done the math and knew what the rest of his morning was to entail.

I put the grumpy slug down, smiling as Mira started to glow. Grabbing the spatula from Eryn, I went back into the kitchen.

Whatever skills Eryn had in being a caregiver for a horde of children, it was obvious cooking wasn't at the top. The kitchen was messy and sticky. Several large pots of gruel sat on the stove.

A bored-looking kid sat on a stool by the tinderbox. While I was watching, he opened the side of the oven and stuck another sliver in. It made sense that they couldn't afford a magical stove, but heat control was nonexistent when you just had a child shoving as much fuel in the firebox as could fit.

"Hey, what's your name?" I asked, grabbing an apron draped over a cabinet. It was always easier to get a child to do what you wanted when you knew their name.

The boy looked up at me with wide brown eyes. "Rust. They call me Rust."

I hoped that wasn't his real name, but when he didn't provide another, I went with it. Applying the spoon to a pot, I quickly started stirring, realizing it was seconds from burning.

"Okay, Rust. You're working with the Master of Mush today." I couldn't help but smile. Funny how perspective worked. "Stop feeding the oven. Can you stand on that stool and get a better view up here? I'm going to teach you how to stir. Did I see apples in the pantry?"

"You want me to stir?" He looked up at me as though I was trusting him with the key to the city.

"Absolutely! If you can fill the tinderbox, you can stir!" I tried sounding upbeat, my favorite tactic with children. The truth, however, is I was pretty sure the gruel was already burnt. The faster we got him away from the tinderbox, the more chance I had to salvage it.

We got to work. Rust stirred while I cored and chopped

some apples. I found some old cinnamon sticks that I grated into the boiling pot. The kitchen started smelling like a proper breakfast was in the works.

Several curious children popped in asking questions. None stayed longer than my promise that breakfast would be ready soon.

The house, however, started waking up with the smells.

"You used the last of our apples, did you?" Eryn asked as she came in to check on our progress. She sounded tired. "I guess Mira's return is worth celebrating, but you used the last of our cinnamon too. You work in a restaurant where food wasn't tight?"

I felt every fiber of her exhaustion, even if I internally cringed at her judgement. It was the same voice my mom used after a long winter, when the pantry was looking bare.

"Aye, my apologies. Was trying to spice it up a bit. Has Tandy talked to you about our donation yet? Where do you keep your dishes? I'll start serving everything up. How many mouths do we have to feed?"

Eryn studied me for another long moment before replying, "Thirty-five, not counting your crew. She did, and apologies. I'm so used to making things stretch that, even with the bounty your team is offering, I'm trying to imagine how to make it last."

Thirty-five mouths. I couldn't imagine trying to run a household that big day in and day out.

"Rust, why don't you get the bowls down?" I said quietly, trying to comprehend the monumental task the woman had before her.

"Elli, get back into the dining room!" Eryn's voice snapped. "You know, no one but Rust is in the kitchen while food is being cooked. Apologies, I'll get back to getting everyone set. Rust can help you with the bowls."

I ladled out spoonful after spoonful, counting the bowls, leaving Tandy and me out. I portioned it out almost perfectly, although the last bowl was mostly the dried, stuck-on remnants at the bottom of the last pot.

Rust took it. I watched as the look of excitement at having apple *and* cinnamon in his breakfast melted away as he looked at the burned mush.

"Take this to Richard the slug," I told him. If Richard had nothing, he had several hydrating tricks up his sleeves.

Children occupied every nook and cranny of the dining hall. They pulled at Tandy's clothes, marveling at its finery. Thankfully, her nettle enchantment was turned off. Everyone looked notably clean, as Richard kept pulsing as child after child brought him *something else* to clean. Andrew crouched over one highchair, spooning gruel into a child's mouth. He had bits of spit-up gunk on his bandana.

"Thank you for the help with breakfast. I didn't mean to sound ungrateful." Eryn stood beside me in the doorframe. As I looked at her, I revisited my estimate of her matronly state. She wasn't much older than I. The gray in her hair had been flour. I noted she hadn't grabbed a bowl for herself either, and her thin frame was as delicate as many of the children's.

"We're going to find you some help," I said. I didn't know how, but I knew it was true.

Richard extended two tentacles back from his perch on the table in agreement.

I didn't need a [System] request to give me this quest.

Chapter 57

NO STATUES FOR SLUGS

"Cole, those kids need our help." Tandy wasn't wrong.

The kids needed help, no argument there. But what could we do?

Also, Leo was invested in the Hunt. My [Heartbeat] skill pulsed with his need to prove himself. If we didn't go, it was entirely possible he'd go without us, and our team would effectively end. There had to be a solution that wasn't just one or the other.

"The invitation, though," I said what we were both thinking.

"I know." Tandy was at a loss as I was. Almost three dozen kids lived in that orphanage. Even with Andrew's help and our dungeon loot, it would not be enough. Not long term. Even if we stayed and tried to help, I wasn't sure it'd be enough.

"Richard, do you have any ideas?" It was a shot in the dark.

I think they should invest in a bathtub.

Gods be damned, slug, I don't know why I ever asked his opinion on anything.

"I talked to Andrew while you were cooking. Apparently, pop-up dungeons have become a thing. He's heard a couple of reports through the [Wayfinder] network of towns getting overrun. It's enough to have me worried about Woodsten. Team Abs wouldn't know the first thing to do about finding a dungeon. The Adventurer's Guild has been noticeably silent. It's the small towns that are suffering."

Tandy was spiraling. She was stuck on it all. Which wasn't great because now we had a third item to add to our list of things we needed to worry about.

"You're not helping," I countered.

We were walking back to Mistress Del's to consult with Meredeath and Leo, our bags significantly lighter. Andrew had insisted we keep a little of the coinage for 'emergencies.' He sounded like my dad.

The Ashborn have always figured out a way to survive. I'm not sure why the two of you think the dungeon outbreaks are your personal problem.

Tandy paused and turned, looking at Richard.

"Is that how you've sat out the last five hundred years, [Immortal]? It's 'not your problem'? The world struggled with the cataclysm for decades, but that wasn't your problem. If you're even [Immortal]." Tandy stomped off.

I'd never looked at Richard's theoretical [Immortality] with that lens, probably because I'd never taken it seriously. Tandy was kind of right, for all that it cut.

It wasn't my problem because I couldn't fix it.

We both stared after her as her boots hit the pavement hard enough to cause heads to turn. Her nettle cloak flapped behind her braids. People parted, giving wide berth to her stormy countenance.

"Tandy hasn't met a problem she won't try to own," I told Richard.

Yeah, fair. What buzzed up her skirt?

I smiled. For all his wisdom and snark, he still had a long way to go before he understood Tandy. You couldn't tell her something wasn't her responsibility. If she was bent on fixing something, it was going to get fixed. Either that or she was going to torture herself and everyone else around her with it. Tandy didn't understand the idea of can't.

I didn't bother rushing after her. Andrew had given us pretty clear directions back to the Red Eaves district. I was going to enjoy a bit of freedom in a new city. Besides, I wasn't in a hurry to have an uncomfortable conversation with Leo.

Eddie's Mill turned out to be much easier to navigate once I took the time to learn it. My internal map had filled in. The central mill and market formed the city's center, with the rest of the city extending like spokes on a wheel.

I passed a flower shop, looking in the window at a collection of fresh-cut and potted flowers. Part of me wanted to pick out a bundle and bring it back to Eryn, to give a little joy to her and the children.

Something about the orphanage had caught my imagination. A different life, a left instead of a right. Fixing up the house with a fresh coat of paint and maybe fifteen room additions for all the souls camped out in the yard. Running the dungeon with Andrew and bringing home the loot.

So, do you have a plan for practicing your skills yet? Richard's question rudely interrupted my daydream.

Uh, nope. I hadn't really considered it.

You need to have a plan.

I started walking quicker. This didn't sound like a conversation that I wanted to have either.

"You're suggesting I kill myself once a day?" A passerby on the street gave me a side-eye as I talked with my mollusk. I gave them a quick, reassuring smile. They frowned harder and quickened their pace. I guess it was an unusual thing to say to oneself.

I'm suggesting you make a plan for each of your skills, including ***that*** *one.*

"*That* one? The one that just morphs me into something a little *less human* each time I use it?" I murmured, this time trying to avoid attracting the notice of another passerby.

Richard didn't respond immediately.

"Don't think I haven't thought about this. I'm talking to a sentient slug with what I'm assuming is a similar class." I let my words sit uncomfortably between us. "What is the natural conclusion to this class? Is [Cheat Death] even a skill I *want* much less want to *practice?*"

The slug on my shoulders sat unusually quiet.

Strolling through the city, window shopping, I smelled spices coming from restaurants and bakeries. I even stopped on a street corner to chat with a young mother and her snuffling kid. It was a wonderful moment to be alive. To be the gelatinous, partial amphibian pet of a slug who could reasonably be mistaken for a human.

"How are we even going to have this conversation with Leo?" I changed the subject. I wasn't really irritated with Richard. I was just feeling trapped. "Excuse me, Leo, but we're going to pass on your ticket to the Hunt, because we've got a houseful of children to feed?"

That's a rhetorical question, right?

I didn't bother replying. His opinion wasn't what I wanted. I just needed a moment.

At the next square, I moved out of the flow of pedestrians. The town square held the local well and a small manicured park space. This one held a dark onyx obelisk almost three meters tall. I walked over to it, reading the inscription. It recounted the feats of those who fell in one battle of the cataclysm. The names etched on the obelisk were old, forgotten.

It was likely we'd be forgotten much sooner than these lost souls.

Elasira Penragon. Richard's mental voice knocked me out of my introspection.

"Excuse me?"

Elasira, she was friendly. Had golden hair that glowed in the sun. She loved to play practical jokes.

"Okaay, context would help." As I said the words, my eye fell on the list of names.

Lira Hesa, Rsan Talon, *Elasira Penragon.* The three Heroes of Eddie's Mill.

The inscription followed with dozens of more names, but hers was third on the list.

That's the problem with caring when you live as long as I have.

A cloud passed over the sun, threatening an early drizzle. I stared at the name. Perspective was a bitch.

"That would be... tough."

I sat on a bench as the first raindrops fell. Richard curled in on himself. For the first time in a while, I felt completely alone.

You'll note you have seen no statues of slugs.

"You'd have to be heroic to have a statue."

Heroic and dead, of which I'm guilty of neither.

"Glad I'm in good company."

We sat for ten minutes, an hour, I wasn't sure. But it hadn't rained enough to get me soaked, just enough to make my gills flex comfortably.

Our introspection was broken with an unrequested [System Notification]:

[Quest Complete: [Missing].

The mystery of Mistress Del's missing ladies has been solved. Meredith Steele has turned in the ring as proof, and the party has received free room and board for the month. Additional rewards may be granted upon talking to Mistress Del. Adventure Onward!]

Tandy and Meredeath must have returned to *The Velvet Box* and delivered the news to Mistress Dell.

An idea blossomed in my head. Maybe we could reroute Mistress Del's reward to the orphans? We were going to head to the Hunt and wouldn't need it. And she was a bit of a softie. Once she got involved with the orphanage, she'd probably take them all on. She seemed a bit like Tandy that way. Something to consider.

I turned towards the Red Eaves district. It was time to sit down and have a good old family meeting.

Floria would laugh at me if she knew I was going to play the unpopular head of the household. Gods help me, she'd be right to laugh.

Chapter 58

FAMILY MEETING

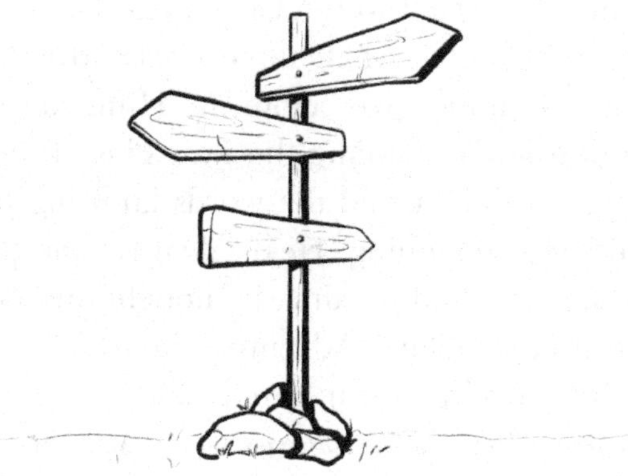

As family meetings go, the setup for this one could have been exponentially worse. Lunch wasn't a busy time at *The Velvet Box*, so we had a large booth to ourselves. Mistress Del had even given us a full spread for lunch.

She'd been grateful for the closure we'd provided.

Everything was great until Tandy revealed she'd donated most of our [Dungeon Treasure Chest] to the orphanage.

"You did *what*?" Leo exclaimed, bits of biscuit flying out of his mouth.

Tandy looked at him as though he were a barbarian. Reddening cheeks betrayed the sense of guilt she felt. She went on the offensive.

"You weren't there. The children were living in canvas tents, eating burned gruel for breakfast." Tandy didn't bother mentioning who'd *made* the gruel. Little Rust had told me it'd been the best-tasting breakfast they'd had in a while, so I kept my commentary to myself.

"But we were going to use that to gear up for the Hunt." There was a flatness in Leo's voice that brooked no argument. He was *pissed*. And I realized he'd never agree to skip the Hunt in favor of helping the kids. The orphanage needed help, but I was going to have to be creative in how I executed it.

"We can still make it to the Ceaparean Drift in time, even without the money. It's what, three weeks to get there? And we've got a little under five before the Hunt starts? Plenty of time to work a few jobs along the way. Plus, Tandy, you kept some coinage, right?" I said the words knowing that Andrew insisted we keep something. He'd taken on the plight of the orphanage himself, and he already thought any donation was too much from a fledgling [Adventurer] party.

"I've got two golds worth, twenty silver," Tandy admitted. It wasn't a ton when spread across four [Adventurers] and an [Immortal] mollusk, but it was a lot more than we'd had when we entered Eddie's Mill.

Leo looked as though he'd bitten a lemon. "You gave it *all* away?" The anguish in his voice seemed mismatched with Tandy's actions.

"These are kids, man. We'd never let kids live in those conditions in Woodsten." I left unspoken what I was hinting at. No one had let *him* live in those conditions once he became an orphan. Not that Uncle Artie was an upstanding citizen, but Leo'd had a roof over his head and food on the table.

Leo looked at me, his eyes blazing. Message received.

"Look," Meredeath jumped into the conversation, putting a hand on Leo's arm. "I'm not thrilled with our wealth evaporating, but we've still got the ability to make it to the Hunt, and we've got free room and board, so we can earn more before we leave. We've got options here."

Tandy and I exchanged a look. Meredeath wasn't helping our end goal.

"So, if we've got a week before we leave, what do we do with the time?" Leo asked.

I want a spa day.

"Do spas even allow slugs in?" Meredeath asked, eyebrows raised. She was obviously egging the slug on.

The four of us looked at Richard, who sat idly in front of a bowl of leafy greens. He was gumming a sprig of dandelion absently. He didn't bother replying to the jab.

"Well, thanks for that suggestion. Anyone else?" Tandy prodded.

"I think we should log the new dungeon with the Adventurers' Guild. There's got to be a reward for finding a new dungeon." This idea came from Meredeath, of all people.

"How about *you,* Cole?" Tandy probed. I knew what she wanted me to say.

Glancing at Leo, I put my heart on the table. "I want to help the orphanage. The house is falling apart. If we focused on fixing it up, it could really turn things around. Honestly, I thought about suggesting we stay here and help make a real difference." Leo opened his mouth to object, so I rushed the rest. "But I know how important it is for you to go to the Hunt. For us. I just want to do as much for the kids as we can before we leave."

There. I'd put my cards on the table.

"We can barely take care of ourselves, much less an entire orphanage." Meredeath noted. She wasn't wrong, I just didn't predict she'd take a hard line against helping orphans. I was about to say so, but Tandy stopped me.

"Don't you feel the need to help?"

"It's not our problem. We didn't create it. This is an Eddie's Mill problem that the general populace is turning a blind eye to. No matter what we do, unless we dedicate our lives to the solution, it's only going to be a temporary fix." Meredeath used her fingers to emphasize each point, the edges of her black nails poking my heart. She wasn't wrong.

"Okay, so how do we get Eddie's Mill to care?" Tandy asked quietly, unwilling to let it go.

"Mind if I join you?" We'd been so focused on our conversation, no one noticed Mistress Del sneaking up on the table. Before anyone could respond, she pulled up a chair at the end of our booth and sat down heavily. "I can leave you be, but it sounds like you've stumbled upon an 'Eddie's Mill problem that the general populace is turning a blind eye to.' Sounds like my kind of problem. Lucky for me, [Overhear] is a skill of my trade."

She made no genuine apology for eavesdropping. Meredeath met her eyes with determination. The older woman stayed calm, though. "Can you tell me about this orphanage?" she asked.

With the question, all the tension at the table melted. Meredeath looked away, crossing her arms against her chest.

Tandy gave me a quick grin of triumph. Both of us had hoped to bring Mistress Del into the plight of these kids. We already knew she had a kind heart, just from taking us in. Tandy and I fell over each other filling the Mistress in on the details of Eryn, Andrew, Mira, Rust, and the rest of them. Even Leo softened a bit when I talked about the state of the house and how Richard spent two hours just cleaning the kids up.

Mistress Del asked questions calmly, drawing out possibilities we hadn't considered. At the end of the conversation, we didn't have answers, exactly, but we had direction, an immediate plan that didn't involve Leo rushing off by himself or the abandonment of the town's orphans.

Tomorrow, we were going to visit the Adventurer's Guild to see what the payout was going to be for the dungeon, then bring the Mistress, Leo, and Meredeath by the orphanage.

"Well, I'm glad that's settled," Meredeath said abruptly, as though she'd been bored the whole time. "I'm going to hang out with some new friends. I'll see you all in the morning."

"It's only settled if we leave on time," Leo said, giving us a steely gaze over his mug. He was like a dog with a bone. *Nothing* was going to stop him from making the Hunt.

I was looking forward to it too, but it'd taken on a deeper meaning for him. Like an adventuring lifeline.

"Yeah, Leo. We hear you. We're going to go to the Hunt." I turned to Meredeath as she stood to go. "Want some company?"

The look she gave me made me immediately regret asking. "You're welcome to join me, but I'm not sure it's your scene." I got the impression she was offering out of obligation.

My heart clenched. Was I going to be brave and go with her? With the possibility of being an unwanted third wheel? Did I back down and stay with Tandy and Leo? Safe, but an outsider to this separate world Meredeath was a part of?

I jumped off the cliff.

It was time to find out what else was in the world, and it started with Meredeath.

It was time to jump — to say yes.

"Yeah, no. I want to go." The words came out less confidently than I had hoped, but I'd said them. I'd taken the leap.

Meredeath and Mistress Del exchanged a look.

"He's going to need different clothes," Mistress Del said, her nose upturned at the state of my Woodsten wool. "And some accessories."

Meredeath's eyes twinkled with mischief. "Do you have anything we could borrow?"

"Oh, honey, the lost and found has better options than this." She waved at me. The two leaned together, talking conspiratorially.

Tandy rolled her eyes, scooting to get out of the bench. She was, no doubt, off to practice. Leo sat sipping his beer, looking amused.

"You want to come with us?" I asked him hopefully.

Leo smiled, taking another draft. "No, I think I'll stay

here. You asked for this, bro." He leaned back, watching as the two women batted about several options, from a fishnet tank top to an eyebrow piercing.

"Eyeliner?" I blurted out, overhearing one suggestion they'd settled on.

I think eyeliner is going to be the least of your concerns. You're going to be wearing a collar by the end of the night.

Oh fuck. I wasn't sure if I'd agreed to a date, a trap, or public humiliation. Odds were good it was going to be all three.

I wonder if they've got a leash I could hold?

Chapter 59

COLLARED

My heart quivered as Meredeath pulled my hand down a set of cramped stairs.

It felt like Minvi, my first girlfriend, was pulling me into the field after school.

We were about to do something forbidden.

The walls of the stairs billowed out, made of a velvet that sensually caressed my bare arms. They'd put me in a leather vest, leaving my farmer's tan on full display.

The stairwell had been in a back alley of the Red Eaves district. Painted black, with dim pinpoints of light from the room above as our only illumination, it felt dangerous.

Meredeath squeezed my fingers as she got to the landing, a large ironclad door barring our entry. She lifted a pale, dainty hand, knocking hard. A slit opened, revealing a dark face with completely white eyes.

I tried to act cool. The man looked as if he was possessed.

Maybe that was the point.

He looked at me and shook his head. "You have the wrong club." The slit closed sharply, dismissing us.

Meredeath looked at me, frowning as though to say, *What'd you do?*

She knocked hard again. This time her hand flared with a green fire.

The slit opened. "I told you..." The annoyed man's voice trailed off as he examined Meredeath's fiery green eyes.

"He's mine," she growled. The statement felt like all the promise of the night rolled into one simple sentence.

Richard licked my ear. *Now you're mine.*

I wiped the saliva off. For fuck's sake!

I didn't want to bring the slug, but we all decided he couldn't be left alone, and Tandy and Leo weren't in the mood.

Richard had acquiesced to a bit of eyeliner, and Meredeath had even turned some of his black spots into mini skulls.

As much as I wanted this night to be special. To mean *something* with Meredeath, I had a sinking suspicion that Richard was going to dampen the mood. It was like when my brother, Hitch, used to follow Minvi and me around like an unwanted chaperone.

"Fine, but there's a cover charge of one silver for him."

The slot closed as the sound of bars sliding filled the confined space. I didn't have any silver. Part of me was relieved the expedition was getting cut short.

The man stood, white eyes eerily glowing in the dark foyer. His muscled arms crossed, with leather strips crisscrossed against his skin.

Meredeath smiled. She slipped a finger between her breasts and pulled out a silver coin. I stopped myself from asking how she'd gotten it.

It was the same bedeviled smile Minvi'd had when she'd snuck a contraband flagon of ale into my loft on solstice. I'd gotten blamed for it later. The next day she hadn't defended me when I'd been accused of pilfering it. What could I say? They found the flagon in *my* loft.

The silver exchanged, the man eyed me once more. He shrugged, as though abdicating all responsibility for my fate. He closed the door behind us, sliding the bars into place.

Who were they trying to keep out? Because if it were me, I could be okay with that.

This is going to be good.

I highly doubted that.

The inner door swung open, introducing me to magically enhanced club music for the first time. The beat was heavy, as a flicker triggered. They usually reserved flicker light shows for large outdoor festivals. This one was blinking a hundred times a minute *indoors*.

I tried not to look directly at it, my eyes already beginning to see spots.

We were standing on a platform, a catwalk of sorts, above a cavern. I should have expected the club would be underground, considering how much the city leveraged the caves. Stalagmites reached up from the ground, casting shadows into the dark corners. Cages dangled from the ceiling, containing scantily clad dancers who gyrated to the music.

I almost asked if they needed rescuing, but Meredeath pulled me down the stairs towards the bar.

The squeeze was tight, and the smell of patchouli heavy. My stomach clenched with unease.

Minvi'd moved in quickly after her parents kicked her out, my tiny apartment squeezed tight with the two of us.

I survived that summer.

I could do this.

The winged shoulders of my vest provided a perfect platform for Richard. He'd adjusted his spotting to darken, matching the aesthetic of the place. My eyelids itched with smoky eyeshadow. I refrained from touching my eyes, constantly in fear of smudging Meredeath's work.

Looking around, I didn't stand out as much as I'd feared. The place was full of people of all shapes and sizes. The only similarity seemed to be a propensity for black.

Several folks seemed to hold minor multicolored flickers dancing around, burning the image of flashing lights into my retinas.

"Let's get a drink!" Meredeath shouted towards me. She didn't have to say that twice.

Two topless, skinny men manned the bar. One had his nipples pierced while the other flexed his pecs, shaking a drink.

"What do you want?" the nipple bartender asked as we leaned over the counter.

Meredeath pulled another silver from her bra and ordered a martini. She pointed at me.

"I'll take a beer," I coughed out.

And a hot pepper.

"And a hot pepper. The hotter the better." The guy gave me an odd look. I pointed at the slug. He shook his head as though he'd had stranger requests.

"A beer, really? We're supposed to enjoy ourselves," Meredeath yelled, leaning back against the bar, as she scanned the dancers. I tried to mirror her nonchalance, awkwardly leaning against the bar trying not to make eye contact with any of the dancers.

The music changed. This time it was high-pitched. I could feel Richard's slime vibrate in time with the screeching tune. I really tried not to wince, but I'm sure I looked miserable.

Meredeath glanced at me and sighed. "I knew this was a mistake."

I opened my mouth to argue. To lie, but I was confronted with a mental flash of Minvi ambushing me.

"I knew you were a mistake," Minvi had said as she left the last time, slamming the door after we'd fought about money.

I just nodded at Meredeath. No part of this night was in my comfort zone, but I was an adult. She could have her fun without me.

"I'm fine. Don't let me stop you from having fun. I'm just going to have my beer and then I'll go." The words tasted like defeat.

Minvi cheated. She'd stolen my last bit of coin. Left the apartment empty, save for the scent of her lavender perfume that haunted me for months. Leo and Tandy had saved me in the aftermath. Leo kept me busy, while Tandy gave me a Richard-worthy side-eye anytime I said something positive about Minvi.

Meredeath's martini arrived. She deftly plucked an olive off the toothpick and held it out for Richard.

I watched in disgust as he ate the salty snack, foaming as it hit his slime. From what I could tell, his eating pickled food was a bit like a human eating a lemon. Sour and weirdly pleasant in small quantities.

My beer came with a hot pepper split like an orange wheel perched on the side of my mug.

I took a quick sip. The beer tasted like the ghost of Richard's pepper floated in the foam. Sheep-cursed slug and his pepper fetish. I quickly removed it, handing it off to Richard.

"You sure you're okay?" Meredeath asked one last time.

"Yeah, I'll just go sit over there," I said, squinting as I pointed to a small empty booth.

She nodded, eyes already on the dance floor. She'd found a giant bear of a man who'd dyed his red beard black and braided a skull bead into it. How could I compete with him?

I shimmied over along the side of the room. The space behind the stalagmites seemed reserved for couples. My face burned as I got a glimpse of two women making out, clothes in disarray.

"Ten-minute break!" a voice called from above as the flicker and music cut. Dim lights snapped on, which, from the groans of the crowd, might well have been dawn.

I quickly grabbed an empty booth before it got snapped up, putting Richard on the table with his pepper. Dull clangs sounded while the stagehands lowered the cage dancers to the floor. The male dancers wore nothing but jockstraps and glitter. The women looked like they'd lost a battle with a pair of fabric scissors. Everyone glistened with sweat, oil, and glitter.

Replacement dancers jumped into the cages. They waved, blowing kisses at the crowd as the cages lifted into the air.

"New here?" A girl slid into the booth across from me. She had pointy ears and short spiky hair.

"How'd you guess?" I said dryly.

"I have never seen a slug walk in before."

I laughed. Gods, it felt good to laugh.

Richard raised his head, the butt of the hot pepper hanging out of his mouth like a cigar. *You laughing at me?*

"Yeah, banana slugs are probably rare in the city."

"Did you know their slime has numbing properties?" She looked at Richard with a glint of avarice.

"You're an alchemist?" I asked. I wasn't anxious. If she stole a little of Richard's slime... well, he left it everywhere.

She leaned forward trying to get a closer look at Richard and bumped my beer. It sloshed over the side.

"Oh sorry, here, let me dab that up." Almost magically, she produced a cloth napkin to soak up the mess. "Yeah, I'm an alchemist of sorts. I just haven't seen a slug like this specimen. Mind if I grab a glob of slime?"

"Go right ahead." I waved at Richard, giving her permission. He didn't seem to mind. She took out a spoon and scraped a bit of goo into a bottle.

"Much obliged!" With a nod, the woman was off.

I took another sip of my beer. The music kicked back up. The noise and flashing slammed into my psyche. I focused on Richard, his tentacles bouncing in rhythm. I could see the slime vibrating off his skin, puddling under his body.

Glancing out into the morass of tight leather and naked chests, I caught a glimpse of Meredeath on the shoulders of the mountain man holding onto the bottom of a cage as it swung in the air.

"Down, witch!" Nipples, the bartender, was yelling.

Meredeath blew him a kiss to the crowd's amusement. She did not get down.

She's just your type.

The problem was that Richard was right, sarcasm aside. Meredeath was mysterious. Dark. I didn't understand her. Minvi was similar, in a Woodsten way. She had a dark streak, a daring edge that drew me like a moth to the flame. I just wanted to know what it was to let go.

My back was firmly locked in place. I took another sip of beer. For a cavern, it was boiling down here. Self-introspection did that.

My head bounced along with the music. The only experience I had with dancing was the prancing ribbon dance of our Maypole festival. The vest had dug in at my armpit, and the chaps I'd thrown on over my normal pants creased awkwardly against the back of my knees.

I'm sure if I told Meredeath she'd just laugh and tell me the pants weren't meant for sitting.

My beer was hoppy and spicy.

"You shouldn't drink any more of that." An androgynous individual slid into the booth across from me. Couldn't a man just have a beer with his slug?

"And why not?" I asked, unimpressed with the person's claim. They had delicate features outlined by the makeup everyone else was wearing. A bull ring looped through their nostrils, and the poetic sliced eyebrow raised at my tone.

"Gimi. She dosed your beer with sweet water."

The room tilted. "What's it do?"

"Loosens you up. Makes you less aware," he said. She said? I couldn't tell.

Honestly, both sounded… tempting. I reached for the mug. My hand danced in the lights.

They leaned forward, their vest split across a small but feminine chest covered by a sheer blouse.

"I think it's what allowed her to take your slug," she whispered conspiratorially.

My vision spun as I saw a smear of slime and the butt of a pepper. No Richard.

My stomach dropped through the cavern. "Richard?"

Chapter 60

WHAT THE SLUG GIVETH, HE TAKETH AWAY

"Where did she take him?"

"Gimi's an alchemist in the Bath Quarter. He's probably fine. She does this sometimes, gets obsessive over an ingredient. The fumes have eroded her brains. I can take you to her place. My name is Liv. What's your name, friend?" She stood, her body stretching unusually tall in front of me.

I blinked. It had to be the drugs.

"My name's Cole." I tried to stand, but the world spun violently.

Liv signaled a server to bring two glasses of water. Sobering up was a good call.

This was turning into an awful night.

"I need to get back to Mistress Del's, get Meredeath." It was the oddest thing to hear myself mumbling but being unable to stop myself. How much of the sweet water had I drunk?

"You're one of Del's? You don't look her type. Crap." Liv snapped her fingers, and I watched as she talked to the server. They looked at me worriedly.

Suddenly Meredeath was there.

"What happened? How is he drunk, he only had one beer?" She snapped her fingers in front of my face. I cringed, shying away. "Oh, fuck, can't I just have one night off?"

Liv and Meredeath helped me up, and we staggered up the velvet stairs. The alley was dark and empty, and thankfully not too far from *The Velvet Box.*

The air smelled faintly of sewage and mint. Meredeath swore nonstop. I wasn't sure why Liv had latched onto us, but I wasn't in a position to argue.

Leo'd been sleeping when we barged in. Tandy had been practicing. They both gave me a look of disgust as I sat heavily in bed, watching Meredeath and Liv explain what happened.

My mind wandered. The silence of the room after the club was deafening. They whispered to each other, debating a plan of action. My heart thumped distantly, stretched thin as it reached for Richard. He was alive. I knew that much. Which was probably a given if he *was* [Immortal].

I took off my vest. It was so *hot.*

"It's the sweet water. He's going to be naked soon if you don't stop him." Liv's voice rattled in my head.

Was she talking about me? I started fumbling with the chaps. I just needed to change. The leather string slid through my fingers.

Leo batted my hand away. "Put this on, big man." He handed me my nightshirt as he helped with the chaps. No one had called me big man since I was a kid, and Floria's job had been to get all of us ready for bed in the loft.

"I'm not a big man. I'm an [Adventurer]." The words made sense in my head. An [Adventurer] was all grown up, not some puffed-up pretend version of an adult. Maybe I wasn't cut out for Meredeath, but I'm sure I could find someone who wasn't an undead princess.

Maybe I should send a letter to Minvi?

Or Liv, Liv's kind of cute.

I blinked, realizing I'd been pointing at Liv. Fuck.

"Leo, take care of him, will you? We're going to move this conversation outside." Tandy took control of the situation. She was cleaning up the mess. Reliable Tandy.

The girls left as Leo stripped me down.

"Did they leave because of me?"

Leo looked at me with… was it pity? Compassion?

"No, you're okay, man. It's just time for bed. We'll get your slug back tomorrow."

I looked at him and reached out, tugging at his beard like I'd seen Meredeath. He looked at me confused. I just patted his cheek and climbed up into the loft.

Distantly, I heard the door crack back open.

"He just climbed into your bed?" Tandy whispered too loudly.

"Yeah, after patting me in the face."

"Drugs do weird things."

"I guess."

Blissful oblivion took me.

The morning was not so blissful. I lay flat out on Leo's bed. Head probably right where his drool pile normally sat.

"Good morning." Tandy had pulled herself up, her head even with mine. She'd poked me awake.

"Please tell me I wasn't a complete idiot," I whispered. My face was burning as I realized I was naked except for my underwear.

"I can't do that, but I can tell you that you now own the top bunk."

Great. Failing up.

"Is it recoverable?" I'm not sure I'd recover my pride, but I had to figure out how to function.

"I mean, for you?" she teased. "Maaaybe… You're fine. Just get dressed before you join us for breakfast. It's going to be a big day."

I came downstairs hungry.

"I mean, Richard is slippery. It's not all Cole's fault," Leo said loudly as I came up to the table.

"Yeah, plus you were there, too, Meredeath. This is partially your fault," Tandy chimed in.

I knew what they were trying to do. It made me feel better, anyway.

"So, what's the plan?" I gave a nod to Liv.

"We rescue Richard, then head to the Adventurers' Guild to lodge a complaint and claim our dungeon," Tandy said matter-of-factly.

"I work with Mistress Del most nights, so she's tasked me with helping you," Liv explained. "Besides, I want to get to the bottom of Gimi drugging you. The club is a safe space. Petty theft is one thing, but you were a helpless babe. If Gimi's drugging people that badly, I need to get her barred from the club. I mean, she should be barred anyway, but I'm not sure the twins are going to care about a missing slug."

"The twins?" I asked, my head still fuzzy.

"The barkeepers, the owners of the place." Liv was much too chipper for whatever o'clock in the morning this was "I've never seen Gimi drug someone so heavily."

So, Mr. Nipples was one of the owners? I needed a new line of work.

"It's my new skill, [Gelatinous Regeneration]," I explained, trying to answer Liv's concern. "It decreases my [Poison Resistance]. On the one hand, I get drunk quicker. On the other—"

"—You get drugged quicker." Liv nodded. "That's a dangerous skill. Hopefully, the regeneration is worth it."

"Did you say gelatinous? You didn't tell me you'd picked

up a new skill." Leave it to Tandy to latch on to the one thing I didn't want her asking questions about.

"Yeah, I picked up two after defeating the last boss." I darted my eyes to Liv, trying to redirect the conversation somewhere safer. "So, what's the plan?"

An hour later, I paced outside an alchemist shop waiting for my team members. My head throbbed. The sun was as bright as a flicker. Whoever invented sweet water deserved eternal boils.

Cole?

"Richard?" I shouted.

I'm in here.

"The alchemist's?"

No, the spa.

I blinked. The spa? I looked around. Sure enough, a giant sign read 'Amidale's Spa Emporium.'

"So you weren't captured?"

I was, but you think an alchemist in Eddie's Mill could hold me captive when the [Lich] Queen of Niyatgra couldn't?

The slug had a good point. I ducked into the alchemist's shop. Leo had Gimi pushed up against the wall. Tandy was holding a wooden cage, pointing at a slime pile.

"Guys, he's next door." The group looked at me. "Hi, Gimi. What are you going to offer us *not to* report you to the authorities?"

Oh, ask for a sample case. And get a jar of the dancing nettles. I could use that for my collection.

Collection? Was Richard an [Alchemist]?

"Uh, I could offer you a nice pouch of moon blossom?" Gimi offered.

Leo growled, shoving her harder against the rack. "And I could push you through this wall and send everything on this rack onto the floor."

The offer was insulting. The woman took one look at our group and assumed we were all partnered up.

"How about a sample pack, some of the white lace, a pack of yarrow, plantain, and all of your dancing nettles?"

Gimi's eyebrows knitted together as we started the negotiations. We had an advantage. Leo applied pressure if Gimi got too stubborn.

We left Gimi's alchemy shop stocked with everything Richard wanted and with a good start to my first aid kit.

Walking into Amidale's, an attendant greeted us warmly. "Ah, such a large group this morning. What sort of service package can I offer you? We have baths, steam rooms, as well as a variety of treatments."

"I'm looking for my slug."

"Excuse me?" The lady was flabbergasted. I didn't blame her.

"I'm looking for a foot-long banana slug," I repeated. "His name's Richard."

This got us escorted onto the street.

"Richard!" I called. "Come join us, or you're going to have to slug back to Mistress Del's on your own."

Screams emanated from the baths as two half-naked customers came running out, wrapped in towels. The attendant was behind the counter with a broom aimed at Richard.

He was fluffed out, slowly undulating forward. His glistening skin was shiny, newly steamed, and no doubt abundantly moisturized.

Stepping forward, I pointed at Richard. "See? I told you my slug was in here."

I kneeled down, picked Richard up and put him on my shoulders.

And that was how we ended up being banned from two establishments in one morning. Might as well aim for three.

Next stop: Adventurer's Guild.

Chapter 61

RED TAPE

Richard was extra drippy.

"Alright, I found your slug. I'm going to head out." Liv walked away, her hips swaying in her leather lace-up pants. A large part of me wanted to follow. Instead, I turned to my slug.

"Have a good time?" I asked Richard as we walked to the Adventurer's Guild.

I did. That was a superior bathing facility. My sarcasm was lost on him.

"Welcome to the—Oh, it's you." The guild clerk's curiosity cut off abruptly. "The green room is open." He went back to his paperwork, studiously ignoring us.

"What door do we need to walk through to log a new dungeon?" Tandy asked quietly, arms crossed.

The clerk didn't bother raising his head. He just laughed.

"You and what army?" He dismissed us before we could even lay a claim.

Tandy inhaled, ready to argue, but I had an idea, more of a gamble.

"Andrew Ashborn, the famous [Wayfinder]," I said.

The man sat back, his chair creaking under his weight. "You teamed up with Andrew, huh? Show me your [Party]," he commanded.

Tandy acquiesced, and I prayed Andrew hadn't dropped out of the party.

"Green door. If you come back with him, I'll let you through to red. You can talk to Monka about your so-called dungeon."

He returned to his paperwork. The ass.

We went downstairs to find the room full of wannabe [Adventurers]. I reworked my estimation of the first group of grungy rat tail collectors. They'd at least *done* some work. The crowd today was pristine. I doubt they'd stepped out of the walls or into the sewers once. They had well-greased unused swords, and their tunics were unstained.

Even I, a glorified slug locomotion apparatus, puffed up my chest, feeling superior. The heavily mustached barkeep eyed us as he served a customer. Tandy marched right up to the quest window.

"Are you here to turn in your quests?" the clerk behind the counter asked sweetly, dipping her book lower. I got the impression that very few [Adventurers] in the green room ever turned in quests.

"Uh, no," Tandy said, put off balance by the question.

"Well, I cannot issue you new quests until you've completed at least one of the two I gave you earlier." The clerk raised her book, *A Stallion's Quest*, promptly dismissing us.

Tandy looked ready to lunge through the barrier and strangle the woman on the spot.

I intervened. "Monka, right? I had two queries unrelated to our quests that I was wondering if you could help us with."

She sighed, put her bodice-ripper book down, and eyed me.

"That's what I'm here for, to teach young [Adventurers] the rules of adventuring. How can I help?" Her sarcasm was so thick that I wondered if she was related to Richard.

"Okay, well, has the paperwork come through for [Your Mom's Party] yet?" I asked. "Are we [Sworn Adventurers] now?"

She gave me a thin smile, which I immediately took to mean no.

Before she could insult me with her response, I jumped to my real question, "Do we need to be [Sworn Adventurers] to log a dungeon in Eddie's Mill?"

"Tell me more about this dungeon," Monka said, opening up a notebook. At least she was pretending to take us seriously.

Don't tell her another word until she agrees to log it.

Tandy moved forward as if she were going to talk, but I held up a hand signaling her to stop.

"How about we log this under [Your Mom's Party] first? Then I can give you the details."

Monka looked up, grinning as she closed her notebook and put her pen down.

"Fine. The answer is no; [Sworn Adventurers] cannot log a dungeon as you are not yet part of the Adventurer's Guild. The likelihood of a [Sworn Adventurer] finding a dungeon in Eddie's Mill is about as high as that slug on your shoulders being sentient. Good day, I think we're done here." She looked over at the bartender. "Gus, I'm taking fifteen minutes, okay?"

Before I could say another word, she slid a curtain across the window, effectively ending the conversation.

"Well, that could have gone better." Meredeath was ever so helpful with her commentary.

"I guess we need Andrew. It's the only way they're going to believe us." It was hard not to see this as a setback. We were going to have to trek all the way back out to the orphanage, but then I realized that wasn't such a bad idea.

"I could just show them my invitation to the Hunt," Leo suggested.

"Nope, let's get Andrew. He can vouch for us as [Adventurers], too. I bet we'll be [Marked Adventurers] by the end of the day." We marched back up the stairs, not waiting for Tandy's opinion. I was going to take the entire crew to the orphanage. Leo and Meredeath would have a hard time ignoring their need if they saw it in person.

The walk was uneventful, but the arrival at the orphanage was everything I'd hoped.

"The Master of Mush!" Rust yelled, running out from under a tent. For once in my life, I didn't cringe at the title.

"Hey, Rust! Are Andrew and Eryn around?"

Leo and Meredeath looked wide-eyed at the canvas strewn about the front garden. Little pairs of eyes peeked out. It was easy to dismiss a situation you hadn't seen for yourself.

As we explained the situation to Andrew, he agreed readily to accompany us to the Adventurer's Guild.

It was Leo who pulled us up short.

"How about we go tomorrow? I think if Meredeath could get a few things from the market for me, I could fix up the house." My tall friend squinted at the sagging soffit. "Do you have any tools or supplies, like nails?"

Tandy looked at me, and I smiled. We'd cracked through. It'd been the first glimpse of the old Leo I'd had in a long time.

"Guess that means I need to get working in the kitchen," I chimed in, not missing the grateful smile from Eryn. "Come on, Rust. Let me teach you how to *really* clean a kitchen."

It felt good to be in a kitchen. Richard was amiable for once, using his [Clean] skill generously. After we finished cleaning, we were ready to start dinner, and I convinced Meredeath to use money from our purse to buy extra ingredients. They were going to have a robust stew tonight with homemade biscuits if I could time it all right.

Mistress Del stopped by that afternoon with a basket of fruit. The conditions of the orphanage appalled her just as much as they had Tandy and me. She left before dinner, promising to come back with entertainment.

I seared the meat, having Rust chase the salivating children from the kitchen. With a liberal application of pepper and a bubbling pot of carrots, parsnips, and potatoes, I pulled off a feast. The [System] must have been feeling generous, because I earned back one of my prized skills.

[You have gained the skill [Steady Temperature]. This skill aligns with [Adventurer]. You have an increased ability to control the temperature of any substance within your direct control.]

After dinner, Mistress Del reappeared with a box of old children's books. She settled down in a rocking chair with dozens of hungry ears.

"Simon was a snail. To be precise," she read as Richard rolled his eyes to the children's amusement. "Simon was a Giant Heltenic Land Snail. Not to say that he was a giant; looming over houses, and barns and villages, but as snails go, he was among the larger…"

The children giggled at Richard's horrified expressions as she read through a children's story about a dancing snail that saves the day.

I went to bed that night with a smile on my face.

The next day, Andrew met us in front of the Adventurer's Guild. He wore his adventuring gear: scale mail over a tunic, a blue bandana, and his black ax strapped to his back. With a grin, he entered the building and smiled at the clerk.

"So, Kile, I hear we've been having problems with a new [Adventuring Party]?" He set his trap perfectly as we waited outside. He'd told us to follow him thirty seconds behind.

"Yeah, these idiots were throwing around your name yesterday—" Kile paused as we walked in behind Andrew.

I didn't bother suppressing my grin.

"I see. You're talking about my group, [Your Mom's Party]?" Andrew did a good job holding a straight face as the clerk floundered. Posturing in front of Andrew was a losing proposition, and I'll give him credit that he didn't bother trying.

Instead, he waved us through to the red door as promised.

We stepped into a much more sophisticated space. It wasn't *just* a holding tank for hungry [Adventurers]. Instead, a small wooden greeting station sat empty, with a *Wait to be Seated* sign dangling. Tables sat empty in a common area. Surrounding the space were a door that looked like it led to a kitchen, a wall full of pinned quest cards, and what looked to be a closed shop with many armor, weapons, and other adventuring gear on display.

"Yeah, this looks about right. Now you guys know why I never come here." Andrew sounded tired. "Give it a minute, and Monka should pop up."

Sure enough, within a few minutes, the clerk from downstairs walked in from the kitchen. There must have been a hidden servant's staircase.

"So they *are* your friends after all? Talk about a plot twist!" Monka addressed Andrew, not bothering with an apology.

Andrew was all business. "Yep, the real deal. Can you open up the shop and give us a consultation? We've got a few things to straighten out with the Guild."

Monka bobbed her head, leading us to a large table that looked more at home in some business suite. She sat us along one side, while she cranked up the iron curtain from the store.

"Is it okay if we do the business first? I've got a bunch of kids downstairs, and they'll get rowdy if it's only Randi down there." Monka sounded more like an exhausted professional than the asinine bureaucrat we'd encountered yesterday.

"Sure," Andrew affirmed.

Today, Monka had used a wire headband to push her brown locks out of her face. She'd thrown on a formal Adventurer's Guild uniform. Brass buttons sat neatly on her wrinkled vest. This was all a show for the red door "official" [Adventurers].

She folded her hands over an official-looking notebook.

"How can I help you today?" Her words were neat, trimmed of all emotion and opinion. The type of voice anyone working in customer service develops after years of practice.

"I have two official requests and a favor," Andrew began. "First, I would like to officially vouch for Leo, Tandy, Cole, Meredeath, and Richard as [Marked Adventurers]."

Monka nodded, looking from person to person before frowning.

"Who's the fifth member?"

"Richard, the [Fanged] banana slug." Andrew said calmly.

Can't an [Immortal] get any respect these days? I need a statue, Cole. A hundred statues. No, a thousand.

I hid my smile, imagining a city full of tiny little banana slug statues. One for every home.

"Of course," Monka opened her book, taking notes. "A [Pet]?"

I am not a [Pe—

"[Animal Companion]," I corrected her.

I'm an [Immortal]! Have her put down [Immortal]!

I gave Monka a polite smile, gritting my teeth as Richard railed against the fates that put him at the administrative mercy of a backwater hick.

"And, Andrew, you witnessed the passage of their [Trial

Dungeon]?" Monka's pen sat waiting over her notes as she lifted her eyes to him.

"No," Andrew said. My heart dropped. Were we going to be held up by more red tape? "But I'd be willing to swear on my rank that I have firsthand witnessed acts of [Adventurers] that someone of a [Sworn] status could not complete. This group *has* passed their [Trial] and received full [System] classes and rewards."

Monka nodded, as though expecting his reply. Her pen scratched in the notebook.

"Very well, I'll lodge this with the central office." She looked at Tandy as though prepared for an argument. "Without the administrator from the Northeast Mountain District weighing in, it will still take a couple of days for them to formally approve this status change."

"That may be a problem." Andrew forestalled Tandy's objections. "My second request is to log a new dungeon in Eddie's Mill and give the founder's credit to [Your Mom's Party]. If I understand the bylaws, however, that won't be possible until they're formally recognized as [Marked]."

Monka's eyes widened. "So, it's true?"

Andrew nodded.

Her pen sat above the book, ink pooling on the tip.

"What does it mean to have a dungeon attributed to the party?" I jumped in, sensing this was my moment.

"Having a dungeon attribution fulfills one of the requirements when seeking the next tier of [Adventurer] rank. There are also monetary fees collected by the Guild for monitoring those wishing to delve into the dungeon." Monka sounded as though she was mechanically quoting some [Adventurer's] rulebook. Maybe she was; we should get a copy. "I expect the collected fees to be hefty, since this is the first new dungeon in our district in a hundred years. It could revitalize the Eddie's Mill Adventurer's Guild."

The [System] had given me Faction Points, and I was

pretty sure the Guild had nothing to do with assigning a [Hero] class, so I boldly continued. "Is there any issue in attributing the discovery to Andrew? I'm assuming, Andrew, all monetary benefits would go to the Ashborn Orphanage?"

Even if my party had a complaint about the solution, no one would speak up against the grinning [Wayfinder] with tears in his eyes.

[Skill Upgraded: [Heartbeat] is upgraded to [Heart]. Not only are you the heartbeat of your team, but your empathetic nature extends to the world around you. Warning: you are *more* susceptible to seeing what you want to see in people, friend and stranger alike. This skill is passive.]

"Now we just have to take on the Ceaparian Drift Hunt," I muttered, self-satisfied.

And solve Leo's emo issues. Oh, and find some marble for my statues. Do you think the children would make good stonemasons?

PART IV

The Hunt

Chapter 62

HOMESICK

We hoofed it to the Ceaparean Drift, eager to get to the zone before the event started. Being five days early meant that we had a luxury none of us had experienced really since becoming [Adventurers].

Down time.

Once Leo had shown the officials our invitation, they'd assigned us a camping spot in a copse of trees. The shade was welcome, as the Ceaparean Drift was essentially a desert.

"What are you going to do now that we've got camp set up?" Tandy asked as she strung up her hammock. We'd worked it out so that someone would babysit the camp while the rest of us could explore.

"I'm going to go see about getting some new gear. I still need some armor." Leo fingered his threadbare tunic. He'd left the pink sweater in his pack since the last dungeon.

My guilt got the better of me. "Here, take this." I threw him one of my two money pouches.

Andrew had insisted I take some winnings from the dungeon after getting the long-term earnings assigned to the orphanage. I'd kept it quiet from the girls.

"Hey, thanks, Cole. That'll help." Leo tossed the pouch up and down, weighing its worth.

Meredeath eyed me and tossed a small bag Leo's way as well. Leo caught it deftly, grinning. Apparently, Andrew had been more generous than I knew. All three of us looked at Tandy.

She stood shaking her head as she tied the last knot on her hammock. "Sorry, I've got to keep the coins I've got left. I've been footing the bill for our travel."

Feeling guilty, I decided to give her most of my other pouch later tonight.

It made sense, but she could have chipped in something. Just for show, in the spirit of Leo's rehabilitation. Minimally, not to look like a jerk. That wasn't Tandy's style, though.

Leo shrugged. "I'm just grateful you all chipped in anything. This should really help." He opened up his own pouch and poured in our donations. Leo casually tossed our empty bags back to us. The blue-dyed leather pouch sat fat on his hip. "How about you two?"

I eyed Meredeath, seeing if she'd speak first. I shouldn't have bothered; she always held her cards close to her chest. She gave a fake shrug, as though she hadn't already planned *something*.

"We're going fishing," I said, patting Richard on the head.

We are?

I grinned at Richard's question as he sleepily raised his tentacles.

Leo's eyes crinkled in amusement. "You are? That's..." His voice trailed off. I knew what he was thinking. That fishing sounded too much like home, too normal for our current life. Too [Mundane].

And that's exactly why I was doing it. I needed a brief escape from the insanity of being an [Adventurer].

The road to the Ceaparean Drift had been long, dusty, and full of minor quests. The [Adventurer] life seemed to be a stream of boring, muddy roads interrupted by absolute terror. I needed fun.

"I know it's *mundane,* but I need a little slice of our old life. A day where the only goo I'm covered in is worm guts. I want to laze along that big ass river we passed and catch trout."

The words sounded whiny as they came tumbling out, but I was tired. Not tired in that all that was missing from my life was a nap, but homesick. Life-sick? Could I be life-sick for my old job as a glorified dishwasher?

"I think that's a grand idea." Tandy had climbed into her hammock as I was talking and gently swung back and forth. She yawned as she waited for the rest of us to leave. She was feeling the same weariness I was.

"I'm going to look for other—" Meredeath caught herself, her eyes shifting around to look at the other [Adventurer] campsites. "Others like me. With this many teams coming together, maybe there's someone around."

Her reasoning made sense and, for her sake, I really hoped that she could find someone. I was not getting roped into that search. After the night at the club, I would no longer just do whatever Meredeath wanted.

So I just nodded, returning to packing my fishing kit. I'd been planning this after consulting my dad's map. I'd gotten a collapsible pole and some basic gear—thread, hooks, some fake bait.

"That's great!" Leo said, breaking the awkward silence. We were all feeling a little guilty that no one was going to help Meredeath, but we all needed a break from the quest life. In a sense, her quest was just a different version of my homesickness.

I watched and saw her eyes glisten. My heart broke a little. We hadn't run into another off-worlder, only whispered rumors. Every town had a tale, but no one materialized when we investigated.

She'll be fine. Richard smacked his lips, still trying to wake himself up. *She'll find someone, eventually. Let's go fishing. What are you using for bait?*

"I was going to dig for worms. Figured I'd scout the riverbank and find a suitable spot first, though. I've got a small jar of sausage bits that came with the hook kit." It wasn't really about catching any fish; it was about fishing. I didn't care whether I caught anything.

I shouldered my pole and walked away from the campsite. I'd made note of the tributaries as we'd walked into town. The Ceaparean Drift sat along a fairly large river called the Tigra. In the desert, the glacial-fed river was a lifesaver.

I just needed to hike upstream, above the camp. The latrines ran off into the river, and I'd had enough sewage in the last month to last a lifetime.

I've got a better idea than old sausage. You find a spot, and I'll handle the bait.

Finding a spot was harder than I thought it'd be. I wasn't the only [Adventurer] who'd had the idea to spend a few aimless hours fishing. Each shady tree with a good vantage point of the river had a couple of souls already fishing it.

Richard sat on my shoulders, fully awake now. His tentacles extended actively tasting the air. The overcast weather was perfect for fishing. I just needed a spot to get my hook in the water.

What about the rock over there? Richard pulsed his body toward a large boulder I'd already examined and decided against. It sat *in* the river, with a ten-foot span of gushing water between me and the rock.

But I was tired, so I gave the boulder a second look.

If I could make it, the rock was big and flat. It'd be a *prime* spot. But I was never a good swimmer, and the current made me nervous. I didn't want to spend the afternoon trying to swim back to camp.

"It's too far." I started moving on when I felt Richard's lips clasp my earlobe. I really hate it when he does this.

Noooo, it's perfect, he purred into my ear, one of his fangs catching on the sensitive skin and tugging my head in the boulder's direction.

"Come on, Richard, I still need to look for bait. I can't dig for worms on a boulder."

I didn't want to admit how worried I was about making the leap or how nervous the rushing water made me. I couldn't stop looking at the current; the water noticeably churned in the mini-chute. The river was wide enough to fit two barges across, but in this spot, it narrowed enough to cause the already swift current to speed up.

Since jumping into the tidemaw, I just couldn't look at rushing water the same. Intellectually, I knew I had [Gills]. But the experience of drowning had stuck with me.

I'm *going to be your bait.*

I stood there dumbly with a tiny slug tooth embedded in my ear. *Richard* was going to be the bait? I hadn't seen that coming.

"Won't you drown? Won't you get eaten?"

You still don't believe I'm [Immortal]? Think of me as one of those fake worms, the ones made of sinew and rope.

The general store I'd perused had some, but they'd been too expensive. Plus, why waste my money on expensive artificial bait when worms are free?

I'd seen enough over the last couple of months to back up Richard's ridiculous claim of [Immortality]. But I just couldn't believe it. It was too undignified.

Plus, *true* [Immortality] seemed a little too far-fetched. Damage resistant? Sure, but not totally [Immortal].

"I don't think this river has a fish big enough to eat you." There was no point in arguing with him on his own [Immortality]. That I had learned.

You've never fished in the Tigra, have you? There's fish that'd eat bait the size of you.

"That sounds like a tall tale." There was no way. It wasn't uncommon for Richard to indulge in exaggeration.

You need to see more of the world, Cole. There are fish as big as wagons out there. This river doesn't have any of them, but there are absolutely fish the size of a horse. And I'm great bait. Irresistible to fish, who wouldn't eat me? I guarantee we'll catch something interesting.

"There's no way," I snorted. "Besides, I couldn't pull a fish that big with this rod. I'd need a bigger hook. And I refuse to believe you're that tasty, even to a fish."

I'll take that bet, and if I win, I get my pick from your share of the next dungeon loot.

"Deal, and if we get a minnow...?"

If we catch something [Mundane], I'll never lick your ear again.

"Deal!" I would do anything to get him to stop randomly licking my ear when he wanted my attention. I had found no leverage that outweighed his enjoyment of making me twitch. This would work nicely. I'd just wanted to fish. Who cared if I caught nothing?

Now, let's hop over to that rock and go fishing. Stop thinking of that leap like you're a [Mundane]. You have stats now. Skills. Use one.

Right. I had skills. [Mind the Gap] would be perfect for this. I still hadn't gotten used to leveraging skills when we weren't in a dungeon or on a quest. I knew we were supposed to practice, but it was impolite to flaunt in front of [Mundanes]. Plus, it was stupid when the errant use of a skill could cause an accidental wound or death.

Here, though, out in the wild, it would be fine.

I eyed the gap, took a breath. The edge of the bank ended

in a rocky cliff, with the water rushing five feet below. The boulder was slanted at a forty-five-degree angle before flattening out. I went for it without thinking further. Backing up, I took five steps and ran.

I looked down as I came to the edge. The water hiccuped, sending up a small splash. A twinge of nerves shot through my skull just as I triggered [Mind the Gap]. The skill fizzled.

What the hell?!

Chapter 63

HOOK, LINE, AND SINKER

I put everything I could into the [Mundane] leap, terror throwing me off the shore. It was my worst nightmare. For a moment I dangled between the boulder and cliff, flying through the gap. My right foot smacked the stone, and I tossed my weight forward, slapping hard against the boulder. My body rebounded, and my feet dipped into the river. I scrambled, trying to gain purchase.

Richard pulsed forward, leaving a thick, blue slime on my hands as he crawled to safety.

"This isn't the time for slime!" I yelled at him. Damn slu—the slime [Glued] my hands to the rock. I stopped my frantic scramble, now anchored to the boulder.

There, you're safe.

Icy fingers grabbed at my legs as I hung limply.

My foot slipped off the underside of the rock. Thankfully, Richard's blue sticky slime pinned me to the boulder.

I would hurry. [Glue] won't hold forever.

Using the leverage I had, I flexed my muscles, pulling my body up. Just as my feet got under me, the [Glue] started to release. I stood carefully. The ridged stone was wet, and the underside had a deep green moss that'd caused my feet to slip. Breathing heavily, I closed my eyes.

It was hard to trust skills when they fizzled like [Mind the Gap].

Skills shouldn't fizzle like that. They should be rock solid. Tandy and I were both having trouble.

You okay, little buddy?

"I'm fine." The audacity of calling me little buddy. I pawed at my backpack. Thankfully, the rod and my gear were safe. It'd only been my face that'd kissed the rock.

With a deep breath, I took a step forward, carefully placing my toeholds, and leaned forward to grip the rock.

I don't know how I was going to get back to the shore, but that was a problem for future me.

Slowly, ridge by notch, I worked my way up to the top of the boulder. It stuck three yards out of the water, and the top held a scruffy-looking tree that was eking out an existence with its roots melding to the top of the boulder.

I sat hard, swinging my backpack next to me. The scorching breeze formed little tufts of whitecaps. The rest of the world melted in the rush of water, fading into the background. I took in the incredible view, relaxing for the first time in weeks.

"Gorgeous, isn't it?"

I jerked almost losing my seat. Looking down, I saw that the far side of the boulder dropped to a small alcove where a young guy sat in the shade. He'd tossed his own fishing line out into the water.

Oh, for fuck's sake.

I came out here for some alone time. Well, alone time plus

Richard, for whatever that was worth, and this guy had been sitting here fishing the whole time?

"Hi." I didn't bother to hide my disappointment. I couldn't get a good look at the guy; an oversized straw hat covered his face. All I could see was a reed bobbing up and down as he chewed on it.

"I hope you brought bait," he replied. "There's nothing on this rock to use, and I'm not too keen on sharing what little I've got left."

"I'm good, brought everything I need." Richard had finally made it to the top of the rock, his yellow antenna extending out in front of him, surveying the view.

Silence hung between us. Honestly, I didn't want to continue the conversation, but it was also awkward just ignoring each other. I watched the guy watch his line.

"You catch anything yet?" I started twisting the two sections of my pole together and stringing the thin line between the loops on the rod.

"Ayup, got a stringer attached to my foot. Nothing too big, but I'll be eating well for the next couple of days." The guy hadn't moved a muscle. I squinted and looked at his foot, and I saw that a rough rope was tied around his ankle. That's one way to do it. I hadn't really planned on catching much, but I brought a stringer of my own.

One day I hoped to get one of the fancy extra-dimensional rings for private storage. Today, however, it was a [Mundane] sort of day.

"Good, I'm hoping to catch enough for dinner for my team. This seems like a promising spot." With the line threaded through the loops, I got out the biggest hook in my kit and held it out to Richard.

"Are you sure?" I whispered.

Richard twirled his eyestalks in the universal sign for rolling his eyes. He didn't even bother saying anything, so I just began looping and firmly tying the hook to the line.

The last thing we needed was for the hook to slip off and send Richard to the bottom of the river. I frowned at the thought. Did slugs float? It didn't matter. Losing him in the river wasn't a thought I wanted to dwell on.

None of these ideas seemed wise to me.

With everything set, I looked at my slug. He'd been sunbathing, stretching out, avoiding the small amount of shade the tiny tree cast.

"How do you want to do this?" I whispered, I really didn't want to explain to the stranger that I had a talking fanged banana slug [Companion]. [Owner]. Whatever.

The last [Mundane] that caught me talking to Richard avoided me for the three days we were stuck in Tresseat. Which was hard, because he'd been the mayor that'd hired us for the job.

I mimed sticking the hook in Richard's lip, like I might if I had a minnow I was using for bait. The hook in my hand was ridiculously large, a whole hand-span big, but even so, I wondered if it was big enough to support all of Richard.

He'd gotten chunkier lately.

I heard that. And no, you're not hooking it through my lip. Now watch.

I held out the hook and watched as he slithered up and wound his body around the metal. He wrapped once, twice, three times and let his tail section trail off into the air. Richard glowed faintly golden, a sure sign he was using a skill. Slime oozed out of his pores, and it seemed to solidify his body into the shape, locking him into place. His tail waved lazily.

There, that should take care of it.

"Will you be able to breathe?" It was a dumb question. I knew it as soon as it came out of my mouth. He wouldn't have volunteered if he hadn't had some way to survive.

No, I'm a land mollusk. I can't breathe underwater. I don't have [Gills] like some sea slugs I know. Before I could protest, he continued. *I can, however, hold my breath for several hours. And before you get all worried, I also have a skill that will temporarily grant me [Gills]. So, I'll be safe, not that it matters. I am [Immortal] after all.*

The more Richard insisted on his [Immortality], the more I questioned its veracity. I looked up to find my new rock buddy staring up at Richard.

"Is that a banana slug?" The man stood, stretched on his toes to see over the ledge of the boulder. He wasn't very tall. The straw hat he'd been wearing had fallen onto his back, attached by a leather cord.

I immediately understood why he'd been using it. The guy's skin was puffy and red. He was far beyond a tan. His dark hair was shaggy, hanging in locks over bushy eyebrows. It was shocking he could see. The style made me think of a nearly blind sheepdog we had back home.

"Yes," I said carefully, still unsure whether I should explain what Richard was. Giving too many details to a [Mundane] kid of a certain age led to the reality I was living out. I didn't want to be responsible for that.

"Is he your [Pet]? I didn't know banana slugs existed here." He watched Richard's tail wave in the wind, then grew suddenly self-conscious. He brushed the hair out of his eyes and gave me a grin.

"Hi, I'm…" He hesitated for a moment, "I'm Ash. You in for the [Raid]?"

I extended my hand. "Cole. And yes, he's my [Animal Companion]. We got here early, so my team split up to explore on a rare day off."

Ash nodded, his eyes still glued to Richard. My banana slug fascinated the kid.

I like him. He appreciates my natural glow.

I snorted.

Ash looked at me confused, so I explained. "Richard, that's the slug, is enjoying the attention. Not too many folks admire his, uh, look."

"Banana slugs are pretty common where I'm from. I just

haven't seen one since I left. It's nice to run into a piece of home. Are you really going to use him as bait?"

I frowned. This guy didn't have the accent of the mountains.

"Where are you from? You don't sound like you're from the frontier, and I thought fanged banana slugs were local only to the Heltenic Forest."

I let the string go a bit, feeling the weight of Richard. I didn't think we'd need a sinker. The slug was heavy enough. I reeled him up, pulling the hook tight to the tip of my rod, getting ready to cast.

Ash watched, eyes fixed on Richard. "Yeah, no, I'm from Oregon. Different region, pretty far away. Our slugs are not fanged or sentient." I wasn't familiar with Oregon, but it wasn't like my dad's map was all-inclusive. The continent was big. There were plenty of places in Akyrima I didn't know about. I tilted my wrist back.

"Richard, are you ready?"

Yes.

With a long, studied snap of my wrist, I cast him out. The line ran from the rod, and everything looked good until a snag caught in the reel. With an utter lack of grace, Richard's momentum reversed, and he swung back towards us, smacking into the bottom of the boulder.

I winced.

Ouch. I thought you knew how to do this.

Ash was trying to be polite, holding back a laugh. I didn't bother, letting the chortle out. The problem was immediately obvious as the line had tangled in the reel mechanism. I started fishing it out, and slowly winding it back in. Richard just hung like a limp slug, bobbing in and out of the water as I worked to untangle everything.

"So, you have a party? You're one of the [Adventurers] here for the Hunt?" Ash asked, watching me work.

"Yeah, two old friends and a new friend. Plus Richard, if

you can count a slug."

I count more than any of you.

"That must be nice." Ash had grabbed the line, holding Richard up so he wouldn't keep smacking into the wall.

I didn't care. I almost had the snag out. The slug had volunteered for this after all.

Ash was glued to Richard. The slug fascinated him.

"You an [Adventurer]?" I asked. "Doing it alone?" If so, he was very good or idiotic. Maybe both. There were many reasons no one tackled dungeons without a team. No build could handle all contingencies.

I swore, the reel had gotten worse.

"Yeah, I'm not the best at delves, but I have a few tricks. Mind if I help?"

I nodded. He couldn't make the tangle any worse.

"[Mechanical Fix]," Ash muttered a skill, and a silver weave of magic snaked up the line, straightening it out. It even fixed my inept tie to the hook. "Reel it in now. It should be good."

Turning the crank, I found everything was smooth. He'd single-handedly not only untangled the line, but the mechanism was smoother than ever.

"Wow," I muttered without even thinking about it. "It'd be nice to have you around with that skill."

I looked down at the kid to thank him and immediately realized my mistake. A set of hopeful eyes looked up at me. "Really? You'd take me on?"

Now look what you've done.

Chapter 64

ANOTHER FISHY TALE

"Uh..." I mechanically reeled in the line and looked down at the kid? Man? The guy had an ageless quality about him. He could have been fifty or fifteen. I twitched my wrist, trying to think of something to say.

"Nice cast!" Ash said.

I looked out as Richard spun through the air. I swear I could see the grin on his face from yards away as he flew end over end.

"Thanks. About your question, I'm not actually the leader of my group, so, if you want in, you'll have to talk to Tandy." I didn't meet the kid's eye as I just kept my focus on Richard as he splashed into the water. I'd cast him towards the middle of the channel. The line continued to run out as he sank into the river.

"I understand." Ash's voice lowered in disappointment. My [Heart] went out to him, but adding someone to our group was a big decision. "So, who's Tandy? You have five of you in your party?"

I sat down on the boulder. Inwardly, I couldn't help but sigh. Fate would not give me the quiet solitude I'd planned for the day.

The line stopped spinning out. Richard had effectively hit the bottom. I watched as the line started drifting faintly with the current. At this distance, and out of earshot? Tentacle shot? Mind shot? I couldn't communicate with Richard, but our bond was calm, so I answered Ash's questions.

"Tandy's our leader. She's a [Mage] of sorts. I've known her for most of my life. She's incredibly smart. A real planner."

"Beautiful? They're always beautiful in the stories," Ash said wistfully. So, he was a bit of a romantic? Mentally, I dropped his age a bit in my head. How he'd become an [Adventurer] so young, I wasn't sure.

"I never really thought of her as beautiful. She's just Tandy. She's like a sister." Had I ever tried to quantify Tandy's beauty? She wasn't ugly, but she was just one of the guys.

I wrapped the string on my line around a finger and closed my eyes. I imagined her on the last quest, auburn hair tightly braided, eyes fierce as she wove a trap for the beast. Her wool cloak flapped back as the *Cavern of Winds* blew at us, trying to disrupt her concentration. The image was impressive, badass, and beautiful.

"You know, she is beautiful. She's the most resourceful, determined person I've met. Loyal. She'd do anything for us."

The line tugged, and my eyes snapped open. I watched the tip of my rod, ready to jerk if I got another bite. Part of my mind worried about Richard, but when no other nibbles happened, I relaxed. The sun had come out in strength. I wrapped a bandana around my neck, covering my gills. The heat felt good, as long as I didn't dry out.

We'd spent waaay too much time in dank underground

caverns. A breeze swept across the river, tugging at my hair. My eyes closed again, soaking up the ambiance.

"She sounds great!" Ash's voice broke my reverie. "Who else is on your team?"

Resigned, I opened my eyes to watch as the tip of his rod jerked in a cast. The guy could not read the scene I'd painted for my day.

"Well, there's Leo. He's the beautiful one." I laughed. Leo had always been a favorite of the women in Woodsten, and now he had stats and skills. If we ever spent more than a night in a city, I'm sure he'd have a small harem of women at his beck and call.

"Ah, I see. You're in love with him?"

I choked. What?! What was it with this guy and Meredeath, trying to pair everyone off with everyone else? I absolutely was not interested in Leo. My admiration of him and his physique was simple jealousy. I'd always been the scrawny guy, and never the looker. Especially standing next to Leo and Tandy.

Sure, he was sexy. But…

"No, he's not my type." I chuckled. Can you imagine? We'd get into *so* much trouble. "And I'm *definitely* not his."

"Okay, so Tandy, Leo, the sentient slug. Who's left?"

"Meredeath." Her name slipped out. "If I've fallen for someone, it's Meredeath."

I hadn't really said it out loud before. She was beautiful and, under the bite and the looks, she had a certain genuineness.

It's too bad I wasn't *her* type either.

"Meredeath? That's a weird name. Tell me about her." I watched as Ash jerked his rod up and down. As though bouncing his bait off the floor of the river was going to help.

I didn't bother, just letting Richard take care of himself. My mind gave in to the luxury of thinking about Meredeath, that way. It was exhilarating.

"She's different. I wouldn't call her weird, but she's very careful about her appearance. And guarded in a way that you know she's been through some shit. She's beautiful, unusual…"

How did one describe Meredeath? The knot of tension that tightened when I thought about her melted.

"You must have it hard for her. Trailing off like that," Ash laughed.

My face grew hot, and it wasn't just from the sunburn I was accumulating.

"Maybe. We haven't known each other for very long. It's just infatuation, and after going to the club with her in Eddie's Mill, I'm not sure we're meant to be. She's different, and it's refreshing." I left it at that. Honest and safe.

Ash jerked his rod. "Getting a bite." We both watched, waiting for the next nibble.

When the bite came, it was on my line. The tip of my rod bent quickly, and I lifted my hand, setting the hook. The monster on the other end of my line ran with Richard, my reel spinning as the line went out.

I grabbed the reel, trying to stop the fish. The line went taut and the rod almost jumped out of my hand.

"Holy shit!" I'd gone fishing, but the largest thing I'd ever caught was a baby gar. While impressive, the fish hadn't come near to pulling like this. Whatever was on the other end of my line was an absolute monster.

I slowly let some more line out, worried it might snap off and that I'd never retrieve Richard.

"Keep it on the line. I'll help." Ash was furiously reeling in.

I ignored him, all of my attention turned to pulling at the fish, then letting it go, pulling and letting it go. We were battling, and my stamina bar had popped active, slowly ticking lower with the effort.

I regretted using Richard as bait on a crappy fishing rod

I'd bought from a cheap general store. It wasn't magical or mechanically reinforced. I did not know that fish like this were even possible in a river.

With each tug and reel in, the fish drew my line back out. We were in a war of attrition; whoever tired first would lose. As my stamina ticked down, I could already predict the outcome. Fuck.

My mind raced through my skills. I had nothing useful for fishing.

Straining against the pull, I looked down at the coil. Half of my line was still out. I made very little progress in reeling Richard in.

My stamina bar was draining hard as I made a big push. I stood up, using all the muscle power I'd gained.

And that was such a mistake. The rod creaked, and I saw a crack start along the groove where the two halves of the rod twisted together.

Stamina bar forgotten, I let some line out, trying to relieve the tension on the rod itself. My mind raced. The crack grew bigger. I let the reel go, reaching to grab the top half of the pole, when Ash's hand latched onto the rod.

"[Mend the Breach]!" His hand glowed with the same silver magic he'd used before. The silver magic crackled through his fingertips and knit the wood back together. "Concentrate on the fish; I've got your gear. [Reinforce]."

Ash's voice had dropped in timbre as he called out his skills, silver magic snaking down the rod and out across the water, strengthening the line.

It was now or never. My stamina had dipped in the last quarter of the bar. My specialty was in dying, not Leo's muscle-bound tasks. I lifted the tip of the fishing pole and dipped it, reeling in the length of line I'd won.

"I'm going to lose them," I said, my teeth gritted together with effort.

"[Boost]!" Ash cried. My stamina surged.

Over and over. Lift the tip, pulling the fish in closer. Dip the tip as I furiously cranked in the line. The entire time Ash stood focusing on holding his skills. He'd fallen into a meditative trance.

Finally, a pull brought the fish up to the surface of the water. Its head was a foot and a half wide, with two enormous eyes sunken on top of its head. The hook was firmly set in its mouth. The barb protruding through its jaw.

Don't let it eat me! Richard's mental notes cried from the water. He'd crawled up the line, clinging above the hook.

As I twisted the rod to the side, time slowed, as the fish's entire body breached the surface. Shimmering green-blue scales reflected in the sunlight, casting a rainbow image across our boulder. The fish was three yards long, with a thick untarnished body. This fish was the undisputed king of the river.

I forgot I was trying to catch it, that Ash was holding everything together, that Richard was in danger. I just watched in awe as it swam on the break.

Rainbows danced, its jeweled scales glittering. The beast was beautiful. It turned, and its panicked eyes locked onto me. I knew, in that moment, that I had it. It was tired, and I'd won. Then time resumed as it jerked its body, trying to dive. I watched it twist in the water, frantic.

I knew what had to be done.

"Richard, bite the line!" The fish put the last of its energy into a dive, thrusting Richard underwater just as I'd yelled at my slug. I held onto the reel, letting some line out.

Sweat beaded on Ash's face. "I don't know how much longer I can hold it," he muttered. We were both coming to the end of our strength.

Suddenly the pressure vanished. The two of us fell backwards in a heap. Ash's skills broke, and his magic went wild for a moment, covering us both. It felt like a cold slap on my sunburn, stinging my jaw. The magic wormed into me and churned my stomach.

The instant passed quickly before it backlashed into Ash.

Even the momentary bite of his magic hurt. My muscles clenched as raw energy ripped across my body in a shockwave. I stumbled away from him.

"What was that?!" The words came out harsher than I intended as I rubbed my stinging face.

Ash ducked his head. "I'm sorry. I lost control. [Boost] is a once-a-week skill. I don't use it often, and certainly not with two other skills active."

I clutched the fishing rod. Without the pressure of the mega fish, I could reel the line in without worrying about it snapping. The line felt heavy as Richard had wound himself around the trailing line.

I glanced at my new friend. His black hair stood in a comical halo around his head as remnants of energy crackled from hair to hair. He looked tired leaning against the rock, as though his joints ached. The magic had taken a toll.

My estimation of his age increased. With those skills, and the tired look of his eyes, he was probably closer to my age than I'd originally thought.

Finally, Richard breached the surface, and as I pulled him in, I could hear his mental complaints.

Almost bit me in ***half****. Licked the slime right off me! Who in the living hell does that? Legend-fucking-ary, my slimy ass!!*

He was cussing but not injured.

"No, I'm sorry. You just surprised me, that's all. Your magic kept us all together. Thank you."

[Achievement Unlocked: The King and I. You have uncovered the [Mythical] King of the River. Few in the last millennium have met this rainbow catfish and lived to tell the tale. You chose mercy over mastery. Friendship over feasting. For this, you will be rewarded:

Skill gained: [Thread of Mercy] - Your bonds now carry intent. Strengthen or release them with purpose.

Skill gained: [Mark of Mercy] - To spare a legend is to

carry its shadow. Mythical beasts are less likely to view you as hostile. You gain a faint impression of the beast's intent.

Skill stacked: [King of the River - Rainbow Catfish] Freshwater creatures no longer register you as prey unless actively provoked. You also regenerate +10% stamina when in freshwater.

Quest Chain Unlocked: [The Mercy Ledger: Beasts] You have encountered a mythical beast, and instead of slaying it you chose mercy. You have found 1/??? beasts. To grow your power, observe other mythical beasts. This is a [Hidden] quest and is unsharable.]

"That was sick! Did you get the [Achievement]? You're going to have to introduce me to Tandy. I have to join your team." Ash was no longer hiding, no longer slumped. His apology and power flare forgotten as he dove into the excitement of a new [Achievement].

I bent down to pick up Richard. "You okay?" He looked less slimy than usual, and his normal bright yellow was muted. He slowly pulsed his body, climbing my arm, and wrapping around my shoulder to settle in his normal spot.

I'm tired. The words carried an exhausted quality that I'd never heard from my friend.

"Rest," I told him. "I think we're just going to lie in the sun for the rest of the afternoon."

Richard leaned close, giving a barely audible burble of agreement. I sat back down, tuning out Ash babbling about his skills. With Richard nestled around my neck, I looked out at the Tigra. Whitecaps formed and broke. A branch floated by. It was beautiful.

A long, wet slurp was the only warning I had as Richard licked my ear.

Just a little reminder that I won the bet.

Chapter 65

CRACKS

Richard moved forward, scrunching down as though stalking prey. I scanned the scene, identifying nothing edible by his standards. Just some dusty sage, red dirt, and a couple of cacti. Nothing vegetative that he preferred.

My yellow companion inched forward, antennae stretched in front of him, as though sniffing the air. Slowly his butt lifted, wiggling like a cat's.

"Are you sure --- Meredeath's death ray --- aimed --- Ash?" Leo asked so quietly I only caught a few words with my inattention.

What had he said? Meredeath aimed her death ray at Ash? That couldn't be right.

He probably meant [Death Bolt], the skill she'd earned trying to throw her knives at carnivorous prairie dogs on the trip here.

I held up a finger, asking Leo to give me a second. Glancing back at Richard, I found him several feet away from his former location. He was smothering what looked to be a small lizard.

"You eat meat?"

What do you think the fangs are for?

"Sorry, what was that?" I asked Leo. "A [Death Bolt]?"

Richard lifted his head. One small lizard leg dangled from his mouth.

Leo shushed me, drawing us away from the team. He kept his voice low, which I now realize wasn't because he didn't want to interrupt Richard's hunt. "Are you sure they should come with us? I mean, Meredeath's [Death Bolt] is useful, but what if she accidentally aims it at one of us? And Ash? He's just weird." This time, his head bobbed over to Ash and Meredeath, who seemed intent on their own morning.

Ash bent down, examining a small white wildflower blooming in the shadow of a rock. He looked like a kid, full of wonder and innocence.

I doubted my decision plenty after I brought Ash back to camp, but I felt like I owed him after he helped save Richard. Plus, his powers were cool. And I wasn't sure anyone would believe my story if I didn't have a witness.

Ash plucked the flower, standing up. Meredeath leaned in, listening to him explain some property of the herb as it zipped into his inventory. He had one of those dimensional storages I'd been eyeing. How he afforded one, I have no idea.

I knew I was more than a little jealous of how Meredeath and Ash hit it off.

"OREGON?" Meredeath yelled out of nowhere, gesturing wildly at Ash.

I was wondering how long it was going to take them. Richard had turned his head towards the spectacle, eyestalks rolling as he burped lizard. *Stupid off-worlders.*

"KANSAS?" Ash looked astounded. Great, they're *both* off-worlders. I should have guessed. I'd never heard of a place called Oregon, and Ash *is* really painfully weird, and this is coming from a guy with a sentient slug.

The two off-worlders hugged, and began whispering intensely.

We're never going to get rid of Ash now.

"Don't think we're going to be leaving Ash behind now, and you know we can trust Meredeath…" I glanced at Leo, frowning. "She's saved us more than once."

"Yeah, but she's a *[Death Knight]* now," Leo whispered. He'd been practicing swinging his axe. His knuckles were white on the shaft as he held it over his shoulder.

I wasn't sure where his sudden stance against [Death Knights] was coming from. Made me tuck my 'Faction Points to Rhi' secret a little deeper. Ash was making some complicated hand gestures trying to convey a theory of world-crossing magic, and Meredeath was leaned in, giving him her complete focus.

I tried not to roll my eyes.

"It'll be *fine*. You can't solo a boss, besides Meredeath's skills have been pretty useful so far," I said, turning to Leo so I couldn't watch the two. Leo's muscled arms flexed as he listened to me. "Look, if I can put up with Ash, you can be fine with her [Death] powers."

Leo might be able to solo a minor boss, but Tandy and I were still pretty underpowered. Even if I had survived a few tough moments.

Meredeath was our highest damage dealer. I suspected that while Ash wasn't a killer outright, he still had some major tricks up his sleeve. If he could magnify Meredeath's output, maybe we wouldn't be completely useless in this Hunt.

The camp had gotten overrun by fancy nobles and [Adventurers] with magical armor and the spending power of a treasury. We looked like kids playing dress-up by comparison.

He sighed. "If she vouches for Ash, I suppose we've got to take him." Leo looked at me, his eyes hardening in a way I hadn't seen. "You need practice. Start taking this seriously. If we're going to reach our full potential, if we're going to make it as a team, you're going to have to progress."

I'd been fairly miserable in the dry heat of the desert. My weakness against heat and intolerance of dry environments combined to make the Ceaparean Drift nightmare fuel. I had a canteen dedicated to wetting my bandana.

"I *am* progressing." I was just a little… slow. He just had to hit things to practice, to progress. He'd picked up six different axe-attack skills on our trip to the Drift.

The inherent defensiveness that I'd carried my whole life, as I'd never progressed in the 'right way', reared its ugly head. With the [Dead Wrong] class, I just couldn't Leo Smash my way into new skills. Progression wasn't as straightforward for me. My build was more decoy than damage, like some weird utility player.

The new [Mercy] skills I'd picked up didn't pack a punch either. Like [Heart]. I wasn't going to hug a dungeon boss into submission. No one got far as an [Adventurer] by talking out their feelings.

Leo's hand came down on my slug-free shoulder, squeezing in a gesture I'm sure was meant to be reassuring. I had to hold back a wince as several points ticked off my health bar. He'd gotten strong. Or maybe my [Gelatinous] nature was getting the best of me.

"Hey, sorry," Leo apologized. "I know you're working as hard as anyone."

I gave him a nod, even though his apology did nothing to silence my inner critic.

"Well." Leo stood, brushing the dust off his pants. "If Ash is coming with us, we might as well get started."

I raised my head, missing his expression as he walked away. His new white and gold embossed armor shone in the sun.

You've all come a long way since we met in that dank forest.

I shook my head at Richard's comment. Leo'd come a long way. I watched as Tandy smiled, talking to Meredeath and Ash. Tandy worked harder than all of us combined, I knew she was on the verge of a breakthrough. And, as long as Meredeath didn't start raising undead, her ability to kill things was unparalleled.

Me? I was good at dying.

Leo had really leaned in since we'd journeyed to the Ceaparean Drift. He'd embraced the "level up" life, and as a "common" [Warrior] he had a lot of options.

"I'm not moving as fast as the others," I said, and I knew my words sounded resentful. I let out a long sigh.

Progress isn't always measured by a number going up. Power isn't always at the end of a hammer. You need a slug's perspective. Thankfully, you have me.

A slug's perspective was awfully slow.

I closed my eyes, feeling the heat of the sun on my face. We were a long way from the dark, dank coastal mountains of the Heltenic Forest.

I'd traded the stench of the kitchen compost for the guts of the latest monster. Linchpin of the team, I was not. But even I had to admit I'd come a long way for a part-time line cook slash dishwasher. I let the breath I'd subconsciously held go, willing my shoulders to drop and my back to unclench. [Self Critic] snapped off.

"I'm going to be an Everbear-damned [Master of Death]." The words were more for me than Richard, but I still waited for a snarky reply. Something like 'a lot of good it's done you' or 'whatever that means.' His biting rejoinder never came, so I finished the statement myself. "Good at dying, less at dealing."

I walked towards my team, ready for what was to come.

"I still don't have the Raid Quest. Can you share it across?" Meredeath asked. She looked out of place in the desert. The sunlight sank into her dark clothes as though swallowed by an abyss.

"I've got it." Leo shared the quest out to the party. "I must say, I'm excited to try out my new class."

[Raid Quest: Legendary Hunt]

Welcome to the Hunt! You have been given access to the [Legendary Monster Quest Chain]. The Ceaparean Drift Canyonlands currently has three Legendary Creatures in residence. Take part in the destruction of a creature to earn loot, decrease the monster's hold on the civilized world, and progress. You have discovered 1/3+1 Legendary Creatures. Your party has killed 0/3 Legendary Creatures. Your party has killed 1/? creatures. Battle on!]

When the notification had first triggered, I'd reread it. I'd discovered [1/3] Legendary Creatures? Then I remembered the [King of the River]. The beauty of his scales glistening in the sun, I gave Ash a furtive glance. He'd gone a shade paler, too.

I had the sinking feeling that [Legendary Hunt] directly conflicted with our hidden quest chain [Mercy Ledger: Beasts].

"Leo, did you say you picked up a new class?" Tandy asked in a distracted tone, which meant she was probably reading the quest text too. She waved the notification away, eyes focusing on Leo.

He grinned. His blond hair shimmered in the morning light. "I sure did. They had class trainers in the camp—"

"And you didn't tell us?" Tandy interrupted, muttering under her breath. "Of course he didn't."

"Uh, sorry?"

I shook my head. We joked that there wasn't enough gray matter to bother a Nirantian brain sucker between Leo's ears.

Tandy waved at him to continue, so he did, digging his grave deeper.

"There were trainers available. I thought there might be something more powerful than [Warrior]. I was right!"

Oh no. Those aren't [Trainers], they're [Recruiters].

We all stood there, sweating as the sun rose higher in the morning sky, waiting for Leo to tell us what his new class was. He waited with a shit-eating grin. I realized he wanted one of us to ask.

"Out with it." Meredeath, per usual, was the first to lose her temper. "What's the new class?"

"I'm a [Paladin]. Technically, a [Provisional Paladin of the Hunt]. My inspiration is [The Huntress]."

Oh, fuck, not that bitch.

Tandy and I looked at each other. [Paladins] were driven by the gods, their inspiration and patron being the source of much misadventure for the heroes in stories. The path of the [Paladin] was one of incredible legends or, more likely, an untimely death.

Leo'd only ever been interested in happy endings. He never calculated the cost.

I spoke up. "Leo, did you not think to question the granting of the class?" The words sounded like Tandy's, but my guilt gnawed at me as I thought of my own hidden quest chain [Mercy Ledger: Beasts].

He turned to me, eyes flaring defensively. "The class will help us on the [Raid]. You both act as if I can't wipe my nose without permission. I'm taking my progression into my own hands. Not all of us are a [Sage] or have a slug at the reins."

My eyes flickered over to Tandy's. We'd both hoped the gap between us and Leo had been shrinking. His mood had improved since we left Eddie's Mill.

Instead, it seemed as though the rift had silently expanded. The cracking of our bond had continued beneath the surface, just out of mind.

That was partially of our doing. Neither of us had really given Leo enough credit to think about this on his own. And my own [The Mercy Ledger: Beasts] [Hidden] quest would not help.

I realized that insisting we needed Meredeath as a damage dealer probably made things worse. And adding Ash to the party was like bringing a stranger to watch a drunk Uncle Artie make a scene on solstice eve.

My [Heart] ached in my chest. There was plenty of blame to spread around for this fracture.

"You're right. I'm sure it'll be a boon to us all. I just wish…" What did I really wish for? Here we were on a [Raid] together as [Adventurers]. Our wildest dreams come true. Except it wasn't.

I still felt like the underpowered loser I'd been back in Woodsten. I couldn't fault Leo for feeling the same. Being [Adventurers] was messy and complicated. It had solved none of our actual problems.

Trying to save face, I finished the sentence in a way that Leo would understand. "I just wish I'd thought of that. It's a cool class. I'm happy for you."

The words hung between us awkwardly, so I held out my hand to shake.

Leo's frown slowly turned into a grin.

"Sorry, man. Next time, you'll have to come along!" He clasped my hand and drew me into a hug. My face pressed awkwardly into his newly acquired ox horn hanging from a leather cord around his next. He smelled of desert pinions and sage.

My eyes caught Tandy's, and she raised one eyebrow in a question. I gave a quick, negative headshake. Now wasn't the time. I was committed to the lie, anything to save our trio.

Can we get this over with? Richard asked, sunbathing on a red rock.

Leo released me from his bear hug, all sins forgiven, all

smiles as he was the first on the trail. Tandy followed as I bent down to retrieve the sunbaked Richard.

I watched as Meredeath and Ash gave each other indiscernible looks.

Cracks ran across the sunbaked land as I tightened the water-soaked bandana around my neck.

Chapter 66

INTO THE SLOT

I couldn't imagine that the giant river Ash and I had fished on ran through such a dry place. As it hit the vast plains, they called it the Tigra, but here, in the canyon lands, they called it the Stonebender.

Back in Woodsten, we couldn't have imagined a river so large. Was this what the Niyat looked like before the cataclysm? People said it was the largest river in the East.

As we walked surrounded by red dust, sage, and juniper, the river seemed even more impossible.

This was not a land of water. The campground for the Hunt was at the crux of the river, but even so it was temporary. The landscape was sparse. No one could survive out in the true wilderness for long.

No wonder it was a haven for beasts.

Richard had settled on my shoulder, his stomach happily burbling as he digested his leggy snack.

"An entire fucking lizard," I murmured.

Did you want me to eat only half of it? Besides, it progressed the quest, didn't it?

Ah, so that's where the 1/? killed beasts came from. At least the kill didn't affect our [Hidden] quest, so maybe we'd be okay after all.

"No, but it was almost as big as you are. Where did you put it all?" I muttered to him, exaggerating only a little.

A lot of judgment from someone who ate a foot-long sandwich from the vendor yesterday.

He wasn't wrong. Just way too observant.

I watched my friends ahead of me. We commonly took the tail of the line because Richard could keep a better eye on what was behind us than anyone focused on putting one step in front of the other.

Tandy led, followed by Leo, Ash, and Meredeath. Leo was humming to himself, his axe resting on his shoulder. When we were out in the wilderness, he always had it out, ready to go.

Unlike him, I had [Guardian's Promise] strapped to my hip. It was too awkward to have out and swinging around as we walked. Richard was always jumpy when I practiced with it, worried he'd get squished.

Which seemed odd for someone who was theoretically [Immortal].

I wiped the beads of sweat from my forehead. The sun was high, and there was no shade. The sage and juniper reached hip height, and miniature cacti and scorpions covered the few shady spots. I heard a telltale lip smack out of Richard.

He'd eaten, he was warm, and he was about to succumb to a full-on food coma.

"You still paying attention back there?"

Of course, why do you ask? I could hear the yawn in his mental projection.

"Because I know you. You're full and warm. I don't need to remind you we're in a beast-filled wilderness, do I?"

Yes, yes, kill the legendary beast. I didn't think you were that interested in succeeding on this quest.

I wasn't, but I hadn't said it out loud to anyone. Slowing my footsteps a hair, I gave Richard and myself a bit more privacy.

My eyes kept seeking Leo's broad shoulders and tousle of straw hair. Had he grown taller since we left Woodsten? Maybe it was just the shoulder pads on his armor. The life of adventure was suiting my friend in ways that it wasn't resonating with me.

"I don't, but we're here. It's complicated."

If you say nothing, you have only yourself to blame.

I knew this. But the thought of bringing it up with Leo burned in my gut. A [Provisional Paladin of the Hunt] couldn't turn away from the Hunt. He'd forfeit his class.

He was becoming a force with his [Superior Enchanted Axe of Singing]. The type of [Adventurer] we'd talked about being as kids. Who needed a [Sponsor] when he could align himself with a goddess?

Getting him to take part in a quest chain for mercy, a collector's quest, seemed as unlikely as a floating castle. The conversation would not go over well, and I'd end up caving, anyway.

The truth was, we needed Leo. We were all specialists. He was our generalist who could deal damage in any situation. Did he need us, though? He could smash and trash with any team across the continent. But Tandy was still figuring her magic out, and I still wasn't sure what role I had to play. I was nearly worthless in a true fight.

I think your [Self Criticism] skill triggered.

"Damn it. Why did I have to keep that one?" I checked my status sheet, and sure enough, it'd been auto-triggered.

"How do you know? You keep insisting you can't read my mind, but—"

Your shoulders tense every time you get stuck in one of those loops. So, I can tell when your ear brushes my back.

Suddenly self-conscious, I tried to lower my shoulders. Stress tended to make my back clench. Tandy and Leo had stopped on the trail, and I quickly caught up with everyone.

"The trail goes this way," Tandy said, stepping down onto something that wasn't much more than a goat track.

"But didn't they say we were going into a slot canyon? It starts right here." Leo'd stepped off the trail to examine a crevasse in the ground. I walked over to what he was pointing at.

The ground opened up, dropping quickly twenty feet. A log wedged in the crack, and I could almost imagine myself hopping down and crawling to the base of the narrow shaft. My brain couldn't help but imagine the ground closing over us, swallowing us as its latest victims.

"I'm not sure I could climb down there that easily." This was Ash, whose agility score wasn't terribly high. As a self-proclaimed mechanic, his physical skills were mediocre.

If I were honest, I wasn't sure I could scramble down the sun-bleached knobby log either.

Tandy stepped over to look. "This looks like what they described a slot canyon to be." She kicked a pebble over the side. It clinked as it hit the log and bounced down to the bottom.

Something slithered under a shaded ledge. A long tongue reached out to taste the pebble before returning to its nest.

"Did you see that?" Ash's voice shook as he spoke. The guy was more [Mundane] crafter than [Adventurer]. I felt guilty, having convinced him to give the [Raid] a try with our group.

"Yes, let's follow the path a little longer, and see if it drops into the canyon. If it doesn't, Leo, we will take your advice,"

Tandy compromised, as she was not keen on jumping into the hole either.

Leo seemed mollified.

"If we have to jump in there, I vote Leo goes first," Meredeath countered.

We walked another ten minutes to find that the trail dropped into a washout leading into the canyon. I stood watching as the team scrambled down the loose gravel slope. Dust and rocks clinked down into the canyon with each step.

"Woah." Leo's voice echoed. "Cole, you've got to see this. It's incredible down here."

I sat on the oddly smooth, rippling sandstone as four sets of eyes swung up to watch *my* awkward descent. I stretched out a leg, shifting my weight. The scree moved under my heel, tipping me forward.

I had planned to watch and learn as the rest of the party made their way down to the canyon floor. Now, I realized as I flung an arm out to catch myself, that I probably should have paid closer attention.

My elbow banged painfully into a rock as I desperately lunged for a scrubby sage bush. My hands wrapped around its prickly branches. As I tried to anchor myself with it, the plant pulled up whole hog. Betrayed by the desert plant, I tumbled down the escarpment.

I toppled end over end.. Richard clung, tucked into my head, his slimy trail gritty with dust and debris. Finally, I landed on my back, dazed, covered in red dust.

Smooth.

Checking my status, I'd taken a couple of points of physical damage. Leo offered a hand, helping me stand up. He patted the dust off my clothes. My face was red, and it wasn't from the sunburn I'd picked up. No, I'd taken most of the damage to my ego.

"Well, we're all here now," Meredeath said dryly. Her black leggings were pristine.

I coughed as I inhaled some of the dust kicked up by my descent. She had to have a skill that kept her clothes black, right? An [Aura of Darkness]? Or a [Pristine] cleaning skill?

Either way, despite Leo and my efforts, both Richard and I were now coated in a claggy layer of dust.

"This is remarkable," Tandy said as she ran her hand along the canyon wall. Ash came over, examining the sage bush I'd brought with me. He picked it up and showed it to Meredeath. The entire bush disappeared into his inventory.

Twenty-foot tall walls towered above us, in rippled sandstone. Layers of red, orange, and yellow rock were stacked like sheaves of parchment. The canyon glowed in the desert sun, but it was cooler down here. Water, even ice, sat in puddles of shade.

"We ready to go back and kill that beast under the log? I could do it myself if you all need a moment?" Leo held his axe like he was ready for action.

I thought of my mercy quest. That creature hadn't been a creature of legend, but it hadn't been a monster either.

"Tandy, was it red on your map?" I asked, trying not to be forceful. Leo could be stubborn when he dug in.

"No, I think it was just an ordinary overgrown lizard." She frowned as she zoomed to our location. "Yeah, it's still there as white, just part of the landscape."

I shrugged. "We should probably leave it, just a distraction. Let's get on with the quest. Let's find a legendary beast to kill!" I said it with false enthusiasm, praying we were too low level to find any legends.

Tandy looked at me, frowning. When we'd been kids, we'd always pull Leo into our schemes by pumping him up about some ordinary task that we needed his muscles for. An enthusiastic facade was one technique that worked every time on our friend.

Now was no different, as Leo smiled. "You're right, let's

focus on the goal." He'd already turned, moving deeper into the canyon.

Tandy looked at me, and I shrugged, bobbing Richard up and down. I didn't want to tell her yet.

The [System] rewarded me for my efforts.

[[Thread of Mercy] experience gained! Sparing the life of the Desert Lizard has strengthened your bond to [Desert Creatures].]

No explanation of what that meant or did. I looked at Ash. He was examining the red stripes in the rock wall with no sign of receiving a notification himself.

Apparently, intent mattered.

Chapter 67

JACKPOT

The slot canyon was unlike any landscape I'd encountered in my twenty-five years. I mean, sure, I'd never been out of the Heltenic Forest, but this was crazy.

We'd been walking on a path in the full sun of the desert, scorched and sunburnt. But here in the canyon, in the shade of its walls, twenty feet below the surface, it was cold. Maybe not cold when compared to an Ursine Wall winter, but freezing compared to the desert we'd abandoned above.

The ground was a sand-pebble mix, stones smooth with wear, and it was oddly damp. An oasis of water in a landscape that had almost none. Even so, we didn't see very many creatures. Ravens watched us from above, flying over the canyon and marking our progress with caws.

Here and there, the walls widened up, and a rare tree sprouted on an outcrop.

"That's an aspen, I think." Ash said, walking over to examine the tree.

The ground rumbled.

"That's not a tree!" Tandy shouted the obvious as the tree ripped itself out of the ground.

The tree monster towered above us, not a legendary beast, but one that'd been lying in wait. It swiped one paw down, grabbing Ash in a leafy hand. The once-dormant tree sprouted a rough face made of foliage. It lifted Ash towards a knotted gap in its trunk full of gnashing teeth.

Ash screamed, and I didn't blame him.

Throw me at it. I can help.

I didn't bother to ask how as I [Slug Tossed] Richard at the top of the tree monster. He hit and clung onto the branches, a yellow disk of goo.

I watched as Leo swung his axe at the trunk. The head rebounding hard, throwing him back.

"That's no aspen, it's ironwood!" Leo yelled.

I shook my head, realizing that my hammer would not be much use if the tree was an ironwood. Only an [Enchanted] weapon could inflict much damage, and Leo's axe suggested that even that might be limited.

Richard dropped onto one of its leafy eyebrows. The face wiggled dramatically, trying to dislodge him. Richard's slime trail glistened in the sun.

Tandy threw a web at the elbow joint of the arm holding Ash. It stuck and hardened, not allowing the arm to bend further. With Ash's movement towards the mouth halted, the tree looked at Tandy and grinned.

Another joint further up the branch popped, twisting to move Ash closer from a different angle. The sharp teeth in its maw glistened with anticipation.

I had to do something. I reached into my bag, looking for anything useful. My hand fell upon the cluster of lucky nails

I'd kept. They were special [Steel Nails] I'd gained through a skill.

I ran at the tree, dodging a root that tried to trip me. Resting the first nail, a fat spike used for heavy-duty construction, against the trunk, I brought [Guardian's Promise] down on its head.

I heard a satisfying split of the wood as the nail slammed into place. Steel *was* harder than ironwood.

The monster screamed, releasing Ash. He dropped to the ground in a heap.

Quickly, I set another steel nail. I'd sentimentally kept half a dozen of them. Looking at the split in the trunk, I placed the second nail higher, just beyond the split. Another swing, and a louder crack sounded.

"Duck!" Tandy yelled, and I hit the floor as a huge branch swung over my head. Grabbing my next nail, I aimed it up into the gap my previous swings had created. Just as I was about to swing, Leo roughly pushed me away.

He triggered a skill, [Precise Strike], and I watched as the blade of his axe hit directly up through the crack. He slammed all his power straight through the weak spot in the trunk.

Meredeath fired a green [Death Bolt] into the eye that Richard hadn't gooped over. Ash ducked as a leafy appendage swiped at Richard, trying to clear its vision.

"Place another nail!" Leo commanded as he ducked, winding up for another strike.

I shoved one into the deep gap in the trunk and Leo took a swing at my last lucky nail.

"[Precise Strike], [Power Strike]," he grunted. I watched as the power behind his awkward swing almost tripled with magical input.

The wood split in an explosion of splinters. A crack threaded through the ragged bark up through the maw that'd been its mouth. The creature slumped over.

We all waited, tense. Ready for a second round. Richard sat on its eyebrow munching leaves and continuously expelling an acidic goo into its eyes.

[Iron tree guard defeated. You have earned experience. Richard used the skill [Final Blow], gaining double experience.]

I still got it!

Of course, he finished the beast off by munching its leaves. The smug slug dropped from his perch on top of the tree's brow with a wet plop. His antennae swung in the air in victory.

I picked him up by his slimy scruff and placed him on his normal roost. Bracing for criticism, I turned towards the team.

"Your slug did it again!" Leo was disgusted.

I didn't blame him. Richard had been using this skill a lot since the dungeon run at Eddie's Mill. Leo had earned the same skill but never triggered it at the right moment. That took planning, and a level of intellect Leo struggled with.

"Richard, you've got to stop stealing Leo's experience," I berated my companion, not for the first time.

Your experience, you mean? His voice was haughty as he began to clean his face.

"I don't know what you're talking about." And I didn't. Leo's the one with the [Final Blow] skill.

It was your nail. I'm your [Companion]. Haven't you realized you get some of that double experience bonus?

"Sorry, Leo," I said as I looked in the crack of the tree trunk. Sure enough, my nail was at the top. I reached in and grabbed it.

[Skill Acquired: You have gained a new [Dead Wrong] skill, [Loot]. You will now be able to use this skill to loot any party kills you touch. At the base level, this skill provides [0%] extra loot.]

Holy shit!

I touched the tree, whispering my new skill, "[Loot]."

[You have looted the iron tree guard. You receive:

3 Used Steel Nails

2 Iron Ingots [Components]

2 Hardwoods [Components]

1 [Heartree] [Component]

The loot dumped onto the canyon floor in a pile. Leo stared at the hunks of wood and iron ingots in surprise.

"Did you just use the [Loot] skill?" Ash whooped. "I've got to be dreaming. Do you know how rare that is?"

It's a big deal.

I looked at my companions, wide-eyed. This could be a game-changer. We didn't have to spend hours breaking down monsters or beasts into components. Or, feel guilty as we left the carcasses unharvested. Selling this to crafters would give us a whole new income source.

Maybe a utility [Adventurer] wasn't as useless as I thought.

"Pretty rare?" I said, wondering what we were going to do with the stack of components.

"All you need is some dimensional storage and *any* [Adventurer] group would take you. Hot damn, I'm so glad we met."

"Wow, all that from one monster?" Tandy chimed in. "This opens up so many more options for us." Her mind was already evaluating possibilities.

"I know I didn't contribute much to the fight, but do you think I could have the [Heartree]?" Ash asked tentatively. I looked at the slight man, wondering what he wanted it for.

"Contributed little, or at all?" Leo rumbled as he walked by with a smirk.

Ash looked down. "Nevermind," he muttered. "I'll try to get one later."

Frowning, I picked up a [Heartree]. I didn't care that Ash didn't take part in the fight. His strength didn't seem to be in direct damage. He'd done okay as a decoy. What I was curious about was what he was going to use this [Heartree] for.

"Wait, don't listen to Leo. He's just being a grump. Why do you need it?"

"I've found a few options. You can make them into mini-bombs, but that takes some other components." What were the 'bombs' this guy was talking about?

Meredeath strolled over. "Bombs? Really?" She looked at my confusion. "They explode, normally dealing massive damage when thrown or as part of a trap."

I nodded, encouraging Ash to continue.

"That's a waste of their potential, though. With a [Heartree], I can use it to power wood-based mechanics. So, like your reel, I could attach one and it would help auto-reel. Or add one to a catapult and have the mechanism auto-reset. I mean, that would probably take a couple, but you get the idea." Ash's enthusiasm was infectious.

With that [Loot] skill, [Heartrees] are going to be raining on you like coppers.

"They're that common, Richard?" I didn't bother hiding my disbelief.

Richard looked up at me, and then a tentacle swung over to Ash. He opened his mouth, fangs gleaming, and seemed to dislocate his jaw.

Suddenly, a dozen [Heartrees]—little round wooden disks with a magical gleam to them—ejected into the space in front of Richard.

"What just happened? Did your slug throw up ten times its body weight in [Heartrees]?" Ash eyed Richard suspiciously, even as he licked his lips at the pile of loot.

I have a dimensional storage tooth cap.

Random behaviors of my slug flashed through my mind. Richard posing on top of our kills. Gnawing on random items with his little fangs. Licking various components in shops.

"Have you been looting our kills this whole time?" I asked, outraged.

Richard didn't bother replying. He just looked up at me with a smug little toothy grin.

"I can have these?" Ash started picking up the [Heartrees], popping them into his own dimensional storage. I really needed dimensional storage. "You can't believe what I'll be able to craft."

"They're that valuable?" Meredeath fingered her onyx ring.

"You have no idea. I wouldn't have to be an [Adventurer] with all of this. I could just craft." He sounded so wistful, as though my nightmare was his dream.

"I have a confession to make," Meredeath said, twisting the stone on her ring. Another two dozen [Heartrees] popped onto the canyon floor.

She had dimensional storage this whole time?! *And* [Loot]?! I knew she was a bit of a loot goblin, but she'd been holding out on us.

I opened my mouth to point this out, but Richard stopped me. *We're all allowed a secret or two.*

"I can't possibly repay you all," Ash said, still picking up [Heartrees] and popping them into his storage. He wasn't going to let the debt prevent him from grasping the opportunity.

"I want bombs," Meredeath said plainly. She gave me an amused look at Ash's avarice.

"You can't repay us *yet*," Tandy chimed in. "But we may need to think about forming a guild sooner rather than later."

A guild. The best [Adventurer] parties had small cities that worked with them, consuming their loot, and updating their gear. It wasn't even a dream I'd considered. Not surprisingly, it looked like it'd been on Tandy's long-term plan.

I looked over at Leo. He'd walked away from the conversation, opting to scout down to the next bend in the canyon. Leo gazed back at our huddle, impatient to get on with the Hunt.

I gave him a shrug and leaned in, wanting to hear more about these 'bombs' of Ash's.

Chapter 68

THE BUTTERFLY EFFECT

The journey through the canyon lands was odd. The path wound in and out of different slots, with varying elevations and widths.

Sometimes the canyon walls grew tall and narrowed so much that we had to climb the walls wedged between two faces. Other times, the space between the walls would widen in a bend, frying us in the sun. The ground went from moist to frozen to baked.

Carve-outs of various heights had formed, little alcoves where insects and rocks nestled. They looked like little altars to the gods of the desert, waiting for an offering. Some of these sat at eye level, while others were halfway up the canyon walls. Some were just large enough for a small offering, and others could have fit our entire party in the mini-cavelike structure.

"I wonder how this landscape formed." Meredeath surprised me with her question. I'd never thought about how a landscape *formed*. "There's no river carving the rock. It's not volcanic."

"Maybe it just is?" I said, tracing my hand along the wall. If I pressed hard enough, dust and sand would scrape off in a puff. The rock was soft.

"Leo, you talked to some of the other groups. Are we supposed to join up with one of the other [Adventurer] teams?" Tandy wiped sweat from her brow, taking a moment to get a sip of water.

We'd been hearing the horns of other groups all day, but our path had been pretty straightforward. The canyon had only deviated into narrow dead ends that were easily explored.

"No, the Hunt coordinators just assigned us this trail," Leo explained, grabbing the canteen Tandy handed him. "They said if we hear a fight, that we have to wait to get permission from the engaged team to jump in."

We're slower than the other groups. They're already ahead of us.

I kept that nugget of wisdom to myself.

"We just got to keep pushing." Leo handed Tandy the canteen back. The break, apparently, was over. The sun had risen to the highest point in the sky.

"How long is the Hunt supposed to be? We're not camping out here tonight, are we?" I asked. We'd need to head back soon to get to our campsite before dark.

Outside of the iron tree guard and a few loose scorpions, we had encountered no real hints that we were on the right track. Worse, we hadn't really encountered anything worth our time. This [Raid] event was turning out to be much less exciting than expected.

"He told me to follow this canyon to its end," Leo insisted, and I realized in that instance a problem. Tandy normally got our quests. Leo wasn't a planner. He didn't care about stupid things like the details.

I looked at Tandy, immediately concerned.

"Yes, we've gone over this, Leo. Everything seems in order, did the guy say something about using horns?" Tandy asked, giving side-eye that told me to keep my mouth and opinions to myself.

"Maybe." It was Leo's turn to look abashed. "But it doesn't matter, because we're on a single-track path. We're supposed to blow our horn," he held up the ox horn strung across his neck, "when we have a creature in sight."

A group of horns sounded in the distance, as though triumphantly announcing a victory to the entire Hunt.

[Raid Notification:

Your [Raid] has killed 1 of the 3 legendary creatures. Your reward will be calculated based on the percentage of your contribution. Caution impact to your [The Mercy Ledger: Beasts] will also be calculated on this measurement.

You receive: 0 experience and 0 loot.

Your [The Mercy Ledger: Beasts] quest relationship status has dropped by 10 points. Although you did not take part in the kill, you belong to a [Raid] who committed the act. If you or your team harms such a creature, it will significantly harm your reputation. Your reputation with Legendary Beasts is +40.

Caution: if you drop below 0, you will lose this quest and all previously earned benefits.]

I gaped at the notification. Seriously? I knew there would be implications, but this seemed extreme.

A quick glance at Ash showed he was frowning. Looked like he got the same notification.

One reason I'd been walking so slow was that I figured it wouldn't be the worst outcome if we missed out on the killing. I didn't realize that simply being in the [Raid] was going to jeopardize my quest.

"Guys, we have to *go*. I just got a notification that my [Initiate of the Hunt] patroness is unhappy. If we don't start moving faster, I'm going to lose more reputation. I don't want to endanger my class." Leo's words triggered a nightmare scenario.

His reputation with his goddess directly opposed mine with the legendary beasts.

"You took a reputation class without consulting the rest of us?" Tandy's voice was sharp. I cringed at her words, being guilty of almost the same thing. She pressed her hands to her temples as she shook her head. "We will not be successful if we don't plan, and I can't plan anything if I don't have all the information." She quickened her pace, leaving Leo in the dust.

So many secrets were stacking up. I still hadn't told them about the Faction Points from the dungeon because of my stupid promise to Richard. And now I had this [The Mercy Ledger: Beasts] quest.

Confusion marred Leo's face. "I didn't realize there was reputation associated with it until they gave it to me."

I felt that. Things weren't always as black and white as Tandy made them.

I decided to keep my secrets to myself for now.

Ash, however, didn't have a filter. "I've got a reputation-based chain quest too." I tried grabbing his eyes as Tandy slowly turned around. For the love of the Everbear he needed to *shut up*. "Cole and I picked it up..." His voice trailed off as he finally met my look.

Tandy and Leo were staring at me.

You've stepped in it this time.

"Is it true?" Tandy asked with the heat of the desert sun.

I couldn't meet her gaze. "Aye, I did, but not by choice."

Originally when I'd told them about our catch, I'd left out the [Legendary] status of the [King of the River]. Tandy had me walk through the story again. I shared the details but tried to keep the exact wording of the quest out of the conversation. I hate secrets, but I knew revealing *all* of them now would destroy Leo.

"I didn't think it was relevant because I couldn't share it. It's a [Hidden] quest you have to discover on your own," I finished lamely.

They looked at me. Leo at least seemed to nod. Tandy, however, split her ire between the two of us.

"Have I been the only one following the rules? We're a *team*, which means *no secrets*." Tandy looked between the two of us, her hurt plain. I crossed my arms, remembering the burn of being Richard's [Pet]. Apparently, I wasn't good at being the [Heart] of the team.

"Yes? Maybe? It's not that I was keeping this from you—" Okay, that was a lie. "—to *hurt* you." There. I could live with that statement.

She looked at Leo. He just shrugged, looking away in guilt.

I pressed on. "The world isn't just black and white. Meredeath didn't tell us she was from Kansas right away. Or tell her class. Richard obviously knows more than he lets on. And they both have been hiding dimensional storage from us for who knows how long!"

None of that, though, was on Tandy.

Don't bring me into this. I promised nothing.

I was really terrible at this team thing.

"What's the problem?" Leo took up the cause. "These reputation stats don't harm anyone. But this is the basis of my entire [Paladin] class. If I don't have a patron, I don't have the class." Embarrassment disappeared from Leo's voice. Instead he stood, arms crossed, eyes stony, as he stared Tandy down.

Leo's statement was a slap in the face. Intellectually, his class-based reputation associated with the Hunt overruled my [Hidden] quest. I just didn't expect to get smacked with the truth. It was like a bucket of ice water had been thrown on me. This was the [Heart] of Leo's build. Of course, it outweighed my quest.

Tandy looked like she was about to pull her hair out.

Meredeath stepped in, a theoretical neutral party. "Look, at this rate, we're not going to find one of these beasts, anyway. Until we meet one, none of these reputation gains or losses matter. Let's deal with the secrets once we are done with the Hunt."

A butterfly caught my eye as it flitted through the air, behind Leo's head. It was incredibly bright orange until it shifted to the side. Then, the red in the undertone of its wings melded it perfectly into the canyon walls. With a twist of her body, she'd disappear, perfectly camouflaged. I wondered how long she'd been following us.

[Achievement Unlocked: Mistress of the Canyon. You have uncovered the [Legendary] Camouflaged Rock Mistress. Few spot the Camouflaged Rock Mistress who hides in the cool air of the slot canyons. She is curious about your intent, recognizing you as a friend of the beasts. You must satisfy her before being granted any rewards.]

Fuck my life.

The butterfly carrying my doom flitted around Leo's head, as though taunting me to say anything. What could I do? It was as though she'd purposefully picked that moment to reveal herself.

You see her, right? What are you going to do?

My back had tightened until Richard bumped my ear.

What could I do? If I shared her presence, Leo would try to kill her. And like the [King of the River], I knew that would be wrong. She wasn't harming anyone here among the rocks. I knew what was *right*, even if it hurt Leo.

"Alright, are we going to venture onward?" Tandy frowned at me, translating my stress as impatience. "Look, we've got a problem here, but like you said. Until Leo finds one of these legendary creatures, there isn't a decision. He may never find one."

[You have received +20 Reputation Points with the legendary beasts. This puts your total at +60.]

I'd made the right decision, so why did I feel so bad? But

as the team ventured forward, my little butterfly friend followed, flitting above Leo's head. This was going to be a *long* afternoon.

The canyon grew deeper the longer we walked. The heat that'd been pelting us all day dropped off. Ice crystals had formed in the puddles sitting in the shadows.

I suspected some sort of ancient water event formed the canyons. Maybe a magical act that produced water in the desert? Looking up, the canyon's tight walls left a narrow ribbon of sky. It had grown darker with gray clouds rolling in. I shivered, the day's sweat cold in my clothes.

Every once in a while, a raven would stand on an outcropping and caw at us. Or a little canyon sparrow would slice through the air in a display of acrobatics, dodging rock outcroppings as it twisted and turned through the canyon.

Outside of the birds and the Rock Mistress, I had spotted no other wildlife. Which in itself was notable. We had heard none of the [Raid] horns since the [System] notification of the kill.

"We've got a problem," Leo called as he stood in a knuckle of the canyon. The rest of us piled up to look. An enormous boulder sat wedged between the walls, blocking the next leg of our journey.

Leo kneeled down, examining the slim gap under the boulder. "I think we can squeeze under it. It looks like the canyon opens up on the other side." I watched as the Rock Mistress flitted up and over the large sandstone boulder.

"Let me send Richard over, so he can check it out for us. Wasn't there a tributary canyon an hour ago? Maybe we were meant to go down that path?" I didn't relish trying to squeeze under the stone. Leo'd begun using his hands to dig out the wet, sludgy soil, trying to widen the gap.

Tandy watched Leo, arms crossed in disapproval. She didn't revel in tight spaces either. "Go ahead, Cole."

I'm not going under that rock either. I'm [Immortal], not stupid. Just toss me over.

At least we were unanimous in our distaste for wriggling under thousands of pounds of rock. I took Richard in my hand and underhand tossed him up, trying to land him at the pinnacle of the rock. He landed with a light squeak and a wet plop.

I waited as Richard slowly glided to the edge to gain a better view. Ash was making hand gestures to Meredeath, muttering about some sort of lever. Leo was still hand-shoveling sand.

Boss, we've got a problem. A big one.

Chapter 69

HEARTBREAK

Why am I only the 'boss' when things are going wrong?

Richard sent me a rudimentary image. I didn't even know he could do that.

The Legendary Rock Mistress we'd been following joined a whole swarm of butterflies over a crystalline pool. They were beautiful, and exactly what I didn't want Leo to see.

Shit.

"I'm not sure there's…" I didn't want to lie outright to my team. I grasped at anything. "There's not much point in going over there. Seems like it's a dead end," I finished lamely. I was not quick-witted like Tandy in these situations.

Tandy caught my eye and gave me a *what's going on* look.

How much damage could a little butterfly do?

Leo had stopped digging and had sat back on his haunches, covered in gritty mud. Meredeath and Ash were leaning against the rock, trying to help Richard climb down.

There wasn't an easy way to tell Tandy what was going on, so I just shared the text of my quest with her. I should have done it earlier, but I'd just wanted a little bit of the adventure for myself, and I was afraid of Leo's reaction.

Tandy's eyes went distant as she read the pop-up. I walked over to Leo, offering my canteen to help clean off his hands.

With the angle and direction of the canyon, the dregs of the afternoon sun beat down on us. We had four or five hours of sunlight left.

"What do you say we go back to that tributary canyon and look?" I tried to make small talk, but Leo looked pretty down.

He waved off my canteen and just sat in the mud. "Yeah, we can." He hadn't raised his downcast face, and from his agreeable words, I got the impression it was the last thing he wanted to do.

"Come on. You didn't think this was going to be as easy as 'follow the path' directly to the monster we're supposed to kill, did you?" I felt like a jerk.

I idly watched Richard pretend he couldn't climb down the sandstone as Meredeath and Ash tried to figure out how to climb up and reach him. At the moment, Ash had gone down on all fours so Meredeath could step on his back and get closer to Richard.

Leo looked up at me now, his hazel eyes squinting in the sun. "I didn't, but I did. This new class I've got, [Provisional Paladin of the Hunt], it calls to me. I thought that if it was truly meant to be, then it'd be easy. My instincts would pull me to one of these beasts. That *this* was my moment."

I felt terrible. He was so genuine that hiding the Rock Mistress felt like I was kicking a puppy. I knew what he was feeling because I felt the same about my quest line. I glanced at Tandy, who was still deep in her notifications, a dark frown painted on her face.

"The day's not done yet. You still have time to find one of the Legendary Beasts. Or we could find success on some other sort of hunt? Maybe one that's less impressive, that doesn't involve mythical creatures?" I tried. The betrayal burned in my chest.

Leo stood, nodding. "Yeah, you're right. Even if I don't get to keep this class, there will be other opportunities." His words agreed with me, but from the slump of his shoulders, I could tell he didn't really believe it.

"Wait, what do you mean *even if you don't get to keep this class*?" Tandy asked, joining the conversation.

"Didn't I tell you? This is a one-time opportunity. The quest for the class is limited to this [Raid]. Apparently, that's why there's so many hunters this time. They said the last time the Patroness of the Hunt put a call forth like this was over a hundred years ago. If I don't hunt down at least one of these Beasts, then the class won't stick." He *had* mentioned this being a unique opportunity, but I did not know it was *that* exclusive.

Tandy looked at me, pinning me in place with judgement. Shame colored my cheeks. I bent down, picking up a pebble. Looking over, Ash was now on Meredeath's shoulders, hands reaching out for Richard, who was still several feet away.

I met Tandy's gaze. I could read her mind. *Why did you make me part of this deception?* I could see it in the absolute disgust on her face. I was a worm wriggling on the street after a long rain, and one of the local kids had handed me to her—rubbery, squirmy, insignificant. Every bit of that smallness sank into my chest.

[Skill Downgrade: [Heart] has downgraded to [Heartbeat]. While you can understand the link between your party members, you no longer embody the responsibility of that understanding.]

No matter what I did, I wasn't winning in this scenario.

Regardless of my quest, however, I couldn't bring myself to regret saving the Rock Mistress. The creature was beautiful, flickering in her domain. She hurt no one in this blasted maze of canyons.

Meredeath toppled over trying to reach Richard. She and Ash sat in the mud, realizing Ash sitting on her shoulders would not work either. Ash looked a little dazed, covered in wet, muddy sand.

"Richard, stop kidding around. Let's go!" I called up to my difficult friend. His tentacles, which had been waving happily in laughter, looked right at me, as though accusing me of spoiling his fun. "Get down here!" I wasn't in the mood for his antics.

He gave a slug equivalent of a sigh and started oozing his way forward, using his extra clingy slime to glue himself vertically as he inched down the rock. By the time he got to a grabbable height, Meredeath had crossed her arms over her chest, giving him a dark glare.

Turned out neither of us was going to be popular today.

I walked over, holding my hand out for Richard, who smugly slimed along my arm to his normal shoulder perch. "Why do you have to be such an ass?"

Why didn't you tell Leo the truth?

Touché.

Everyone got to their feet, and we began the trudge back. It shouldn't have felt like defeat. There was every reason to think that the side canyon still would deliver something, some sort of creature to make the journey worthwhile. Some hint of adventure, something to satisfy the ever-burning guilt in my chest.

A hunting horn sounded behind us, obviously on the other side of the boulder. My heart sank as Leo turned to look at me in disbelief.

"How could someone have found something back there?"

Richard didn't help. He retreated guiltily behind my neck.

I didn't know what to say. There weren't words that were going to make this better.

"Why?" The betrayal in his eyes burned in my memory.

My mind thrummed with words. *It's wrong to kill the Rock Mistress. This isn't the way.* But the words stuck in my chest. Coward. An ooze of slime dribbled down my back.

"He has a competing quest line. That's why he didn't tell you." Tandy found the words where I couldn't. Her explanation made me sound so selfish. Maybe I was.

More horns sounded.

Leo drew his axe. He stood tall, muscles flexed. Dust, sand, and sweat marred his new armor. He looked every bit the hero. Ready to spring into action.

"You betrayed me for a quest?" Leo's voice broke. He walked towards me, axe held out. For a moment, I wondered if he was going to use it on me. Anger flared in his eyes.

Before his rage, my reasoning was useless. This feeling of *wrongness* was inexplicable.

Tandy opened her mouth to deflect, to make an excuse for me. Anything to make it better. Leo's look made her mouth shut with a snap.

"I want to hear it from *him*."

There was nowhere to hide. No excuse to duck behind. Leo, big, lovable Leo, stood towering over me, a pinnacle of righteous rage. He'd been my best friend.

My body trembled. I clenched my muscles hard. My throat closed up. What could I say? Yes, I hid the legendary beast from you for my own personal gain? That killing the beast—the very quest we were on—felt wrong?

My mind raced, throwing all the reasons at his stony face.

I went with the only thing I could really say. "I'm sorry."

Even as I said it, I knew it wasn't enough. My apology was simply an admission of guilt. Not a reason for the betrayal. I'd dug the hole so fast.

He rounded on Tandy. "And you *knew* too? You knew the details of his quest?"

Tandy's eyes were wide. "I just found out. I..." Her voice trailed off. What could she say?

He turned back to me. "How long have you had this quest?"

"S-since I went fishing with Ash."

He rounded on Ash and Meredeath. Ash had shrunk back, displaying his own guilt by hiding behind Meredeath.

As for Meredeath, she stood firm, unintimidated. "I didn't know, if it makes you feel better." She stared him down, dark eyes unblinking.

It looked like Leo'd gained a battle rage [Berserker] skill. Something changed in him as his musculature grew. He turned his back on us and took large, sand-eating steps back toward the dead end we'd vacated.

Tandy and I looked at each other for a moment. Her face mirrored mine. Guilt and horror.

We followed our friend. Tandy had to jog to keep up.

"What are you going to do?" she called to Leo.

He jogged, ignoring us both. His axe swung freely as horns frantically blew. The fight with the creature had obviously begun and wasn't going well.

Blasts of sound echoed off the canyon walls. A raven added its own caw to the cacophony. I looked up, seeing a lone raven perched on a ledge examining our party. Watching. Foretelling.

We got to the dead end, but Leo didn't stop. Instead, he swung his axe singing through the air.

"[Unstoppable]," he called. The axe hit the boulder, and half of it disintegrated in a shower of sand.

He'd used his rarest skill for a chance at the Rock Mistress.

Leo looked back at Tandy and me. My jaw was on the floor. I couldn't believe the power he'd just unleashed on the rock.

"The funny thing is, I'd been holding back for the two of you."

[Leo has left your party.]

He swung again, the second swing pulverizing the rest of the boulder as he strode forward in the dust. Leo joined the chaos of the Hunt.

The harried team waved him into the fight.

Leo took his axe, activating another skill as he swung. He joined the battle as a wave of energy hit the butterflies. They'd already been stunned by the blast of his entrance. Half fell from the sky. Leo began spinning and batting the creatures out of the air. Energy attacks flew from the other side of the canyon.

The resentment that had been building up over the Hunt drained out of me as he destroyed the Rock Mistress and her swarm. He was right. We'd been holding him back. Neither Tandy nor I could inflict that kind of carnage on a foe.

Leo deserved to be a proper hero. His build was fixed. If he hadn't been [Broken] in the first place, he'd have been on Team Abs all along.

I couldn't look away from the slaughter. He was also wrong. This wasn't how one ascended to the ranks of heroes.

Darts of magic picked off the magical butterflies from the other side of the canyon, relentlessly assassinating them while Leo swung the flat of his axe across the swarm.

The queen sat at the center of the horde. She was several times bigger than her harem. A bolt of orange magic shot from her. The assassin [Mage] cried out in pain. More than half of her swarm lay broken on the sand.

The queen turned towards Leo. Ten of the butterflies broke rank, formed into a wedge, and dive-bombed him from above. He laughed as he ignored the peppering magic bouncing off his armor.

I realized at that moment the truth of this Hunt. They were hunting the Rock Mistress not because she was difficult to kill, but because she was rare. This wasn't a hunt for a marauding leviathan. This was a purposeful snuffing of a unique beast.

I watched in outrage as Leo realized the kill was available for taking. Several more parties had joined the fight, sending arrows and magic bolts at the swarm. It was only a matter of time before they hit her.

A resentment burned. This wasn't why I'd become an [Adventurer], this wasn't heroic. This was a slaughter for the sake of glory. They should have cut the line and let the Rock Mistress go.

With each moment, as the battle drew out, more of her swarm lay out on the red ground. Fragile wings broken. My anger blazed. I fed my shame and guilt to it.

Even so, I didn't defend the creatures. How could I stand against a proverbial army of [Adventurers]? My hand tensed, knuckles white against the shaft of my hammer.

Leo took one last look at us and, with his maniacal, berserker grin, he turned back to the queen. He triggered his final skill and leaped. The air cracked with the velocity of his swing.

The Rock Mistress must have known her death was imminent as she triggered one last spell. A ball of blue light, too painful to look at, shot out at the ground as Leo's axe went straight through the legendary beast.

[You have failed to protect the legendary beast: [Rock Mistress of the Canyon]. Consequently, you lose 100 reputation points. Your reputation with legendary beasts has now dipped below 0 reputation points. You have lost [The Mercy Ledger: Beasts]. You have lost [Mark of Mercy]. You have lost [Thread of Mercy].]

A new shame burned in my chest. I should have acted.

The queen's brilliant death pillar faded, leaving us with a monument of her life. A glass-tiled perfect hole sat in the clearing. The molten shards of glass glowed with her defiance. The swarm of butterflies that had been working on defending her dropped to the ground, collectively dead. A dull rumble sounded.

I think we'd better leave.

The rumbling grew louder. I agreed with Richard when a geyser of water shot up from the hole. Leo was in the blast zone. His body flew, hit by a gush of water. One of the other teams ran in and pulled him away.

Steam came off the water as a pool formed. The depression in the landscape caused by the battle was quickly filling as the geyser kept shooting in the air.

"Guys, I think we need to leave now." The forceful statement came from Ash, of all people. I looked back. He was tugging at Meredeath. "Really, guys. I think I know how these canyons were formed."

I looked back. The geyser was not slowing down. Another rumble, and the ground cracked. More hot water leaked through the earth.

Tandy tugged at my elbow.

Part of me wanted to stay. We had to save Leo. I didn't deserve to survive this. My heart lay out on the sand, broken with the delicate insects. A third of it was simply missing. Another tug pulled at my elbow.

"Let's go. He'll be fine." Ash pointed at the [Adventurers] picking up Leo to take him with them. Water had filled up the crevasses, and another quake hit. A small wave hit my feet, burning them.

The pain woke me up. I let Tandy's next tug pull me backwards.

The ground shook this time, knocking us all sideways. I slammed into the wall to my left, hitting my elbow hard.

I think you need to run faster.

Looking back after Richard's comment, I had to agree. The narrow canyon was filling up with water *fast.* A knee-high wave was headed our way.

"Run!" I screamed, seeing the steam rise above the hot water.

Each step took us closer to safety and further from who we used to be. We sprinted away from the trio of childhood friends who spent summers building tree forts.

Each step was further from Leo. From what he'd done.

A powerful earthquake rocked the canyon walls. Dust and debris choked the air. A lone raven cawed its last judgement as it took flight.

When the wave of water hit us, I finally felt like I was getting what I deserved.

Chapter 70

BRUISED

The water hit *hard*.

It was a nightmare as the hot water rubbed us against the slot canyon walls like a washboard from hell.

I felt Richard glue himself to my shoulders. I wasn't afraid of drowning. My [Gills] loved the hot water after days in the desert air. I could breathe, but not much else. My stamina bar was draining dramatically as I tried to fight the current.

I shot through narrow slots in the canyon. My shoulder slammed into a wall. Friction scraped the skin off my knee.

I desperately tried to keep Tandy, Meredeath, and Ash in view.

A knuckle of the canyon bent to the left. Suction pulled me into an errant eddy. I found myself trapped in a whirlpool vortex. It outstripped the tidemaw's death throes in violence as I spun around like a rag doll.

Do something! I'm going to be sick!

My body twisted, the pressure pulling at my [Gelatinous] nature, but suction prevented me from breaking free. The only counterforce was my hammer at my hip. Its weight dragged me *down.*

I caught a flash of black in the chaos. Meredeath was trapped too. Her brilliant green eyes flared with magic. She flailed, losing the same fight with our watery foe.

She didn't have gills to survive. Several seconds passed. As my body tossed, I watched Meredeath in the chaos.

[Guardian's Promise] pinned me to the floor as water and debris tore at my body. Helpless, I watched Meredeath's desperate struggle.

Ash and Tandy bumped into our hell, but the current stripped them away immediately. Apparently, this vortex was full.

An iron tree guard slammed into the wall next to us. Limbs flailing, the current took it downstream too. I didn't bother trying to break free. All I could think about was Meredeath.

I saw the moment she gave up. She looked down, her green eyes flaring one last time as she slowly closed them. She mouthed the words *Sorry, Cole* as though she owed it to me to survive.

I unclipped [Guardian's Promise]. Leaving it, I kicked off from the floor. My shoulder hit Meredeath hard. Richard took the brunt of the impact.

Oof, you ***could*** *warn a slug.*

The vortex flung us sideways. I twisted, trying to get an arm around her.

Oddly, my body resisted. I felt weighed down as awkward as a misshapen snail.

I've got her. Get us out of here!

I loved that gods-be-damned slug. He'd glued us together!

I spun slower in the vortex with the increased mass.

Aiming my feet, I kicked against the wall. I could see a break in the funnel keeping us in place.

My hand passed through. The suction pulled us back.

A golden light grew in my vision. Silver snaked through it. Tandy and Ash.

A rope passed through my hand. I grabbed on with all my strength.

Immediately the rope snapped taut. We were yanked out of the whirlpool.

I'd been so focused on freeing us, I hadn't prepared for re-entry into the current. We slammed into a wall. Sandstone scraped at my back as water grated us against the side of the canyon.

My hands, raw, clenched on the rope. I held on, unable to protect my body.

It pulled us in like a fishing line. To what? Safety? Would it be in time for Meredeath? Could Richard's [Glue] hold?

The flash flood slowed as the canyon opened up.

Meredeath and Richard broke the surface of the river. My head was still under water. My [Gills] worked overtime. I kicked in the direction we were being pulled. Anything to help.

This was it.

Something grabbed my foot.

The immediate tension threatened to rip me in two. Something in my abdomen ripped. [Gelatinous] was great when getting stabbed, but not so much under torque.

Looking down, I saw a leafy, fibrous hand latched onto my foot.

An iron tree guard gave me a barky, demonic smile. The tree pulled at my leg. My calf muscle stretched unnaturally.

Could I hold on, or would I be ripped in two? Letting go would doom Meredeath. She couldn't survive the soup unconscious. Even if [Cheat Death] triggered, I was pretty sure I'd lose my grip on our lifeline.

I kicked at the tree appendage. The boot slapped ineffectually against the bark.

My stamina was dropping dramatically. Every muscle was tensed just to hold my body together.

The rope went slack. Our anchor had given way.

I was in the middle of the iron tree guard. It had won the tug-of-war match.

The maw of the beast was close. Fuck this. I hoped it choked on me.

It tried to snake an arm around my waist. I kicked out, surprising us both as my boot went *into* its maw. I stomped down. My heel connected on the back of the beast's throat.

The monster, shocked, gagged and let go of us.

The current whipped it away. The rope I desperately clung to went tight again.

When my head breached the surface, I saw Tandy and Ash at the other end of the rope. I saw safety.

They'd pulled themselves into an oversized alcove just barely big enough for the four of us. Ash had braced himself against a ledge that looked human made. He was using his magic to bolster Tandy's. They'd reeled us in like a legendary catch.

Ash immediately took Meredeath. He worked on clearing her lungs while Tandy took charge of me.

"I'm fine. Really," I said as she inspected me. My health and stamina were almost nothing. My abs and calf ached. I was raw and bruised, but the only thing broken was my heart.

She bought the lie, giving me an awkward hug before turning her attention to Meredeath.

The water was still rising. It was only a foot away from our cubby. We weren't out of it yet. But as I breathed in genuine air, I couldn't bring myself to think. To move. I was safe.

Be glad one of us has a brain.

Richard was still problem-solving. He started running a line of slime across the front of the alcove. It'd built up two inches already. A slimy barrier to the encroaching water. Would that even work?

I sagged against the wall, unable to bring myself to ask.

[Skill Acquired: You have gained the [Dead Wrong] skill, [Not Today]. Death may be a constant companion, but not when you need to live to save your friends. Gain [+25%] Stamina, Health, and Mana for [5 minutes] when trying to save another's life.]

Considering all the losses, the [System] notification seemed like a cruel joke.

[Gelatinous Regeneration] kicked in. My body pulled uncomfortably as it glued me back together.

Meredeath coughed, a gush of water coming from her mouth.

Good.

I laid my head back against the sandstone. I could let go.

Darkness took me.

The flood lasted for hours, but eventually it receded. We soggily trod back to the campsite.

Tandy was worried about Leo. I probably would have been too if I hadn't been so tired.

Darkness had fallen, and each step grated at the raw blisters on the bottom of my feet. My damaged calf made me limp. Step after slow step.

Richard huddled close. His slime barrier had saved us. The flood crested a good foot higher than the floor of our cavern. His sticky barricade had worked.

Even Ash was quiet, which I didn't think possible.

Meredeath leaned on him. She was still in shock from the near drowning.

I haven't looked forward to a bedroll more in my entire life. Even during harvest season. I'd never *hurt* this much.

The lights of the Ceaparean Drift Hunt staging ground were a sweet balm to my weary soul. The flood hadn't affected them. Most of the water just fed the Tigra. A few teams gave us sympathetic looks as we staggered past their campgrounds.

Tandy stopped to ask a few times if anyone had seen a tall, blond-haired new [Paladin]. She got only shrugs in reply. Her description matched a third of the Hunt participants.

We figured out Leo's fate when we made it to our site.

Tandy's hammock swung in the night breeze. My bedroll lay next to our cooking pots. Meredeath's charcoal pack was tied neatly to a tree.

But Leo's laundry that had been drying on a line was gone, along with his pack and bedroll. The only evidence that he'd been there was a neatly folded pink sweater left on Tandy's pillow.

I fell asleep to Tandy's sniffles that night.

I only saw Leo once in the ensuing days.

The Hunt included multiple days and objectives. [Your Mom's Party] didn't bother taking part in anything else.

We were just biding our time waiting for everything to end. Tandy had made a deal with a merchant. We'd be guards for them as they made their way back to the Eastern frontier.

I'd been buying sweetmeats from a kebab vendor when I saw him.

He stood tall, straw hair tousled waving in the breeze. He had new armor on, with even bigger shoulder pads. It gleamed in the sun. Leo looked like a full [Paladin]. He'd been walking with two friends, decked out in slightly less impressive armor. They looked to be some sort of nobles with noses in the air as they scanned the vendors.

His 'friends' commented about how the Hunt had gone downhill, all the country bumpkins had come in to watch this year.

Leo's eyes met mine. I stood frozen, kebab in one hand, juices dripping down my arm. Bruised and scraped, I looked a mess. I did *not* belong here, just as his sneering companions suggested.

I smiled with a polite nod, trying to bridge the gap between us. He frowned.

Leo hesitated for a fraction of a second before dismissing me with cold eyes as they bounced to the next stranger in the crowd.

He may be a [Paladin] now, but I was an [Adventurer]. I stood a little straighter. A country boy, sure, but one that'd fight a dungeon for a missing girl, feed a house full of orphans, help a [Lich] hold the line, and cut the line to let the [King of the River] go.

I was Cole Moldboard Thornsfield. No one was going to write a story about me, but that was okay. What I was doing was still worthwhile.

I watched as his broad back receded.

He didn't look back once.

I didn't either.

Chapter 71

AFTERMATH

Our exit from the Ceaparean Drift was uneventful. No bandits bothered us on the first leg of the caravan.

Tandy and I mourned the breakup of our trio. For all my resolve that my version of an [Adventurer] was right, it still *hurt* that Leo had turned right when I went left at the fork in the road.

We headed back east. Maybe not to Woodsten, not without Leo. How could we have explained his absence?

We were moving slowly, stopping at the small towns that peppered the western expanse.

Every time we entered a town, Tandy would pick up minor quests at the Adventurer's Guild.

Tandy would wake up early and hit the quest board. Meredeath and I weren't naturally early risers, and Ash didn't seem to care.

I don't think anyone would have trusted me to pick up the quests, anyway. I sure didn't.

Tandy had changed. Instead of late nights, she tortured herself by getting up at the crack of dawn. She'd go into the courtyard, or step away from camp, and *practice.* Over and over.

I'd been cursed with a lethargy that sucked any will to practice. I barely got up for breakfast unless I was in charge of the meal. Ironic that the thing I enjoyed the most was cooking.

Today, however, we'd found a cheap inn that included a basic breakfast for all. I was going to skip it, but the window in our room sent a shaft of light right onto my pillow.

So I was up and being served watery eggs by the time Tandy'd returned. I thanked the server, trying not to let my expression give away my opinion of the soggy food. Even the potato hash looked burned. I absentmindedly pushed both around on my plate, trying to work up the courage to eat either.

Meredeath would be down in a bit—or wouldn't. She *really* wasn't a fan of mornings.

Ash slid into the booth. "Where's Richard?"

I glanced up, wincing as I put a forkful in my mouth. At least it wasn't cold. I swallowed, like the eggs were a shot of shitty vodka. "He's finding his own breakfast."

I wasn't really embarrassed that Richard dumpster dived for breakfast, but every time I'd admitted the fact to someone new, they always gave him the *poor Richard* routine as though I didn't feed him proper food. The slug *preferred* compost and trash.

Ash signaled that he wanted his own plate of under-achieving eggs and looked at me with the eyes of a man with a thousand questions. I didn't regret inviting Ash onto our team. I really didn't. His skills had saved us a dozen times already. Nothing about him was particularly objectionable. He just wouldn't stop *talking*.

"How did you sleep?" Ash asked, and without waiting for a reply, continued. "I thought those beds were hard. However, I've found most beds to be hard since I've been here. I need to figure out an improvement, maybe a magical camping mat that repels bugs? I hate it when we're out on the trail and I wake up with bugs in my bedroll. How're the eggs?"

I opened my mouth to reply, but he overrode me again. "They look good, like they've got real herbs in them."

I forked some more into my mouth, swallowing quickly. They were getting cold. If these were *good* to Ash, I shudder to think how bad the food in his world had been. "I miss orange juice. You all don't seem to have it."

"What's orange juice?" I asked, taking a mouthful of the cool minty tea they'd served with the eggs.

"Oh, uh. It's juice made from oranges."

"The color?" I took another bite. I loved doing this to the guy. There seemed to be a lot about his world that he'd never really thought about. He was so earnest, too. He never caught on that I was ribbing him.

Kind of like Leo.

Ugh.

Leo was walking his own path. Death and glory, shiny armor and riches. Every once in a while, we'd hear some rumor of Leo Patch the [Paladin of the Hunt]. He was making a name for himself. The Beast Slayer, they called him.

I poked at the eggs on my plate, moving them around.

We'd found a couple lost children, defended a caravan from bandits, and escorted a herdsman to their summer pastures. They weren't *big* jobs, but they were important.

I'd rather be an Andrew Ashborn, [Wayfinder] for the Lost, than Leo Patch, The Beast Slayer.

I still couldn't shake the sense that Leo was lost. That we'd find him. Fix this.

"No, it's a fruit called an orange because it's well, orange. It's a citrus fruit, like lemons but much sweeter. It was common for us to have fresh orange juice as part of our breakfast." The server delivered Ash's plate. His eggs were a little overcooked, looking almost rubbery.

"So, you have orange trees in your yard, and you make fresh orange juice every morning?" I knew it was unlikely. From all the things Meredeath had told me, they lived in cities where no one farmed their own food.

It'd always sounded a little odd to me, but there was much about their world I couldn't imagine.

Ash had turned pink at my question. "Um, no, the fresh orange juice comes from a carton." I frowned. What was a carton? Sensing this, he rushed his explanation. "It's like a box that you keep liquid in, but it's small. We can buy them at the store. They're made of, um, like magically bound wood chips. But instead of magic, it's glue."

My eyebrows raised, and I tried imagining a rectangular wine barrel full of fruit juice with floating woodchips. They must really enjoy orange juice.

"We used to put the images of missing kids on milk cartons," Ash continued.

I tried imagining a wine cask with the image of a lost child, but I failed. What a strange memorial for a child.

"How's breakfast?" Tandy interrupted my thoughts, scooting onto the bench across from me.

I moved over for a trailing Meredeath. Tandy always dragged Meredeath out of bed before giving us the mission details. Meredeath poured herself a cup of tea, holding the cup between her fingers as though it were the only thing keeping her alive.

Tandy scanned the table, grimacing as she examined the quality of our 'free' breakfast.

"Maybe we shouldn't prioritize the 'breakfast included' inns," Meredeath said, looking at our meals. "The last three have been really terrible."

I nodded heartily in agreement.

"Yeah, we can look into it, but it has saved us a lot of money," Tandy countered.

My eyes swung over to Tandy, frowning. I hated when she was right.

Then I saw it.

A ghostly smudge of powdered sugar at the corner of her mouth. She'd gotten a pastry for breakfast. This, our penny-pinching leader, had skipped the crappy eggs and spent our hard-earned money on a pastry.

I eyed her. "That's easy for you to claim. Since you don't eat breakfast, right?" That'd been her excuse for months. She wasn't a "fan" of breakfast food.

With a smile, I reached across the table and dabbed at the corner of her mouth with my napkin. Ash looked confused, but Meredeath read the room.

"You've been sneaking out to buy pastries?" Tandy was unwilling to meet any of our eyes until Meredeath let her off the hook. "*Without me?* I'd get out of bed for a good donut hole."

"That's what he said," Ash trailed off as we looked at him.

His goofy grin was infectious. We all burst out laughing. It felt *good* to laugh.

Tandy was going to have a lot more company in the mornings when the inn's food was suspect.

"Alright, back to business, everyone. We've got a quest. There's a missing kid, and we've got to find him." Tandy's words brought us all back to reality. "The kid's friends admitted to daring him to go into what the locals call the *Slime Cavern*. Our job is either to pull him out or confirm his fate."

I cringed at the euphemism. We all knew what *confirm his fate* meant, and it wasn't anything good. Ash's face turned green. He really wasn't cut out for the [Adventurer's] life, the kid had such a weak constitution for the reality of death.

"If he's passed, maybe we can have Ash paint him onto a wine barrel." Everyone stared at me as if I'd grown horns.

Even Ash. I waved at Ash. "Like your milk carton graves, Ash. It'd be nice."

Ash stared at me for once at a loss for words. He mouthed the words *milk carton graves.*

"You said your people put images of missing kids on milk cartons, right? We don't have these milk boxes, but we've got wine casks."

He gave a long, "Ohhhhh." Meredeath clutched her stomach as she laughed. Tandy and I just sat, missing the joke.

Tears streaming down his face, Ash just choked out, "No, I think we're okay. We'll let the family handle the grave."

"What am I missing?" I asked, confused by these off-worlders.

"The kids on the cartons are presumed missing, not dead," Ash explained. "They're not graves. They're made with the assumption that it'll work out and they'll find their way home. It's possible the kid's just run away and needs a reminder that they're missed."

Huh. How optimistic.

"More likely they're kidnapped. Or dead." Typical Meredeath commentary.

Ash's interpretation sat with me. This idea that a kid could run away and just needed a reminder they were missed. Maybe we *should* put Leo on a wine cask or two.

"Enough of milk cartons, let me share the quest," Tandy cut in.

[Local Quest: Slime Cavern Rescue

The populace at Hunt's Rest has issued an Adventurer Quest to search the Slime Cavern for Raif Leais, a 10-year-old child of the village. If found alive, recover the child and return him to the parents. If dead, return with news of Raif's death and any belongings recovered. Reward: 5 gold, potential other rewards depending on quest criteria fulfillment.]

There it was. The duty of an [Adventurer]. I'd thought

about going home a lot these last couple of months, but if I did, who was going to save this kid?

It sure wasn't going to be Leo.

Not today, anyway.

I set down my fork.

"You all ready?" I asked. A twinge of excitement threaded through my chest. It was time to save a kid.

A slime cavern? Did you guys pick this quest just for me?

The story continues on Royal Road, a free serial platform, and Patreon! If you want to find out what happens next, get caught up on the action.

Stumbling Up: A Loser's Guide to Progression, Book 2 is available now! https://www.royalroad.com/fiction/121984/stumbling-up-a-losers-guide-to-progression

Stumbling Up, Book 2 will be released on Amazon, Kindle, and Audible in Spring 2026!

For Stumbling Up bonus content, visit our website! https://dragontomespublishing.com/stumbling-up-bonus-content/

Acknowledgments

This past year has been rough, and it is a minor miracle that I've written *Stumbling Up* at all. There are many people I'm thankful for and who have helped in innumerable ways in making this book become a reality. If I miss you, please know it is not intentional.

First, I want to say thank you to my spouse, Jen Kirmer. You've been here this whole time listening to me babble about slug tentacles, helping me print out the slug army, formatting the book, being my alpha reader, and talking me off the ledge when Richard makes me want to quit. Thank you.

There are a few people in my life who helped give me the shove out of the plane. Mark Whelan, Mark Nolan, Roger Butler, Seamus Nugent, Thomas Laffey, Emily Cummins, Rachael Cordero, and Laurie Nicoletti for telling me I had a worthwhile dream. Cheers to the BEARS who let me go and are still cheering me on.

Alisha, you've been here the whole time in the fluffy red chair. My writing bestie, I can't wait to see what you do next! Kat, thanks for all the work on promoting Stumbling Up. Geneva, my friend, thank you for all the support over the years and your patience with my anxiety and willingness to help me stumble up.

Jay Krauss, the short king. Appreciate every message you drop, encouragement, and willingness to talk about how much noise plate armor actually makes as you try to sneak around in it. To Tommy, for boldly volunteering to be my first interviewee, and for being a friend. To Lance for not canceling on me, and a friendship that brought Fritter and Muffin into the world. Thanks to all the authors in the community (Erin, Jason, Doug, Rose, Dasha, KT) who've had a kind word over the last year.

Thank you for those in the growing cornucopia: PopPop, Pianoninja, Chatbox_Brian, Stacy F, Gary Bradley, BJ, Kels, Meph, Rob, Isaiah (see I can spell it), Evan, TheBusyBard, RJ-Wilkie, Kristen, pengtron, ninikomis, Astyanax, Ayo, Mesa, and the indomitable Hannah. Specifically, Piano and Brian, my two alpha readers. You've pulled me out of a few spirals, amped up the comedy, and nudged in all the right ways. May Briyain live on forever!

To the girls' group — Kat, Jen, Emily, Elizabeth, Yari, Dominique, and John — you convinced me a bunch of dick jokes might sell after that first fertility statue incident and choosing to put lube into the infinite bag of liquid.

Thanks to Richey for being with me this whole journey and adding his own love into the story. To Jeremy Frazier for taking up the banner and adding his passion to the narration. Jessica Threet's talent and professionalism are unmatched; thanks for putting up with us amateurs. Jamie Garner for giving me the confidence to give this a go. Appreciate Morpheuz's detailed chapter and cover art. I still marvel at the amount of expression you've fit into a banana slug. Additionally, Stacy Fontenot much appreciative of your help with transcribing and making sure Stumbling Up is available in braille, you've been invaluable!

Finally, thank you to my mom for encouraging me to write (and read) even though she doesn't understand any of it. To Al, Kathleen, and Deb for their support and encouragement, and early edits. And for Donna, the best sister a goblin could ask for - thank you for the banana slug pics, the late-night Bigfoot theories, and all of our adventures.

A book takes a village, and I'm grateful for every member of mine.

About the Author

Reck Well is the author of *Stumbling Up: A Loser's Guide to Progression* and *Potions and Perils: An Evermoss Cozy Fantasy*. Known for character drive, humor-forward fantasy, Reck writes for readers who want found family, heartfelt moments, and laughter tucked between dungeon runs and snarky sidekicks.

Reck, a true chaos goblin (they/them), lives in Kansas with their spouse, houseful of cats (Dragon, Nancy, Chester, and Fluff), and dog (Mrsha). An avid hiker and wannabe [Adventurer], many of the landscapes they explore end up in books.

Having a reluctant green thumb, they are also often found in their herb garden chasing away slugs.

Reck is proud not only to be known as “that slug guy” in the LitRPG community, but also as a frequent podcast host on the *ChattinStats* podcast interviewing authors about their releases and journey, and for the *Reck and PopPop Show*, a reader-focused LitRPG podcast.

While Reck writes fantasy, they also publish science fiction under the name MJ Douglas, including the novels *Augmented* and *Echo*. No matter the pen name, their work blends humor, heart, and immersive world building that draws readers in and makes them feel at home even in the strangest of worlds.

Reck is happiest when swapping stories with readers, championing the genre and convincing people that yes, a fanged banana slug *can* be a compelling sidekick.

instagram.com/@wellrecked

facebook.com/dtp.reckwell

tiktok.com/@reckwellauthor

MORE LITRPG

A very big thank you to those who run the LitRPG facebook group. I've been a part of this group for years as a reader and now an author. If you're a fan of LitRPG it's the place to be.

Also a thanks to other Facebook groups: LitRPG Books, Game Lit Society, the LitRPG Authors' Guild, and the many other groups that allow authors and readers to intermingle. Check out PopPop's LitRPG World, *The Reck and PopPop Show, The ChattinStats Podcast* on Youtube, and the *In Other Worlds Podcast.*

Made in the USA
Coppell, TX
19 January 2026